FREEDOM'S SLAVE

ALSO BY HEATHER DEMETRIOS

Exquisite Captive

Blood Passage

BOOKS ONE AND TWO OF THE DARK CARAVAN CYCLE

FREEDOM'S SLAVE

BOOK THREE
of the
DARK CARAVAN CYCLE

HEATHER DEMETRIOS

BALZER + BRAY
An Imprint of HarperCollinsPublishers

Balzer + Bray is an imprint of HarperCollins Publishers.

ISBN 978-0-06-231862-6 (trade bdg.)

Typography by Torborg Davern
Map art © 2014 by Jordan Saia
17 18 19 20 21   PC/LSCH   10 9 8 7 6 5 4 3 2 1

First Edition

For Brenda Bowen, honorary Ghan Aisouri

QAE MOUNTAINS

FOREST OF SIGHS

RIVER SORROW

TAVRAI TRAINING CAMP

DJAN TERRITORY

ARJINNAN SEA

WATER TEMPLE OF LATHOR

MARID TERRITORY

FISHING VILLAGES

IBLIS

ARJINNA

The Arjinnan Castes

THE GHAN AISOURI: Once the highest caste and beloved of the gods. All but annihilated, the members of this female race have violet eyes and smoke. They are the only jinn who can access the power of all four elements: air, earth, water, and fire.

THE SHAITAN: The Shaitan gain power from air and have golden eyes and smoke. They are scholars, mages, artists, and the overlords who once controlled the provinces.

THE DJAN: The largest caste and the peasant serfs of Arjinna's valleys. They have emerald eyes and smoke, and their power comes from earth—the sacred soil of Arjinnan land. They are manual laborers, denied education or advancement.

THE MARID: Caretakers of the Arjinnan Sea and fishing folk, these serfs draw their power from water. Their eyes and smoke are blue. They are the peasants of the coast, as uneducated as the Djan and subjected to equally brutal labor.

THE IFRIT: Long despised throughout the realm, the Ifrit have crimson eyes and smoke. Their power comes from fire, and they use its energy for dark magic. They are soldiers and sorcerers.

The Jinn Gods and Goddesses*

GRATHALI: Goddess of air, worshipped by the Shaitan
TIRGAN: God of earth, worshipped by the Djan
LATHOR: Goddess of water, worshipped by the Marid
RAVNIR: God of fire, worshipped by the Ifrit
MORA: Goddess of death, worshipped by the Ash Crones of
    Ithkar

* *Because the Ghan Aisouri can draw power from all four elements, they worship every god, though individual Aisouri have their favorites.*

If you are the dreamer, I am what you dream.
But when you want to wake, I am your wish.

—Rainer Maria Rilke

PART ONE

Vi fazla ra'ahim.
You are a sword, nothing more.

—Tavrai mantra

1

BOTTLES.

They were the only illumination in the pitch-black room. Hundreds of them, filled with jinn of every caste. Clear bottles, pulsing with the light of their prisoners' magic. Emerald, sapphire, gold, ruby: the jinn energy swirled inside, trapped.

They covered the shelves that had been carved into the lapis lazuli wall behind the throne, just one of many changes Calar had made to the palace. She had taken to calling them her court. When faced with a decision, Calar would smile, brilliant in her cold beauty, and say, *Why don't we ask my court?* She'd caress a bottle or two, speak to the miserable jinni inside it. *What do you think I should do?*

From where Kesmir now stood, hidden in the shadows, he could just make out the shape of the naked bodies stuffed into the vessels. A curved spine, head on knees, eyes closed in order to block out what was happening. It was a small miracle Calar had decided not to line the bottles with iron, the sickmaking element that would have killed most of the jinn by now. She claimed she was being merciful by allowing them to keep their *chiaan*, but Kesmir knew the truth: she liked seeing them in pain. Liked making them watch what she did from the throne. It was no fun if they were dead.

Several bottles were so tiny, they could have rested in Kesmir's palm. Others were grotesque—tall, but incredibly thin, so that the jinn inside had no choice but to stand with their arms raised above their heads. There were bottles that were so squat they resembled discs more than vessels, and the jinn inside these looked like contortionists, their limbs held at painful, impossible angles.

They hadn't noticed Kesmir yet. He couldn't bear to see their accusing eyes. He might as well have put them in there himself. He'd often considered setting them free, but there was little good that would do. Calar would just kill them all, then find some horribly inventive way to punish her disobedient lover.

It was already too late for the prisoners whose bottles no longer emanated light. The corpses inside were slowly decaying, their spirits finally free of the bottle's confines. He'd tried to get Calar to take the dead jinn away, but she wouldn't.

They're a message, she'd said, *to anyone who dares to defy me.*

Just last night, Kesmir had been present when an Ifrit peasant begged Calar to spare his daughter's life. Begged on his knees, forehead touching the mosaic floor in deference. Sweaty skin against tiles that curled into elegant geometric stars and vines. Kesmir had been standing in his usual spot: three steps to Calar's left. The Royal Consort, His Wretchedness Kesmir Ifri'Lhas. *Royal Whore, more like it,* he thought.

He faced the great hall as moonlight streamed through the latticework windows and climbed the carved pillars covered with ancient Kada scrollwork—prayers to the gods for the safekeeping of the Aisouri who were long dead. The high, vaulted ceilings were covered in mother-of-pearl mosaics made to look like the sky at dawn, when the Aisouri had once trained in their ancient martial art, *Sha'a Rho*. It was the most magnificent place Kes had ever been. Yet in the three years since taking up residence in the palace, Calar had turned it into a slaughterhouse. The throne room stank of dark magic, fear, and blood. The coming day would be no exception.

"Why should I spare a traitor's life?" Calar had said. She spoke in a wine-drenched drawl, more interested in the *savri* in her hand than the agonized father at her feet.

She was toying with him. Kesmir had already seen what Calar had done to the jinni's daughter—this false hope she was dangling before him was nothing more than the amusement of a bored tyrant. He shuddered and Calar's eyes flicked to his. He gave her a small smile, the cruel one they used in their games. Only he didn't want to play the games anymore. She returned the smile and Kesmir relaxed. She hadn't noticed his revulsion. Gods, when had that happened—*revulsion*? Not so long ago his sole purpose in life had been to love her, and love her well.

"Not a traitor, My Empress. No," the jinni had said. "A silly child in love. The boy's a Djan, yes, but not a *tavrai*. I swear it. My daughter is a good Ifrit."

"What would you tell your daughter right now, if she could hear you?" Calar had said, her voice going soft.

This, Kesmir knew, was her favorite part.

The Ifrit began to cry. "I . . . I'd tell her I love her and that I will find a . . . a good Ifrit boy for her. No more Djan. A . . . a soldier from My Empress's army, perhaps."

Calar smiled, false benevolence. She gestured to one of the bottles behind her. Inside, an Ifrit girl's mouth was open in a silent scream, palms against the glass. Her face was bruised, lips swollen and bleeding. Like the other jinn in the bottles, she was naked. The bottle was just big enough for her to sit on her knees, her arms covering her breasts, a useless attempt at modesty. Her eyes were full of terror and shame.

The old jinni looked past Calar. Even now, Kesmir could still hear that father's precise howl of pain. It echoed in his heart and would not let him sleep that night. Not that he would have, anyway.

A sound from a far corner of the room brought Kesmir out of the memory. His hand went to the hilt of his scimitar, waiting. A figure in a dark cloak strode toward him, wearing a wooden mask that disguised the jinni's features—a peasant mask from the harvest celebrations, this one depicting a fox. Necessary precautions when you were trying to overthrow an empress who could read minds.

"I heard a phoenix cry tonight," the jinni said. A male this time.

Kesmir drew closer, his hand still gripping his scimitar. "I'm surprised it still has tears," he answered, voice soft.

It was a different jinni each time, but the same code. Kesmir suspected the jinni behind the mask was a Shaitan—he had the soft cadence of the jinn aristocracy, the perfect diction only the wealthy could afford to have.

"We've found someone who can help you," the jinni said.

"There are many jinn who offer to 'help' me."

The jinni slowly lifted his index finger to the side of his mask and gently tapped twice near his temple. "This kind of help, General," he said.

Impossible. It was too much to hope for. And, yet, what this jinni presumed to offer was what Kesmir's whole plan hinged on: the first step on the path to wresting Arjinna away from his lover was for Kes to control his own mind, build a wall between his thoughts and her own. It would be pointless for Kesmir to overthrow Calar until he knew how to keep her in the dark, to protect his mind from being ravaged until he begged for death. Reading his mind was a pastime of hers. It used to be a way for Calar to be closer to him, but not anymore. Her mind was a weapon pointed at him as often as not. He couldn't influence her anymore, couldn't hope that her tyranny was just a phase. If he didn't depose her, someone else would. And, unlike him, they would kill her. Fool that he was, Kesmir still had hope that once she no longer had power, Calar would return to herself, to the girl she'd been when she rescued him long ago.

"Calar killed every Aisouri trainer during the coup. There is no one left with that knowledge." Disappointment tinged

Kesmir's voice—he couldn't hide the desolation of yet another hope dashed.

Anyone who knew how to protect the mind had been burned in the massive cauldron that now sat before the palace.

"That is what you were supposed to think," the jinni said evenly. He took off his mask, revealing a gaunt face with too-large golden eyes and a mess of burn scars covering nearly every inch of his skin. Even so, Kesmir recognized him.

"You're dead," he said, taking an involuntary step back. "I saw Calar set you on fire, saw her kick you off the cliff."

"My daughter is the last living Ghan Aisouri," Baron Ajwar Shai'Dzar said. His eyes glimmered in the wan light of the bottles. "Did you really think there was no one who wanted to keep me alive long enough for me to see my child on the throne your imposter empress has claimed?"

"Your daughter is barred from Arjinna. The portal—"

"The gods will find a way," Ajwar said. "She is their eyes, their voice, their sword in the darkness."

Before Kesmir could say another word, the baron pressed a golden whistle into Kesmir's hand. "Blow this from the top of Mount Zhiqui when the sun rises."

Without another word, Nalia Aisouri'Taifyeh's father evanesced. Golden smoke swirled around him and then he was gone, leaving behind nothing but wisps of honeyed evanescence and the whistle in Kesmir's palm.

He'd seen such whistles on the Aisouri, when Kesmir and the others had fastened the ropes around the dead royals' necks before hanging them from the palace gate, where they remained to this day.

It was how they'd summoned their gryphons.

Kesmir's eyes settled on the throne. The Ghan Aisouri dais had been replaced by one made of pure volcanic rock, a massive thing with hard edges and evil spirals that spilled around it like a demon's halo. Its smooth surface reflected the light of the bottles, and Calar's dark energy hung about it like a shroud.

His mind drifted to his daughter, wondering what the gods had planned for *her*, this child of luckless love.

Calar wouldn't understand what Kes was doing, but it didn't matter. She'd left him with no choice. The jinni who'd taken him in after he'd lost everything, who had shown him tenderness and a loyal, fierce love that brought down a kingdom, was still inside her, lurking in some forgotten corner of Calar's heart. But if he didn't act quickly, the best parts of Calar would be gone, stamped out by her increasing dependence on dark magic and her obsessive need to kill Nalia, whether or not the portal was closed.

Kesmir was trying to overthrow the jinni he'd once loved more than anything in the worlds not because he wanted to destroy Calar, but because it was the only way to save her.

2

BLOOD AND ASH AND DARKNESS, FOR HOURS ON END.

Raif was nothing more than a scimitar that slashed through the endless night, a hoarse voice that directed the jinn around him.

The Eye of Iblis was a corner of the universe the gods had forgotten about, a black hole. Impossible to escape. *Here* was nowhere, a void so vast, so incomprehensible, that it was as if he'd been flung into deep space. By his calculations, they'd been traveling across it for over a month, using his sister's *voiqhif* to guide them toward Arjinna. They'd fought the whole way through, but today's battle with the ghouls was the worst by far. Not only were there more of the monsters than usual, the army was on its last reserves of *chiaan*. The Eye had nothing for them to replenish their energy with. If they didn't get to Arjinna soon, they'd be stranded here forever—or at least until they died of hunger, thirst, ghouls. The supplies they'd brought with them were running out, but Zanari promised they were close to home, a day or two away at most. *Home.* Gods, it'd been a long time since he'd seen Arjinna.

The only light on the battlefield came from multicolored streaks of *chiaan* as the jinn grappled with monsters twice their size. The circular formation protecting Nalia and Zanari—the empress and her seer—had long since been breached as more and more ghouls descended. The lamps the Brass Army had carried were now mangled bits of glass and metal that littered the floor of the Eye.

Raif ducked as a stream of violet *chiaan* hit the chest of the ghoul running at him. He turned and Nalia grinned at him, her hands burning with Ghan Aisouri magic. Behind her, the Brass Army and the ghouls they fought made a terrifying tableau.

"Show-off," he said, laughing despite the death surrounding him. The terror, the blood on his hands, the *chiaan* pumping through him—this was where Raif belonged. In the fight, a whisper away from death.

"Come on. Tell me watching me kill ghouls isn't sexy," she said. Battle pillow talk, charged with adrenaline, with the knowledge that everything could end at any moment.

In answer, Raif pulled Nalia to him, his lips crushing hers. The battle disappeared, and it was just the jinni he loved more than anything and her *chiaan* that filled him with liquid light. After far too little time, he stepped away, though gods knew that was the last thing he wanted to do.

There was a shout behind them and he pulled Nalia to the ground as Tazlim barreled past, golden lasers shooting from his fingertips. The commander of Nalia's army was a remarkably well-trained warrior for a jinni who'd just been rescued from a bottle he'd been trapped inside for thousands of years. *Nalia's army.* How quickly Raif had gone from antiroyalist *tavrai* to nearly bending the knee.

"Keep killing these ghouls and there's more where that came from," he murmured against Nalia's lips.

Her eyes gleamed, wicked and lovely. "Promise?"

"I always keep my promises."

She stood, eyeing the battlefield around them, the sight of her causing something fierce and primal and terrifying to rise up in his chest.

He grabbed her hand. "Hey."

Nalia glanced back at him, eyebrows raised, but before he could say anything, there was a roar and Nalia whirled around, launching herself at a ghoul that towered over them, the monster outlined by the *chiaan* of the fighting around them. Its needle-sharp teeth gnashed at the air, moving toward her neck, saliva and blood dripping from its gaping mouth, but before Raif could move to help Nalia, the creature froze. Nalia pushed it to the ground with one hand, pulling her Ghan Aisouri dagger out with the other. Paralyzed by the spelled blade, the creature could do nothing but watch as Nalia speared its heart. She stood, wiping the blood on her leather pants as she turned to Raif.

"Better keep that promise, Djan'Urbi," she said. She winked before throwing herself back into the chaos.

Raif would remember this moment every night for months and months to come—that wink, the way it made him feel like a boy in his first blush of manhood. Nalia, his Nalia, who disappeared into the Eye without a trace, taking his heart and every bit of hope inside him with her.

3

KES WAITED UNTIL THE INKY DARKNESS OF THE ROOM
he shared with Calar turned gray in the coming dawn before
he slipped out of the bed's warmth. The small form that slept
between them sighed and turned over, throwing her little arm
over the pillow her young father had just vacated. She slept the
kind of deep sleep granted only to children who had yet to be
weighed down with cares. Kes leaned down and kissed his daughter's forehead, casting one more glance at Calar sleeping beside
her as he straightened up. He hated leaving them alone together.

Calar had been especially restless during the night, and Kes
had half thought he wouldn't be able to meet the gryphon after
all. At one point, she'd gotten out of bed and taken long drags
of the *gaujuri* pipe that sat on a low table nearby. Its rose scent
filled the room, the smoke encircling her head like a crown. She

stumbled over to the freestanding flames in a corner of the room that hovered above the thick carpeting, igniting the air with Ifrit power. Kes feigned sleep, one eye slightly open as he watched her sit before the fire, soaking her hands in it, the flames reflected in her anxious eyes. Gradually, they went glassy and dull, the drug sweeping her cares away. He was attuned to her every movement as prey is to predator, his body tense and still. Kesmir had lain beside Calar like this night after night, his fury mounting. This was the only time when his thoughts were his alone. As she slept, he could think about resistance and the end to her reign of terror. But if she were even half awake, he was in danger of her slipping into his mind, taking a peek, as she often liked to do.

She'd spent the better part of her nights tossing and turning, moaning in her sleep. The secret work she did with the Ash Crones was affecting Calar more than she let on in her waking hours. Gods knew what those dark, ancient witches deep in Ithkar's volcanic caves were conjuring with their hellish spells. It was whispered they were as old as the volcanoes themselves, the first Ifrit to be created from Ravnir's smokeless fire. As soon as she was born, Calar's mother gasped her last breath just as Calar drew air into her lungs for the first time. Calar's now-dead father, having little interest in raising a child, had dropped his daughter into the Ash Crones' gnarled, clawed hands. She nursed at their teats, milk soured with the tang of death magic. Was it any wonder she had become the cold, cruel mistress of a land that had tried, and failed, to annihilate her?

It wasn't until the faint sound of a horn blowing for the change in the watch in the latest hours of the night that she had finally returned to their bed. Now she slept on her side, eyes closed, breath shallow. The crimson linen curtains that covered the arch that led to Calar's private balcony rustled in the slight breeze that carried the salty tang of the Arjinnan Sea on its breath. Kes drank deeply, filling his lungs with its rich, clean scent. He would never get used to this. In Ithkar, there had only been fire and ash and rot. The first thing he smelled the night of the coup was the amber oil that burned from intricate lamps that hung from elegant hooks along every hallway in the palace, a sweet, rich gift from the earth.

Between the curtains' folds he glimpsed fragments of the land that lay below the palace. Each blade of grass, each strip of velvety bark and drop of water and grain of tilled earth had been fought for with the blood of his people. Calar had no love for this land, rarely venturing beyond the walls of the palace. But Kesmir reveled in its beauty, in the non-Ithkarness of it. He liked nothing more than to take Yasri to his favorite haunts, where he taught her joy and kindness, instilling in his child a desire for beauty and peace, not the bloodlust of her mother. It was all he had to give her. That, and protection from those who would harm her if they knew what she really was.

Kes reached for his tunic and drawstring pants, opting for soft Djan cotton over the formal uniform that the highest-ranking members of the Ifrit military wore. If he hurried, he just might make his meeting with the gryphon. For much of the night, he'd lain wide awake, so angry at his restless lover that he could have killed her in her sleep. He wondered, belatedly, why he hadn't just done it while she slept and his scimitar was within reach, before

Yasri was brought into their room by the nanny, inconsolable after a nightmare, arms reaching out for her papa. Always her papa.

Why, *why* couldn't he just end this?

Because you haven't given up on her yet, he reminded himself. *Because she's the mother of your child. Because killing her would only solve part of the problem.*

He tied a belt around his waist and filled its notches with poisoned daggers before throwing his scimitar over his shoulder, where it rested against his back, a familiar weight. A coup, as he well knew, was more than just eliminating the leaders. The dead needed to be replaced with jinn who weren't tyrants. And how was he going to find those leaders, organize his jinn, earn the trust of the resistance that he prayed would spread like wildfire among the Ifrit, and ensure the safety of his people—all without Calar having a clue?

Then there was this shame he carried around with him, this weakness that could shatter every hope he had for peace: he wasn't sure he'd be able to go through with killing the jinni he'd once called his *rohifsa*. A stubborn part of Kes still loved her—not in the way he once had, but enough to shudder at the thought of being the one to stop Calar's cruel heart from beating. And Yasri—dear, sweet, unexpected Yasri. He'd been less than twenty summers old when she came into his life, her mere presence reorganizing all that he believed about the world and his place in it. He didn't want her to inherit a life of blood and revenge. A life of being hated and feared because of her birthright. And so he'd vowed to the gods that he would end the war among the jinn and give his life for the land if they would spare his daughter and place her in loving hands that would help her grow into everything her mother was not. A reckless bargain, and one he'd be happy to make again and again.

Kes crossed to the wide double doors leading out of the bedroom—thick slabs of lapis lazuli inlaid with a repeating teardrop pattern made of pure gold. To his right was the bathing room, hidden from view by a floor-to-ceiling lattice carved from a single piece of marble. Tall candles inside the room glowed, the warm light flickering behind the delicate floral pattern of the latticework. He longed for the hot waters of the submerged bathtub, the musk-scented steam. Once, the pleasures of the palace had been enough for him. But that was years ago, before his daughter was placed in his arms for the first time.

Kes hesitated, his hand on the golden knob of the doors leading into the sitting room. A part of him was tempted to stay—this whole meeting could be a trap. Nalia's father could be planning to ambush him and punish Kesmir for the death of his son, Bashil. Kes had been against Calar's killing the boy, but she'd wanted to hurt Nalia and that was the best way she knew how. Pain was not something Calar could ever resist inflicting. Of course, the problem could come not from Nalia's father, but from within the palace itself. All it would take was one of his enemies at court to see Kes skulking through the hallways and have enough idle suspicion to follow him. Then again, Calar might have read Kes's mind without him knowing it, and this was her chance to catch him in the act, to make a lesson of him.

But in the end, the opportunity to train his mind was too good to pass up. Kes didn't know if he'd ever again have a chance to keep Calar out of his head. And until he could do that, a coup was next to impossible. He glanced once more at Calar before leaving the room. Her white hair spilled over the black pillow like a giant spider's web, a beautiful trap. When she was asleep, he could almost remember what it had felt like to love her. Kes turned away. There was no point in longing for the past. All he could hope for now was a chance to change the future.

He turned to go when he heard her voice from across the room.

"Where are you going?"

Terror seized him, a freezing burn that crushed him in its grip. He turned around, his face bland. She was still lying down, her eyes heavy with sleep, one hand absently playing with Yasri's hair. That one act of affection toward their daughter was enough to throw Kes into confusion. How could he hurt the only family he had left? Perhaps the price was too high to pay. And yet.

"I just need a walk—can't sleep," he said. "I'll be back later."

She studied him for a moment. He waited, searching for that calm he'd once had in her presence. The sun hadn't even risen and his nerves were already frayed.

"Very well." She turned on her side, eyes closing as she threw one arm over Yasri, pulling their daughter closer.

Kes slipped from the room, sighing in relief as the door shut behind him. The weight of her power, the fear of her wrath and how it would affect their daughter, just two summers old, threatened to overwhelm him. Being in Calar's presence was akin to being suffocated without the hope of death's kind release.

Calar's maid shot to her feet when he reached the hallway

outside Calar's rooms, her scarlet eyes struggling against sleep.

"What does My Empress need, sir?" she asked, her face flushing as it always did when he looked at her.

Calar had nearly killed the girl after reading her mind and discovering the jinni's attraction to Kesmir. He had never been sure what it was that made Calar more furious—that someone else could want Kesmir, or that her maid hadn't desired Calar herself. The only reason Kesmir had managed to save the girl's life and her position was to remind Calar how much she hated training new servants.

"Nothing, Elvka. I'm just out for some air. When the empress awakens, please let her know I'll return after the morning meal."

She nodded, and he could tell she was trying not to look at the deep scar that ran along his left cheek, a present from one of the Aisouri who'd burned his village down when he'd been a child.

"Have a nice . . . walk," the jinni said.

Kes raised a hand in farewell and hurried down the hall, making his way to the palace's highest dome. It had become his place of refuge, nothing more than a small, unfurnished room made of alabaster stone with a *widr* roof, the wood covered in prayers to Grathali, goddess of air. It was unclear what the Ghan Aisouri might have used the tower for, but it was perfect for Kes's purposes this morning. From the keyhole window cut into the wall just below the dome, he could see the Qaf ridge, dark against the lightening sky.

Kes fixed his eyes on Mount Zhiqui, then closed them as the image connected with his will. Crimson evanescence filled the small room, surrounding him in a cloud of smoke that smelled of burning *widr*, a campfire in a secluded clearing. He felt the chilling breeze of the mountaintop as he touched down seconds later, the cold wind as restless as his own heart.

Dawn as seen from the top of the Qaf Mountains never ceased to amaze Kesmir. He'd often come up here as a child, gazing longingly at the land he'd been exiled from. He'd never been entirely clear just what it was exactly his ancestors had done to piss off the Ghan Aisouri so much, but it'd been enough to get Kes's entire race banished for thousands of years to a lifeless region of rock and fire.

As the sun rose behind the palace in the far west, rays of light spilled over the Infinite Lake, turning it into a shimmering sapphire. The palace blazed with golden light, a collage of onion domes and spires, elegant arches, and elaborate windows. He could imagine Calar where he'd left her, sleeping in the bed they shared in the room directly above where Antharoe Falls tumbled into the lake below.

The Forest of Sighs spread out beneath him, still wreathed in shadow. He'd never seen the *tavrai* camp. Despite their small numbers, the forest was well fortified. Though its *bisahm* was strong, it wasn't the magical shield that protected the *tavrai*—it was the forest itself. Whether from some ancient magic or the gods, the forest served those who took sanctuary in it. An Ifrit army intent on ridding the forest of its *tavrai* was met with a solid, invisible, impenetrable wall that no number of weapons or mages could get past.

Kes waited until the sun sat just above the palace's highest dome, then put the golden whistle to his lips. It emitted a strange sound, something between that of a crashing wave and a hawk's piercing cry. Within seconds, a large shadow was moving toward him across the sky, following the line of the northern ridge of the mountains. Kes had the good sense to be nervous. He'd seen the viciousness of the Aisouri gryphons in person many times. Teacher, bodyguard, war horse, and companion—the gryphons had been all these things, and more, to their Ghan Aisouri mistresses. He well remembered the purple-eyed witches riding the creatures into battle and, later, the fierce struggle they'd put up when Calar and the Ifrit stormed the palace. Many of his own Ifrit soldiers had died of merciless claw and beak wounds, gutted, their innards spilling to the marble floor. In the end, it had taken five Ifrit soldiers per gryphon to bring them all down. It was anybody's guess how this one had survived.

Kes hoped, belatedly, that it had eaten breakfast already.

The shadow drew closer, its form materializing as it prepared to land. The creature was enormous, twice Kes's height, powerfully built. The front half of its body was reminiscent of a hawk, with eyes that seemed to look into his soul, ringed in blue feathers, but the bloody beak with bits of flesh still clinging to it reminded Kes of the creature's animal nature. The lower half of its body was that of a lion, with huge paws and a whiplike tail, strong enough to push Kes off the mountain if its owner so desired. As the gryphon landed, its muscles rippled beneath its fur. It paused before him, taking the measure of Kes in one glance. Its eyes were unlike any Kes had ever seen, dozens of colors that swirled together.

"So," it said, its voice a building avalanche, "you wish to undo the mess you made three years ago."

Kes settled into a defensive stance, his eyes straying to the blood on the creature's beak. "We both know that's impossible."

The gryphon looked at him for a long moment, then seemed to nod.

"Good answer." It settled onto its haunches, surveying the land. "Still, I'm not sure why I should help your attempt at a second coup. You tried to kill my mistress in the first one, and you destroyed not one but two races that night."

"I was not one of the executioners of the Ghan Aisouri."

That had been Haran's job. Kes had never liked Calar's ghoul, but he'd been a force to be reckoned with. The Ifrit empress had been none too happy that the last Ghan Aisouri had killed Haran before he'd managed to make a meal of her. The night of the coup was a collage of memories: cutting down guards in the palace throne room, blood coating the stairs as the gryphons were sliced open, one by one, Calar exuberant as she took the crown off the dead Ghan Aisouri empress's head and placed it upon her own. Kes, his bloody hands tracing her jaw, her lips—he'd had to resist taking her right then, the corpses of guards and gryphons that littered the floor be damned.

"That you were not in the killing room of my slain charges is of little comfort to me, boy," the creature said. "The royal race's blood is on your hands—I can smell it. But their deaths will be avenged soon enough by my mistress, may she reign with light and power."

Kes went utterly still as the ancient expression—and that one word: *mistress*—washed over him. Fate. Destiny. There was no other explanation for what he was hearing.

"You're—you're *Nalia Aisouri's* gryphon?"

Each gryphon had but one mistress, the two souls bound when the Aisouri was little more than a babe. Was this one able to survive because she had?

The creature seemed to grow taller as it answered. "Yes. And her life is to your advantage. If she had perished that night, you would be in my belly by now."

Kes did not doubt the truth of this statement. The gryphon pawed at the ground and Kes felt the stone tremble beneath him. It gave an agitated flap of its wings, and again, Kes was reminded of how easily he could be tossed from the mountain's peak.

Kes nodded. "Fair enough. And what shall I call you?"

"Thatur."

Of valor. What an apt name for Nalia's battle companion.

"Ghar lahim."

Thatur raised his eyebrows. *"Nice to meet you?* No jinni ever thinks it is *nice* to encounter my kind." Thatur stepped closer. He smelled of the verbena that coated the fields in spring and a musty, animal wildness. "Baron Shai'Dzar says you're gathering a resistance already. Is this true?"

"Yes."

"And after you dethrone Calar, will you kill her?"

Kill. He already knew he wouldn't. No matter the evil in her, Kes couldn't watch the *chiaan* spill out of his lover and disappear forever. Yasri would never forgive him, murdering her mama. Even if he was the favored parent. Kes was a coward and would need someone else to do it for him, if it came to that. Which he hoped to the gods it wouldn't. He'd do everything he could to save her life. Everything. It was the least he could do for the little jinni she'd once been, the girl who'd taken him in when he'd lost everyone he'd known and loved.

"It needn't come to that," Kes said.

"Calar gets to live while an entire caste of jinn does not? While every gryphon but myself is but ashes? You want my help and Calar doesn't perish? That will never be an even trade," the creature said.

"It is all I have to offer." *Please*, he begged silently. *You are my only hope.*

"You are one jinni," the gryphon said, impatience leaking into his voice. "What makes you think you will be able to defeat the woman who annihilated the royal caste in one night—*without killing her?* Do you expect Calar to return to Ithkar to live out her life in peace?" He snorted, a leonine huff. "Absurd. I'm wasting my time."

Thatur turned and Kes rushed forward.

"I'm the only person she trusts," he said, desperate. "If she has no other choice, I may be able to reason with her. And I'm not just trying to end Calar's reign. I want my people to have a chance to make real lives here in Arjinna. We can't have that while she rules, I agree. But there has been too much death—surely you must recognize that?"

"*Peace.*" Thatur shook his head. "And how do you propose doing that?"

"In any way possible. Once she is no longer able to read my

mind, I can set my plans in motion. I can think about them whenever I want. I can *lie* to her." He held out his hands in helpless supplication. "I'm tired of shedding blood and burning bodies. Aren't you?"

Thatur's eyes scanned the sky above and he was quiet for a long time.

"My mistress used to come to these mountains on her own," the gryphon said softly. "It was one of the few places she could just be herself. Her mind was beautiful—not a shred of hatred in it."

Just his head swiveled to look at Kes. One move, one wrong word, and Kes knew the gryphon would kill him. He could sense how much he wanted to. *Yasri.* He must tread carefully. His daughter had no one else, no one she could truly depend on.

"Killing me won't bring them back," Kes said. "I don't even think it will make you feel much better. But . . . I suppose it would be a kind of justice."

It wasn't until a year after the coup that Kes had bothered to think of the Aisouri as anything but the monsters he'd always known them to be. Now he knew differently. Thatur raised his eyebrows, watching him for a long moment with his bright, intelligent eyes.

"Justice," the gryphon repeated, as if to himself. His eyes fastened on Kes's. "If I train you, boy, you must promise me one thing."

"And what is that?"

"That *you* will kill her. It will hurt her far more than any other death possibly could."

Anything less than death is unacceptable.

The gryphon did not say the words out loud and yet they were as clear as if he'd whispered them in Kes's ear.

"You've been reading my mind this whole time," Kes said, an edge slipping into his voice.

"Of course." Thatur seemed to snicker, his tone self-satisfied. "Who," he asked quietly, "is Yasri?"

Kes swallowed. "My daughter."

"*Calar's* daughter."

"Yes." Kes tried not to think about her, about the magic that had been required to protect her.

But Thatur sucked in his breath. "Tell me it's true," he demanded. "Tell me what I just saw is *true*."

Here, then, was the biggest risk Kes had ever taken in his life. A sharp pain gripped his heart. It was too late—he could no longer hide her. And maybe, just maybe, her existence would convince the gryphon to train Kes without the promise of Calar's death.

Kes nodded. "Yes," he said, soft. "My daughter is a Ghan Aisouri."

Thatur sank to his haunches, disbelief and joy warring in his eyes. "Does Calar know?"

"Yes."

"She'll hurt the child," he growled. "How can you—"

"Calar is many things," Kes interrupted. "But she loves our daughter. Yasri is the only . . . the only happiness she has."

"How old is she?"

"Two summers."

"You will bring her to me in one year's time, if not before," Thatur answered. "By three summers old, a Ghan Aisouri's power begins to reveal itself. No matter how you've disguised her, you won't be able to hide that. She belongs with me. As far from the palace as possible. She must train, learn to control her powers—"

"I will not have my child taken from me," Kes snarled, chest heaving, crimson *chiaan* spilling through his fingers. "The Ghan Aisouri no longer lay claim to every child born with purple eyes. I am her *father*. Nobody gets to tell me how to raise my child. *Nobody*."

Thatur's feathers ruffled in agitation and he prowled the length of the cliff for many long moments, deep in thought. Finally he stopped before Kes.

"Be here every morning at dawn. The first time you don't show up is the last time I will."

Kesmir nodded and Thatur took a step back, sitting on his haunches.

Now, he said in Kesmir's head, *we begin.*

4

THE GHOULS HAD BEEN UNBELIEVABLY FAST, THEIR
sense of smell allowing them to navigate the darkness with chilling efficiency. The jinn had been outnumbered three to one, and
by the time it was all over, nearly every soldier had depleted their
chiaan. Zanari—their only guide—had been wounded, perhaps
mortally, and nearly every lantern had broken, casting them into
a dark abyss they would never be able to see their way out of.
There had been losses on both sides, including Anso, one of the
Dhoma jinn who'd accompanied Nalia in the cave beneath the
Sahara. The Brass Army had won the battle in the end, if this
could be called winning. The air stank of rotting flesh, drying
blood, and the bitter odor of magic.

Taz crouched over Zanari, feeding her yet another tonic.
There was no Phara to care for her: the Dhoma healer was back

in the Sahara, tending to the jinn who'd been too traumatized by the brass bottle to consider traveling through the Eye. It wouldn't have mattered. Taz didn't need to be a healer to know that if Zanari didn't replenish her *chiaan* soon, she would die.

"Has he found her yet?" Zanari whispered.

Nalia had gone missing and Raif was combing the surrounding area, his terror for his *rohifsa* so palpable, Taz could feel it from their makeshift camp.

"No," he said quietly.

It was impossible to believe that she'd been killed. Taz had seen her on the battlefield; Nalia fought like a righteous, damning goddess. An empress intent on taking her rightful place on the Arjinnan throne.

"She'll turn up," Zanari said. "She always pulls through."

But even Taz could hear the doubt that had begun to creep into Zanari's voice. It'd been a full day since the battle with the ghouls. The Brass Army was still fighting the occasional monster, but many of the soldiers were already beginning to rave from too much time in the darkness. It was too close to what they'd experienced in the bottles Solomon had trapped them inside. Taz feared if they didn't leave the Eye soon, they never would.

"How are you feeling?" Taz asked.

Zanari grimaced. "The truth?"

He nodded.

"I can't hold on much longer, Taz. If we wait too long . . . I won't be able to get us out of here. I can already feel things getting . . . muddled . . . inside me." Her voice broke. "But Nalia . . ."

Taz patted Zanari's hand absently as he stood. "I know."

They'd all accepted that going into the Eye was a risk, that getting out wasn't guaranteed. He'd been prepared for losing soldiers to the ghouls, but Taz hadn't let himself imagine losing Nalia. It was impossible, after she'd told him her story. She seemed . . . immortal, almost. How could they leave the empress of Arjinna in this godsforsaken place?

Zanari moaned, and Taz once more held the bottle to her lips, parting them so that he could get the tonic into her mouth. When he was finished, she gripped his hand.

"Get my brother, Taz. We have to leave."

"He'll never forgive you."

Her eyes were full of misery. "I know."

They would have to make the impossible choice for Raif because he'd never be able to make it himself. Taz had only known the *tavrai* commander for this past month in the Eye, but it was the one thing he was certain of: Raif Djan'Urbi would rather die than live without his *rohifsa*. Taz knew because he'd once had that same look in his eye, when his own *rohifsa* had slipped into the god-lands without him.

Taz scanned the darkness. In the distance, he could see the lights of the search parties, *chiaan* that flickered like sputtering candles. Long ropes had been tied to a jinni in each team that left in search of Nalia, the other end held by a jinni in the temporary encampment. It was too easy to lose soldiers when there was no light to see by. He could hear their cries to one another as they searched, faint shouts that were swallowed up in the thick black canvas of the Eye.

"Bring them in," Taz said to the jinn who stood with the ropes.

"But, sir, they haven't found her yet," one of the rope handlers said, looking back at Taz, confused.

"Bring them in," Taz repeated. "Before our guide dies."

There was no way out of the Eye without Zanari. It would be like trying to find a specific grain of sand in the bottom of the Arjinnan Sea. Only her psychic powers—her *voiqhif*—could see the invisible road that ended at Arjinna's Gate of the Silent Seers.

Sudden understanding dawned on the soldier's face. "Yes, sir."

It wasn't the first time Taz had been forced to make such a choice. He'd led soldiers in the Ifrit border wars and then, later, commanded Solomon's jinn in the Master King's battles against his human enemies. No matter how important Nalia was to Arjinna, they couldn't sacrifice the lives of every jinni in the Eye for her.

There was a caw above and then a burst of Marid blue evanescence, feathers turning to skin: Samar, chief of the Dhoma, reverting back to his human form. The shapeshifting *fawzel* came to stand beside Taz.

"Anything?" Taz asked.

Samar held up a jade dagger. Taz had seen it in Nalia's hand during the battle, and he knew it to be a Ghan Aisouri weapon. His own sister had been an Aisouri, taken from his family at birth, and she'd had one just like it.

"I fear the worst," Samar said. "I can't believe that she . . ." He trailed off, shaking his head.

Samar didn't need to explain to Taz. The ghouls were canni-
bals: likely, what was left of the last Ghan Aisouri was in the belly
of a monster. Taz ran a hand over his eyes, surprised by the tears
that threatened to leak out.

"One of us will hold Raif down while the other sedates him,"
Taz said. "It's the only way we'll get him out of here."

"It'll take more than two of us, brother. And Touma will
fight just as hard," Samar replied.

Touma had become Nalia's shadow, the very first jinni who
had been released from his brass bottle. When he'd learned that
it was only through Nalia's power that the discovery of Solomon's
bottles had been possible, he'd pledged his life and sword to her.
Touma had already demonstrated his fierce loyalty to the empress
on more than one occasion.

"Well, that's two of the most stubborn jinn in this army.
We'll be ready," Taz said.

Samar signaled for Noqril, one of the other *fawzel*. He'd been
in the cave with Nalia and the others when they'd gone in search
of Solomon's sigil. Not only was he a shapeshifter, he also possessed the power of invisibility.

"We're going to need your assistance, Noqril," Samar said.

The other jinni nodded, for once solemn. Gone were his
usual off-color remarks and swaggering. The absence of both
underscored the chilling task at hand.

A cloud of Djan green evanescence hurtled toward them from
where the search parties had been combing the land, a plume of
Ifrit red just behind it.

"Here we go," Taz murmured.

The evanescence had hardly dissipated before Raif was stalking toward them, barely more than an outline in the darkness.

"Why are you calling the search parties in?" he growled, jabbing a finger in Taz's chest. His eyes were wild with fury and terror.

Taz held his ground, sick with dread. He didn't want to see the look on Raif's face when he realized he was losing Nalia forever. None of them did.

"Raif," Taz said, gentle. "It's Zanari."

He'd already determined this was the best way to start: catch Raif off guard, play to his love for his sister.

"What's wrong with her?" Raif asked. The panic in his voice showed just how on the edge he was. Perhaps already over it.

"She's very ill," Taz said. "We need to get her to a proper healer in Arjinna. And . . . if we don't leave soon, she won't be able to lead us there."

"Of course," Raif said.

Taz's eyes widened. *That was easy.*

"Choose who will accompany her to Arjinna," Raif said. "As soon as she's healed, she can lead soldiers back here to pick the rest of us up."

Or not.

Touma arrived then, eyes bright as he looked over Taz's shoulder. "We found her?"

"No," Raif said. He turned to Samar. "I'll need one of the *fawzel* to stay. And Touma, you can be my second."

The Ifrit's devotion to Nalia had once seemed to wear on

Raif, but the loss of her had created an unlikely bond between them.

Samar shook his head. "Brother, how would Zanari ever find you again once she's healed? Her power works in images—there is nothing here to see."

Raif stared at them. "Are you suggesting we leave here *without Nalia*? Have you lost your fucking minds?"

His voice rose and the jinn nearby gathered closer, watching the terrible drama unfold.

"Raif."

Taz turned at the sound of Zanari's voice. Two jinn were on either side of her, holding her up. Already, a patch of blood was blooming through the bandages around her middle.

"Zan . . . there's a way, right?" Raif said. "We can figure it out."

The plea in Raif's voice was unmistakable. He and his sister looked at each other for an endless moment. Raif suddenly seemed a child then, completely unmoored.

Zanari's eyes filled and a sob escaped her throat. "I'm so sorry, little brother," she whispered.

"No." Raif's eyes went from her to Taz to Samar to Noqril, his face filled with a growing horror. "*Please.* She's alive, I know it. I can feel her out there, she's my . . . my . . . I just need more time. Zan, *please, please* don't do this."

Raif trembled as he backed away. Touma's hand went to his scimitar and he moved to Raif's side. Noqril caught Taz's eye and Taz nodded, once. The jinni disappeared. Seconds later Raif was struggling against Noqril's invisible arms. A stream of curses shot out of his mouth, and Noqril cried out as Raif reared his head back and bashed the invisible jinni behind him just as Touma aimed a kick at where Noqril's back would be. Noqril became visible as he fell to the ground, a sizable bump already forming on his forehead. Two other jinn pounced on Touma, holding him to the ground. Raif bolted into the never-ending night, but Samar was ready. He sent a stream of electric-blue *chiaan* to Raif's feet and Raif hit the ground, hard.

Zanari screamed. "Don't hurt him!"

Samar pounced on top of Raif and they struggled in the thick gray dust of the Eye. Raif had managed to get on top of Samar, his fist drawn back, but Taz leaped at him, his own arms wrapping around Raif's torso and pulling him off the Dhoma leader. Noqril appeared in front of Raif.

"I'm sorry, brother. And I truly mean that." He pulled back his fist and hit Raif so hard in the face that the sound echoed.

Raif's body went slack in Taz's arms as he slid into unconsciousness.

"He's gonna be one angry jinni when he wakes up," Noqril said.

"Yes, but he'll wake up alive, in Arjinna, with an army," Taz said.

"But without Solomon's sigil," Zanari said quietly.

Taz whirled around. *"What?"*

"He asked Nalia to carry it. Thought . . ." She took in a shuddering breath, closing her eyes as a wave of pain washed over her face. "Thought it would be safest with her."

Taz didn't want Raif or any jinni to ever put that ring on. It was an evil thing, and though it had freed him and the rest of the Brass Army from their bottles, it would have been best if Nalia and Raif had left it buried beneath the desert. But Raif was right about one thing: it was collateral. Once this Calar who Taz had heard so much about knew Raif possessed the ring, she would have had no choice but to surrender. Only a few people knew Raif had no intention of ever using it, Taz included. But now . . .

Taz looked down at where Raif lay slumped on the ground, unconscious. With Nalia gone, this was the leader of Arjinna. Taz could either focus on his own army and the Dhoma who were even now rotting in Ithkar's prison or try to be to Raif what Taz had intended to be to Nalia—an adviser, protector, friend.

There was one thing Taz was certain of. Now, more than ever, Raif would need to be surrounded by people he could trust.

Taz grunted as he grabbed Raif and threw him over his shoulder. He spared one last glance at the darkness, sending a quick prayer to the gods that they'd accept Nalia's body without the ritual burning, even though he knew they wouldn't. Then he joined the other jinn as they followed Zanari out of the Eye.

5

THE LATE-MORNING SUN FILTERED PAST THE HAZE OF smoke from cooking fires and burning rubbish that clogged the narrow lanes and alleyways of the Ghaz—Arjinna's hub of commerce halfway between the palace and the Forest of Sighs. Shirin pulled the hood of her cloak over her long braid and kept her head down as she navigated the familiar streets. She couldn't afford a run-in with an Ifrit patrol, not when she was carrying a bag of contraband weapons she'd stolen from their stores the night before. Not when they knew she was Raif Djan'Urbi's second, his most trusted warrior. With the portal between the realms closed, it was likely Shirin was now first in line on Calar's list of jinn to murder. It would have been far easier to evanesce to the Vein, her destination for the morning, but with the increase in Ifrit surveillance, the risk of being ambushed was too high. Shirin's palms were sweaty, her empty stomach a mess of knots. Being outside the safety of the forest was a death wish.

Grandmothers in layers of frayed clothing sat on low stools against the wall, hawking their wares. This was what freedom looked like in Arjinna: old women, cold and hungry, forced to earn a few *nibas* selling the luxury goods of their former masters, stolen after the Shaitan were carted off to the palace or the prison in Ithkar. No one knew for sure what had happened to the overlords. Some said they were executed immediately. Others said they were wasting away in the palace dungeons. A few lucky ones were in Calar's employ; Shirin knew that for a fact—mages forced to do her bidding. Despite Calar's dark powers, there was no one in the realm more knowledgeable in alchemy than the Shaitan mages. Shirin wouldn't trade places with them for anything in the worlds. She shuddered, remembering the stories she'd heard of Calar's policy of torturing those in her employ when things didn't go her way. Or throwing them in the great cauldron of fire that burned in front of the palace, an Ifrit addition to the former home of the Ghan Aisouri.

Like all the Marid and Djan in Arjinna, the grandmothers were starving—they had no choice but to risk their lives in the Ghaz, day in and day out. If they were lucky, an enterprising, kind Ifrit merchant would throw them enough coin in exchange for the goods. More likely, the Ifrit would steal what little the grandmothers had, threatening to turn them in to the next patrol that came by for selling stolen goods. It was a strange sight: these beautiful items, artifacts from another age, sitting in reed baskets in the mud, their shine worn off after passing from hand to hand.

Vases from Earth, the images painted in blue ink by the skilled hands of infinitely patient artists. Mirrors in golden frames, the glass a view not of one's face, but of anything in the past of their lives. Precious jewels, ancient books—all of it a treasure trove now that it was illegal to manifest anything, even food or clothing.

This was Calar's newest decree, all part of her war against the *tavrai*. It was obvious that this most recent law was an attempt to turn the jinn against the revolutionaries and quell any desire for an uprising. Because informants were rewarded with land and manifestation privileges, the entire realm was filled with spying neighbors and family members who turned on one another. Though the *tavrai* had taken to manifesting food and clothing and leaving it all over the countryside for people to find, many jinn refused to avail themselves of it, for fear they'd be caught and sent to Ithkar or worse—executed.

It didn't matter what the *tavrai* did anyway—they'd all be hanging from the palace gates soon enough. With Raif gone and Calar's fear-mongering reaching new heights, the revolution was doomed. The best they could hope for at this point was to take down as many Ifrit as they could when they staged their last battle. This time, Shirin was all in. By her calculations, she had about twenty-four hours left to live.

A faded poster clung to the wall of a bakery and Shirin stopped for a moment, staring at the face fashioned in bold black and white: Raif, staring off into an unseen future, his eyes resolute. She remembered when the artists started putting them up all over the city, long before the Aisouri had been killed. It had been their act of resistance in the hopes of adding to the revolution's meager ranks. Raif had actually blushed when they came upon the first one. He'd reached up and tried to take it down, but Shirin had slapped his hand.

I look a right ass, he'd said. *This isn't about me, it's about all of us.*

Shirin had pulled him away. *It gives the people hope, knowing you're out there, fighting for them.*

What she'd wanted to say was that it gave *her* hope, gave her a reason to wake up in the morning, when the dreams were too real, the past too close. Now, everyone just assumed he was dead. With the portal closed, he might as well be. Shirin took one last look at the poster, then moved on. That was all she could do now—keep moving, keep fighting.

Once again, Shirin saw the look in Raif's eyes when he defended the *salfit* he'd traveled to Earth to find. A Djan'Urbi, in love with a Ghan Aisouri. *How could he?*

She could still feel Raif's lips against her own, the heat of him, battle lust and something else. Shirin walked faster through the mud that coated the alley. There wasn't time for these pointless thoughts, this exercise in torture.

To hell with them both, she thought, adjusting the heavy burlap sack she carried over her shoulder.

Shirin smelled the Vein before she saw it. The downward slope of its cobblestoned lane acted as a gutter for the butcher stalls located along it, filling the air with the stench of death and decay. Shirin was well acquainted with the alley. In addition to being the home of the jinn black market, it was lined with harems and taverns, both of which continued to do a booming business despite the hard times. As such, they remained the best places for spreading information and finding new recruits for the *tavrai*. Jinn with thin faces and too much rouge leaned over the balconies that fronted the harems and called down to possible customers.

"Hey, brother, I can grant you a wish for that loaf of bread."

"Sister! Come upstairs and share that bottle of *savri* with me. I'll give you a good price."

That could have been me, she thought. If it hadn't been for Dthar Djan'Urbi rescuing her all those years ago, Shirin didn't know if she'd even be alive now.

An emaciated jinni stepped out of the shadows gathering in a nearby alcove, his Djan eyes bright with fever. "*Gaujuri*, pretty girl? Forget your troubles, eh? Grant me a wish or two?" He smiled, his teeth yellow, rotting from the potent herb. The last thing Shirin needed was to get high. And granting wishes these days could land you in Ithkar faster than you could say *screw the empress.*

"I'm good, brother, thanks," she said, shrugging off his dirty hand.

The alley was crowded, the scent of unwashed bodies mixing with the ghastly perfume of slaughtered animals. All around her, jinn traded what they could for food, clothing, *savri*, candles.

"Genuine Ghan Aisouri artifacts!" called a large Marid jinni.

She stood behind a table that sagged from the weight of jade daggers, leather cloaks, and gryphon harnesses. The goods had been showing up ever since the Aisouri had been killed, brought into the markets by palace servants and Ifrit soldiers who'd raided the palace in those early, chaotic days of the new regime. More often than not they were fakes—cheap things that broke the minute you tried to use them. From the looks of this table, though, the Marid had the real deal. Which meant she had an Ifrit backer. Shirin hurried past. That would just make a bad day worse, being recognized by an enemy collaborator.

She reached the Third Wish and ducked inside, searching for her contact in the half-light of the tavern. It was early, so only a few tables were occupied. Most of the drinkers were the drunks of the Ghaz and merchants conducting business over steaming bowls of watered-down goat stew, fragrant with coriander and cumin despite the little meat they contained. The Wish was one of the few places where all the castes mixed: rich, poor, Marid, Ifrit—it didn't matter, so long as the *savri* kept coming. The bar had been started by jinn on the dark caravan who'd granted their human masters their third wish and had then been set free from the magic that bound them. There were a handful of them in Arjinna, free jinn who the Ghan Aisouri hadn't known what to do with. For years they'd been running a brisk trade in the Ghaz as merchants and madams, drug dealers and black market mavens. The main room of the Wish had walls covered in fading swaths of velvet with shabby matching curtains that were drawn across private alcoves tucked away from the main floor, in dim corners. All kinds of things happened in those alcoves. Candles hovered in the air, the tallow evaporating rather than dripping. Long wooden tables occupied the center of the room, with smaller ones on the outer periphery.

Shirin caught the eye of the bartender, a Djan with one golden eye, one emerald—a *hagiz*. She knew his story—the child of a slave who'd been taken by her overlord, with no choice but to bear his child. Yurik's mixed parentage was unusual among the jinn. Though no one could prove it, most jinn feared that a child with mixed blood would have weaker *chiann*. The *hagiz* were pitied by most, but Yurik had done well for himself at the Wish and was indispensable to the revolution.

He set down the goblets he'd been drying and inclined his head toward the stairway. Shirin nodded and made her way to the second floor, knowing Yurik would be close behind. She pushed open the door at the top of the stairs, letting herself into his familiar quarters. The single room was cozy and lived-in, the floor's rough wood planks covered with thick rugs. A simple space, it contained little more than a bed, a small table with chairs, and a shelf filled with contraband items Yurik sold as needed: potions that changed jinn's eyes in order to disguise their appearance, poisoned daggers, iron-tipped arrows—deadly and sickmaking. Iron was one of the few things that jinn could not withstand, and so the metal was a precious weapon smuggled in from Earth in the days when the portal was still open.

Shirin heard his light tread on the stairs just before he joined her, a bottle of *savri* in hand.

"Fancy seeing you here, love," Yurik said, grinning.

"Well, I was in the neighborhood." Shirin returned his smile. Something about him lessened the weight on her heart, just a little. No matter how bad things were, that grin rarely left his face.

"That bag wouldn't, by any chance, have something to do with the raid on the Ifrit stores by the Infinite Lake, now would it?" he said as he uncorked the bottle of *savri*.

"Fifty guns, fully loaded, with extra ammunition."

Human weapons such as these were impossible to manifest, as they required the jinn to produce steel. Because steel was derived from iron, the Ifrit could only get these weapons from Earth—attempting to manifest one could easily result in death. Since the closure of the portal, guns had become a rare, precious resource. They worked faster than magic and killed instantly if aimed with precision. The guns that were not made of steel were difficult for the jinn to copy or manifest, as the materials—plastic, carbon fiber—were unknown in the jinn realm. The few mages who would have been able to manifest them had been killed by the Ifrit in the first wave of purges.

Shirin dropped the bag of weapons on the floor with a heavy clunk, then took a long, hearty swig from the bottle Yurik offered her.

He grabbed a chair and turned it around, sitting with his arms resting on its back. "That's my girl," he said. "I can always tell how things are going with the resistance by how you drink your *savri*."

Shirin wiped her mouth with the back of her hand. "What does this tell you?" she said, holding up the bottle, emptied of nearly half its contents.

His eyes twinkled—*twinkled*. "That we're screwed to all hells."

"And yet you're just as relaxed as ever. You are one twisted jinni, you know that?"

He shrugged. "Takes one to know one, *raiga*."

Wolf. It was what the *tavrai* called Shirin—Raif's *raiga*. Did Raif and Yurik see her that way, too—all bared teeth and snarls? *Focus.*

"I need you to distribute these throughout the Ghaz today— can you do that?" she asked, gesturing to the bag.

"To what end?"

"You know to what end, Yurik," she said quietly.

She was tired of arguing with him about this. For weeks they'd been on the verge of a shouting match over the *tavrai*'s plan for one more last offensive. He called it suicide; she called it honor.

Yurik stood and crossed the room, then tugged the bottle out of her hand. "I've been going over some maps. I found a route that—"

"You're still on about this mass exodus to Ithkar?" She shook her head. "There's a reason the Ifrit wanted to get the hell out of there so badly."

"But they survived, didn't they?" he said. "Don't you think living on the other side of the Qaf is better than arming grand-mothers and telling them to kill the first Ifrit they see?"

Shirin rubbed her thumb over the jagged scar that cut into the skin around her wrist, a nervous habit she'd had since child-hood. It was a constant reminder of what she'd survived, of why she could never give up this fight. The memory of that long-ago night was embedded deep inside her: the dagger she'd stolen from her overlord, biting down on a knotted sheet to keep from crying out as she sliced into the delicate skin just above her shackle. It was the only way she could imagine gaining her freedom—she'd rather lose her hands than spend one more minute on the over-lord's plantation. He'd tied her to his bed, a treat for later, but the ropes he'd used were too loose on her skin-and-bones body. Shirin lost consciousness when the blade hit her bone and her overlord found her there, bloodying his sheets, half dead. *Foolish little whore,* he'd said to her. *You thought all you needed to do to get rid of me was to cut off your hands?* He'd grabbed her injured arm, pressing her hand against the bulge in his pants. *This hand belongs to me,* he'd hissed. *And I shall do with it as I please.*

She'd been nine summers old.

"Shirin," Yurik said, his voice gentle.

He knew she'd gone somewhere he couldn't follow. He knew how to bring her back. When she turned to him, his eyes were searching and he held out the bottle of *savri* again, the only med-icine that ever helped her.

Shirin grabbed the bottle and took another long swig. "What makes you think Calar would even allow us to take over Ifrit ter-ritory? It's still *theirs.* I, for one, don't want to fight over a useless patch of rock and fire. We don't know Ithkar at all, never been there. We'd be sitting ducks when the army came after us. At least this way, we go out on our own terms."

"Our terms . . . or Raif's?"

She growled, frustrated. "This has nothing to do with him!"

"Doesn't it?" Yurik said softly. "This has Djan'Urbi's stamp all over it. Go out in a blaze of glory, right?"

There was no mistaking the feeling in his eyes—that hint of unearned jealousy. Shirin had never given Yurik a reason to think he was anything more than her friend. And yet what he wanted was plain as day, there if she wanted to see it.

She didn't.

Shirin crossed to the soot-stained window and looked down on the street below, filled with indecision. She didn't know what was right or wrong anymore.

"I'll never live up to your idea of me," she said. "I'm not good or noble. Just a *raiga*, after all."

"You don't care what anyone thinks—that's what I like about you. You know that."

The compliment warmed her, but only because it was something Raif would have said—*had* said. It was part of why he'd chosen her as his second.

"I need to get back to the forest." She turned to Yurik. "Will you do it?" she asked, gesturing to the guns in the bag.

"When have I ever *not* done something you wanted, Shir?" Yurik said, his voice laced with bitterness.

"Yurik . . ."

She heard everything he wasn't saying, but she refused to listen. He was her only friend—she wouldn't take him as her lover. Not because she didn't care for him, but because she knew she'd close her eyes and pretend he was Raif. He deserved more than that. Much more.

Yurik waited a moment, his hope a palpable thing in that tense silence. Then his lip curled as he threw open the door. He turned, one hand gripping the knob, his eyes sadder than she'd ever seen them.

"You make one hell of a beautiful martyr, Shirin Djan'Khar."

Shirin headed east, toward the *tavrai* headquarters in the Forest of Sighs. She took the long way through the forest, wending her way past overgrown sugarberry bushes that perfumed the air with their soft, sweet scent and elder pines that vaulted toward the sky, their thick trunks covered in moss. As she moved deeper into the forest, Shirin looked for markers cut into the wood of the pines, careful to stick to the path. To veer from it would be folly. Though the forest was selective about who was allowed inside it, little protection was given to its guests once they passed through the invisible barrier that acted as wall, gate, and weapon all in one. Thus far, the forest had refused to let the Ifrit inside, as though it instinctively knew Calar's soldiers meant only harm. The inability of the Ifrit to enter the forest was the only miracle Shirin had witnessed in her young life, aside from the Djan'Urbi family's unbinding magic.

The forest was at the heart of the ancient story of Jandessa and Rahim, the doomed lovers from different castes. Long ago, Jandessa had sought refuge in the forest, fleeing her Shaitan family after her father murdered Jandessa's Djan lover. It was said that before her time, the forest had been open to all. But the gods had heard her cries for solitude and barred all but those seeking protection from entering the forest. Thus, the forest gifted the *tavrai* asylum and denied entrance to those who would do them harm. The protection of this fearsome landscape was what had allowed the *tavrai* to avoid engaging in full-scale battles with the Ifrit. Instead, they worked at slowly wearing their enemies down through small attacks and raids.

Still, the forest itself could do plenty harm. Deep holes lurked beneath the brush, hiding snakes whose venom wiped away every memory from the victim's mind, and carnivorous plants that craved jinn flesh. None of this particularly bothered Shirin. She'd learned long ago how to appease the pines, so as not to receive a whipping from their branches. She recognized the sour scent the snakes gave off and knew where all the pools of quicksand lay.

Shirin was halfway back to camp when she stopped on the forest path, gutted. Just before her stood a *widr*, a swath of its bark missing and replaced with Raif's determined handwriting, a skill he hadn't acquired until he was ten summers old. He was one of the few *tavrai* who could write. SHEEREN + RAF WAZ HEER.

She reached out and traced the letters with her fingertips, the ache for him traveling up her arm, into her heart, a suffocating thing that had held power over her for nine long years. She closed her eyes. She would not cry, she would *not*—

"Godsdamn you, Raif Djan'Urbi," she whispered.

Raif.

Raif.

Her first thought, when she opened her eyes in the morning.

Her last when she closed them at night.

She'd tried to erase the feel of his lips against hers—that one kiss she'd given him just before he'd left for Earth. A kiss nine years in the making, a kiss he'd returned, surprised at first, then soft and warm. His callused hands on her cheeks, his body pressing hers against a wall. It was impossible to blot that memory from her mind—or the one that had cemented her feelings for him, so long ago.

Shirin has been free for six months. The wounds that bracelet her wrists have healed into scars, only one of her body's many reminders of those years on the overlord's plantation. She sits in the shadows, outside the firelight where the free jinn dance.

It is the harvest festival and she can only tell that Raif is across from her by the way he holds his body, bony shoulders thrown back, so sure of his place in this world of the tavrai. *He wears a dragon mask, of course—he loves dragons. She has chosen that of a wolf—teeth in a snarl, fur white as snow. Yet somehow he knows it's her behind that ferocious face.*

"Shirin, come on! They're going to start the reel," he says, crouching before her.

They are ten summers old, too young to join in most of the dances. She shakes her head, silent as always. She has not spoken for two years. She will not start today.

"Come on, little wolf," he says, more gently now.

Inside she is wild, just like the wolf on her mask. Snapping teeth and bloodlust. Raif knows this and yet he still reaches out to her. He knows she will not bite him. Never him. They are the same age, but he is somehow older than she.

In some ways.

She slowly stands, then takes a step back. Uncertain. Before she can run away, he grabs her hand and pulls her into the circle of swirling jinn. His skin is warm and his chiaan *feels like a summer meadow. Safe.*

She knows the steps, has watched this dance all her life. They kick up their feet, sending dust into the sky. Shirin throws back her head and laughs, a wolfish howl from her belly, and she can see the smile in Raif's eyes, the happiness behind his dragon mask.

When they are finished she opens her mouth, and for the first time since the overlord did what he did to her and to her mother, since the time she saw her mother's ashes fly away on a gust of autumn wind, she speaks. The sound travels from her heart, up her throat, syllables made of gold and hope. The word she speaks is medicine. *A cure.*

"Raif."

His eyes widen and he pulls off his mask.

She is a locked door. He is the only one who can open it.

The night after Shirin had discovered Raif was in love with a Ghan Aisouri, she pulled her second, Jaqar, deep into the forest. They were not two lovers on a tryst, but animals letting off steam. Rough bark against her back, teeth against skin. Both of them covered in blood and sweat, the grime of a battle they'd just lost to the Ifrit. It was surprising how easy it was to bed someone she wasn't willing to die for. Shirin couldn't pretend he was Raif; there was no gentleness in his eyes, no softness in his touch.

Thank gods.

Later, she'd bathed in the freezing River Sorrow and only let the tears come when she was underwater, holding her breath, wondering if she should just let go. Open her mouth, give up. It'd be so easy.

But she was Shirin Djan'Khar: if she could survive an overlord who had done such despicable things to her, she could survive anything. And though it was Raif who'd given her back her voice, it was she—Shirin—who had kept her own heart beating, her lungs filled with air. No one owned her. No one.

Nalia sighed, content, eyes closed against a soft sun, her skin lapping up a gentle breeze.

The sand was warm beneath her towel and she sank into it. The waves crashed on the shore, a lull that filled her with a delicious drowsiness. She hadn't felt this good in a long, long time. Maybe ever, come to think of it. Somewhere above her, a seagull cried, a child laughed. The faint strains of Edith Piaf filled the air: Non, je ne regrette rien.

Dying felt like a trip to the Riviera.

"Hayati, *wake up*," said a soft voice. Clove-scented lips brushed her ear.

Maybe it was the Riviera. Malek had a home there, where he took Nalia several times a year—he'd always said it was one of the last bastions of civilization. Of course he'd found a way to swindle the gods into giving him his version of paradise. Her silver-tongued captor, always on the make. The world had been his personal playground—why not the afterlife, too?

"Hayati, I'm not going to ask a second time."

Nalia smiled, her eyes still closed. "Or what? We're dead—you can't punish me, and we both know you wouldn't, anyway."

She reached up an arm to push him away. Malek caught her hand and held it. There was the gentle pressure of his lips against her palm and then he let go.

"I'm dead," he said, his voice quiet. She could feel his hot breath on her lips. "You, however, are not. Yet, anyway. Now Wake. The. Hell. Up."

He pressed his lips against hers and the warmth, the ocean, Malek—all of it disappeared. She was in a roiling sea, dark as midnight, and she couldn't find the shore.

6

THE SUN TUMBLED INTO THE OCEAN'S HORIZON LIKE A swirling ball of molten gold that had fallen out of a god's hand. To the north, the Qaf Mountains towered against the darkening lavender sky, lapis lazuli blue against a backdrop of Ghan Aisouri purple, with shots of green, pink, and orange: the Arjinnan aurora. The Three Widows rose together, dancers called to the stage to perform an ancient series of steps. They glimmered above the highest peak. One moon waxed, one waned, and the third was full.

Arjinna.

Taz stood just beyond the Gate of the Eye, its twisting bars bent from the force of the hundreds of hands that had just pushed through it with their last remaining *chiaan*. An army flowed beneath its arch, a river of flesh covered in dried blood and the gray dust of the Eye. The Ifrit soldiers who had stood guard outside the gate lay slumped against its columns, dead. Their blood dripped from the dagger in Taz's hand and the scimitar Samar held loosely in his fingers. Taz's eyes scanned their surroundings, but there was no sign of the Ifrit. Their presence would be noted soon enough. Two thousand jinn weren't easily camouflaged.

"So this is Arjinna," Samar said.

Taz nodded, overcome with the sight of his land after so many years of exile. When he'd left, he'd been angry and in love and eager to be as far away from his overlord father as possible. Returning after so many years gave him vertigo. Taz swayed, his body trying to remember this place, to comprehend that it existed while everyone he'd once known here was long dead. His throat tightened and Taz didn't know if he wanted to sob from joy or utter horror.

I shouldn't be alive was all he could think.

Samar clapped him on the back. "Welcome home, brother."

Home.

"It's your home too, you know," he said, with a sideways glance at the Dhoma leader. If he felt unmoored, he couldn't imagine how the Dhoma who'd never seen Arjinna before were feeling.

"We'll see," Samar said, his voice uncertain.

They moved farther afield as the army swarmed the clearing before the gate. Most of the soldiers immediately found their element in order to replenish their *chiaan*; others simply stared, dumbstruck, at the Arjinnan sky. Taz looked to where a small group of his soldiers surrounded Zanari. She'd collapsed as soon as she'd led them to the gate. They wrung their hands, faces ashen. There wasn't much time left to save her.

"We need to contact the *tavrai* immediately," Taz said.

Samar frowned. "Easier said than done."

Zanari and Raif were both unconscious. As the only jinn who were *tavrai* and had been in the realm during the past three thousand years, they were the Brass Army's point of entry into the *tavrai*'s secretive world. Though Touma was trying to revive Raif with increasingly harder slaps to the face, the revolution's commander had been heavily sedated and continued to appear as though he were in a deep sleep.

Taz sighed, weary. "If we can't revive him within the next few minutes, we're going to have to send messengers to the forest."

From what Taz knew of the *tavrai*, the chances of the scouts gaining entrance to the impenetrable forest were slim. It was more likely that his Brass soldiers would be captured by an Ifrit patrol.

Raif needed to wake up soon.

"It looks like this every night?" Noqril asked in disbelief as he joined them.

Taz smiled. "Every night."

How many times had he dreamed of this sky, the smell of the gentle breeze that blew around them? Taz headed toward a secluded patch of land, then leaned down and pressed his lips to the soil. He'd been waiting so long to do that. He raised his arms to the sky and let the wind surge around him, his element bringing him back to life. It was nothing like Earth. The very air here was charged, the *chiaan* igniting his blood, sending currents of energy roaring through him. He wondered if the Master King would have been able to bend the jinn to his will had he been in Arjinna. Solomon may have had a ring fashioned by his god, but the jinn gods ruled here. Magic lived in this air, wild and fierce.

Off to the east, he could make out the water temple of Lathor. Its walls of water glimmered beneath the moons, catching the wan tangerine light of the setting sun. Taz stared at the sun until the final rays disappeared, the moons and stars now jewels in the crown of the sky. Taz stood still, his body tensed, waiting. He would only feel at home if he heard the sound he'd tried more than anything else to conjure in his memory when he was stuck in the bottle. Silence settled over the land in expectation.

There it was—faint at first and then louder: the evening prayers began. The low bass of the haunting chants thrummed against him so that Taz felt the words in his very bones. It was as if the entire realm froze in awed wonder, allowing the words to fall upon it like a soft spring rain.

First were the Shaitan prayers in Grathali's temple high in the Qaf Mountains, where her worshippers could best access their element. Taz's golden eyes closed as the *pajai* calling the prayer finished the final lines of the evening *sadr*:

Restless goddess of the skies, send us your spirit on the wind. O Grathali, fill us with the power of your ever-changing, ever-shifting grace.

The priest's magically amplified voice carried across Arjinna, to the ears of every Shaitan in the realm. Taz could imagine the other *pajai*, who sat at the four corners of his caste's main temple, whispering the words of the evening *sadr*, their palms raised to the sky as the head chanter's voice soared to the very ears of the gods. For most of his life, all Taz had wanted was to become a temple priest, to make those sacred vows that would consecrate his life to Grathali. He craved their peace. He wanted to be good. It had been his father's worst nightmare, a son giving up his birthright as a Shaitan overlord, choosing instead the monastic life of the *pajai*.

As soon as the last notes of the Shaitan prayer faded, the Djan *pajai* in the temple at the entrance to the Forest of Sighs began the Djan *sadr*, a similar prayer, but this one directed to Tirgan, god of earth. Taz listened to that one, too, its low earthy notes that crashed against one another like an avalanche. Then the Marid call to Lathor, goddess of water, the prayer swirling around him, a storm that turned to mist. Finally, the deep bass of the Ifrit call, once barely discernible over the range from Ithkar, but now piercingly loud, coming directly from the palace. Their *pajai*'s words burned and their edges were sharp, prayer as battle call. A temporary stillness rested in the wake of the prayers, and in that stillness, Taz reached deep inside himself for courage.

He would need it more than ever now that his empress was dead. Taz had been quick to fall in line with Nalia, a welcome relief from the prospect of beginning his life anew, alone and adrift on Earth.

And now?

He turned to where Raif was finally showing signs of consciousness. Was this the future of Arjinna, a grieving boy and an army of orphans?

Raif opened his eyes, bleary. "Whatshappening?" he mumbled, confused. "Wherearewe? WheresNalia?"

"Just a little more of this tonic, brother," Touma said. "This should clear your head in no time."

Raif gagged as the liquid slipped down his throat, then rubbed his temples, moaning. Though he was able to stand on his own, he swayed slightly and Touma stood behind him, one hand held out in case he should fall.

"Perhaps we kept him spelled too long," Samar said.

Taz shook his head. "We didn't have a choice. There's no way we would have gotten him here otherwise."

Suddenly Raif went still, silent. His head snapped up, eyes clear and furious as he looked first at Samar, then Taz. Whatever Touma had given him was undoubtedly working now.

"Where is she?" His voice was cold, deadly.

How to break a heart without shattering it completely?

"She's gone, brother," Taz said, soft. "You know that."

Without a word Raif turned toward the Gate of the Eye, a ruin now, and began pushing through the ranks of jinn who continued to stream through it.

"Raif!" Taz hurried after him, grabbing hold of him just as Raif reached the pitch-dark of the world beyond, sprinting in the opposite direction of the army.

Raif whirled around and drew back his fist in one swift movement. He stood there, poised to fight, breathing heavily.

"I didn't travel through hell after three thousand years in a bottle to play nursemaid to a child," Taz growled. Tough love was the one thing he'd learned from his father. "Your sister's dying and you have an army stranded in a field. Get out there and contact the *tavrai* before Calar kills every last one of us."

Raif's fist fell to his side. "What do you mean, Zan's dying?"

"That last trip through the Eye nearly killed her after she got wounded by a ghoul—remember? She needs the best healer you can find." Taz stepped closer to him, barely able to distinguish Raif's features in the darkness. "I lost my *rohifsa*, too. I know I'm asking you to go against every instinct you have. But you can save your sister's life. Hurry, or she's gone as well."

Raif turned to the Eye, his hand reaching into the darkness. It hovered there for a moment, as though Nalia could simply reach out and grab hold of him.

"She died for you," Taz said. "You must live for her. Anything else would be dishonoring the one you love."

It was painful to see the battle Raif fought, as though he were being shredded on the inside by a vicious, clawed creature. Taz knew this was an impossible choice, that he was telling Raif to move a mountain, to run across the sea. Raif doubled over, hands on his knees, as one gut-wrenching sob tore from him. Taz turned away. No matter how much he understood what Raif was going through, this was a private grief.

Taz runs through Solomon's palace, keeping to the shadows as he searches the harem. He needs to tell Lokahm that they're really going to do it: rise up against the Master King. Tonight. Taz's worry mounts as he fails to find Lokahm in any of the usual places. All the other eunuchs have been accounted for—where is his rohifsa?

He enters the bathing room. The air is full of fragrant steam and the sound of dripping water. The marble walls sweat.

"Lokahm?" he whispers.

Then he sees the body. Taz falls to his knees, his agony echoing off the walls around him.

Raif straightened, his eyes dead. "I will never forgive you for taking away my choice back there, for letting them drug me."

Taz nodded. "I know."

Raif turned to the light of his land and walked toward it.

Nalia, *a voice whispered.*

The broken jinni remained still. The gray dust of the Eye coated her body, a shroud. Her clothing was drenched in blood, now stiff and dry. One arm was bent at a sickening angle. The corpse beside her had begun to decay, filling the air with the scent of rotting flesh.

Nalia.

The jinni stirred, just barely. A twitch of a finger, a fluttering eyelid.

Rise, empress of Arjinna. Your land awaits you.

A strangled gasp, lips parted.

Will you desert those who love you in their time of need?

Nalia Aisouri'Taifyeh opened her eyes.

7

"SHAME, SHIRIN DJAN'KHAR. *SHAME.*" FJIRLA DJAN'URBI'S
eyes—nearly the exact shade as Raif's—sparked with anger. "My
husband did not give his life in battle so that the *tavrai* could kill
themselves."

Shirin met the elder's gaze with her own fierce, stubborn one.
They had been disagreeing about the *tavrai*'s last stand since Shirin began planning it.

"I can think of nothing more honorable than dying in battle,"
Shirin said. "You want us to wait here like cowards, hide from the
Ifrit for the rest of our lives?"

"It takes more courage to live than to die," Fjirla said.

Godsdamn her, Shirin thought. It was easy for the widow of
Dthar Djan'Urbi to hand out criticism as though it were a daily
ration of bread—she never had to get her hands dirty, never had

to make the tough choices.

Shirin's face warmed, her resolve slowly cracking. A voice spoke up from behind her—Jaqar.

"Ever since Calar's law against manifestation, the people have turned on us almost completely," he said. "With the Ifrit continuing their offensive, our only advantage is the element of surprise. They'd never expect an attack of this size. This is war, grandmother. And wars are meant to be *fought*."

Fjirla shook her head, disgusted. *"Ma'aj yaqifla."*

I wash my hands of it.

Raif's mother walked away, toward the *ludeen* that had once held her whole family. Now all of them were dead, or as good as dead. *I know what that feels like,* Shirin wanted to say. *I know your loneliness, what you carry inside you.*

A shout went up near the entrance to the encampment and Shirin turned, her heart stopping as she took in the jinni striding toward her. Joy—so much of it and so fast—rushed through Shirin, a flood that threatened to drown her.

"Raif," she breathed. Once again, it was the only word she could say, the only one that had ever mattered.

Against all the conceivable odds in the universe, he was home.

His eyes found hers, a darker shade of green than she remembered. No, not darker—dull, vacant. It was as if the fire burning inside him had gone out.

"Raif?" she whispered.

He looked at her for a long moment, as though he couldn't understand her. As though he didn't know her. It seemed as if he'd come from the depths of hell, his clothes tattered and bloodstained, every inch of him covered in what looked like ash. He sported a sizable bruise on his cheek. Gods, what had happened to him?

Raif, Raif. Her heart beat out his name, but she hated herself for it. He was here with *her*, no doubt. The Ghan Aisouri. She'd done this to him. Raif was hurt—broken in some way Shirin didn't yet understand. But he was here, and that was all that mattered now.

There was a cry behind them. Fjirla was running toward Raif, her long white hair flowing behind her like a flag of surrender. She threw her arms around her son, sobbing. Raif stood there, unmoving, unmoved. After a few moments, he maneuvered out of her embrace.

"Zanari needs our best healers. Now. She's in danger," he said.

"Where is she?" Fjirla asked, moving from overwhelming emotion to intense focus—the *tavrai* way, born of the constantly shifting tides of war.

"The Gate of the Eye," Raif said.

He'd hardly got the words out before his mother was sprinting toward the healers' *ludeen*, one of the few tree houses of the forest built within a trunk and not the branches in order to better accommodate the wounded and ill.

Shirin stared. Now the gray dust and the haunted look in his eyes made sense. "Raif, you didn't . . . I mean, you didn't come *through* there. Did you?"

"Not everyone made it out," he said, his voice flat.

"But how—"

"Antharoe and the Blind Seer."

It took Shirin a moment to get what he meant, but when she did . . . *Gods and monsters.* He was saying that the ancient story of the legendary Ghan Aisouri, Antharoe, and her blind seer had come to life. Until today, they'd been the only jinn to cross the Eye and live to tell the tale. So *Zanari* had used her *voiqhif* to get them through the Eye, just like the blind seer? But Antharoe—who could possibly—

Bitterness filled Shirin: of course—Raif's Ghan Aisouri. The new Antharoe.

Emerald evanescence began to plume under Raif's feet. "I'll see you at the gate," he said. "We have . . . visitors."

"Visitors?"

Gods, what other horrors had he brought with him?

"I'll need your help settling them in," he said, not bothering to explain. "They're going to draw a lot of attention, so make sure we have *tavrai* keeping the Ifrit well away from the gate."

Then he was gone, just smoke in the cool night air.

The *tavrai* camp was all confusion. Jinn were running in every direction, shouting and grabbing weapons. Shirin stood in the center of it all, stunned. It took her a minute to process what was happening around her. After what felt like minutes but was only a matter of seconds, she put two fingers in her mouth and whistled. Instantly, all activity stopped. The *tavrai* looked to her, frozen in place. Shirin felt a faint glimmer of satisfaction. She'd done well in Raif's absence—there was no question who was leading their ragtag army.

"To your stations!" Shirin called, signaling for her best jinn to join her—ten battle-scarred males and females who she trusted with her life.

"What in all hells is going on?" Jaqar said.

She filled them in on the little that Raif had told her, the words clipped, edged. He was here, then he was gone. That was really all she knew.

"And if the Ifrit attack in full force while these 'visitors' are here?" one of the *tavrai* said.

"I didn't expect us to live out the night, so any time afforded us beyond that is a little something extra from the gods," Shirin answered. "Now get out there and spill some Ifrit blood."

She didn't wait to see them off. Shirin grabbed her scimitar and evanesced to the gate in a swirl of earthy smoke. When her feet touched down on a small mound of earth overlooking the Gate of the Eye, she couldn't help but stare. The Three Widows shone silver over the spectacle before her.

"Fire and blood," Shirin breathed.

The gate was . . . *open*. Not just open—utterly destroyed. The Ifrit guards who'd been standing before it lay in puddles of their own blood.

But that was nothing compared to what was streaming out of the gate itself—jinn. Not the ghouls from the stories of her childhood who lurked in the impenetrable darkness of the Eye. Hundreds of jinn—thousands, maybe—poured out of the gate.

They were dressed in the uniform of the *tavrai*. Had Raif truly recruited all these jinn for the war? Many of them looked the worse for wear, but this was no surprise, not if they'd just crossed through the Eye. But how in the gods' names had Zanari managed it?

"Who are they?" asked Jaqar, coming to stand beside her. His bright-blue Marid eyes were glued to the unknown jinn.

She could almost see the calculations he was doing in his head: how many could he cut down if he had to?

"I have no idea."

Her eyes searched frantically among the crowd and then— Raif. A tall Shaitan with molten-gold eyes and a strange-looking jinni with a white stripe in his hair stood near him, deep in conversation while Raif leaned over his sister. Zanari was lying on the ground and Aisha, the *tavrai*'s most experienced healer, bent over her. Shirin made her way toward them, unease unfurling in her stomach like a tattered flag.

The jinn surrounding Raif looked her over, each one as battle-worn as Raif seemed to be. Raif himself didn't register her approach at all, but that was to be expected. He was crouched, staring intently at his comatose sister, his lips moving in a soundless prayer as his mother and the healers worked over Zanari. With the ash covering her braids, his sister looked like an old woman. A nasty wound cut across her stomach and Shirin covered her nose at the stench of rotting, infected flesh.

"Ghouls," Aisha explained at Shirin's questioning look.

"I'm Shirin," she said to the jinn beside Raif, "second in

command of the *tavrai*. Now who in all hells are you and why are you wearing our uniform?"

The question was a growl. *Little wolf.*

"I assume only a jinni of the most wonderfully ruthless character could take over the revolution in this one's absence," the Shaitan said, nodding toward Raif, who was entirely focused on Zanari.

"And you are . . . ," Shirin said, eyes narrowing.

"Tazlim Shai'Majdak," he said with a small bow. "Former slave of Solomon, the Master King, and prisoner of a terribly small bottle hidden in a cave for three thousand years. And," he added, gesturing to the scores of jinn roaming around the broken gate, "the commander of the Brass Army. As to your other question: we wear the *tavrai* uniform because we are joining you in the fight against Calar." The jinni's smile was forced, an attempt to ease the tension.

It didn't work.

Shirin had no doubt that this Tazlim had experience leading soldiers. He carried himself with the delicate grace of his aristocratic caste, but there was hard, trained muscle beneath his tunic, and authority in his voice. His gold eyes shone in the darkness and the moonlight danced on his skin—a light brown, the color of a *widr* tree's wood. He wore the white armband of the *tavrai*, but his was braided with purple fabric. What did it mean?

"Raif recruited you?" she asked, careful to keep her voice low so as not to disturb Aisha's work.

The healer worked quickly, eyes filled with worry. Zanari

looked in a bad way. Shirin didn't know what it would do to Raif to lose her. It was only a few years ago that he'd lost his best friend, Kir. Shirin herself had felt that death like a wound to the gut.

"It's a little more complicated than that," said the jinni with the long white stripe of hair and bright Marid eyes. He stood beside an Ifrit with an orange stripe in his hair and a playful glint in his eye. What kind of strange company had Raif been keeping on Earth? And what was with the stripes—some strange Earth fashion?

The jinni with the white stripe caught her stare. He pulled at his hair. "It signifies our gift. We are *fawzel*."

Shapeshifters. *Godsdamn.* Raif *had* been busy.

"Well you can't stay out here," Shirin said. "If Calar hasn't sent troops over to find out what's going on, she's bound to at any moment. You need to gather your soldiers and . . ."

And what?

"We were hoping you might have some room to spare in your camp," Tazlim said.

Shirin bristled. "It doesn't look like we have much choice."

Gods, Raif, she thought. *Would a little bit of warning have killed you?*

Zanari gave a rattled gasp and her eyes snapped opened as she cried out in pain. Raif and his mother exchanged a brief, relieved glance.

"I made it?" Zanari asked, her voice full of surprise as she took in her mother's face.

"Yes, *gharoof,* you made it. The worst is over, thank the gods," Fjirla said.

Raif rested his forehead on Zanari's shoulder and whispered something to her. "I'm okay," she answered, soft.

Zanari's eyes slid to Shirin's. "Hey, sister."

"Hey, there." Shirin gave Zanari a tight smile. "You and Raif have a lot of explaining to do." Fjirla frowned and Shirin added, "But first, you know, feel better."

Zanari snorted, a faint smile on her face. "Thanks, *raiga*."

Shirin shrugged. "I've never been good at . . ."

"I know."

"*Antharoe and the Blind Seer*?" Shirin asked, a small corner of her lip turning up.

Zanari's face darkened. "Something like that." She turned to her brother. "Raif, there was no time. I swear, I never would have left Nalia if there'd—"

"You let them knock me out," he said, his voice low and hard.

The conversation was unbearably private and yet Shirin couldn't walk away. Who was Nalia?

A shard of fear cut into Zanari's eyes. "I'm sorry, little brother. I loved her too—"

"Don't," he said. "Don't use the fucking past tense." His jaw tightened and he stood abruptly, walking across the field and toward the forest.

Shirin watched Raif, the cracks in her heart growing longer, wider. What had happened to him out there?

A stream of tears slid down Zanari's cheeks. Fjirla shooed the jinn away. "Go. All of you."

"Who's Nalia?" Shirin asked Tazlim, as soon as they were away from Zanari.

"Your empress." Tazlim pushed past her, his eyes on Raif. "She's dead."

The Ghan Aisouri. She was dead. *Dead.*

"I have no empress," she said, but the words were lost in the din and it didn't matter because the Ghan Aisouri was gone and yes Raif clearly wasn't happy about that, but maybe, just maybe she'd feel his lips against her own again, someday.

But did she still want that? *Love,* Zanari had said. *Love.*

"What happened to him?" Jaqar called to her, glancing in Raif's direction.

"Nothing he won't recover from," Shirin said. *Tavrai* died every day and they kept going. Why should an Aisouri's death be any different?

She organized the Brass Army into groups, barking out orders to the *tavrai* as they corralled the Brass soldiers, keeping physical contact with them so that they could evanesce together to the forest. She caught up with Tazlim and pulled him aside.

"I need to know what happened out there," she said. "I can't have my *tavrai* see Raif like this."

"It's almost impossible to explain the Eye," he said. "Long story short, we were attacked by ghouls."

"They killed the Aisouri?"

"I don't know. I assume so. We couldn't find her after the battle." He shook his head, grief etched into the lines of his face. "We had no choice but to leave. *Gods.*" Tazlim cleared his throat, looking away.

Shirin looked over her shoulder, into that gaping maw of darkness.

Serves her right, she thought. It was a fitting punishment for an Aisouri. They'd given the overlords the power to rape little girls and kill their mothers. Each one of them belonged in the belly of a ghoul.

"How long has Raif been like this?" she asked.

Tazlim seemed to know what she meant by *this.* "Since yesterday—at least, I think it was yesterday. Time doesn't really exist in the Eye."

Jaqar joined them then, his eyes cold as he glanced at the Shaitan commander. He pointed to Shirin. "She's in charge until Djan'Urbi gets his shit together. Forget that and I'll make your jinn regret it."

Her lover turned on his heel and stalked toward the group of jinn he was responsible for, throwing angry glances at every jinni from Earth he encountered.

"A jinni of few words, that one," Tazlim said. "I take it we have some explaining to do?"

"Yeah, something like that."

Shirin took one last look at the gate before pushing ahead, leading her group into the safety of the forest.

8

KES FORCED HIMSELF TO WATCH.

It was a monumental effort to resist vomiting, to keep himself from running as far and as fast as he could. Take Yasri and never come back.

"He's not bleeding enough," Calar said to the soldier who was whipping the naked jinni tied to a pillar in the throne room. She motioned for him to stand down. "Not nearly enough." Her voice was dangerous, soft.

This time the victim was a low-ranking Ifrit soldier with nothing in his head but the memory of his lover dying in one of the purges. Kesmir had warned Calar this would happen: the purges had been intended to wipe out resistance among the Ifrit, a reminder to return to their values of solidarity—not an excuse to murder at will. The purges had the opposite of their intended effect: they created resistance where there had been none before and had sown hatred—and fear—of Calar into the hearts of many Ifrit.

The hours of this evening's torture had been a waste. From what Kesmir gathered, Calar had learned of only one tiny cell tucked into the Qaf Mountains. Just a few deserters from her army who had stockpiled human weapons hoping for . . . what? A chance to assassinate her? Fools, every last one of them. This was what happened when his contacts went against Kesmir's advice. He'd told them to be patient. To wait a little longer. Kes himself was unscathed, if only because he wore the peasant mask for his clandestine meetings. Only his closest advisers in the resistance knew they were being led by Kes. Calar didn't know how big the rebellion was—the jinni tied to the pillar had been the first of Kes's recruits to be caught. But he'd never be able to give Kes up—all Calar would see in his mind was a jinni wearing a mask.

"Human weapons," Calar purred, practically skipping toward the jinni.

Kes ground his teeth. The poor man's flesh was already in ribbons—in some places, the bones were visible.

"You wanted to use them on me, didn't you?"

"No," the jinni managed. "Never, My Empress—"

Calar's eyes glowed and Kes knew what would happen next. Dear gods, he knew.

The jinni screamed then, the sound of a tortured, braying ass. Blood began to flow from his nostrils, the corners of his eyes, his ears. Calar stepped away, breaking her connection with his mind. The jinni's head slumped forward. He'd either fainted or died.

She turned to Kes, licking her lips. "That felt good." She grabbed Kes's hand, then turned and motioned for the guards who'd brought the prisoner three hours ago to take him down. "Kill him. He's of no use to us now. Wasn't much use to us before."

Kill him meant throwing him into the cauldron. It meant a slow, agonizing death by fire laced with dark magic. It burned yet kept the victim alive for hours, even after the skin had melted off.

It was, Kes thought, the absolute worst way to go.

Calar pulled him onto the balcony that overlooked the Infinite Lake, leaning against it, her eyes shining as she watched the soldiers cut the prisoner down and drag him from the room. She tipped back her head and laughed, a joyous peal. Kes stared at her, horrified.

Calar moved Kes's hand to her breast. "I want you to take me," she whispered as she pressed herself against him, her breath hot against his ear. "Right now."

"Cal . . ."

Inside, he recoiled with disgust. This was new—her absolute pleasure in watching a jinni suffer, the way it made her laugh, made her rip off his belt and slide her hand into his pants.

She touched him, frowning. "No one can see us, my love." She slid her tongue along his jaw, kissed his chin. The things that once drove him wild with desire. She'd always found a way past his barriers—even when he was at his angriest with her, he always succumbed to the beauty of her body, the way her eyes would soften when he held her close. But he couldn't do it this time. He couldn't do what he'd been forced to for months now: pretend she was the maid who waited outside her bedroom door or imagine her hands were those of the handsome jinni who shined his shoes and gave Kes seductive, inviting smiles when no one was looking.

How could she want this, after what she'd just done? He took Calar's hand and withdrew it from his pants.

"What's wrong?" she asked, genuinely confused.

This—her cruelty, the way she'd come to hunger for pain— could only be the result of the dark magic she was drowning in, her work with the Ash Crones.

"Calar. What you just did—"

She cocked her head to the side. "Yes?"

"Was the pain necessary?" he asked quietly.

"I've never known you to get squeamish at the sight of blood."

It was one of the things she'd always loved about him, Kesmir knew: his rage had been nearly as bottomless as her own. They'd once danced in puddles of Ghan Aisouri blood. Literally. He could still remember how easy it had been to slide across that floor, reveling in their victory.

But then Yasri came into their lives.

From the moment Kes saw his infant daughter's eyes, everything changed. He'd cut down anyone who wanted to dance in *her* blood simply because her eyes were purple. And it got Kes wondering—*had* every single one of the Ghan Aisouri been evil? What would have become of his Yasri if she'd been forced to train under someone like Calar? He realized he no longer knew the difference between his lover and the Aisouri who'd slashed his face just so that the scar would always remind him of her "mercy" at allowing him to live after Kes's entire family was slaughtered right in front of him.

"When blood flows justly," he said now, choosing his words with care, "I have no cause for concern."

"That jinni was a *traitor*," Calar growled. "One of our own Ifrit, stealing our weapons and plotting against me. Can there be a more just reason to execute someone?"

"I'm not talking about the order for execution." It was a pity the jinni had to die, but he knew the risk he'd been taking. Kesmir couldn't save him, not without putting his fledgling rebellion at risk. "I'm talking about what just happened in this room." He ran a hand over his face, hoping to hide the disgust there, the fear. "Calar, what you did to his mind . . . he screamed like an animal being butchered."

"I had to know what was in there." Her voice turned cold. "If you'd been doing your job, perhaps I wouldn't have needed to question him at all."

Kes stiffened. "Do *not* put this on me," he said, finally losing his temper. Ifrit blood ran hot and thick, rage always on the surface, unless held in check. There was only so much he could take before giving in to its siren song. "I told you what would happen if you continued like this."

"Watch yourself," she said softly.

"Or what—I'm next? Our daughter?" He turned his crimson eyes on her, not bothering to hide the disappointment in them. "The portal's closed and that Ghan Aisouri nothing but a memory." He forced himself to soften his voice. "You've won, my love. It's time to stop fighting. Let's build the world we've always wanted. We can—"

"That's enough, General," she snapped.

General? When had she ever called him that? He had always been Kesmir, her *rohifsa*, ever since the day they met, two children on the outskirts of a burned village.

Kes gave her a curt nod, his voice suddenly formal. "Apologies, My Empress."

And when had he ever called her that, except in bed, the words spoken against her lips as he willingly obeyed her every command? They'd become strangers.

Kes pushed off the wall, but instead of moving closer to her, he crossed to the other end of the balcony.

"Your father . . ." He let his voice trail off.

This was very dangerous territory. But hadn't she once said, *Kes, don't ever let me be like him*? Kes would never forget how her father had hanged a little boy for stealing a piece of bread. How he'd beaten the Ifrit into submission with his notoriously cruel work camps. Or his dark pleasures too horrible to name.

"What about him?" Her voice was cold, verging on hatred.

"The way he . . . You once said—"

"Stop right there. Stop or I swear to the gods I will throw you off this balcony."

Kes's blood ran cold. She was gone. Well and truly gone.

He didn't have to turn around to know she was searching with her mind until she found the spark of his consciousness, by now nearly as recognizable as her own. It'd been a long time since she'd looked inside him in anger. Kesmir sucked in his breath, praying he could hide the rebellion. He threw thoughts of resistance behind memories of Yasri as a baby. It was all he could do until his training with the gryphon started in earnest.

"There was a time you would have asked," he said as her mind latched onto his.

He faced Calar, ready, and her ruby-tinted lips turned up. Accusatory. Chilling. "There was a time you had nothing to hide."

Cold terror swept through him. He remembered what the gryphon had told him this morning, during their first session.

If you try to hide something, she'll know, Thatur had said. *The key is to fill your mind with so much that she will tire of looking. The truth will be out in the open, but there will be so much to see that she won't find it.*

Kes knew his mind was full of the horror he'd just witnessed—she would expect that. He added worry about his troops who fought the *tavrai* in the Qaf range. The gryphon and the secret meetings with his co-conspirators, these Kes gently guided to the farthest reaches of his mind, hidden behind mundane things like court gossip and memories of Ithkar. He thought about Yasri, how much she looked like her mother, especially with her glamoured eyes, a perfect Ifrit crimson. Even the child didn't know what she was, what power lurked inside her. And as long as Calar reigned, she never would. Kes hastily pushed the worry about Calar someday hurting their child behind one about dinner and how the *savri* had been off—sour, like vinegar. He already knew that one day soon he'd have no choice but to take his daughter to Thatur for safekeeping. It was only a matter of time before Calar turned on her, threatened.

Kes felt the moment when her consciousness slipped into his. Calar waded into Kesmir's mind, slow, but steady. Before the coup, Kes had cherished these moments with her. It had felt as though they were together in a secret wood, where nothing could hurt them and no one could find them.

It had been a long time since Calar had been so intimate with him. For weeks, the closest she'd gotten to him were bouts of frenzied lovemaking, a distraction, nothing more. Feeling her inside the landscape of his mind was like getting a visit from a long-lost friend, someone who was both utterly familiar and a stranger.

She pushed deeper, prodding for the things he'd tried to hide. There were doors there she'd opened long ago: memories of the coup, flashes of happier times in his childhood, before he'd lost everyone he loved. She glanced at his memories of their early days together: that first, fumbling kiss, the sound of her ecstasy as they made love, Kes watching her sleep beside him. She pushed deeper. Calar was like a blind woman in a room full of familiar objects, searching for the one thing that didn't fit.

He knew she could only sustain her connection for so long. He just had to wait her out. Kes added a disagreement he'd had with one of his officers to the front of his mind, fear that she no longer loved him—she'd like that. After a few more minutes, Calar broke the connection.

"Leave me be," she said, brushing past him. She didn't turn to look at him and, after a moment, he left the room without a word.

"If Yasri wakes up in the middle of the night, bring her to my rooms," he told the guard waiting outside the throne room. The young sentry nodded, eyes wide. Kes knew she had heard that jinni being tortured, seen the broken, bleeding body being dragged down the hall toward the cauldron.

After what he'd just witnessed, Kes couldn't leave Calar alone with his daughter. Not anymore.

As soon as he entered his rooms Kes flung off his cloak, burning with rage and shame and . . . relief. Gods, he'd done it. He'd actually hidden something from her. He crossed to his private balcony and stepped outside. The throne room and Calar's chambers were around a bend, far enough away that she couldn't sense him.

He stared out over the land he'd helped to conquer. It still felt foreign, despite its loveliness. Kes almost missed the soot-filled skies of Ithkar with its volcanoes spitting lava and the black, shining rock that covered its barren plains. Terrible in its beauty, each day a struggle to survive. But it was home.

Without the smoke that had blanketed Ithkar's sky, he could finally see all the colors in the aurora that splashed across the gods' midnight-blue canvas. This swath of rainbow each night was too cheerful by far. The Three Widows were bright, bathing the meadows in the south and the sea beyond in misty silver. The Widows, at least, were familiar, though in Ithkar they'd been transformed by the smoke in the air into three blood-red discs, their presence ominous. On this side of the Qaf, the Widows were mysterious sisters of the night, enigmas shrouded in iridescent gowns. He could only remember fragments of the old legend. The sisters were wives to the three gods of the sun: the god of dawn, the god of day, the god of coming night. Jealous of one another, the gods fought among themselves, arguing over whose sun burned the brightest. Kes couldn't remember the rest—there were no books in Ithkar, no people of letters. All he knew was that the three brothers burned to a crisp, their souls combined into one ghost sun, leaving their moon wives forever widowed, lonely keepers of the night.

So many of the jinn legends were stories of broken hearts. He shouldn't have been surprised, then, when his own heart was ripped to shreds by the one person he thought he'd always be able to depend on. He leaned against the banister, running a hand over his close-cropped hair.

Below him was a perfect reflection of the palace on the still surface of the Infinite Lake and the soft roar of Antharoe Falls tumbling over the mountain cliffs. The palace never failed to intimidate him with its glorious domes and masonry, the gold and mother-of-pearl tiles that shimmered in the moonlight. For so long it had been a place of terror, where the Ghan Aisouri sharpened their weapons, waiting, he knew, to kill every last Ifrit. Then it briefly became a place of victory and pleasure, where he and Calar were finally free to begin building the life they'd always dreamed of. Now it was once again a place of terror.

Kes's crimson eyes moved beyond the lake, to the patch of darkness in the east, near the base of the Qaf range. The Forest of Sighs. According to the Ifrit spies who reported to both him and Calar, it'd been well over two months since Raif Djan'Urbi had graced the land with his presence. More likely than not, he was stranded on Earth with the Ghan Aisouri Calar so desperately wanted to kill. He had to admit, it'd been a rather brilliant move on Calar's part, forcing the Shaitan mages in the palace to close the portal using the Ash Crones' death magic to destroy the ancient doorway to Earth. He'd thought that would be enough to temper Calar's madness, but it had only served to strengthen it. He realized now that the only thing that kept Calar in check was the threat of someone more powerful. With the Aisouri stuck on Earth, there was no one to challenge her. Not until Yasri came of age.

There was a knock on the door to his rooms and Kes turned. "Enter," he called.

One of his scouts crossed the threshold. "Sir, something's happened at the Gate of the Eye."

"Can you elaborate on that?" Kes said, barely keeping his annoyance in check. It wasn't this jinni's fault he was coupled to a madwoman.

"There appears to be . . . well, an army coming through it."

"An army."

"Ye—yes. Led by Raif Djan'Urbi."

Kes's heart quickened. Had the Ghan Aisouri returned, then?

He reached for his scimitar and the richly embroidered tunic that Calar insisted he wear as the Royal Consort.

"Let's go."

For the first time in a long, long while, Kes felt something like hope stir in his chest.

9

KES KEPT TO THE SHADOWS, GROWING INCREASINGLY concerned as jinn streamed into Arjinna from the Eye. The gate was little more than twisted metal, and the jinn who came through it kissed the soil before scattering along the wall to replenish their *chiaan*. Were these the Dhoma he'd heard so much about? But from his soldiers' reports, their numbers hadn't been nearly this plentiful.

Every now and then Kes's eyes strayed to the wall that kept the monsters of the Eye out of Arjinna, its stones as ancient as the land. Try as he might, he'd never been able to cover or erase the images the *tavrai* had painted on it. They glowed at night: colorful renderings of Dthar Djan'Urbi and his son holding up a broken chain, *sadrs* from the jinn holy book, the *Sadranishta*.

Give ear to us, o gods, hear the cries of our blood.

After an hour crouched in the long, lavender grasses that covered the hills overlooking the wall, Kes told the squad he'd taken with him to return to the palace. There'd be no fighting tonight. From his vantage point behind a boulder, he could see the Djan'Urbi boy and his sister, and, other than a handful of *tavrai*, he didn't recognize any of the other jinn. How had they managed to cross the Eye? Calar had been so certain that closing the portal would keep the Aisouri away.

Kes looked harder. The Aisouri must have been in disguise— a smart move on her part, given the unhappy welcome she was sure to receive from the *tavrai*. Djan'Urbi had his work cut out for him, that was certain, but recruiting an army that rivaled the numbers of Kes's own ensured he was off to a good start. As the jinn made their way into the Forest of Sighs, it was clear that Calar could no longer be assured a victory. Kes's heart lifted at the prospect of defeat—then he wouldn't be the one to bring her down. Maybe he could salvage his little family. It was an unlikely prospect—gods knew what would become of Calar if she were once again brought low by an Aisouri.

And what of this supposed daughter of the gods? From all that he'd learned about her, it seemed Nalia and Djan'Urbi had forged some kind of bond with one another. Her unexpected alliance with the *tavrai* leader suggested she might be different from her dead sisters. She might be someone his daughter could even look up to, learn from. Kes shook his head. What was he thinking? This Aisouri had been taught to kill Ifrit, to subdue all the castes. If she wanted the crown, she'd very likely get it. And the Ifrit? They'd be sent back to their hellish life in Ithkar, or systematically destroyed. How to broker a peace while Calar still had leverage, that was the real question. Yet if he aligned with the Aisouri in any way, it would kill Calar just as surely as that purple *chiaan* that had wiped out whole Ifrit families, including his own. Would he go so far as to dishonor the memory of the Ifrit dead, to give in now that his people were so close to building a world that included them? Kes grabbed fistfuls of the grass beneath him, tortured by the choices he would soon have to make. He wasn't nearly qualified enough for this task.

He waited until the clearing before the gate was empty, then evanesced back to the palace, his heart heavy. Calar was waiting for him in the throne room, her hands clutching the onyx arms of the new Arjinnan seat of power. For once, she was more afraid than him.

"Well?" she asked, her voice sharp.

"I didn't see her. But she'd likely be in disguise," he said.

"So it's true, what your scouts told me?"

"Yes. Somehow Djan'Urbi was able to get through the Eye."

"*Antharoe and the Blind Seer,*" she said to herself. "I bet they used that sister of his. Her *voiqhif* is how they found the Aisouri in the first place."

Kes rested a hand on his scimitar. "So what would you like to do about this?"

Calar stood and began pacing before the throne. Her heeled slippers echoed in the empty chamber.

"The Aisouri must be killed. *That* I will do myself." She frowned. "Somehow."

"We'll have to come up with a strategy—we have an awful lot

more jinn to fight now," Kes said.

"We'll do that tomorrow. For now, leave me be."

He gave her a small bow. "As you wish."

Calar had resumed her pacing and she merely waved a hand without looking up. "Go. I'll see you when I come in."

Kes made his way to Calar's rooms, his heart heavy. *When I come in.* Obviously he was expected to share Calar's bed tonight, despite what had happened mere hours ago. He was a whore then, his body to do with as she saw fit. He used to look forward to his nights with her, filled with love and laughter, the chance to see a side of Calar that no one else was privy to. There was gentleness in her, vulnerability. He'd seen her cry, and she him. She'd loved Kes so well for so long. But now she was only a monster in pretty packaging.

He sat heavily on the bed and his head fell into his hands. Kes wanted her back. But they'd chosen different courses after Yasri was born. He couldn't follow Calar to the dark places anymore.

Hours later, Calar slipped into bed beside him. Kes lay on his side, feigning sleep. Calar leaned closer and wrapped her arms around him. Her scent, so familiar: campfire and some unidentifiable musk. He felt the dampness of tears on his bare skin.

"Kes . . . I'm sorry," she whispered. He lay there, silent. "I don't know what came over me. I . . . I'm not really like him. I *can't* be like him." A sob slipped out of her and he turned and gathered her into his arms. No matter what she did, a part of him would always want to protect her, love her, help her.

Please let her come back to me, he silently prayed to Ravnir.

"You scared me," he said quietly, his lips against her glossy white hair.

She tightened her hold on him, burrowed into his chest. "I know. I don't know what's happening to me."

Gods, what was he supposed to do? One minute she was a creature fashioned from darkness itself, the next a frail girl, terrified of the blood that ran in her veins.

She looked up, her crimson eyes wet. "I love you so much. I don't ever want to hurt you—or Yasri. I swear it."

He was silent.

"Kes, you believe me, right?" Panic tightened her voice. "You two . . . you're my heart."

He was saved from answering by frantic pounding on their door. Kes instinctively pushed her behind him and reached for his scimitar, where it leaned against his bedside table.

"Who is it?" he called.

"Fazhad, sir."

He relaxed and slipped out of bed, pulling on a pair of drawstring trousers. "Enter," he said.

The light from the torches in the sitting room outside the bedchamber outlined a reed-thin jinni with auburn hair that fell to her waist. Fazhad was one of Kes's inner circle, an Ifrit captain who'd seemed nothing but loyal to Calar until Kes accidentally discovered she wasn't loyal in the least. He'd never expected her to turn, but when he caught Fazhad sobbing in a broom closet after watching Calar torture a child who'd been helping the *tavrai*, he knew he'd found an ally.

"My Empress," the captain said, catching sight of Calar. She bowed before turning to Kes, her eyes bright. "The scouts you asked me to keep near the forest have just returned." Fazhad paused. She was a jinni of few words and would never have come to the empress's rooms in the middle of the night unless it was absolutely necessary.

"And?" he said.

"The Ghan Aisouri is dead."

Kes's breath caught in his throat. Hopelessness washed over him. *Fool, don't let Calar see.* Behind him, he felt her stiffen.

"Explain," Calar said.

He turned, his eyes resting on her face, its contours lined by the moonlight that bled into the room from the floor-to-ceiling windows. Her fists gripped the black silk sheets, the softness she'd shown him moments before disappearing entirely, though her face was still wet with tears.

"We're not entirely sure of the details yet," Fazhad said. "The scouts overheard the newcomers discussing it. They suspect she was attacked by a ghoul in the Eye. No one could find her and they had to leave her behind."

The light went out of Calar's eyes. "No one can find her. And you think this means she's dead, do you?"

To her credit, Fazhad didn't flinch at the sudden harshness in Calar's voice. "My Empress, to my understanding, it would be impossible for any jinni without Zanari Djan'Urbi's powers to cross the Eye. I believe it is safe to assume the Aisouri dead, yes."

Calar's eyes narrowed. "Maybe I should send you into the Eye to find out."

Now Fazhad blanched. She bowed her head once more, taking a moment before she straightened. "As you wish, My Empress."

Kes turned to Calar. "She's my best captain. There's another way to find out whether or not the Aisouri is dead, am I right?"

"Her true name," Calar said softly. *Hahm'alah.*

Jinn only exchanged true names with their spouses during the wedding ceremony, and with their closest family members. It allowed them to contact one another, no matter how far away they were. Calar had stolen Nalia's true name from the girl's brother. Even now the memory of what Calar had done in Morocco to that innocent child filled Kes with sorrow and disgust. Bashil hadn't been much older than Yasri. He'd grieved for that boy. But with Nalia's true name, Calar would be able to keep track of her, torture her with endless threats through the images that jinn passed to one another when using *hahm'alah.*

Kes turned to Fazhad, anxious for her to leave before Calar ordered her into the Eye. "That will be all for now, Fazhad. We'll discuss this further in the morning."

She bowed once more, then turned on her heel, hastening out of the room. When the door shut behind her, Calar slipped out of bed and crossed to the flames that licked the air in the corner of the room. She set her hands inside them, waiting for the fire to fill her with its *chiaan*, then dropped to her knees, closing her eyes. Kes watched her, tense. Did he want the Aisouri to be dead? He wasn't so sure anymore. Since Calar had closed the portal, there'd been no way to use Nalia's true name. The portal's closure had effectively cut off all communication between Arjinna and Earth, a barrier to their magic. But the Eye was a loophole. If Nalia were alive, Calar would know.

After a few long moments, Calar's eyes snapped open and she began shaking. She turned to him, her hands pressing against her cheeks. "I can't . . . I can't contact her. She's *dead*, Kes. She's gone."

Laughter spilled out of her then, a girlish trill, pure delight. She jumped to her feet and vaulted into his arms. Disappointment washed over him, but he tried to mask it—Calar would feel that in his *chiaan*. It was muddled up in a confusion of other, conflicting feelings: relief that the Ifrit wouldn't go back to royal subjugation, fear that Calar would continue her reign.

She pulled back and Kes searched the face he knew so well. Her emotions moved like a bird of prey on the hunt, fast and fleeting. Joy, anger, sorrow, all in one moment.

"You're not happy," he said.

"I am. I just . . . really wanted to kill her myself." She tilted her chin up, searched for his eyes in the darkness of their room. "But I'll take what I can get." She pressed her lips against his, as though she were a soldier just come home from a long, hard war.

He felt nothing. The tenderness of those moments before Fazhad had knocked on their door had been washed away by her maniacal glee over Nalia's death, this unending desire to take life.

Kes pulled away. "What about this new army? We still have to reckon with them."

"*That* I am most displeased about." Calar frowned. "If we move quickly, we should be fine. My work in Ithkar is almost finished. The creatures are absolutely magnificent. Everything I'd hoped for—and more."

Her shadows. Kes's skin crawled just thinking about them. Calar was the only one who controlled those monsters of hers. Even the Ash Crones who'd helped her create them had no power over them. There'd be no way for Kes to predict how Calar would use her newest weapon. What little advantage he had was slipping through his fingers. As quickly as she was working to ready the creatures for battle, he had to be that much faster.

She moved toward him again, but he dodged her. "Calar. The *tavrai* may outnumber us now. We should consider the possibility of a peace treaty—"

Her lips curled. "A *peace treaty*?"

"Yes," he said, his voice more forceful than he'd had the courage to make it in years. "They could slaughter our people. Gods know what they've brought back with them from Earth."

Her eyes bored into his, narrowing.

"Get out."

"What?"

Calar pushed him. "I said, *get out.* I can't even look at you right now."

He crossed the room and angrily donned his uniform. "Why are you fighting this war, Calar? Who are you fighting it for? Because it's sure as all hells not for any of us."

Pain—slicing through his head, needles plunging into the soft tissue of his brain. Kes dropped to his knees, his palms against his temples, but before he could scream it was gone.

He looked up to where Calar stood across from him, so thin and fragile in her black shift. Her eyes glowed crimson, but she was staring in horror at him. Kes felt something drip off his chin and he lifted a hand to wipe his face: blood. He grabbed a hand-kerchief and held it against his nose.

"I'm sorry," she whispered. "Kes—" Her bottom lip trembled and he stood, turning away.

"Good night, Calar."

Leaving her right then was selfish. He was supposed to stay and placate her, make sure she trusted him. Now that the Aisouri was dead, Kes just might be the only hope Arjinna had of ridding itself of Calar.

But he'd be damned if he spent one more second in her company tonight.

10

RAIF WANTED TO DIE.

He sat on the edge of his bed, the one he'd hoped to share with Nalia, staring at the wall of his *ludeen*. He'd awoken hours earlier from a drug-addled sleep after drinking an entire bottle of tonic. Whatever Aisha had given him, it'd been strong enough for a squadron. His body was made of lead, he was a sinking stone. He'd first stumbled out of bed an hour before, confused—*Nalia, Nalia*—and his mother had sprung from a nearby chair, blocking his path to the door. He'd been hoping the memories of those last moments in the Eye had been a nightmare: Taz and Samar, saying they were leaving Nalia. Hallucinations, that's all. A side effect of a ghoul's bite, perhaps.

But then he remembered, all at once in a rush: Nalia was dead.

The sound that came out of Raif then was more animal than jinn and when his mother tried to comfort him, he pushed her toward the door. He was breaking he was breaking and she had to go before he hurt her—

"Get out," he snarled.

She stared at him, as though Raif were a stranger.

"Get. Out."

She lifted her hand and ran her fingers over his cheek. "I felt the same way when your father died," she whispered. Her hand dropped to her side. "Mourn tonight, my son, but tomorrow your people need you."

He waited until the door had closed behind her before he started throwing things.

Now he sat on the bed, surrounded by shards of glass and splintered wood. His hands were bloody with stinging cuts. He went from being numb to feeling everything at once. Raif leaned forward, gripping his hair in shaking fists. They should never have gone into that cave, into the Eye. He should have run away with her as soon as the portal closed. They could have hidden anywhere. Calar never would have found them.

And now she was, she was . . .

"Fuck, fuck, fuck, *fuck*."

Nalia's beautiful skin, shredded by a ghoul, her heart in its mouth, her blood dripping down its lips, her soul trapped in the shadowlands, forever stuck in limbo because her body didn't burn, he'd never see her, never again—

Raif sank to the floor and curled into a fetal position as the memories tore through him, each one cutting deeper than the one before.

"Can I kiss you?" she asked, her lips inches from his own. "Even though we can't be together? Even though it will be the last time?"

He reached up and tucked a small strand of hair behind her ear. "It won't be the last time, rohifsa. Not if I can help it."

"Whoa," he said, looking down at the sheets. "What's this?"

"Silk." She blushed. "I wanted it to be nice."

"Ah, so this is what it's like to spend a night with the empress," he said with a wicked smile. "A lowly Djan like me . . ."

"Shut up," she said, hitting him. He laughed and pulled her closer.

"Come on. Tell me watching me kill ghouls isn't sexy," she said.

In answer, Raif pulled Nalia to him, his lips crushing hers. The battle disappeared and it was just the jinni he loved more than anything and her chiaan that filled him with liquid light. He pulled away, though gods knew that was the last thing he wanted to do. . . .

"Keep killing these ghouls and there's more where that came from," he murmured against her lips.

Her eyes gleamed, wicked and lovely. "Promise?"

"I always keep my promises."

But he couldn't keep this one.

The evening prayers began and he screamed at the gods, screamed until his throat was raw.

A brown glass bottle sat a few feet away from him, remarkably still intact. Another sleeping tonic. He reached for it, threw off the cap, and poured its contents into his mouth. He was out in seconds.

The dead empresses of Arjinna surrounded Nalia, towering over her in their regal gowns. They were incandescent, glowing with wispy violet light, spirits from another plane. Each wore the Amethyst Crown, each had Nalia's purple eyes. They'd saved her life, their voices pulling her from the shadowlands, where she'd been lost in that midnight sea. Now they regarded her, silent witnesses to her resurrection.

"Thank you," she said.

Her voice was a barely audible whisper. Her kingdom for a glass of water. But this was the Eye—she could search a whole lifetime and never find a drop of water.

The empresses remained expressionless as they began their retreat. It seemed their work was done—for now, anyway. Before Nalia could utter another word, they disappeared, the black arms of the Eye enfolding them. For a few moments, bright spots of white and violet light danced before Nalia's eyes and then those, too, were gone, leaving her in utter darkness.

"Raif?" she whispered.

There was no response. She reached out a hand, hoping to feel his warm body nearby—perhaps everyone was sleeping, resting after the long battle. Maybe this was all a strange, Eye-induced dream. Her skin grazed flesh, but it was not Raif. It was wet and cold and her finger snagged on what could only be a claw. Nalia jerked up, crying out as blinding pain traveled up her left arm—only a ghoul's claws could do that.

There was no Raif, no Zanari, no army—just the rank

smell of death, the dust in her mouth, her nose, covering every inch of her skin.

She remembered now: the ghoul, so fast, dragging her through the Eye, Nalia screaming as the lights of the jinn grew fainter. The vicious fight with the monster. She couldn't find her dagger, must have dropped it along the way. She'd wounded the ghoul, but it seemed it wanted to stay alive long enough to take her into the godlands with him. She grappled with the enormous creature for what felt like hours, until the last of her chiaan bled out of her. She felt the moment of total depletion, like the last gasp of a drowning person. Her magic was gone. It was all too easy for the ghoul to break her then. The darkness was its ally, and while she stumbled about, blind and bleeding, it latched onto her scent, then pounced. When the ghoul snapped her arm, the agony nearly knocked her out. The creature used the last of its strength, bashing her head against something hard and unyielding before crashing to the ground beside her. She didn't remember anything after that.

Awake, she could feel that the ghoul was dead. She could smell its flesh decaying.

"Raif," she said again, louder. Her body began to tremble with fear—fear like she'd never felt before, a monstrous wave of it crashing down on her—

"RAIF." She screamed his name this time, consequences be damned. He wouldn't be far. He'd never leave her, she knew that. They'd find each other.

But the darkness swallowed her cries; deafening silence was its answer.

Nalia pulled herself to her knees, crying out when she accidentally put weight on her broken arm. The bones in her wrist, too, seemed to be shattered.

She wouldn't give in to the panic. He was alive, somewhere, he was looking for her. Raif would never leave her, never.

The Brass Army shouldn't be hard to find. She'd see their lanterns from miles away. She just had to start moving. Nalia struggled to her feet. Yes, they were looking for her, and soon she'd be in Raif's arms and a healer would fix her broken bones and someone would have water and food—gods, food!—and this would all be one more bad memory in a string of bad memories.

Nalia raised her hand and the tiniest flicker of chiaan answered her call for light. Not nearly enough to get her through the Eye. She could taste the burnout in her mouth, like charred meat. The emptiness inside her felt too much like those desolate days of grief after Bashil had died. If Malek were here, he'd be smoking one of his infernal clove cigarettes and cursing the entire Brass Army for their incompetence. She would have died in the Sahara if it hadn't been for him. Now she was in the same position—no chiaan, no water, no food.

No Malek.

You are not going to die, she growled to herself.

"You are not going to die," she said, aloud.

Water. Food. This had to be her priority. The Eye had little of either, but the ghouls had been able to survive on more than the occasional jinn tourist in their midst. The ghouls: her wan light would be a beacon in this darkness. But she had no choice. She was adrift, waiting for a rescue that might never come.

I am Ghan Aisouri.

The dead empresses of Nalia's realm hadn't woken her just so that she could die. Unless they'd been a dream. But they'd seemed so real.

I am Ghan Aisouri.

One foot in front of the other, so slow. So hungry. Parched. It was like being back in the Sahara, back in the bottle, the darkness, pressing closer and closer and gods what was out there? The panic built, a bird trapped in her chest, gnashing its beak against her skin, desperate to be free. Nalia fell to the ground, her broken arm wedged beneath her body. She screamed as the pain shot through her. Tasted blood in her mouth.

Nalia rolled onto her back and, for the first time in her life, she gave up.

Raif!

He sat up in bed, gasping. Cold sweat covered Raif's body, the sheets twisting around him, the blanket thrown to the floor. He'd heard her, plain as day, as though Nalia had been right beside him.

She'd been terrified. Pure, unadulterated fear was in that voice that called to him.

"Nal?"

The room was empty. He knew it was, but he just wanted to hear her name.

Judging by the moonlight drifting in through the window, it was still the middle of the night. Raif grabbed a pillow and screamed into it. He'd go crazy, maybe already *had* gone crazy, knowing that she was out there, alone and scared and maybe hurt and there was nothing he could do because he was a useless Djan and fuck the gods, fuck them all to the depths of hell.

Raif got out of bed and crossed to where a small throne to Tirgan, the Djan god, sat. He drew back his bare foot and kicked it, relishing the pain. He kicked it again, then again.

The earth flew in every direction and the statue hit the wall, shattering. "You're a useless piece of shit god if you can't even bring one jinni back."

Anger felt good. Felt right. He'd almost understood when the gods took his father: Dthar Djan'Urbi had been ready and his son was left to complete the work he'd set out to do. But there was no one *no one* who could replace Nalia.

He left the pieces of the altar where they were and slipped on a pair of shoes, then evanesced to the far eastern portion of the wall separating Arjinna and the Eye. It was a deserted section he could be certain wasn't guarded by the Ifrit. His destination was the gate, but it was best to approach with caution, as Calar's patrols often went past it. He headed west, walking along the wall, careful to keep well away from the main roads. The stone was covered with *tavrai* graffiti, the colors faded but still swirling. There was the image of his face, an iconic sketch over the words *Kajastria Vidim*—"Light to the revolution." A repeated image of broken shackles in a swirl of rainbow-colored evanescence—a symbol that had begun to crop up the year before—filled much of the wall's empty space, as well as a few crude remarks about Calar, scratched into the stone itself. As he neared the gate he noticed a lone figure standing before it. Raif went still, but when the jinni turned to face him, he relaxed—Touma. He'd once been annoyed by the jinni's devotion to Nalia, but since losing her Raif had found that this Ifrit was the only jinni carrying the same hope for her survival that Raif had within himself.

Touma stepped back as Raif drew closer. "Just in case," he said, in explanation for his presence at the gate.

Raif understood.

"I'll leave you be for now." Touma put a hand on Raif's shoulder for a moment, then walked toward a nearby hill covered with lavender grass. It wasn't until he'd disappeared that Raif stepped up to the gate.

He wanted to be alone with her.

It was hard to breathe, knowing Nalia was out there. She was his *rohifsa*. He'd know if she were gone. She wasn't. He felt her . . . somehow he could feel that the thread between them hadn't snapped, not yet. Raif held on to his hope like a life raft.

He refused to let go. To let *her* go.

Raif wrapped his hands around the bars, now repaired in order to keep any ghouls from venturing into Arjinna from the depths of the Eye. The iron burned, sickmaking, but his body barely registered the pain. The gate itself had always terrified Raif. It was an evil-looking thing, made of Ithkar's volcanic rock and the iron so anathema to jinn, with spires that ended in deadly points. The star-studded night sky stopped just above those points, the blues and greens and purples of the aurora shifting instantly to black. He remembered childhood dares to touch the gate or stick a hand through it, the thrill he'd gotten from not knowing what was going to happen burning through him. Kir had once claimed to hear breathing on the other side of the gate, but Zanari, only nine summers old at the time, their elder nonetheless, had refused to believe Kir by virtue of the fact that his hand hadn't been eaten.

"*Rohifsa*, where are you?" he whispered.

Raif had wanted to see the look on Nalia's face when she first stepped onto Arjinnan soil. He'd imagined it a hundred times. How he'd say *welcome home*. Nothing grand, probably not what you were supposed to say when an exiled empress finally returned to her kingdom. But she would have heard everything behind the words, as she always had.

His gripped the gate harder, relishing the pain as the iron seeped into his skin. The Eye shredded his hope until none was left. Standing here before its impenetrable darkness, Raif could finally see what the others had accepted days ago:

Nalia was dead.

Her voice had felt so real in his dream, as though she were just across the room. But he'd woken up, alone. And that feeling in his gut—that she was still out there, fighting for each breath because that's what she did, she fought against incredible odds—wasn't that just his heart, protecting him from the truth? But how could he believe she was dead when everything in him screamed she was alive?

"Nalia," he whispered. "Nal, please . . ."

It did her no good, his curling up into a ball and giving up. He had to act. For her. For Arjinna. It was what she'd demanded of him, time and again. He'd let her down so much. He had to do right by her now.

He had to do the hard thing. He used to be so good at that.

"Hey, little brother."

He turned. Zanari stood behind him, eyes big in her pale face. He wanted to be angry at her for the way she'd let the others force him out of the Eye, taking away his best chance at finding Nalia. But all he felt was cold inside.

"It had only been a day," he said quietly. "We might have found her."

"I was dying, Raif." He hated the softness in her voice, the pity. "If we hadn't left then, every last one of you would be stuck in the Eye right now."

"I told you to leave without me."

Zanari sighed. "I couldn't let you die for nothing, Raif."

"It wasn't *nothing*," he growled. "I would have found her—I know I would have."

But even now he could feel the hopeless desperation that had stolen through him during those last hours in the Eye, searching and never finding. She'd vanished.

Zanari slid her arm over his shoulder. He leaned into her for a moment, then pulled away.

"And your *voiqhif* . . . nothing?" He cringed at the pathetic hope in his voice—of course there was nothing.

"Just darkness," she said gently, gesturing toward the Eye. "You know that."

He stared through the gate's bars, as though he'd somehow see her from here. A form running toward him, arms outstretched. He gasped, turning away from Zanari, a fist in his mouth.

I can't, he thought. *I can't live without her.*

If Zanari weren't here, he'd get through that gate somehow. He'd run until he collapsed.

"Raif . . ."

"I heard her. In a dream," he said, his eyes once more on the endless dark before him. "She called for me. She was scared. Terrified." He turned to her. "What if she's still out there, Zan?"

His sister tried to hide the pity on her face, but he caught it. This was worse than death, this not knowing, this wanting.

"I can't do it, Raif." She shook her head, not even bothering to wipe the tears that poured down her face. "The Eye isn't like other places. It operates under a different set of rules. The only reason my *voiqhif* got us through the first time was because I could focus on a fixed location outside it. And I think the only reason I could do *that* was because I had an army's energy to draw from and we were going to a place I knew like the back of my hand. Arjinna helped us through just as much as my *voiqhif.*

But to find something *in* the Eye—one jinni with no *chiaan*? Raif, what you're asking is impossible. The minute we stepped in there," she said, pointing beyond the gate, "we'd just be wandering. Losing energy. We'd never find her and we'd never make it home alive. I'm sorry, little brother, but I'm not going to kill you, even if you do want to be put out of your misery."

The words filled his chest, hard, cold stones stacked one on top of the other. *So this is it,* he thought. His future without Nalia stretched before him, years of . . . nothing. Existing, at best.

"There won't be anyone to burn her body when she . . . when she . . ." He choked on the words. He couldn't say it. "I won't even see her in the godlands—"

Zanari took his hand. "I know."

They stared into the Eye for a long time.

"I want to die," he said.

"I know."

The endless night seeped into Raif until every bit of light in him dimmed.

Zanari laid her head on his shoulder. "Are you scared?"

"Of what?"

"Whatever's next?"

He was scared of living in a world where Nalia didn't exist. That was all.

"No. We have the Brass Army." He paused as a new thought came to him. "We don't have the ring, but . . . this is how Nalia wants it. She thinks no good can come of the sigil."

Past tense: *wanted, thought.* He couldn't do that. Not yet.

Raif could still see the fear in Nalia's eyes, feel the terror lancing her *chiaan* as she begged him to turn away from the altar where the sigil had lain.

Solomon's ring would have made this fight against Calar too clean, too easy. Raif didn't want easy. He wanted battles and blood. He wanted to make the Ifrit suffer.

11

EVER SINCE THE COUP, THERE HAD ALWAYS BEEN A PAL-
pable sense of fear—paranoia, even—in the Ghaz. There was no
telling how or where the Ifrit would strike. Though most of the
jinn had never seen Calar, gossip from the palace reached the
public relatively quickly. Her erratic, increasingly violent behavior
was attributed to her alliance with the Ash Crones of Ithkar and
an addiction to *gaujuri*. Calar's decrees and arrests were so varied
that the Djan, Marid, and Shaitan seemed to walk with slightly
hunched backs, as though preparing for a blow to strike. Even
the Ifrit civilians had begun to shrink into themselves. It wasn't
unusual to hear doors in the villages being pounded on at night
and the sudden sound of Ifrit boots as Calar's soldiers evanesced
into the narrow streets.

Everyone was afraid of being named a collaborator. Friend

turned on friend, family against family, relationships thrown to the fire to save a jinni's own skin, or someone's else's. Where once the Ghaz was filled with lively shoppers and a bustling trade, it now held furtive glances and whispered transactions. Tonight it seemed as if something were different, a shift in energy that Shirin couldn't quite put her finger on. Hope, perhaps, but from the murmured conversation around her, it was clear no one knew quite what to make of the past day's events. Still, it was strange to see light in eyes that had long been full of terrified resignation.

She could get used to hope.

Though it was so late at night that it was nearly morning, the Third Wish was full when Shirin pushed open its creaky doors, the chorus of voices a comforting din that drowned out the endless pacing in her mind. That was why she was here, wasn't it? The noise that wouldn't let her think, the way no one here expected anything of her, least of all Shirin herself. Well, almost anyone— Yurik had expectations. She just wasn't quite sure what they were and, at any rate, it didn't matter whether she lived up to them or not. Though, if she were honest with herself, a tiny part knew it did matter.

The bar smelled of unwashed bodies and *savri*, stale. Every table Shirin passed was talking about the same thing: the mysterious army that had arrived through the Gate of the Eye. Shirin crossed to the bar and leaned against the end, careful to keep the hood of her cloak up—the last thing she needed was an informant tattling to the Ifrit. She was ready to fight whatever came her way, of course, but she wanted a break. For one godsdamned day she wanted to *not* fight. Yurik was busy pouring drinks at the other end of the bar and she caught his eye and held up one finger. He nodded, his eyes lingering on hers. She looked away first.

"The whole thing was melted," a Marid fisherman in a loose linen *sawala* was saying. "I heard that the Ifrit blasted the gate down so the ghouls would kill us all."

"Aw, come off it," said a toothless Djan. "I saw the jinn coming through it with me own eyes. It's an army, I tell you! The *tavrai* carted them off to the forest right quick."

The Marid laughed. "An army from *where*? You've been taking a bit too much *gaujuri*, friend." He poured more *savri* into each of the clay mugs.

"I'm telling you what I saw!" the Djan insisted. "Hundreds of soldiers and they all had white and purple armbands."

"Purple, you say?" asked the third jinni at the table, another Djan. He was quite a bit younger than the others and his hand shook slightly as he sipped from his glass. An informant, Shirin had no doubt—that nervousness was a telltale sign. Her hand moved to the dagger concealed beneath her cloak.

"Ghan Aisouri purple." The old Djan leaned forward. "Maybe the rumors are true, eh? Maybe one of them's alive. Maybe she's come to fight that snake on the throne."

The fisherman's eyes filled with fear. "Keep it down, brother. You want a vacation in Ithkar?"

"What did you say your names were again?" the young jinni asked, voice tight.

Rookie mistake. Sometimes they made it so easy.

Before the jinn could answer, Shirin was at the young Djan's side, her dagger inches from his heart. She leaned over him, pretending to hug an old friend.

"Move and you'll sorely regret it," Shirin murmured.

The Djan went still. "I think there—there must be some mistake—"

"What did the Ifrit promise you for squealing?" she asked, her voice still low. The other jinn at the table stared at her, open-mouthed.

"No! You've got it wrong—"

"I don't think I do." Shirin shifted forward, and the jinni gasped as the blade made the slightest bit of contact with his skin.

"Okay, okay," he said. "Please. They took my father. They said if I helped them, they'd let him go."

The Marid's eyes narrowed and he stood, his chair toppling behind him. "I'll kill you with my own hands, you little *skag*."

Several heads turned to stare. So much for keeping this quiet.

"Is there a problem here?"

Shirin glanced over her shoulder. Yurik was standing behind her, holding a bottle of *savri* by the neck, an improvised bludgeon. She kept a firm grip on the traitorous jinni's shoulder but sheathed her dagger.

"An informant," she said quietly. "You want to throw him out of your bar or should I? And by 'throw him out,' I mean kill him." She gave the jinni who trembled beneath her hand a look of pure loathing. "Your father's already dead. You were a fool to believe the Ifrit."

Yurik motioned for a large Djan who sat near the Wish's

entrance. He moved across the bar with surprising speed. When he reached them, Yurik roughly pulled the traitor out of his seat.

"Take this one out back," he said. "I'll be there in a minute."

Within seconds, the jinni was gone.

"Drinks on me," Yurik said to the men at the table. He started toward the stairs and Shirin followed him to his room.

When they got inside, Yurik rested a hand on her shoulder, his eyes searching hers. It was heavy and warm, solid. She shrugged it off. Shirin couldn't bear it, this tenderness. Unwanted. Undeserved.

He sighed and crossed the room, away from her. Whether she intended to or not, she always insisted on that distance. Being touched had not always been a good thing in her life—even now, it was hard to shake those childhood memories.

Yurik leaned against the table, identical to the larger ones downstairs, watching her.

"Are the rumors true?" he asked.

"Depends on which ones you're talking about," she said. "Raif's back and he has an army—jinn from Earth."

She wasn't going to tell him the other part, that Raif hadn't left his *ludeen* in two nights. If anyone but the *tavrai* found out, the jinn would lose the shred of hope Raif's reappearance was reigniting within them.

"Did they really cross through the Eye?"

She nodded. "And they had a Ghan Aisouri with them, but she's dead now, thank gods."

Yurik let out a low whistle. "Maybe things aren't as bad as you thought, eh? You've got your commander, an army . . ."

She wasn't sure if she was imagining the slight sneer underneath the word *your*. Or the tension around his eyes.

Shirin shrugged. "We'll see."

There was a pause, heavy with all the things neither of them were saying. The bar below was only a soft roar up on the second floor. Despite the Wish being the most popular place in the land, Shirin always felt more at peace here, as though Yurik's room was a secluded retreat deep in the Qaf Mountains.

"What happens now?" he finally asked.

"I don't know. Everything's different." She sighed. "Raif is . . ."

Shirin pursed her lips, shook her head. She felt like a traitor just thinking the words—she couldn't say them out loud because if she did they'd be true: *I don't trust him anymore.* That was what it was, then—that hard thing in her belly. She loved Raif, yes. Always. But for the first time, she didn't feel safe around him. Maybe he was even as unpredictable as Calar.

"Let me ask you something," Yurik said. "Let's say, by some miracle of the gods, the *tavrai* win the revolution. The Ifrit go back to Ithkar, if you're lucky. Then what?"

"Then we . . . we . . ."

Shirin frowned, her gaze shifting from Yurik's tanned face to his shelves of contraband, things that kept him and countless others alive even in the leanest times. Like her, he was a survivor. He'd been on the dark caravan, granted his master's third wish, and come back to a war-torn land, a free jinni trying to ease the burden of everyone around him. He could have stayed on Earth and lived it up. But he hadn't.

She lifted her chin, defensive. "After the war, we'll . . . see what the people want. If it's a leader, they'll choose one—and of course it'll be Raif."

Yurik snorted. "Of course."

She ignored his derisive tone. "If they don't want a leader, then . . . fine," she said. "At least we won't be slaves of the Ghan Aisouri or Calar's playthings."

"Shirin—" Yurik stopped, growling. "Can't you see how endless this war is? As soon as you defeat one enemy, another takes its place. What have you gained by fighting as you do?"

"What have I gained? My freedom, my *life*. Before the Djan'Urbis found me . . ." Her voice caught and she swallowed, hard. Yurik's eyes softened, but that just made her glare all the more at him. "Let's be honest—I'm going to die sooner rather than later. I just want it to be on my own terms."

"It doesn't have to be that way," he said.

"What other way is there?" she spit.

Yurik crossed to her, tentative steps that made her want to flee and yet she waited, her heart beating faster the closer he got.

"There is an infinite number of ways to live out your years, love," he said. "Infinite." He reached out a callused, work-worn hand and placed it against her cheek. Her eyes shifted away from his, from the kindness in them. He knew her inside and out without her having to say a word.

"Look at me," he whispered.

She forced her eyes to meet his—one gold, one emerald, both seeing right through her, past every defense she'd built up. She sucked in her breath as his *chiaan* swirled over her lips and he stepped closer.

"*Shirin.*" He said her name as though it were the answer to a question he'd been asking all his life.

She wanted to run, but her body wouldn't move—no, it was moving, but *toward* him, *what am I doing?*, and then his lips were on hers, warm and gentle and his arms held her body against his and she was melting, tumbling, swirling.

For one perfect moment, Shirin forgot the war. She forgot the past. She forgot Raif.

Raif.

"Stop," she gasped, pushing Yurik away from her. He stumbled back, eyes wide. "What the hell was *that*?" Her voice was too loud, her breath too short.

He sighed and looked down, hands gripping his waist. She could feel the sadness and frustration and . . . and something else, that infinite, perfect moment of sweetness, rolling off him.

"From the moment I met you, all I've ever wanted to do is make you happy," he said, quietly, looking up at her. "To take care of you."

"I don't need anyone to take care of me," she snapped. A *raiga* through and through.

"I know," he said, one side of his mouth turning up. "But wouldn't it be nice?"

She laughed then, the sound too loud, cruel. "I've never liked nice. When are you going to learn that?"

She threw open the door and bolted down the stairs.

Shirin didn't stop running until she collapsed on the edge of the forest, breathless, sweat and tears streaming down her face.

They were both fools—him, for thinking she was someone worth kissing, worth taking care of, and her, for realizing that a small part of her wanted him to.

12

KESMIR STEPPED OUT OF HIS CLOUD OF CRIMSON EVA-
nescence, not breaking his stride as he crossed the wide expanse
of the Cauldron. Once the Ifrit seat of power in Ithkar, it was now
Calar's laboratory where she and the Ash Crones could experiment with the darkest magic in the land. Wrought from a warped
dream, the palace had been brought to life by the first *shirzas* of
the Ifrit thousands of years ago. Lacking a royal family, the Ifrit
had long regarded their generals as the true royalty of their race.
Calar was the last in a long line of *shirzas*, and it was her cruelty
and power that allowed her to be the first Ifrit to wear the Amethyst Crown.

Kes had never liked the Cauldron. He'd lived there since he
was a child, brought to the ebony stronghold after he lost his
family. Built entirely of shimmering volcanic rock, the Cauldron

got its name from its location above the volcano's caldera. Unlike the other volcanos in Ithkar, Ifrit *chiaan* kept the fiery mountain from erupting so that the castle could be built over it. A still lake of lava filled the crater, covered by a thick layer of steam that pooled over the edges so that the Cauldron seemed to be smoking day and night. It was an improbable structure, held up by stilts fused to the rim of the volcano and towering over Ithkar's eastern border, close to the setting sun and buffeted by the harsh, dry winds of the volcanic plain. The sun rose over the palace in Arjinna and fell when it reached the Cauldron. The metaphoric implications of this had never been lost on Kes.

The sun had risen hours ago—between the sunlight and the Cauldron's fire, the heat was nearly unbearable. Kes found himself longing for the cool halls of the Ghan Aisouri palace, the sweet winds that blew through its delicate arches. There was nothing delicate or sweet about Ithkar. In the distance, Mount Ravnir, the largest of the volcanos that dotted the ashy plains, was spitting fire into the sky. Lava burst from its circular top, flowing into the lake bed surrounding it. Other volcanos simply belched black sulphuric smoke into the sky, while still others rumbled ominously. This was the land of fire and blood, shadows and terror. A beautiful nightmare.

He'd be happy never to see it again.

Kes turned from the plains and made his way across the Cauldron's open-air courtyard that stood before the entrance to the castle, the wind so strong he had to brace himself against an onyx pillar or be thrown over the edge and into the fiery lake itself or, even farther, into the moat of lava that flowed at the base of the volcano. He hadn't forgotten the way the wind clawed in Ithkar, filling his nostrils with the scent of sulphur. He wanted the lush fields and forests of the south, protected by the mighty Qaf from Ithkar's misery. It wasn't until Kes had moved to Arjinna that he realized just how terrible Ithkar had been. How cruel it had been for the Ghan Aisouri to banish an entire caste to this hateful land. For this reason alone, he was glad the Ghan Aisouri were dead.

The heavy double doors swung inward as he approached, and Kes stepped into the entryway, cooler than the outdoors but warm enough to keep Ifrit *chiaan* in balance. The hall was lined with the skulls of long-dead enemies. Fires blazed along the wall, a torch on either side every few feet. Kes ran his fingers over the flames of the one nearest him as he awaited Calar. The fire's energy coursed through him, refreshing.

He heard the empress before he saw her, the heeled boots she wore every day cutting across the stone, like an axe to a chopping block.

"They're ready," she said as soon as she saw him, breathless, her ruby eyes alight. She wore a glittering black kaftan with red stitching at the neck. "They're finally ready."

Kes felt his horror at what she'd just said in the pit of his stomach, an oozing, living thing that had grown inside him like a tumor these past three years. He'd begged Ravnir, the patron god of the Ifrit, for this mad experiment to fail, but either he had refused to listen or Mora, the goddess of death who Calar had been cavorting with, was more powerful. Kes tried to muster up some enthusiasm, but Calar scowled, his reaction too slow for her pleasure.

Gods and monsters, Kesmir, he thought to himself. *Get it together.* He was slipping. It was getting harder and harder to feign his allegiance to her. She'd see through him before he'd changed a damn thing.

"I'm sorry, was the fact that I created hundreds of soldiers who cannot die not impressive enough for you?" she said.

Calar's hands shook, ever so slightly. It had been happening more and more now, these little tremors, cracks in her strength. This ignited both sorrow and hope in him, dueling emotions that he would never be able to resolve.

"My love, you know how I feel about what creating these creatures has cost you," he said, forcing himself to draw closer to her. Not a total lie. If she read his mind right now, she would see his concern over the toll this dark magic took on her.

Calar awarded him with a small smile and took the hand he offered her, mollified. "Do you remember the night we made love right in this very hallway?" she said.

"Of course." The smile he gave her this time was real, not for the Calar before him, but for the one on that night so long ago. "I distinctly remember the scent of burned hair."

She laughed, the sound echoing in the silent caverns of the Cauldron. "I hadn't even realized it was on fire until the guards were throwing water on us."

"Your father was furious. He threatened to throw me into the moat," Kes said.

"He threatened to throw everyone into the moat."

Kes had always been terrified of her father, and had not grieved at all when the Aisouri did away with him. Calar had learned her cruelty at the knee of that necrophiliac *shirza* who delighted in dark atrocities. Along with the Ash Crones, he'd molded Calar's power, whittling away at the good in her until, finally, the Calar Kes had fallen in love with had disappeared altogether.

She swept through the Cauldron, its dark interior even darker now that the bulk of her staff was in the Aisouri palace. He pointed to the intricate tapestry that ran the length of the wall off the council room they'd planned the coup in.

"When do you imagine this will be finished?" he asked.

The tapestry told the story of the Ifrit in garnet thread against a black velvet background. The earliest days, when they were a powerful tribe among the jinn. The war with the Aisouri that resulted in Ifrit banishment and the beginning of Aisouri rule. Centuries carving out a life in Ithkar—if it could even be called that. The last panel showed the beginning of the dark caravan. A wizened jinni sat in a room off the hallway, painstakingly working on the final tableau: the coup and Calar's coronation.

"Oh, not for a year, I'd say," Calar said. "He tried using *chiaan* but it simply didn't come out right. Some things you have to do the hard way, I guess."

Kes thought of his secret meetings in Thatur's nest at the top of an impossibly tall elder pine in a grove near the coast. Learning to build a wall in his mind that would keep Calar out was like creating this tapestry. It required intense concentration and careful attention to detail. It had to be done the hard way.

She motioned for a nearby guard. "Take a torch and help us downstairs," she said.

He followed Calar into the Cauldron's depths, a labyrinthine series of cells, both dungeon and lab. They didn't speak and he wasn't sure if it was because they had nothing to say to each other or too much. Silence, he'd learned, was best.

For years Calar's father had been working on his shadow army, but his attempts had had little success. It wasn't until the coup that Calar had been able to garner the power necessary to create her monsters.

The room is locked from the inside. Only Calar, Kesmir, and the matriarch of the Ash Crones, Morghisi, are present. The dead bodies of the royal caste lie in piles, where Haran and his executioners left them after being ordered to contain the civilian population. Kesmir wonders if this room is what the underworld smells like: a butcher's wet dream.

"Has anyone been in here since they died?" Calar asks.

Kesmir shrugs. "Who knows? It's been total chaos."

Morghisi narrows her eyes at him. They are as black as the tar gardens in Ithkar. "Can you be a little more specific for your empress, boy?"

He stiffens. Why did Calar have to keep such awful company? "Haran and the others left an hour ago—that is all I know."

Later, much later, Kesmir will realize that the hour between Haran's leaving and Calar's arriving with Morghisi had been precious indeed: those minutes had enabled Nalia Aisouri'Taifyeh to be "rescued" by a servant, a notorious slave trader Calar would later execute herself.

"Is it too late?" she asks, turning to where Morghisi has placed thin white stones over the eyes of each Aisouri.

Before answering, the crone rests her palm over the stone on the nearest body, muttering in a language Kesmir has never heard. It sounds evil, even to his ears: crushed bones and dark teeth glinting in the night. The crone lifts her hand. The rocks now glow with dark amethyst light, pulsing with life.

"No, My Empress," Morghisi says in her reedy voice, "it is not too late."

Before the guard pushed open a door at the end of the underground passageway, Calar turned to Kes and slipped a gold chain over his neck. A familiar white stone dangled from it. The *yaghin* had been set into a disk of gold so that it looked more like a strange piece of jewelry than a dark magical object. Calar, he now saw, had taken a similar one and placed it around her own neck.

"Why do I need to wear this?" he asked.

She smiled, a carnal upturn of the lips that made him shiver. "You'll see."

The guard stood beside the door, fear radiating off him, a stench that turned the air sour. "Is there . . . is there anything else I can do for you, My Empress?" His voice shook and Kes wondered just what exactly had been going on here.

"One more thing, if you will," Calar said.

She drew an elaborate key from the pocket of her kaftan.

"Open the door." She reached out and grabbed the torch from his hand.

Her eyes shone, greedy, and the flames danced in their crimson depths. The guard took the key with a shaking hand. Whatever was about to happen, Kes knew it wouldn't be good for the guard. The jinni turned and threw Kes a desperate look, a cornered animal. Kes's stomach turned and he forced his face into the mask of cool detachment that had kept him alive all these years.

"Your empress has commanded you to open the door, swine," he said. "So open it."

Calar leaned closer to Kes and rested her head on his shoulder for a moment. She loved him this way: cold and cruel.

The guard turned the key in the lock and the door swung inward.

"In you go," Calar said. He reached for the torch and she shook her head. "There's no need for that."

The guard's hand dropped and he moved forward into the pitch-black room, his steps reluctant, a jinni walking to his execution. As Kes's eyes adjusted, he could see that the room wasn't dark as in the absence of light. The space writhed, the darkness a living thing that pulsed. It smelled of death, like a battlefield. Calar pulled Kes into the room with her and shut the door behind them.

"My Empress?" the guard said, his voice barely a whisper. Naked, unabashed fear.

"*Sahai,*" Calar whispered in the old tongue. *Awake.*

The whirling mass of shadows instantly broke up into individual columns of onyx evanescence, conscious energy that sought to feed its hunger. A hundred screams pierced the air, distinct and somehow one at the same time. A chorus of terror. Kes forced himself to stand still as the shadows descended on them.

Calar turned toward him, her eyes the only light, a terrible beacon. "It's the sound of their victims' screams," she shouted above the agonized wails. "Isn't it gorgeous?"

He didn't bother to attempt an answer. It was all he could do to keep from running from the cell, screaming himself.

Though the shadows had no form, the smokelike substance of each creature made its intention felt. Nausea overcame Kes as the swirls attempted to feed on him, but the *yaghin* around his neck began to glow, a dull pulse that repelled the creatures.

The guard, however, was not so lucky. He howled as the shadows surrounded him, their substance strong enough to wrestle him to the stone floor. Kes looked away as the jinni's *chiaan* was violently ripped from his body. Shreds of crimson energy flew into the air, electric blood that the killing shadows gorged on, the sound of their feeding like a howling wind. They lapped up his soul like spilled milk.

Calar laughed, clapping her hands in delight. "Yes, my darlings! *Yes!*"

Kes doubled over, resting his hands on his knees, dizzy. How would the *tavrai* be able to fight this? He should just try to kill her now, wrap his fingers around her neck—

Calar placed her hand on Kes's back. "My love, are you ill?"

He nodded and she spoke once more into the room, this time calling the shadows to her. *"Ðæl."* Sleep.

They obeyed, flying into the *yaghin* around her neck. The stone absorbed them, throbbing with black light, its surface swirling as though it contained a roiling ocean.

"I want to try them out," she said. "Let's pay a visit to one of the villages, shall we? See if their precious *tavrai* come to save them." She grinned, white teeth glinting like pearls in the darkness. "I hear there's something of interest in a Marid village in the south."

Something of interest. Gods, he knew what that meant.

Kes glanced at the necklace around Calar's neck. There'd be no time to warn the villagers. It'd be a massacre.

He forced himself to match her sadistic joy. "Lead the way, my love."

13

JUST AS RAIF WAS ABOUT TO ENTER THE *LUDEEN* WHERE the *tavrai* council was gathered, someone grabbed his arm. He turned, expecting a *tavrai* with a message of some kind, but it was Touma, the grief in his eyes echoing Raif's own.

"A word, please," Touma said. "Sir."

Raif nodded, motioning for Zanari, Taz, and Samar to wait for him before entering the council room. He walked a few paces away, Touma at his side.

The jinni took a long look at Raif, then shook his head. "You've given up."

"Yes." Even to his own ears, Raif's voice sounded hollow, dead. Shame pooled in his gut.

"Do you really believe she's gone?"

Raif gazed at the bright green stars above, which now always reminded him of Jandessa and Rahim. Maybe every time two jinn tried to change the stars, it ended badly.

"I can still feel her," Raif said quietly. "She's my *rohifsa*. I think that even if I stood beside Nalia's burning body I would still feel her." He sighed. "Even if she lives, we can't get to her. And she can't get to us. I'd hoped for a way, but Zanari said it's impossible. I have to . . . to let her go, Touma."

"Would you permit me to remain at the gate?" Touma asked. "If her . . . if her spirit wanders, she will know we have not forgotten her."

If her spirit wanders.

It would wander. There was no one in the Eye to burn her. Raif closed his eyes for a moment. *Oh, gods, Nalia. Come home to me. Please. Please don't be gone.* He'd make sure to die where no one could find him, where there wouldn't be a body to burn. They could live out the ages together, ghosts forever joined in the in-between. It was the only future that gave him any hope.

Raif nodded, then cleared his throat. "A year and a day?"

It was the traditional mourning period for jinn. Touma nodded. "I will guard her—body or spirit—with my life."

Raif placed his palms together and gave a slight bow. "You honor her. I'll never forget it."

Before Touma could say anything more, Raif returned to where the others waited for him. Without a word, they followed him into the *ludeen* in the center of the camp. He wasn't prepared for the comfort that initial sight of the room would give him. When Raif stepped inside, he was enveloped in a familiar warmth and the barnlike scent of unwashed bodies and hundreds of meals long since eaten.

The large tree house served as both mess hall and war council room. Raif well remembered late nights sitting on the floor, leaning against the wall while his father planned Arjinna's future. Ever since he could remember, he'd been allowed in the room, inducted into the secret club of the men and women who'd raised him.

Now it went utterly silent as Raif made his way to the long tables that had been pushed together in the center of the room. As Zanari, Taz, and Samar filed in behind him, Raif could feel the power in the space shift, settling upon him and the three jinn who flanked him like a mantle.

He'd been wrong when he'd first entered the room—there was no comfort in this place, not anymore. It reeked of defeat and rebellion.

Shirin stood and offered Raif the chair at the head of the table—was he imagining that hint of reluctance in her slow movement?

Stop it, he chided himself. Shirin had every reason to be upset. He hadn't exactly been the leader they needed him to be since his return from Earth. She was a good soldier, his best. He wanted to keep her on his side.

Raif squeezed Shirin's shoulder as he passed her. "Thank you for taking over while I was gone," he said quietly.

He wasn't just talking about the time he'd been on Earth. The past two days, when he'd done nothing but rage in his *ludeen* or sit vigil beside the Gate of the Eye—those were the hours he was most grateful for. And sorry about. Not because of grieving for Nalia, but for leaving the *tavrai* on the brink of surrender, caring little if any of them lived or died. It'd been impossible to see beyond the gaping hole inside him. Still was. He was just getting better at hiding it.

Shirin gave him a curt nod, then slid into the chair beside Raif, the one she'd occupied ever since he'd made her his second. This was not the Shirin who'd kissed him so many weeks ago or the one who'd stayed up late with him for the past few years, planning and drinking their way into the possibility of peace and justice. This Shirin was hurt, confused. Furious. But as her eyes roved over his face, he saw something in her soften.

"Welcome back, *tavrai*," she said.

Raif didn't sit down. Instead, he looked around the room at the jinn who'd bled for him. Who he'd fought beside since he was a child. They were his family, blood brothers and sisters who he'd pledged to protect. He met each of their eyes in silent apology, lingering on his mother's sea-green ones the longest.

"I went to Earth in search of Solomon's sigil," he began.

The reaction of the *tavrai* was almost comical—jaws dropping, eyes bulging in surprise.

There was a derisive snort to his right. "Bullshit."

Raif went still, only his eyes sliding toward the jinni who'd spoken. Jaqar, the one chosen to be Shirin's second while Raif was gone, a wonder on the battlefield but a heartless *skag* who Raif had never liked or trusted. If he took Jaqar's bait, he'd say something . . . regrettable, at least in terms of keeping the peace. And, Raif had to admit, Jaqar wasn't in the wrong to say what he had. It was more *how* he said it. The insolence, the mocking upturn of his lips.

Raif looked away. When he spoke, he weighed each word, channeling his father's razor-edged dignity. There would be no debate.

"My companions and I found the ring and used it to free the soldiers I brought with me," Raif said. There were gasps around the table, but he pressed on. "They'd been trapped by the Master King for three thousand years and yet they have agreed to fight with us against the Ifrit. These are true warriors who deserve our respect."

Raif glanced at Jaqar, who simply shrugged. He'd have to deal with him soon. The jinni stank of mutiny.

"Are you saying you have the ring?" asked one of the elderly jinn, voice incredulous.

Raif shook his head. "No. During our battle in the Eye against the ghouls it was lost." He paused, his throat tightening. "As was the Ghan Aisouri who carried it."

The reaction was immediate, violent in its intensity: outrage that the ring had been lost, that a Ghan Aisouri had been entrusted with it in the first place. Raif let the shouting and table pounding go on for a few moments—they'd earned the right to it after he'd abandoned them in his grief. He had an army behind him and the blood of Dthar Djan'Urbi within him—there was no reason why Raif couldn't at least keep control of this meeting, whichever way the council voted. He turned to Shirin and tugged his right earlobe—their old sign. She looked at him for a long moment—she'd had no idea whatsoever about the ring. Despite the shock and anger in her eyes, she managed to tug her earlobe in response. They were on the same side. Raif turned back to the *tavrai*.

"Enough," he said. His voice cut through the din and the *tavrai* went silent. All except for one voice.

"I don't know about anyone else," Jaqar said, drawing out his words, clearly relishing the chance to take Raif down a peg or two, "but it's becoming pretty clear to me that our commander is no longer certain which side he's fighting for. Tell me, *tavrai*," he said, turning to Raif, "was it your choice to entrust a royal with the most dangerous weapon against our kind, or did she force your hand?"

Raif's future with the *tavrai* hung in the balance with this question: one wrong word and what was left of his life would fall apart. He hadn't even answered yet and he could already tell the council smelled blood.

Screw it.

"Yes, it was my choice," he said.

The table erupted. Shirin stared at him, something like grief settling into her features. If he lost her, too, that was it—they'd hang him by sunrise.

"Listen to me," he roared. Silence—at least he still commanded *that*. "I made the wisest decision I could, given the circumstances I was in. She is—was—the most powerful among us. It stood to reason that the ring was safest with her."

"But she's dead, so it actually *wasn't* safest with her," one of the jinn said.

All he heard was that one word: *dead*.

"I can't be perfect all the time, sister," Raif said. "The only reason I would entrust *anything* to a Ghan Aisouri was if she were *on our side*. I planned to come home with the ring, a Ghan Aisouri who intended to kill Calar herself—and could very easily have done just that—and an army, which, by the way, we *still have*."

Jaqar hit his palm against the table. The sound was like thunder, reverberating through the room. "This is *exactly* what I've been telling you," he said, his eyes on Shirin's. "All those jinn he brought with him—royalists."

Shirin held Jaqar's furious eyes but made no reply, her face stony and unreadable. She wasn't speaking against Raif, but she wasn't sticking up for him either. This was a very bad sign.

Raif turned to Jaqar. "Say your piece and then hold your tongue," he said, seething. Best to be out with all of it. Jaqar might be an insubordinate ass, but Raif knew he wasn't the only jinni at the table with these concerns. He'd hear them out—it was what his father would have done.

Jaqar's eyes glittered with malice. "While you were busy with your *salfit* and her army, we've been making plans. Without you."

Raif gripped the table, letting the slur slide. Hadn't he himself called Nalia that? He'd had to fall in love with her to rid himself of the impulse. If she were here, Jaqar wouldn't have dared.

Jaqar's eyes flicked to Raif's hands, satisfied with the tension he'd created. He addressed the others at the table.

"I say Raif's a traitor. He's guilty of collaboration with the enemy," he said, "and extreme stupidity. He's a fool to have trusted her—we should be thanking the ghoul that ate its fill of royal flesh out there."

Raif didn't care if it was murder, he was going to kill this jinni. Stab him in the back on the battlefield, suffocate him in his sleep—it didn't matter. He wanted to watch the light go out of those eyes.

Enjoy this while it lasts, he thought.

"Raif," his mother said, her voice soft, "is this true? Was she planning to be empress? Is this why the Brass Army has purple armbands?"

Purple and *white,* he thought. Pure-white armbands would have been greeted with joy, as it was the color of the revolution, symbolizing a future Arjinna where the color of one's eyes did not determine their fate. But purple—that had only ever symbolized the royal Aisouri. Jinn weren't even allowed to manifest clothing or jewels of that color before the caste's end.

Was Nalia planning to be empress, his mother wanted to know. How to answer that question? It was too difficult to explain those stilted, fearful conversations he and Nalia had had after they'd left the cave. Too terrifying to explain those words he'd said to her—*long live the empress*—just before he planned to die in her place.

This was the truth: if Nalia walked through that door right now, he would bend the knee.

Raif sighed, heavy. "She didn't want the throne."

"That's not what I asked," Fjirla said, the warmth disappearing from her voice.

He met his mother's eyes and in them he saw something he'd never seen before: disappointment.

Raif turned to the rest of the group, all jinn who had fought in his father's day along with a few of the most accomplished soldiers Raif had trained himself.

"I know it's hard to see that I put my faith in an Aisouri. Believe me. I saw the royals murder my father, saw them condone evil after evil. I'm glad Calar killed them—it was justice. But we're lucky she didn't manage to kill the one who's out there right now, lost forever in the Eye. The army I brought was saved by *her* for *us*." He took a breath, then another. *Help me, Nal.* "It's true that the Brass Army originally planned to fight for her, but Nalia herself was never interested in ruling. She only would have taken on that burden *if* that was what Arjinnans wanted." He paused. *To hell with it.* "I've never encountered a jinni more worthy of a crown."

Raif could feel the very air around him bristle as the *tavrai* heard that word: *crown.* He ignored it. All his worries over whether or not Nalia was the true empress had disappeared. She was—and he'd lost her.

"I agree with my brother," Zanari said. "I was with him on Earth and I both supported and helped him in all of these decisions."

Raif shot her a grateful look and she nodded. The silence that followed was awkward, heavy with uncertainty.

"This is precisely why my people have never felt that Arjinna could be a home to them," said a voice near the door.

Raif glanced at where Samar leaned against the wall, his expression one of profound disgust and disappointment.

"We Dhoma have created the society you claim you wish to have. All the castes live peacefully together. We break bread with one another, we marry who we love regardless of their caste, and we care for everyone in the camp. This is what you say you bleed for and yet you shun the Ifrit in this forest and look down upon the Shaitan courageous enough to join your fight." Samar stepped into the light. "The choice isn't whether or not you want Raif to continue leading you. It's whether or not he's willing to command an army of bigots."

Raif nodded his head in thanks, overcome. How quick his *tavrai*, who he'd known all his life, had been to discard him. Samar was here only to rescue the Dhoma from the prison in Ith-kar and yet he spoke up for Raif, supporting his brother-in-arms, a jinni he'd known for a matter of weeks.

"If this Brass Army wanted a Ghan Aisouri on the throne," said one of the older *tavrai*, "how can we trust that they won't try to put a Shaitan in her place?" The jinni had been close with Raif's father, a hardened old soldier who'd seen more than his fair share of suffering. "You talk of fighting, but what happens *afterward*?"

"Our army," Taz interjected, "has members of every caste. Our empress is gone and we fight for what she said she always wanted: an end to masters and slaves. We want the same thing."

Jaqar's eyes narrowed as a cruel smile twisted his lips. "All I can gather from this conversation is that it's time for a new leader," he said. "One who doesn't fuck Aisouri whores while *tavrai* are being cut down on the battlefield."

"You are out of line," Raif said, his voice low. It took everything in him for Raif not to pummel Jaqar.

"I wonder if I am." Jaqar's dagger lay on the table in front of him. He picked it up and twisted its point idly into the wood, spinning the blade in lazy circles as he looked at Raif. Shirin stood, her eyes on that dagger as her hand moved to her scimitar. Raif didn't need her help. He knew better than anyone how short a fuse Jaqar had—and how good he was with a dagger.

"Believe me when I say that you are," Raif said, his voice full of cold fury.

Jaqar stared at Raif, and the room sizzled with their energy, *chiaan* just barely under the surface.

"It's too bad about her being dead and all," Jaqar continued, ignoring him. "It would have been a nice distraction for all of us, too. Taken our minds off the war. I, for one, would have taken her as many times as I could before we hanged her. Or maybe we would have cut her up, nice and slow like those Aisouri witches did to my brother—"

In seconds, Raif had leaped from his chair and had Jaqar pinned against a wall. "That line I mentioned a moment ago?" Raif said. "You just crossed it."

He grabbed Jaqar's head and slammed it against the wall. Once, twice. Jaqar's eyes rolled to the back of his head and the light wood of the *widr* wall turned red where his skull had hit it.

Raif let go and the jinni crumpled to the floor, unconscious.

"Just so we're clear," Raif said, turning to the *tavrai* in the room, "I won't tolerate insubordination any more now than I did in the past." He looked at Shirin. "Keep him in line or he hangs."

Shirin glanced at the bloodied wall, then back at him, her eyes troubled.

"As you wish, Commander," she said.

Raif returned to his seat at the table and took in the shocked faces of the *tavrai*.

"Now," he said, his voice calm and his eyes hard, "where were we?"

Nalia had only seen Raif asleep a handful of times in her life. She watched him now, the way he lay on his back, one hand beneath his pillow, one hand on his bare chest. His lips were parted, his long lashes brushing tanned cheeks. She reached out and ran her fingers through his hair and he sighed, leaning into the touch, recognizing her even in his sleep. It'd been a long time since she'd seen him in anything other than pitch-dark. He was too thin, the bones in his face jagged, too defined. Thick stubble covered the lower half of his face and she gently ran her fingers over it, remembering the night when she'd helped him shave. The way he'd picked her up and carried her to bed. Nalia glanced at her wrists—no shackles. Just two thin scars, like bangles. This boy had saved her in so many ways.

Moonlight trickled in through the windows, a soft breeze rustling gauzy curtains. There was a tinge of salt on the air blowing in from Malibu, carrying the low rumble of the traffic at the bottom of the hill, out on Sunset. It was the middle of the night and still the wishmakers were honking their horns, impatient to get to the next after-party. The neighbors across the way were having a party of their own—loud pop music blared, the sound grating.

Nalia's eyes scanned the familiar room. It looked the same as it had the day she left Malek's mansion, all those weeks ago. The wallpaper with velvet fleurs-de-lis, the carved bedpost. The clothes on the floor that she'd left in a pile, in a hurry to escape the Ifrit. She could almost smell Malek's clove cigarettes.

She used to hear him at night, pacing up and down the hallway between their rooms as he chain-smoked. Now she knew what had kept him up, why he couldn't sleep. Malek. The distinctive scent of those cigarettes was exactly what his evanescence would have smelled like, if he'd been a full jinni. But Malek wasn't out there—she knew that: Malek was dead. He'd told her so himself.

She sat up, her breath catching in her throat. Malek was dead. But how could she be in his home when she was in the Riviera—no, in the Eye. She was in the Eye, so how could—

Nalia turned to Raif, panicked.

"Raif." She shook his shoulder and his eyes snapped open. He blinked. Shook his head. Stared at her. And stared, and stared.

"You're alive," he breathed, drinking her in.

Raif thought she was dead. Gods, he thought she'd left him behind, gone straight to a land of not-life without him. A smile snaked across his face as he reached out a hand and ran his fingers through her hair. It had grown past her chin now, no longer as short as it had been when she'd cut it off, grieving her brother.

"Yes," she breathed, reaching for him. "I'm here. I'm here."

His face fell. "I'm having another dream."

But that didn't make sense. If Raif was having the dream, why had she woken up first? Why could she think, feel—touch him? If she were only a figment of his imagination, then wouldn't she be unaware of her presence in his mind?

"Raif, I don't think—"

He sat up in one swift movement and pressed his lips to hers.

Whatever she was going to say was lost in the feel of him, so real. His earthy, spring scent, the tang of savri on his tongue. He pulled off the thin shift she wore, running his hands over her body, his eyes full of wonder, marveling at the beat of her heart under his palm.

"I love you," he whispered into her ear as he leaned in, his lips warm and soft as he pressed them against her neck.

She pulled Raif closer, until he was on top of her, his breath ragged as she slipped off her underwear, pulled down his pants.

Their lovemaking was frenzied, the threat of one of them waking from this dream, from this whatever-it-was, hanging over them. Raif never took his eyes off her. He whispered her name again and again, moaned as she wrapped her legs around him, holding on, silently begging the gods to let them stay here, to let her keep him.

There was sweat and tears, his breath on her skin, kisses she never wanted to end. They finally collapsed, still holding one another. Nalia gripped him as the moonlight vanished, as, one by one, every item in the room was consumed by a swirling cloud of darkness.

"No," she whispered. "Please. Please."

"Look at me," Raif said, his fingers under her chin, gently turning her face toward him.

Her eyes found his, bright green, the only light left in the darkness that was smothering them.

"Don't go," she begged him. "Raif, don't leave me here."

Silent tears streamed down his cheeks as his fingers traced the lines of her face.

The Eye pulled at her and she slipped out of his arms, no matter how hard he tried to hold her.

"I love you," she said. "Raif, I love you."

The Eye swept her away.

14

THE ALARM SOUNDED IN THE MIDDLE OF THE NIGHT.

Shirin's eyes snapped open and she sprang out of bed, fully clothed. She couldn't remember the last time she'd worn night-clothes.

She evanesced to the center of camp, clouds of smoke surrounding her as the *tavrai* stumbled out of bed. She grabbed one of the jinn guarding the camp's border.

"Is it us? Are they attacking the camp?" she asked.

The *tavrai* shook his head. "We're good. There's something happening by the coast."

She turned toward Raif's *ludeen*: he was already striding toward her, eyes glinting. Gods, she loved that look on his face, that maniacal battle glee.

"What do we know?" he said.

"Right now, next to nothing."

He hadn't spoken to her since the meeting with the council. Once they'd gone over their strategy for rescuing the prisoners in Ithkar—one Shirin thought had little chance of success, and she said as much—he'd left the *ludeen* with Tazlim, Samar, and Zanari. She couldn't help but feel she'd been replaced. She was his second in name only.

Shirin put two fingers in her mouth and whistled, getting the attention of a group of jinn near the camp's main entrance who were sticking weapons into every available slot on their belts. "Where are the godsdamned scouts?" she yelled. The jinn raised their hands, uncertain, and Shirin scowled, turning back to Raif. "It's something by the coast. Maybe it's—"

A jinni hurtled toward them, his body pushing out of his cloud of blue evanescence. "A Marid village," he gasped, sweat dripping down his face. "They're killing everyone."

"How many Ifrit?" Raif asked.

"A few hundred is my guess," he said.

Tazlim arrived with Samar and Noqril behind him. "Do we need eyes?" Samar asked.

"Yes," Raif said. "Take care, though."

Shirin was confused until she saw what Samar meant: in seconds, he and Noqril began to evanesce, only instead of leaving, they hovered above her, transformed into two large black birds, one with a white breast, the other with an orange one.

"Report to one of us as needed," Raif said.

Samar cawed in answer and then they shot toward the clouds, disappearing into the black night.

"Shirin, gather the vanguard," Raif said. "Taz, have every soldier ready, but only bring a regiment. Have runners prepped to bring reinforcements."

Zanari rushed toward them. "Calar's at the village, or at least she's planning to be," she said. "I saw her in my *voiqhif.* Something's not right."

"Of course something's not right," Shirin snapped.

Zanari glared at her. "I *mean* she shouldn't be there. This seems like a routine raid. Something's . . . off. I don't know. What if this is some kind of trap?"

Shirin frowned. She was well acquainted with Zanari's inaccuracies due to her lack of psychic training. The jinni had a gift, no doubt, but Shirin wanted only knowns. These foggy possibilities simply set the *tavrai* on edge, made them fight blind and sloppy.

Shirin pulled out her scimitar. "Well, I guess we'll see what's there when we're on the ground."

"I wish I could come with you," Zanari said.

Shirin could see that she wasn't healing quickly from the ghoul's wound. Her face was pale, eyes drawn.

Raif leaned in close to his sister and Shirin had to strain to make out his whispered words. "Even if you were okay I wouldn't let you go. I can't lose anyone else, Zan. I can't."

Zanari hugged him, hard. "Neither can I." She pulled away and rested a hand on Shirin's arm. "Take care of him, sister."

Shirin forced a smile. "Always."

Zanari headed back to her *ludeen,* walking slowly, slightly bent over.

Raif glanced at Shirin. "What's your count this week?"

"Five. You?"

His lips turned up, the old cocky Raif, if only for a moment. "Fifty-four. *Ghouls*, but who's comparing?"

She laughed. "Looks like I have some catching up to do."

Happiness pooled inside her, warming Shirin from the inside out. Maybe she could bring him back. Maybe there was hope for her. Shirin left Raif to organize the *tavrai* while she went in search of her most trusted fighters. If Calar was there, Shirin needed her best on the field. She found Jaqar replenishing his *chiaan* on a pile of rocks at the edge of camp. He glanced up at her, wary.

"You going to bash my head against a wall, too?"

She shrugged. "If you do something to deserve it again, then yeah." *His sweat on her skin, his hands up her shirt.*

As if he knew what she was thinking, Jaqar gave her a twisted grin. "Got any plans after the battle tonight?"

"Calar's come out to play," she said, ignoring his implied invitation. She was done screwing him in the forest. "Want to take a crack at her with me or not? Your choice, of course. If you're too busy licking your wounds . . ."

He laughed, a harsh bark. "That's the Shirin I know. You worried me earlier with Djan'Urbi."

She stiffened. "You were asking for it."

"I was. The bump on my head was worth the look on his face." Jaqar stood, huge and looming. "How do you think our esteemed commander will fare tonight?"

Shirin looked to where Raif was giving orders in the center of camp. He looked more himself than ever. Colder, though. She wasn't quite sure what he was fighting for anymore.

"I think we'll find out." She hit Jaqar lightly on the arm. "Don't die on me."

Shirin crossed back to Raif. "You ready?"

He nodded and held out his hand. "Same as always, right?" he asked.

She slid her hand into his. "Ye—yeah. Same as always."

Raif's *chiaan* simmered against her skin, nothing intentional, just the result of bare skin against bare skin. She nearly stepped back as it flowed into her, searing, unlike any *chiaan* she'd ever encountered.

"What?" he asked, noticing the expression on her face.

"It's just . . . your *chiaan* feels different, somehow." She'd known Raif since they were kids, was well acquainted with his *chiaan*. It wasn't the same.

He stared at her, asking the question as though her answer were the most important thing in the worlds. "How?"

"It's . . . like . . ." She paused, searching for the words.

"Lightning?" he whispered.

Her eyes widened. "Yeah." She looked more closely at him. His eyes were too bright, his cheeks suddenly flushed. "Are you okay, brother?"

He shook his head, joy and terror flitting across his face. "I don't know." He looked out over the camp, but he wasn't seeing it, he wasn't there.

"Let's go," he said, his voice far away.

In seconds, clouds of evanescence surrounded them, Raif's smelling of sandalwood, hers of cedar. She squeezed his hand as the magic pulled their bodies into the air and they became a whirlwind of smoke, racing across Arjinna. In seconds they'd landed on a small bluff overlooking the village, shifting automatically so that their backs were against each other's, affording them the best defensible position. Shirin could hear the screams even from this distance—women, children, frail old fisher-jinn. Red *chiaan* blazed over the few bits of blue Marid magic that tried to defend the village. She hated that a part of her was also aware of Raif's warmth and how good it felt to be fighting with him again.

Raif swore under his breath. "See a maniacal ruler anywhere?" he asked.

Shirin scanned the field below—the empress was nowhere in sight, but she could easily have been hiding.

It was a bloodbath down there.

She felt the air shift and then Jaqar landed beside them, smoke billowing around his feet. "Where do you want me, Shirin?" he asked.

"Ask your commander," she said, her voice even.

Jaqar ignored Raif, who was hardly paying attention anyway as he scanned their surroundings with hawk's eyes. "Do I have to ask him for permission to go into the forest with you, too?"

Raif turned to him, eyes blazing. "Get the fuck down there and kill some Ifrit."

Jaqar gave him a half-assed *tavrai* salute, a fist over his heart. "As you wish, *Commander*."

As he evanesced, Raif gave her a questioning look. Shirin shook her head, mortified. "Not important."

"If he's giving you a hard time, Shir—"

"I'm fine," she snapped. "Let's go kill things."

In seconds Raif was a swirl of emerald smoke, descending on the village, Shirin evanescing just behind him. She landed with her scimitar pointed out, stabbing an Ifrit in the stomach before shooting a blaze of *chiaan* at a soldier dragging a jinni out of her home. The whole place smelled of fish and blood, and it was difficult to gain purchase on the sandy floor of the coastal village.

"Hey, pretty girl," said a deep voice behind her.

"Who, me?" she said, turning around and affecting the helpless voice of a Shaitan overlord's daughter.

The soldier was thick and neckless, his armor reflecting the hut that blazed behind her. He smiled, hungry, and she grinned back, deftly sidestepping his hands that burned with poisonous *chiaan* while at the same time reaching into her boot for the dagger she kept there. The Ifrit swung toward her and she feinted, driving the dagger point into the exposed flesh just under his armpit, where the armor couldn't reach. She felt the knife enter his heart, a satisfying pressure on the blade.

As the Ifrit went down, she caught Raif out of the corner of her eye. He was like a machine, his eyes dark, devoid of all emotion. An ear-splitting shriek behind her made Shirin whirl around. An Ifrit was exiting a hut, something hanging from his hand. The jinni behind him was grabbing at whatever the Ifrit held and the soldier turned, slitting her neck in one quick movement. There was a wail and Shirin looked down, realizing that the Ifrit was holding an infant by its foot. She threw herself at the soldier just as the woman had, but it was too late: he'd already thrown the baby. Time seemed to stand still as the child catapulted through the air and landed in a crumpled heap on the rocks near the shore.

Shirin stared in horror, rooted to the spot as the battle waged around her. She saw a blur in the corner of her eye and then Raif bashed his body against the soldier, throwing the Ifrit to the ground. Shirin blinked, back in the fight, and when she had a clear shot, she sent a needle-sharp stream of *chiaan* to the Ifrit's face, giving Raif time to stab his neck. Raif didn't bother to retrieve his dagger as he stumbled to where the infant's body lay at the base of the rock.

Shirin pulled his dagger out of the dead Ifrit's throat, wiping the blood on her pants as she crouched beside her commander. "Raif. *Raif.*"

He was staring down at the child, whose eyes gazed unblinking at the sky above as blood pooled around her head.

"Purple eyes," he whispered.

The child was a Ghan Aisouri.

15

RAIF LEANED OVER THE INFANT, STARING AT THOSE EYES.
Nalia's eyes. The first truly innocent Ghan Aisouri he'd ever seen.
What did it mean that a Ghan Aisouri child had been able to live
in a Marid village without Calar ever knowing? Gods, were there
more?

Maybe that's why Calar's here.

"Did you know about this child?" Raif asked Shirin, his voice
hoarse.

She shook her head, speechless.

He could still taste Nalia from the dream the raid on this
village had woken him from, smell her on his skin. *Don't leave me
here,* she'd begged. What a mindfuck his nights had become. And
yet there was a flicker of hope inside him. Shirin had felt Nalia in
his *chiaan.* Maybe she'd always been there, inside him, or maybe

he hadn't been dreaming. It was impossible, he'd woken up in his *ludeen*. But nothing was strictly impossible where Nalia was concerned. Yet having hope, only to have it be dashed again—Raif wasn't sure if he'd make it through that.

A dream, he reminded himself. *Just a dream.*

He made himself look at the child, to bear witness to what the Ifrit were capable of. He felt sick, the bloodlust draining away and replaced with horror. This was what they'd come to: infants getting their heads bashed on rocks, mothers having their throats slit. Why had he ever thought the jinn race was worth saving?

They should never have come back.

Or Raif should have put the sigil on the moment he found it in the cave. If he had, this child would still be alive. Raif had tried to do what Nalia wanted, but without her here, without her power, Arjinna was a death trap.

"If I'd put on that ring when I found it, then—"

"Shut up," Shirin said. She placed her hands on either side of his face and forced him to look at her. *"Vi fazla ra'ahim."*

You are a sword, nothing more.

It was something he told his soldiers, when they lost faith on the battlefield. He nodded and Shirin let her hands drop. He closed the baby's eyes with the tips of his fingers. He was glad Nalia hadn't seen this—it was the only good thing about her not being on the battlefield with him right now.

"To your left," Shirin said.

An Ifrit had caught sight of them and Raif ducked, narrowly missing the ball of poisoned fire that flew toward him. Samar dove down from the sky, pecking out the Ifrit's eyes, just as he'd done with the sand soldiers in Morocco.

"Holy gods and monsters," Shirin said. "I thought I'd seen everything, but . . ."

"Pretty handy to have them around," Raif said, his voice still dazed. He wouldn't think of the baby, of Nalia. *You are a sword, nothing more.*

All around him, the battle raged. The Brass Army proved to be a formidable opponent for the Ifrit. Taz commanded with ease, his voice calm as he shouted orders to the soldiers. For once, it was a fair fight. Raif dove back into the battle, relishing these minutes, then hours, free of grief and thought. Both sides brought in reinforcements and somehow this little village was becoming the site of the biggest battle that had ever been fought between the Ifrit and the resistance. There was only the *chiaan* in his body, the scimitar in his hand. Sweat and adrenaline.

Looking across the sandy beach, he caught sight of a large jinni with a scar that cut across the left side of his face. Raif recognized him instantly: Kesmir Ifri'Lhas, Calar's lover and general of the Ifrit Army. Unlike the other Ifrit military leaders, who normally stood off to the side while their forces toiled against the enemy, Kesmir was in the thick of the fight, indistinguishable from his soldiers except for that telltale scar. Like Raif, he was covered in blood, his uniform sandy and torn. A burst of *tavrai chiaan* surged toward one of the Ifrit wounded and Kesmir threw himself in front of his soldier, taking the brunt of the magic's force, which would have killed the already-injured soldier. He went down, hard. Raif moved toward him, but before he could take advantage of Kesmir's fall, the general was on his feet, a scimitar in each hand, wielding them with chilling efficiency. The blades sliced through the air, but when they came down he stopped short of killing the *tavrai* who ran at him from all sides. Instead, he disabled his opponents, slicing into skin so that the soldiers were too hurt to attack a second time, but still alive.

What? Why wasn't he butchering Raif's soldiers?

Before Raif could help the *tavrai* who bled over the sand, a female's cry pierced the air and Raif whirled around, his stomach turning as he caught sight of what was happening outside one of the burning Marid homes. Two Ifrit soldiers had a jinni pinned to the ground. One of them was already on top of her, pants around his knees. He shoved into her and Raif took careful aim, then threw his scimitar. The blade turned over and over in the air, then landed squarely in the Ifrit's back just as the soldier who'd been waiting his turn for the Marid cried out, a burst of crimson *chiaan* colliding with his chest. Raif turned. Kesmir was stalking toward the soldier, blood dripping off his scimitars, his face filled with fury. The remaining Ifrit stared at Kesmir in fear and dropped to his knees, his hands held out in supplication.

The Ifrit commander did not slow his pace as he raised his scimitars and slashed through the air, crossing them just as he neared the soldier's head. The blades landed on either side of his soldier's neck, instantly decapitating him.

Raif bolted across the sand dunes, dodging *chiaan* daggers and leaping over corpses as he made his way toward the Marid woman, who lay sobbing beneath the body of the soldier who'd been raping her. He raised his hand, emerald *chiaan* pooling in his palm as he prepared to force Kesmir away from the woman.

He didn't know why Kesmir had helped her—didn't trust it was for any good reason. Maybe he wanted her for himself, Raif didn't know. Calar's lover wasn't capable of mercy—Raif knew that for a fact.

He and Kesmir reached the woman at the same time and they both halted, staring at one another.

"Get away from her," Raif snarled. He pulled the corpse of the soldier off the sobbing jinni, then bent down to help her up, his eyes never leaving the scimitars Kesmir still gripped in his hands.

"*Shundai, shundai,*" she sobbed, looking from Raif to Kesmir. *Thank you.*

Kesmir dropped to one knee before the woman. "I will not burn their bodies," he said, his voice low and surprisingly soft. He looked up at the woman, his crimson eyes fierce. "You have my word."

He would condemn the soldiers to an eternity outside the godlands—a just punishment, one Raif himself would have given if he'd caught a *tavrai* behaving in just the same way. Still . . .

Raif kept one hand on the woman, the other holding his scimitar. "I'd kill you right now," he said, "but I have my hands full at the moment."

"Until next time, then," Kesmir said.

The general bowed and backed away, red evanescence swirling around him. Then he was gone. Raif stared after him for a moment—he didn't have time right now to consider what it meant that the leader of the Ifrit army didn't seem to enjoy killing *tavrai* but was quick to execute his own soldiers.

"You're safe now," Raif said to the woman, drawing her to a section of the beach the *tavrai* had set aside for civilians who escaped the battle.

He couldn't have been more wrong.

The sky was beginning to lighten when the fighting stopped. Raif only knew they'd won because when he turned around, there was no one left to stab. The dawn prayers began then, a mournful song to the gods, each *pajai's* singular voice undulating, crying out, high then low, swooping over the jinn on the beach. *Do you see this?* Raif wanted to scream to the gods. *Do you see what's become of us?*

The dead Ifrit lay around them like uprooted weeds. The Marid villagers crouched on the beach in terror, nearly as frightened of the Brass Army and the *tavrai* as they'd been of the Ifrit. It didn't feel like a victory. Not with all these bodies.

Then he saw her.

Calar stood atop a low hill, her pale skin glowing, her lips and eyes red as fresh blood, her general standing beside her. Kesmir looked less like the fearsome warrior Raif had encountered earlier and more like an uneasy witness. That was new.

"Come on," Raif said to Shirin as she came to stand beside him. "We've got big game to kill."

He headed closer to the beach, skirting the village, taking care to crouch below the boulders that stood between the village and the shore. He caught Taz's eye and nodded toward the hill before pushing down the beach. A few seconds, later, Taz had joined them. Raif could see Samar and Noqril flying above, scouting the area behind Calar.

"What's the plan, brother?" Taz asked.

"I want to know what Samar and Noqril see before we do anything," Raif said. "This doesn't make sense. Her soldiers have just been massacred and she doesn't seem to have reinforcements on hand. So what's she here for?"

"I doubt she's their clean-up crew," Shirin said. "Feels off to me."

"If Samar and Noqril give us the go-ahead, Shirin and I will try to intercept them on their way back to the palace," Raif said. "You and the others defend the village and deal with anything she sends your way."

Taz nodded toward a bank of trees behind them. "Samar's back."

They waited for the *fawzel* jinni to join them, watching as he crept along the line of trees, careful to stay out of Calar's range.

"I evanesced in the trees so my smoke wouldn't draw attention," Samar said, crouching down beside Raif. "She has a small company of soldiers in the glen—about five minutes' walk away. That's it."

Raif peeked over the boulders. Calar still stood there, a smug smile on her face. She turned and said something to Kesmir. He frowned and backed away slightly.

"Whatever it is, we need to be prepared," Raif said.

Something was very wrong—but what? The beach was littered with the corpses of her soldiers and yet the empress seemed so . . . *pleased* . . . with herself. Raif started forward, motioning for Shirin to follow him.

Taz went to rejoin the soldiers in the village, while Samar

made his way back to a thick stand of trees so that he could make his transformation in secret. Raif and Shirin cut across a wheat field, the stalks rustling slightly as they drew closer to Calar's location. It was a gentle sound, out of place in this death-filled terrain. Like skin moving against sheets. *Nalia.*

Raif was exhausted, which was precisely where Calar wanted him to be. Still, he couldn't throw away this chance. She was so rarely away from the palace.

Shirin scooted closer to him as he gently spread the stalks of wheat aside. Calar was several feet away—too far to kill before she realized their presence. All she seemed to be doing was observing the scene below, silent. Utterly still. Raif set his hands on the bare earth, drawing its energy into his skin, his eyes never leaving Calar. This was the woman who'd killed Bashil, who might as well have killed Nalia. He wouldn't rest until there was nothing left of her but bits of flesh for vultures to feast on.

Calar picked up the small stone that hung from a chain around her neck and began whispering over it.

"What is that crazy bitch doing?" Shirin muttered.

Just as Raif was about to release his *chiaan*, Calar's general turned his head. For a moment they looked at one another, frozen. Raif raised his hands, preparing to fight, but the jinni simply nodded slightly and slowly stepped away from Calar. Was he *helping* Raif kill her? Raif didn't wait to find out. Emerald *chiaan* flew from his fingers just as a writhing mass of black evanescence burst from the stone around Calar's neck. The smoke surrounded Calar, absorbing his magic, protecting her. Kesmir disappeared in a cloud of crimson evanescence.

Shirin fell to her knees, clamping her hands over her ears as a chorus of high-pitched screams emanated from the darkness Calar had conjured. The cloud hurtled away from the empress, toward the *tavrai* and Brass soldiers below.

Raif watched in horror as the shadows descended on his troops. From where he stood, all he could hear were agonized cries as the black smoke swirled through the village. Every time the smoke cleared, all that was left behind were dead *tavrai*. And when the *tavrai* attacked them with *chiaan*, it only seemed to make the creatures faster, as though the *chiaan* were fueling them. Gods, what was *happening*? For a moment, he stood there, undecided. He needed to go down there and help his troops, but he'd never been this close to Calar. He had a clear shot now that those creatures were on the beach.

"Stay here," he said to Shirin. If he did nothing else, at least he'd keep her alive.

"Like hell I will. Who's gonna have your back?"

No one, if I can help it. Kill Calar or die trying. Sounded good to him.

"Stay. Here," he said. "That's an order." Then he charged toward Calar.

The empress turned, a smile on her face. "Why, hello there."

Her eyes narrowed and Raif crumpled to the ground, clutching his temples as his head filled with blinding pain, as though someone were dragging sharp fingernails across his mind.

This was the power Nalia had told Raif of—Calar's psychic weapon, which had killed Bashil and tortured Malek. He felt the empress's presence inside him, her mind cutting into his, slashing

it to pieces with her searing magic. Tearing through his memories as though they were the wrapping on a gift.

Get out. He screamed the words at Calar, knowing there was no need to say them aloud.

Her laugh reverberated inside his skull, high and cruel, drowning out all other sound. Raif writhed as the pain split him in two, struggling against the presence that had slithered into his head. Dimly, he heard her speak somewhere in the deepest recesses of his mind. *Oh, I couldn't have dreamed this up,* Calar said. *You and the Aisouri—lovers?*

He tried to hold on to the memory of Nalia, terrified Calar could somehow take her away, erase Nalia from his mind. He gripped those memories like precious jewels, but a white-hot pain pulsed just behind his eye, drilling into the soft tissue of his brain. Nalia, her lips against his, neither of them caring about the battle that waged around them. Raif saying, *I always keep my promises.* Nalia, a grin that made his blood run hot, then . . . nothing.

You miss her, Calar's voice said, echoing inside him. *You stupid, lovesick fool.*

He could feel her exultant rush, Calar giddy with joy, and then, in the distance, he heard a familiar caw. Raif felt her pull away then, tearing through his mind, leaving nothing but a raw, insistent pain in her wake. Head throbbing, Raif looked up just in time to see Calar screeching at the diving *fawzel.* She raised her hands, grinning as Samar sped toward her.

There was a flash of crimson light and then an explosion of feathers rained over Raif. He looked up. Samar's body—back in

its jinn form—was somersaulting through the air. Seconds later, he fell to the hard earth, his blue eyes open, his chest still.

"Your turn," Calar said, standing over Raif. Her eyes shone. "What an unexpected pleasure."

Just as she prepared to cut him down, a stream of dark-green *chiaan* aimed at Calar shot toward the empress: Shirin. Calar let out a roar of rage, then threw a fiery ball of *chiaan* that hit Shirin square in the stomach. She fell to the dirt, convulsing. Raif expected Calar to finish them off then and there, but she swayed on her feet, her face deathly pale. Even evil tyrants, it seemed, could overdo it. Raif suspected her *voiqhif* worked much the same as Zanari's: great power, but a magic hangover like nobody's business. In seconds Calar had evanesced, the place where she'd stood deserted but for wisps of crimson smoke.

Raif crawled to where Shirin had rolled onto all fours, heaving. He was barely holding on to consciousness—a beheading would have been a mercy right then. It felt as though Calar had sliced a scimitar down the middle of his head.

"You okay?" he croaked.

"Yeah," she gasped. "This just . . . hurts . . . like a bitch."

"Maybe try following orders next time," he said, groaning as his head throbbed.

She grimaced. "Raif?"

"Yeah?"

"Shut up."

He bit back a smile and together they managed to stand, arms around each other's shoulders. They huddled over Samar—noble, selfless Samar, who had lost everything because of Raif's search for the sigil. The Dhoma lay in a pile of his *fawzel* feathers, his long hair splayed out beneath him.

"Fire and blood," Raif cursed, staring at the place Calar had been just seconds before. "We almost had her."

All he wanted to do was kill Calar. He'd never felt so violated, his memories stolen, sullied. *Nalia. Nalia.* Calar had seen so much. And now she'd taken Samar's life.

"I'm going to kill her eventually," he said, placing a hand on Samar's chest, then closing the Dhoma's eyes. "You will be avenged, brother."

"I have no problem helping you out with that," Shirin said.

Two clouds of evanescence swarmed toward them: gold, and red. Moments later, Taz and Noqril were standing beside them. Noqril caught sight of Samar on the ground and let out a rough cry, falling to his knees beside his tribesman.

"We're retreating," Taz said. Raif started to shake his head, but Taz pointed to the battle below. "Look at the village," he said. "Look and tell me we should stay here and fight."

Raif looked.

All he could see were shadows ripping through the jinn that remained. The field was littered with corpses. *Tavrai* and Brass soldiers lay crumpled above the bodies of the Ifrit they had killed only minutes before.

I did this, Raif thought. He'd known something was wrong about Calar being there. He should have gotten his jinn out. But instead he'd stayed because the desire to punish Calar for Nalia's loss had been stronger than his desire to protect his troops.

Shirin's fingers tightened around his shoulders, a hoarse cry all she could manage as she took in the scene below them.

"How?" Raif asked, cold with horror. *"How?"* It was as if Calar had somehow bottled the Eye and could unleash it upon them at will.

"I don't know and I have no idea how to fight them," Taz said. "They . . ." His face went pale. For a moment, Raif thought Taz was going to be sick. "They were . . . were . . . ripping out their souls." He grasped his head with his hands as though he could somehow tear the memory from his mind. "It didn't matter who it was: us or Ifrit, the shadows just . . . *consumed* them. We have to retreat, Raif. We cannot fight this."

"But all those villagers—"

"The shadows went for the jinn on the beach first," Noqril said. "They're dead. There's no one to save."

A whole village, wiped out, just like that.

Raif swore, his body shaking with rage. He'd been so gods-damned close to killing Calar, closer than he'd ever be again. He reached up and threw a burst of white *chiaan* into the air. Immediately, the few soldiers they had left began to evanesce. From where he stood, it looked as though they'd lost over half of the troops they'd brought to the beach with them—a third of the *tavrai* and Brass Army.

Shirin, still doubled over from the *chiaan* Calar had hurled at her stomach, grabbed his hand. "You're gonna have to get me out of here, brother."

It was the one thing he could do. Raif envisioned the *tavrai* camp as Shirin leaned against him. In moments they were gone, leaving the burning village behind.

When they touched down in the camp, Raif collapsed, exhausted. He didn't even make it to his *ludeen*. Instead, he lay on a soft tuft of grass, closed his eyes, and prayed he'd dream of Nalia again.

Before she opened her eyes, Nalia knew that something was different. Instead of the Eye's scent—something akin to the cold air of human ice rinks—she smelled burning wood.

Raif.

She sat up, her body sore from what appeared to be a stone floor she'd been sleeping on. She didn't know how long she'd been there, or how she'd arrived. There was very little light, just a flickering orange glow from two pillars of flame that stood on either side of a familiar gate. She knew where she was: the City of Brass.

No matter that it was forever hidden beneath the Sahara. No matter that all its entrances had been destroyed before Nalia had ever set foot in the Eye.

Raif.

She had to find him before the Eye took her away, had to tell him that she was alive, she was almost sure of it. Something was bringing them together.

Nalia stood, running along the wide avenue that led to the palace she'd spent a night in not so long ago. Sleeping on a pallet she'd manifested, Raif across the room because she wouldn't let him near her.

"Raif," she whispered, her voice hoarse from lack of use and quiet for fear of the cave's monsters she knew all too well. But Haraja was dead—the hideous creature that had stalked them on their quest for Solomon's sigil could no longer hurt her.

"Raif!" she called. There was the sound of feet pounding against hard-packed earth and then he was there, running out of *the alley where he'd once kissed her.*

Raif didn't stop running until she was in his arms. Nalia clung to him, shaking, sobbing. She didn't know if she'd survive being taken from him again. His lips found hers, his tongue gently lapping up the tears that streamed down her face. She kissed him with a ferocity that surprised her, as if she could somehow absorb him into her, take Raif into the Eye and never let go.

She hadn't had her fill of him, but Nalia forced herself to pull away, her arms still entwined around his neck. "Raif, something's happening to us. I don't know what it is, but . . . I think we're really here."

He pressed his lips to her forehead. "That's exactly what I'd want to hear," he murmured. "I've imagined you saying those words so many times, Nal." Pain lashed his face. "But . . . this isn't happening. I'm going to wake up and you won't be there—just like I did last time." He held her tight against him. "And you won't be lying next to me, no matter how much I wish you were."

"Raif . . ."

"Shhhh," he whispered. "We need to make the most of this time. We don't have much. And I don't know if we'll ever have it again."

He picked her up and she clung to him as he made his way to the palace. He was right, of course he was right.

The room they'd once slept in was empty, but her pallet was still there and he sat down on it, still holding her to him. He smelled like smoke and sweat. Flecks of dried blood coated his arms.

She ran her fingers over his skin and he sighed.

"What happened?" she asked.

"A battle. The Ifrit. They killed a—" He stopped himself, shook his head. "Never mind."

"What?"

Raif's eyes went dark with sorrow. "Not now, rohifsa. I don't want to be there. Let me be here with you. Just you."

He kissed her cheeks, her eyelids, the tip of her nose. Her lips traveled the length of his jaw, his neck.

"Tell me our story," she whispered, laying her cheek against his heart.

"After the war is over," he said softly, his lips against her hair, "we'll have a house and some land. We'll make love in our field under the Three Widows, as much as we want, whenever we want. Our two children will look exactly like you. . . ."

This time, when the darkness descended, she closed her eyes against it and held on to Raif until the Eye snatched her out of his arms.

16

GOLDEN EVANESCENCE SWIRLED AROUND TAZ AS HE prepared to leave the battlefield. Below him, the jinn were shifting into smoke one by one, desperate to get out before the shadows could feed on them. Taz leaped off a cliff, his arms extended to the sunrise, and evanesced in midair. But instead of returning to camp as he should have, Taz's mind refused to picture anything but the one place he was simultaneously dreading and longing to go: home. His family's plantation was the site of some of his best and worst memories. It was impossible to imagine the *kajar* without his family, without the serfs who'd crushed the grapes for *savri* beneath their feet, skirts and pants pulled up high to avoid stains from the fruit.

Taz gave himself over to his magic as his evanescence turned him into a ball of cinnamon-scented smoke. He'd been fighting for hours and he needed to rest. Exhausted, he closed his eyes, but just as his body was about to disappear, Taz felt a tug on his arm and realized in horror that one of the Ifrit, hidden, no doubt, among the cliff's rocks, had managed to grab hold of him. There was nothing Taz could do as skin turned to smoke. All he could see was a cloud of crimson evanescence mixing with his golden smoke and then—

He touched down at the edge of a large, burned field. As his body began to materialize, Taz reached for his scimitar. The hold on his leg disappeared, and through the wisps of evanescence, Taz spied the Ifrit who'd caught hold of him: the jinni who'd been standing beside Calar—her general.

Taz raised his weapon, but the other jinni immediately held up his hands and backed away. "I'm not here to fight," the Ifrit said.

Taz snorted. "I find that difficult to believe."

The jinni wasn't handsome by any means: he had a crooked nose, as though it had been broken several times, and an ugly scar across one cheek. But his eyes were distracting. The ferocity in them, those long lashes that skimmed his bronze skin . . .

"Let me guess: you're Calar's lapdog," Taz said.

The Ifrit raised his eyebrows. "Good guess."

"I saw you on the hill." Taz stepped closer. "Tell me, were you sufficiently entertained by Calar's monsters?"

"No."

"Really? You seemed riveted."

The Ifrit sighed, his eyes filling with the sadness Taz had seen in the eyes of his fellow enslaved jinn—it was an epidemic, this hopelessness.

"The pain of another brings me no pleasure," the jinni said. "Not anymore. I've seen enough horrors for one lifetime. I tire of violence."

"And yet you still fought today."

"There was no choice but to fight," the jinni said. "If I hadn't joined my soldiers, Calar would have grown suspicious. And if she had, this conversation we're having wouldn't be possible."

Taz had to admit that the jinni's performance on the battlefield seemed to support this. The Ifrit general's skill at killing his enemies was exceptional, but he did so only in defense, only when necessary. More often than not, he'd been reprimanding his soldiers for hurting civilians. Taz had noticed this many times throughout the battle.

"Be that as it may," Taz said, "I'm not leaving this field without shedding your blood." He raised his scimitar in one hand while the other held a ball of glowing *chiaan*.

The other jinni simply stood there, a far too easy kill. Taz lowered his weapon.

"If you aren't here to fight me, then why in all hells did you come?" Taz asked, exasperated. He was tired, anxious to see his family's plantation, and he wanted to go to sleep for a very long time. But before that, he wanted to see how many of his jinn had survived the battle in that village and honor the ones who hadn't. *Samar.*

Gods, he was tired of death.

"I need a meeting with Raif Djan'Urbi," the Ifrit said. He took a step forward, hands still outstretched plaintively, but stopped when Taz raised the sphere of *chiaan* he was still holding. "Please. I need your help to end this war."

"Do I look easily fooled?" Taz said.

"No. You look like a commander who doesn't want to see any more of his jinn die," the jinni said. "I saw you on the battlefield. Killing you would be a waste of a good soldier."

Taz frowned. "Then you would know I have no interest in surrendering. I fought your kind long before you were born, and I suspect that I will continue to fight Ravnir's children long after you are gone. Pray to your fire god, swine, because I've no more patience."

"My name is Kesmir," the jinni said. "But *swine* is not entirely inaccurate."

Taz paused, yet again. It was harder to kill a jinni once you knew his name.

"I've been waiting a long time for a chance like this," Kesmir continued when Taz remained silent.

"A chance to die in the middle of an abandoned *kajar*?" Taz said.

"No. A chance to join the resistance."

Taz stared. "You would betray your empress?"

"To follow her any longer would be to betray my people," Kesmir said. "Betray myself." His eyes latched onto Taz's, his gaze unflinching. "I've begun training with . . . someone . . . to protect my mind against Calar. We've been building up our own resistance in the Ifrit ranks, but it's not nearly strong enough. If we combined forces, we might have a chance at peace."

Taz looked at him, thoughtful. It was possible the Ifrit commander was telling the truth. His face was drawn, weary. Lips pulled in a permanent frown. He didn't have a cunning look about him. But it was the sorrow in his eyes that made Taz believe this conversation wasn't just another strategy of Calar's. His was not the face of a jinni who'd just won a battle.

"Why did Calar choose to attack that village?" he asked.

Kesmir closed his eyes, his expression pained. "They were harboring a Ghan Aisouri infant."

Taz went still. "Is she alive?"

Kesmir shook his head. "No. Killed in the battle. I . . . couldn't get to her in time." He looked away from Taz, his eyes glistening.

"You nearly annihilated the entire Aisouri race and yet you're concerned about one child?"

Something passed over Kesmir's face, a hurt of some kind, something fierce, but Taz couldn't place it.

"Any Aisouri born from now on is an innocent. They aren't being trained to hate and kill." Kesmir met his eyes once again. "I'm not a butcher. Not anymore."

Taz stood there, unmoving, trying to understand what it meant, that an Aisouri had lived, however briefly. The loss was crushing. A child—the only Aisouri left now that Nalia was gone—cut down before she could even speak. Taz hadn't dared to hope any Aisouri had been born in the past three years. The birth of a royal child was incredibly rare. Sometimes decades would pass before one was discovered. And without the Aisouri themselves to claim them . . . A thought occurred to Taz, so suddenly that he couldn't believe he'd never considered it before.

"What happens when a Ghan Aisouri is born among the Ifrit?" he asked.

To his knowledge, the Aisouri had ventured into Ithkar as often as they could in search of their own kind, but breaching the border between the two lands was never an easy task, and to Taz's knowledge, they'd never discovered a purple-eyed child among the Ifrit. It was possible there were Ghan Aisouri children there, hidden away in the crags of Ithkar's volcanic mountains. The royals had always been worried the Ifrit would brainwash any Aisouri gifted them by the gods and send the children to destroy their sisters in Arjinna. But it had never happened and so the worst was assumed—the Ifrit were killing the babes that so resembled their greatest enemy.

"As you must know, in Arjinna, the Aisouri were always taken from the parents and brought to the palace to train," Kes said. His eyes flashed. "A despicable practice, taking a child from its father. Its mother. But in Ithkar, it's even worse. The Ash Crones claim the child. They drain it of its energy, using the power for dark magic, and then . . ."

"It dies," Taz whispered. An atrocity so horrible, he could hardly comprehend what he was hearing.

Kesmir nodded. "Yes."

All those centuries of meditation and chanting *sadrs* were of little help to Taz right then. Pure hatred scorched through his blood, destroying the inner peace he'd spent so long cultivating. Children. They'd killed their own innocent children.

"You disgust me," Taz spit. "How dare you ask for our help—"

"We were wrong," Kes said. "All of us were raised to hate, don't you see? Me, you, every jinni born in this cursed land. Calar is brutal, our army is brutal. I know this. I want it to stop."

"Why?" Taz asked. "Because you suddenly realize your empress is just as happy killing Ifrit as she is any other caste? You're just trying to save your own skin."

"I have a better reason," Kes said quietly.

"And what is that?" Taz growled.

He shook his head. "Get me a meeting with Raif Djan'Urbi and I will tell you then."

Taz frowned. It would be folly to dismiss helping Kesmir out of hand. If he was telling the truth, there was a chance to stage a coup, end the war.

"I need something better than that," Taz said. "To begin with, why don't you tell me about those shadows?"

Kesmir's eyes hardened. "Abominations. Calar's been working on creating them ever since we slayed the Aisouri. It's the dead caste's energy that powers them."

Taz took a step back, appalled. Things were far worse than he'd thought. And the situation had been rather hopeless to begin with.

"How is that possible?"

"When a jinni dies, their *chiaan* flows back into the earth," Kesmir said. "Calar captured that energy—dark energy now because it came from dead jinn—and discovered a way to create these creatures. It's ancient magic, still practiced by the Ash Crones."

There was a kind of logic to what Kesmir was saying.

Everything had its opposite. Light and dark. Life and death. If *chiaan* came from life, from the living force of all that existed, then it only made sense that its opposite existed, as well: the energy of death and decay—just as powerful, but with a far different agenda. Only in Ithkar were there temples to Mora, the goddess of death. There she was worshipped as Ravnir's equal, the patron goddess of a lifeless land.

Kesmir held up a white stone that hung around his neck. "This is the only thing I know of that can protect us from Calar's shadows. It's a *yaghin*. I'm not sure how it works—I only know that it absorbs the creatures. Other than the ones Calar and I wear, the Ash Crones have the few that are in existence."

"Is there no way to fight them?" Taz asked.

"Not that I know of. You saw what they can do."

Yes, Taz had seen. The creatures couldn't be harmed, at least not through conventional means.

"They obey Calar, yes?" Taz said.

Kesmir nodded.

"So the only way to destroy those creatures is to kill their empress and keep them entrapped in her *yaghin*." Taz finally let the ball of glowing *chiaan* in his hand bleed into the ground below. He sheathed his scimitar, staring down the other jinni. "Is this what you're offering to do for us?"

Kesmir swallowed, his expression pained. "Before the shadows, I couldn't. But now, after seeing . . ." He sighed. "Yes. I will kill Calar."

Taz softened at the pain and despair written over Kesmir's face.

"Tell me your story," he said, gentle. It was a question he'd asked Nalia not so long ago.

Kesmir hesitated, then began to speak, the words pouring out of him. Taz wondered if this was the first time the other jinni had given voice to the tumult within him.

It was a tale so sensational Taz had to believe it—only the most fanciful of jinn could have made it up, and Kesmir did not strike Taz as fanciful.

A jinni in love with the girl who'd rescued him from his burning village, their love forged in the wake of a Ghan Aisouri slaughter of the Ifrit. The careful planning to rise above their oppressors and install the boy's *rohifsa* on the Arjinnan throne. Calar being crowned empress after dancing in a pool of Aisouri blood. Then: her swift decline into madness and a power that only served to erode her sanity and increase her cruelty.

"I thought I would have followed her anywhere," Kesmir said, his eyes dark and haunted. "But she's gone to places no one could follow, not even me. The power didn't free Calar; it created a prison she can't escape from."

He spoke of torture, paranoia, and an increasing need to control the minutiae of the Ifrit government.

"It's her *voiqhif*," Kesmir added softly. "The more she uses it, the worse she gets. It's doing something to her. The best parts of her are . . . rotting. I'm not the only one who sees it."

When Kesmir finished, Taz had to ask the obvious question. "Do you still love her?"

It took a while for the jinni to answer. When he did, his eyes were full of grief. "Enough to make sure she's taken down with as little pain as possible. I owe her that much." Kes wrung his hands, pacing. "My teacher—the one who's helping me control my mind—he's told me time and again that I have to kill her. But I've always refused. It wasn't until today that I knew for certain all hope that she could change was gone. And yet, it pains me." He glanced at Taz. "That must sound crazy to you."

"No," Taz murmured. Wouldn't he have done the same for Lokahm? It would have been impossible to slit his *rohifsa*'s throat. He didn't envy Kesmir that task, though it was a just punishment—an *easy* punishment—after the Ghan Aisouri genocide.

"I have to be honest," Taz said, "I'm not sure Raif or the *tavrai* are going to be thrilled with any kind of alliance with you—or amenable to sparing Calar pain. You assisted in the execution of the Ghan Aisouri, and that's a bit of a sensitive subject with our commander right now."

"We all have 'sensitive' subjects, do we not?"

Taz had expected Kesmir to show some remorse over killing the Aisouri, but there seemed to be none. "You don't regret making an entire race of jinn extinct?" he asked.

This time, Kesmir did not hesitate before he answered. "No. The only way to take the power away from the Aisouri was to kill them all. You've seen what havoc just one Aisouri can cause."

Kesmir looked at Taz, magnetic eyes that called to something inside him that had been dead for thousands of years. Eyes of blood and fire, garnet eyes that didn't look away.

"What of that child who died this morning?" Taz asked. "You say you would have saved her. But if you had, Calar would find out. And where would that leave you and your resistance?"

"If I'd been the one to discover her, I could have hidden her. Faked her death," Kesmir said. "Most of the Ifrit soldiers would never dream I was capable of that mercy—they'd never suspect. I've done it before."

Taz stepped forward. "What do you mean you've *done it before?*"

It was too much to hope for. He had to be misunderstanding.

Kesmir's expression became closed, as if he realized he'd tipped his hand, revealed far more than he'd intended. "There's a jinni in the Vein. He . . . helps. That's all I can say. It's his story to tell and I don't want to put him in more danger than he is already."

His voice caught and Taz widened his eyes. Where was this emotion for the Aisouri coming from?

"Have you ever been to Ithkar?" Kesmir asked unexpectedly.

"I fought in the border wars, long ago. Never on the Ithkar side, though," Taz said.

That had been a brutal year full of bloodshed and the endless chill of the Upper Qaf. But there'd been warmth, too. Long nights with Lokahm and the thrill of illicit love, or fighting alongside Erah, his Ghan Aisouri sister.

"I didn't know any Ifrit until I went to Earth," Taz continued. "Now, some of my closest friends are from your caste. Our late empress's most devoted guard is an Ifrit."

Late empress. Did he really believe Nalia was dead? It seemed so impossible, after the stories he'd heard of her survival.

Kesmir cocked his head to the side. "You lived on Earth?"

"A story for another time," Taz said.

"So there will be . . . another time?" Kesmir asked. The jinni was unable to keep the hope from his voice.

The sun had risen higher in the sky and it brought out the gold in Kesmir's bronze skin, turned his eyes rusty. Taz could see that there were several shades of red to those eyes, just as there seemed to be several layers to the jinni they belonged to. There was kindness in his face, lines from countless worries. Did he ever smile? Laugh? Despite his uniform, Kesmir didn't look like a killer when he was off the battlefield. Taz wanted to know more, but he wasn't entirely sure why.

"I need to consult with Djan'Urbi. Meet us here tomorrow— midnight," Taz said. "Alone, it goes without saying. We need to burn our dead, have a few meetings. I'll be here either way."

Kesmir nodded and crimson smoke began to pool at his feet. His evanescence smelled of campfires, not an unpleasant scent. It reminded Taz of late-night secrets and shared bottles of *savri*. He held Kesmir's eyes until his unlikely accomplice disappeared, swallowed by the morning sun.

It was possible, of course, that the whole conversation was part of an elaborate trap. Raif would certainly think so. But Taz's instincts about people were never wrong.

"Gods help him," he muttered, his eyes on the few remaining tendrils of Kesmir's evanescence that hung in the air.

17

KESMIR KNOCKED SOFTLY ON THE WIDE DOUBLE DOORS that led to Calar's rooms. They opened immediately, one of the servants peeking out. When she saw Kesmir, she motioned for him, frantic, and he slipped inside.

"How is she?" he murmured.

"A little better," the girl whispered. The bruise on her cheek and the quiver in her voice told a different story. "She wants more medicine. Will you sit with her while I call for a healer?"

"Of course," he said.

Kes moved farther in. The lights in the opulent sitting room were out, but a fire burned in the grate, hearty flames that licked the stone.

To his left was the large bathing room and to his right the bedroom he shared with Calar, though it'd been quite some time since they'd made good use of it. *Thank gods,* he thought.

His mind turned over the promise he'd made to the Shaitan commander: *I will kill Calar.*

He had to. He knew that now. The knowledge threatened to crush him. If he lived through it, he would one day have to tell his daughter that he'd killed her mother. Would Yasri ever forgive him? Could she possibly understand?

Kes straightened his shoulders and entered the bedroom. A cold breeze slipped past the window on his left, causing the candles in the room to flicker, and yet the room still felt cramped and stuffy. Calar lay in the center of the large bed that took up most of the room. She was propped up against several pillows, her eyes closed.

"Who's there?" she said, not bothering to open her eyes.

"It's me." He crossed to the elaborately carved cabinet beside her bed, knowing what Calar wanted before she asked for it.

"Can you—"

"Yes," he said.

The *gaujuri* water pipe was made of a single sheet of wind-blown glass with a small silver bowl placed above the pipe's small opening. Filled with fragrant *gaujuri* leaves, its smoke would travel through the bowl to the pipe below. A sheet of foil dotted with minuscule holes sat atop the leaves. Kes grabbed a coal out of the fire with his fingers, the *chiaan* from the burning ember coursing through him, a comfort. He placed it on the foil. A tube dangled from the side, fused to the glass, with an ornate mother-of-pearl mouthpiece. This Kesmir placed in Calar's hand as he had so many times in the past three years. She inhaled the drug's fragrant smoke, one of the few things that eased the pain of using her gift.

"You went too far tonight," he said. "You could have hurt yourself."

A day spent in the Cauldron with her shadows and a fight with Raif Djan'Urbi—what had she been thinking?

"I'm fine," Calar said, her voice heavy.

It wasn't love or pity, this hollowed-out feeling that pushed itself into his consciousness whenever he was near Calar—it was grief.

"Do you remember when we first met?" she said, her voice thick. The *gaujuri* was already doing its work.

"Yes," he said. Kesmir slid to the floor and sat with his back against the bed.

He held his head in his hands as the memory washed over him. A memory he had just betrayed in a burned plantation with the commander of the Brass Army. He'd never forget her gentleness that day. He'd lost everything, everyone. And then Calar was there, in his head, in his heart. All that hate and horror was cast aside by this bloom, pushing through the ashes.

Calar was mumbling and he had to move closer to hear.

"What?" he asked softly.

A strand of her white hair was plastered to her forehead, and he reached out and gently tucked it behind her ear. Gods, how could he betray her?

" . . . so . . . good . . . to me. . . ." She reached her hand up, grasping at some invisible object the *gaujuri* had conjured. She laughed softly, a girlish, carefree sound. "For you."

Kesmir held out his hand and pretended to accept whatever she'd given him. Like this, he could almost believe she was still the Calar he'd fallen in love with. Those wine-red lips, skin like snow. She'd been a vision that day. And what of the day when Yasri came into the world, the pain Calar endured, her tears of joy when her daughter was placed in her arms? The purple eyes hadn't mattered—the little miracle in her arms was theirs. Love, pure and good, filled that room. Their little family.

Calar gazed at him, her eyes growing heavy. "You and Ri are the one good thing," she whispered. Her eyes closed. "The one. Good. Thing."

Kes waited until Calar's breaths became deep and even, then slipped out of her room.

Kes looked over his shoulder before ducking into a small shop, the door beneath a swinging elaborate sign that read The Dragon's Lair, and then smaller, beneath it: We Grant on Demand. Small advertisements for granted items hovered in the window: animals, fine jewelry, items from Earth, foods fit for an empress. Under each was its value in *nibas* or "even trade wishes." There had been several of these shops in Arjinna, but this was the only legal one currently in operation. Ever since Calar had banned manifestation for all castes but licensed Ifrit, such establishments were few and far between in The Vein. And even if she hadn't instituted the ban, only the most educated jinn knew how to manifest items beyond the very basic necessities for living. A jinni couldn't manifest something he'd never seen before, so the former serfs of Arjinna, now free of their masters, remained as destitute as ever.

A small bell hovering in midair above the door jangled as Kes entered the shop.

"Bartering today?" said the boy at the counter without looking up. His eyes widened when he caught sight of Kes and he scrambled to stand. "Sir General. *Jahal'alund.*"

"*Jahal'alund,* Quan," he said, holding back a laugh at the greeting. For nearly two years the boy had been calling him that, unable to choose which word to refer to him by.

"Your friends are in the granting room," Quan said, gesturing to a door down a short hallway to his right. "Would you like some *chal*?"

"Yes, thank you," he said. "No sugar."

A hot cup of tea, something that scalded a little—that was just what he needed.

Quan smiled. "I know."

Kes reached out and ruffled his hair and the boy beamed, pleased at the attention. He was an orphan Kes had taken under his wing after the boy's parents died in a skirmish with the *tavrai*. He knew of no one more loyal to him than this child and trusted Quan with both his life and one of his biggest secrets—the meetings that happened in the shop's discreet back room with high-ranking members of the Ifrit military.

He started to walk past the boy but stopped when he noticed a gun tucked away on a small shelf beneath the counter. "Where did that come from?" he asked.

"A jinni bartered it for a new house," he said. "My master said that was a good deal for us. A very good deal."

"He's right," Kes said. "These are extremely hard to come by." He frowned. "Did the jinni who bartered say where he got the gun from?"

"I overheard a little. There's a jinni in the Vein," he said. "He gave guns to many jinn."

"What did this jinni with the guns expect in return?" Kes asked.

"Nothing," Quan said.

Somebody was arming civilians—the *tavrai*, of course. And he had a pretty good idea who was helping them.

"Who's giving the guns away?" Kes asked.

"There are some rumors, but . . ." Quan grew uncomfortable. "I do not wish to say. If my master knew I was speaking about his business—"

Kes placed his hand over his heart. "I swear on my life I will not harm this jinni or let anyone know where I got this information," he said. "And you know I keep my vows."

The worry on Quan's face swept away. "Yes, Sir General, I know."

Kes could still remember this scrap of a boy huddled outside a burning house, cheeks stained with tears. He'd lost his whole family in one night. *I'll take care of you for as long as I live,* he'd promised the boy. As soon as it was safe, he planned to move Quan to the palace. Yasri could use an older brother.

"His name is Yurik," Quan whispered, even though they were the only ones in the front portion of the shop.

"Yes, I know him. He's a good jinni. If anything ever happens to me, you go to him. Tell him I sent you."

The boy smiled. "He gave me candy."

"Did he now?" Kes reached into his pocket and pulled out a fifty-*niba* piece. "I suppose you could use some more?"

Quan nodded, grinning. "Oh, yes, Sir General."

Kes had long suspected Yurik of involvement with the *tavrai*, but he'd never had proof. When he was ready, he'd bring Yurik into his circle of conspirators—the jinni would be someone who could procure arms, help with logistics. But would the enigmatic owner of the realm's most popular tavern be willing to work with the Ifrit on that level? Yurik appeared to take no sides in the ongoing civil war—his tavern was frequented by jinn of all castes. And yet now Kes knew he was an agent for the *tavrai*. Despite that, he'd helped Kes hide Aisouri children. An interesting character, Yurik.

"Make sure you bring enough tea for everyone," Kes said, patting Quan's shoulder as he moved down the hallway.

The circular meeting room behind the shop was lit by torches placed in elaborate wall sconces. An enchanted trough of lava bubbled in the corner, there for Quan's master to replenish his *chiaan* after granting. The jinni sitting in the granter's thronelike armchair stood as Kes entered. It wasn't Quan's employer, Ahmi Ifri'Or, but one of Kes's most trusted soldiers, here for the first time.

"General," the jinni said with a slight bow. Halem was one of his best captains, but Kes had long suspected the jinni's dissatisfaction with the way Calar was running the realm. It was why

Kes was here tonight, risking his life to recruit him for the Ifrit revolt. Leaning against a wall were the twins—Xala and Urum. The mage and Fazhad had yet to arrive.

"Thank you for coming," Kes said, nodding first to Halem and then the twins.

"We told him nothing," Xala said.

"Though we were tempted," Urum added.

"I admit, the mystery is intriguing," Halem said. "I, of course, serve at the pleasure of the empress."

Xala and Urum exchanged a glance.

"How are your troops?" Kes asked. The door opened and Fazhad slipped in, nodding her greetings.

Halem ran a hand over his unshaven face. "I'm sure you can imagine the rumors about this army that came out of the Eye."

Kes nodded. "Empress Calar's recent work with the Ash Crones will likely dispel some of that fear."

He hated the shadows, but there was no doubt they would ensure Ifrit victories. No one in the realm had the power to defeat such evil. *How do you kill an enemy that can't bleed?*

Halem crossed his arms, worry flashing in his crimson eyes. "I welcome the empress's assistance, of course, but . . ." He hesitated, and it was this hesitation Kes had witnessed so often in his captain that gave him the confidence to set up this meeting in the first place.

"But . . . you're concerned about the effects her plans might have on our people?" Kes said.

"I would never . . ." Halem coughed slightly and tiny beads of sweat broke out on his forehead. He cast a nervous glance at Xala and Urum. "What I mean to say is—"

Kes moved closer. "Halem. You can speak freely here. You've been called to this meeting because we believe that you can assist us in our efforts to heal Arjinna." He felt Xala and Urum shift closer, their bodies unconsciously taking on defensive positions, ready to attack if Halem showed any sign of being loyal to Calar. "I no longer believe that Calar should be empress of our realm," Kes said. "I'm hoping you feel the same way."

Halem stared, his mouth opening and closing like a fish's. It would be comical, if such a conversation wouldn't lead to the firing squad.

"Sir, you speak . . . you speak treason," Halem stammered.

"Yes, I do."

Thus far, Kes had found that being direct was the best approach. If a jinni did not have an itch for rebellion or was content to suffer under Calar, he could always say he'd been trying to entrap them, a clandestine effort to root out the disloyal from his ranks. So far, though, Kes's hunches had proven to be correct.

"There's a small group of us," Kes continued, motioning to Xala, Urum, and Fazhad. "We're planning to overthrow her. But right now, our numbers are too small and I fear Calar will find out before we have a chance to take her down."

There was a soft knock on the door and Kes held up a hand. "Yes?"

"It's me, Sir General," Quan said. "And the old Shaitan."

That would be Ajwar Shai'Dzar, Nalia's father and Kes's closest Shaitan contact. They hadn't seen each other since their encounter at the palace, but Thatur passed messages back and forth between them.

"All right," Kes said, his heart rate slowing. He hated putting Quan in this danger. He'd never forgive himself if something happened to the boy because of him.

Quan came in with a tea tray, followed by Ajwar. He glided in, silent, and went to stand beside Fazhad while Quan set the tray on the stone table in the center of the room. The boy bowed, then retreated, closing the door behind him.

Halem stared at Ajwar. "You," he breathed. "You're supposed to be dead. I heard Calar issue the order myself."

"The gods protect those who serve the realm's true empress," Ajwar said.

He had that soft, lilting tone of scholars accustomed to few words and hours of silent contemplation. Now, in the room's light, Kes could see the Shaitan more clearly. Three years ago, he'd been a handsome jinni, dressed in the finest *sawalas*, lover of a Ghan Aisouri, father to another. All that had changed under Calar. Now he was gaunt, his hair long and gray, and he had a hunted look, shoulders slightly hunched, eyes shifting continually. But that was nothing compared to the burns that disfigured his face.

Kes turned to Halem, who was now watching him closely. "Tell me your thoughts, Captain."

"You could be trying to test my loyalty," Halem said. "Although, I must admit, that is unlike you."

Kes had worked hard to prove to his jinn that he was more than Calar's *rohifsa*. The success of the coup was, in large part, due to Kes's efforts as commander of Calar's forces. Since then, the Ifrit Army had entrusted their lives to him without question.

"It would be a poor way to repay you for your blood pledge," Kes agreed.

He watched Halem's face, keeping his own neutral, impassive. Had he made a mistake in thinking this jinni would fight with him? The other jinn in the room watched in silence, their bodies tense. He could feel their hope, their fear. And Kes knew if he was wrong about this jinni, he'd have to kill him.

"I lost my sister in the purges last month," Halem said softly.

Now it was Kes's turn to be surprised. "Why didn't you tell me she was arrested? I would have spoken to Calar for you—"

"By the time I found out, it was too late. She was already gone." Halem shook his head, his lips turned down. "Besides, would that have made a difference?"

Calar had rarely shown mercy, but Kes had usually been able to convince her to accept a less violent path. Not anymore. His influence with her was waning—and it seemed his soldiers knew it.

"Perhaps not," Kes said. "What was she executed for?"

"An informant claimed she was secretly working for the resistance," he said. From Halem's tone, it was clear he didn't believe this to be true. He ground his teeth, holding back a rage that Kes knew well. "Is killing Calar part of your plan?" Halem asked, his voice hard.

"Yes," Kes said.

His accomplices looked at Kes in surprise. He hadn't had a chance to fill them in on his change of heart after seeing what her shadows did in that Marid village.

"Then count me in."

Kes felt the tension drain out of him. "Good. We need you."

Halem addressed the room. "What's the plan?"

"We'll hopefully be working with the *tavrai* to coordinate our attack," Kes said. "We still need more Ifrit to come over to our side—a lot more. I'm training to protect my mind against Calar's power. As soon as I'm certain she can't get in, we'll set everything in motion. If I try too soon, I'll have ruined our entire operation. This . . . may take a long time. But we have to do it right. I won't try to assassinate her until my teacher believes I'm ready." Thatur had been sure to let Kes know in their last training session that he was far from ready. "Right now, we're just trying to get recruits, do reconnaissance."

"Why not just kill her now?" Halem said. "Forgive me for my bluntness, sir, but . . . don't you share a bed? Why not just smother her in the night?"

This time Ajwar spoke, his soft voice barely discernible. "Calar is incredibly powerful, as you know. There can be no room for error. If Kesmir's thoughts of killing her are too strong, it could wake her and her mind could incinerate him instantly unless he knows how to block her attacks. Once he can properly protect his mind, then we have a greater chance at being successful. Not only that, it does us no good to assassinate her without a clear plan for what comes after. All we'd be doing is creating another civil war."

That was Kes's greatest concern. Right now, the war had two fronts: the Ifrit and the *tavrai*. Kes's resistance within the Ifrit ranks was adding a third front. But once Calar was gone, what would happen? If there was no plan, there would still be three fronts to the war, and little gained. Utter chaos.

Halem leaned forward, his eyes bright. "But Calar would be dead, no? Surely any future that doesn't contain her is preferable to the lives we lead now."

"My concern is for our people," Kes said. "If we don't do this right, hundreds—maybe thousands more—will be killed. I don't want to give Calar the chance to crush us before we've even started."

"She won't," Xala said with conviction.

"Not if we can help it," Urum added.

A low laugh escaped Halem's lips.

"You all right there, Captain?" Fazhad said. She glanced at Kes and raised her eyebrows.

Halem looked up, and the weight Kes had seen around Halem's eyes and mouth disappeared. "Forgive me, but . . . we're going to kill the jinni who murdered my sister," he said. "My wildest dream is about to come true."

18

RAIF STUMBLED INTO HIS *LUDEEN* AT DUSK AND FELL into bed. He didn't take off his clothes, even though he'd spent the past day in them, burning the dead and fighting a battle before that. He smelled of ashes, blood, and sweat. He smelled of failure.

There'd been hours chopping wood, stacking it, standing beside each pyre, blaming himself for every loss. He'd allowed Calar to lure him into her trap because he'd needed to stop thinking of Nalia, because he wanted to prove to the *tavrai* that he was still himself, despite loving an Aisouri. All he'd wanted to do was kill as many of Calar's jinn as he could, and he'd jumped into the fray, heedless of the cost.

And so, as usual, he'd learned the truth the hard way. Raif wouldn't be able to fight this war and honorably lead the *tavrai* if even a small part of him believed Nalia was still alive out there, waiting for him to rescue her. Seeing the eyes of that dead Ghan Aisouri child had decimated him. He'd gotten so used to Nalia's eyes looking at him with love or fury or defiance. Her eyes were epic, crushing. He saw them every time he closed his own. And now. Now all he could see was that dead child, and he wondered if this was what Nalia's eyes looked like, wherever she was.

Stop it, he told himself.

There was work to do, decisions to be made. If there were more Aisouri children out there, he had to find them, hide them—for Nalia. It was what she would have wanted. Taz had told him about the Ifrit who wanted to be their spy and that there were more Aisouri—if Calar's *skag* general could be believed. Lot of good it would do them, since the bastard didn't know how to fight Calar's shadow army. *Funny how he waited to offer his assistance until* after *those monsters massacred our jinn,* he'd said to Taz, before turning away. *You can tell that jinni to go fuck himself.*

Taz had gently clapped him on the back before going to throw more bodies onto the flames. *I'll let you sleep on it, brother.*

Now Raif lay on his back, too worn out to fall asleep. He hadn't been entirely honest with Taz; much as Raif hated Kesmir, he admired a jinni who placed the lives of innocent jinn above his own soldiers. One who wasn't afraid to execute those soldiers when they did despicable things. And he couldn't forget how Kesmir had all but tried to hand him Calar on the battlefield. Unless he'd just wanted it to appear that way? It had all happened so fast, Raif didn't know what to think. And then there'd been Samar, dying midair. He was one of the few jinn who had come to really know Nalia, to have spent more than a few fleeting days with her in the Eye. Now it was just Raif, Zanari, and Noqril who knew the real Nalia—not the demigoddess Taz and Touma and all the rest made her out to be. They knew the girl who laughed in delight when she saw something beautiful, the one who collapsed from grief, too broken to be a daughter of the gods. Her gentle counsel, the fierceness with which she protected the people she loved. And then there were all those things only Raif knew. Memories of her sighs and her taste and the feel of her body beneath his own were stored up inside him like precious jewels in a locked box.

What would Nalia have done?

He'd caught himself asking this question, over and over. Before he met her, Raif had rarely second-guessed his decisions. Now it was all he did. He tried to imagine her, sitting on the edge of the bed or pacing the room, arguing with him.

People change, she might say. *Kesmir's our only chance at getting close to Calar. An alliance with him would only make us stronger.*

No, Nalia wouldn't say that. Kesmir Ifri'Lhas was Calar's lover, her right hand. Other than the Ifrit empress, he'd be the first on her list to die. But was that true? Nalia didn't like killing—look at the kindness she'd shown Malek. And if anyone had deserved to die by Nalia's hand, it was that *pardjinn* who'd stolen three years of her life. That slaver had tortured her every day of her years in captivity and she'd grieved him, even burned his body so that he wouldn't have to wander the shadowlands as she now did. His *rohifsa's* greatest weakness—and greatest strength—had always been her ability to show mercy.

Don't be so stubborn, she would say. She'd sit in his lap, give him that wise, all-knowing look of hers. *You know what you have to do.*

Raif dug the heels of his hands into his eyes as the tears threatened to come again. He was thinking of her in the past tense—when had that shift happened? His mind knew she was gone; why didn't his heart? Those dreams. He'd been in Malek's mansion last night, the City of Brass when he'd collapsed this morning after the battle. He was certain of it. And Shirin had felt Nalia's *chiaan* inside him just hours after he'd made love to her in that first dream. She was a daughter of the gods, magic incarnate. It could be real. It could be.

His heart beat frantically, his mind spinning, faster and faster. Was it possible? *Was it?*

"Please," he whispered, "if you actually give a shit at all, would you please give me a sign?" Talking to the gods was a waste of time, but he was desperate—two seconds away from walking-into-the-Eye desperate. "I just need to know, one way or the other."

He could hear the faint song of the mourning round outside. It was an old Djan tradition: those who'd attended a burning sat in a circle, drinking and singing songs around an elder pine fire, the perfumed wood and the song honoring the spirit on its journey to the godlands. They would be at it until dawn. He should be out there, but he didn't have the heart.

Raif lay awake for hours, knowing he should be thinking about the battle he'd lost, the jinn who'd died, the monstrous creatures Calar had created. But all he could see were those dead baby's eyes.

So Raif prayed and, for once, the gods decided to answer.

Sleep came, and when it did, it was heavy, pulling him under so fast it felt like drowning in pure night. And then he realized: it wasn't sleep, it was the Eye.

This was real. He knew it in his bones. This wasn't an imagined landscape, an illusion. Raif was in the Eye—in the present. He recognized its cold scent, the wrongness of its lack of sound or shape.

The gods had brought him to her.

He could barely make Nalia out in the dark, but he saw a faint tendril of purple *chiaan*, so dim it would sputter out at any second. He didn't dare risk using his *chiaan* for more light—he couldn't see the ghouls, but he knew they were out there. She started as he approached, terror lashing her face. But then she recognized him and immediately began weeping, this jinni who'd once refused to cry, ever.

"You're here, you're really here," she sobbed. Her voice was so hoarse, he could barely understand her. "I'm not sleeping, I'm not. I know it. You have to believe me, Raif, please—"

"Nal. Nal, look at me."

She did.

"I know. I *know*." He pulled her to him, his entire body shaking. She cried out in pain and he jumped back.

"What? What happened?" he said.

"My . . ." She curled into herself, her body shuddering as though pain were a knife slicing through her. "My arm . . . the ghoul . . ."

"What can I do?" he asked, frantic.

She was in pain, so much pain. He'd only seen Nalia a few

hours ago in the City of Brass, but Raif realized that the Nalia he'd seen in those two dreamlike meetings wasn't the real Nalia in the Eye. Five, almost six, days without food or water. A broken arm and gods knew what other injuries. She was emaciated, her lips parched, gray dust covering every inch of her. Her clothing was in rags, blood all over her. She smelled like a ghoul and he could imagine how intense that fight had been for her to be drenched in its scent.

"Nal, tell me what to do," he whispered again, helpless.

She tried to smile, but it was more a grimace than anything else. Even now, she was trying to be strong, to downplay her pain.

"Get me out of here?"

He laughed softly, bent down, and brushed her lips with his own. "I will. We're gonna make it. Just hold on, *rohifsa*. Hold on."

Raif looked around, as though a solution would suddenly present itself. The gods had confirmed everything he wanted to believe: she was alive. They'd brought him here, so obviously he was meant to save her. The relief warred with his concern over Nalia's health. She swayed on her feet, her eyes fluttering as she fought to remain conscious. He had to get her to a healer immediately.

"Rest, Nal. I've got it. You don't have to be brave anymore, okay?"

She nodded and he helped her sit down. She drew one knee up and rested her forehead against it, her breath shallow.

What the hell was he going to—

Zanari. Of course. *Hahm'alah*. Since he was here, maybe he could bring her—

But he'd be putting his sister's life at risk. It was so much to ask—she'd yet to recover from that first trip into the Eye. And she'd told him that even if they found Nalia, Zanari would need the energy of thousands of jinn to traverse it and return home alive.

"That's it," he said.

"What?" Nalia's voice was barely a whisper.

"Zan can bring the army with her. And our healer. Since we're here, she'll have an actual location. If we hurry—"

He lifted his hand, connecting his energy to his sister's. He felt her, faint, because they were so far away from each other, then stronger. It was the middle of the night—she'd have been sleeping. A puff of emerald smoke appeared on his palm. Zanari's face, eyes heavy with sleep.

He heard Nalia gasp and he whirled around, the connection with his sister lost as Raif ran to Nalia. She'd collapsed. He fell to his knees, cradling her, careful not to touch her broken arm.

"Please." He grabbed her hand, pushing his *chiaan* into her as tremors wracked her body. He barely felt her energy, and just like in the desert when she'd first arrived at the Dhoma camp, all he had wouldn't be enough. He tried, anyway. "Stay with me. Please. I love you so much—"

Raif felt a tug, as though invisible fingers were pulling him from behind. He shouted as Nalia slipped from his grasp and he fought like hell against gods knew what. Nalia's eyes followed him, her lips turning up in a sad, resigned smile.

"Nalia!" he screamed. "Nal—"

And then, suddenly, he couldn't move, couldn't speak. He felt whatever had been grabbing at him let go. He pushed toward her, but it was as if he were in quicksand. Raif could do nothing but look down at her, blinded by a blazing white light that suddenly filled the space above her. He could see more clearly now: Nalia was lying on her back, arms and legs splayed out, the left arm at an unnatural angle. Her face was covered in cuts and bruises, her bottom lip swollen. And her eyes . . . her eyes had closed.

He watched her, sick to his stomach. When he saw her chest rise, he nearly sobbed with relief. He was going to lose his mind, just lose it completely—

The light over her pulsed and Raif was able to make out a shape in the stark illumination, then . . . more than a shape.

A white phoenix: harbinger of the death of a hero.

No! Get away from her, you fucking bird, get away—

But the words could only be thought, no matter how badly he wanted to speak them.

The phoenix flew closer to Nalia, then stood over her body, protective. Possessive. Its ancient amber eyes met Raif's in a challenge, claiming Nalia as one of its honored dead.

The phoenix parted its beak, and as the first trill of its song fell on Raif's ears, the Eye closed around him, the light disappeared, and Nalia was gone.

The sign from the gods couldn't have been more clear: Nalia was about to die.

Singing.

Wordless and enchanting, the song seemed to slip under Nalia's skin, twine itself around her bones. It was a call, but to what or who Nalia didn't know. And then Raif was gone; she felt him go. Despair rushed through her, worse than ever before—

Nalia forced her body upright through an agonizing act of will. When she opened her eyes, there was a blinding sunburst of white. It took a few moments for her eyes to adjust, to see more than the light. She stared.

No. Please, no. Not yet.

In the old stories, the heroes saw the white phoenix just before they were taken to the godlands. Having a white phoenix appear at one's death was an honor, a favor of the gods. Like any Aisouri, Nalia had hoped that one day she would be worthy of the phoenix. But she thought she'd be centuries older, not a mere eighteen summers old, longing for her rohifsa *a world away.*

The palace temple is bordered on all sides by pillars carved from lavender marble. They reach toward the vaulted lapis lazuli dome that arches over the mosaic floor. Each pillar belongs to an empress who has passed into the godlands. They tower over Nalia, ancestors set in stone, looking down on her with disapproval. She is twelve summers old and has a lot to learn. Suddenly self-conscious, she crosses to her favorite pillar, where Antharoe looks out from the stone, eyes fierce, cape billowing behind her. Above her likeness is the white phoenix. Made of hundreds of diamonds, its body shimmers in the sunlight that streams through the thousand-pane lotus window. Its wings are outstretched and flames made of glittering rubies burst from behind the bird, a halo. Antharoe has one hand raised in victory and in her hand is her jade dagger—the actual dagger—embedded in the stone. But it is the phoenix that most interests Nalia. She reaches up, tracing her finger along its outstretched wings. Nalia wonders what it would be like to see such a creature.

19

RAIF HADN'T SET FOOT ON HIS FORMER OVERLORD'S plantation since the night Dthar Djan'Urbi freed his son from the shackles that had once bound Raif to his cruel master. He hated this land, wanted to see it burn. The moment he evanesced, he spit on the ground.

Zanari shuddered as they slipped past the unguarded gate that circled the property.

"I don't know if this is such a good idea, Raif."

"We won't be long," he whispered. "Promise."

"I mean," she said, "I don't know if it's a good idea for you to be—"

"Zan, drop it."

She'd come rushing into his *ludeen* the night before, trying to figure out why he'd briefly contacted her using *hahm'alah*. He'd told her everything, then lain down on his bed without another word. There had only been one comfort, but it lifted a great weight from his heart: the presence of the white phoenix meant that Nalia was in the godlands, with Bashil. He no longer had to worry about her unburned body, an eternity in the shadowlands. The phoenix would do right by her, and for this Raif was grateful.

This morning he'd made himself get out of bed. He trained, harder than ever. He didn't speak a word unless it was absolutely necessary. Then he went to the gate and told Touma what he'd seen. The Ifrit was still there, refusing to leave until the year and a day was up.

There was no good way to grieve the love of your life.

"We're here to do a job," Raif said now. "Let's just focus on that, okay?"

"All right, little brother," she said, her voice soft.

Neither of them had good memories of the plantation—they had the scars on their backs to prove it. Since Calar had freed the serfs, many plantations had become refugee camps of sorts, filled with crime, disease, and fear. Raif and Zanari were here because word needed to go out to all the plantations and villages about Calar's shadow creatures. *Tavrai* all over Arjinna were doing the same. The jinn deserved to know what had been unleashed.

"Gods, I hate this place," Zanari muttered.

Even though it'd been years since Raif had tilled the fields and carried water jugs twice his size, the sense of being trapped, the loathsome feeling of injustice, hit him just as hard as it always had when he'd been under the Shaitan overlord's thumb.

"Listen," Zanari said. She crossed her arms, bit her lip—small tells that she was about to say something he didn't want to hear. "I know this isn't great timing, but I'm hoping you'll . . . okay, I . . . I've been thinking—about the portal, the Dhoma, all of that."

"Yeah. . . ."

"So . . . as soon as the portal opens again . . ." She had a wild look about her, as though she were going to jump off the highest cliff into the Arjinnan Sea. "I'm going back to Earth. I think you should come with me."

Raif stared, all the breath leaving him in one burst. "What do you mean you're going back to Earth?"

"I'm . . ." She swallowed. "I'm leaving Arjinna. As soon as the portal opens."

Raif's hands curled into fists. "You've gotta be kidding me, Zan."

She shook her head, her bottom lip trembling. "I love you so much, Raif. So much. But . . . it's over, little brother. This place— Calar and her shadows, all the ghosts here. I'm done with it. I'm done fighting my dead father's war."

Zanari reached out her hand, but he pushed her away. "Don't touch me," he snarled. "Don't . . . gods, I can't believe you'd— after what happened last night—"

The dark hole in his chest stretched wider, deeper. He'd never find his way out. He bit back a scream, pure rage that would have made their stealth pointless.

"That's why I'm saying it now. Raif, being here, it's *killing* you." Zanari's eyes pooled with tears. "It's killing me, too."

"It's our home, Zan. Everything we have is here."

"Not everything," she whispered.

Ah. Phara. He should have realized that right away. A part of Raif knew that was bad of him, not to have remembered his sister was in love with a jinni on the other side of a closed portal.

"If Nalia were on Earth and you had the choice—"

"But she's not. She's dead. She died so that we could save our land, our people—"

Zanari shook her head. "No she didn't. She died for *you*. There was nothing here for her to go back to."

It was like being shot, only worse. This wasn't something a healer could fix. *I have no one left.*

"I'm sorry," she whispered. "I shouldn't have said that."

Raif turned away, hands on hips, looking out at his old prison. This whole land was a prison.

"I made the choice to leave Phara," Zanari began. "At the time, there was really no question. I was so certain we'd win this war, that Nalia would reopen the portal, that everything would . . ." She sighed. "I loved Nalia, Raif. I love you. And I . . . I love Phara. And Earth, for that matter."

He turned, eyes wide. "You *love* that hellhole? With its iron and wishmakers and dirty air?"

He'd hated every second he'd been on Earth. Nalia had been the only good thing about it.

Zanari flushed. "I liked cheeseburgers. And the desert. Most of all, I liked the Dhoma. I don't mean just Phara," she hurried, when he rolled his eyes. "What they're doing, the way they live— it makes sense to me. It feels right. And I think . . . I think you could find peace there. Maybe even happiness."

Peace and happiness . . . not for him. But maybe for her.

And she deserved that. Raif had never considered the possibility that Zanari would leave him, that she'd choose another person or another realm over him. It hurt. He wanted to be angry at her, to lash out. *What would Nalia say?* He could almost hear her voice, gentle but firm: How many times had his sister risked her life, forgone happiness, so that she could stay by his side? How many times had he *not* done the same for her?

If Zanari felt for Phara what he felt for Nalia . . .

"You should go," he said.

"Raif—" Zanari's voice was choked and he pulled her to him.

"I don't mean now," he said, more gently. "When the portal opens. You're right. This land, it's a lost cause."

"Come with me. We'll get as many jinn out as we can."

He shook his head. "No, I've gotta see this through. You know that."

He motioned for Zanari to follow him across the dew-spattered land. He could have found his way to the serf cabins in his sleep. The simple wooden structures were situated on the far edge of the property, behind a grove of *widr* trees. He stopped when he reached the stand of trees, the sight calling forth his father.

"Do you remember when—" Zanari began.

"Yes," he murmured. "I remember."

He was seven summers old again, planting the *widr* seedlings with his father, both of them on their knees in the rich dirt, coaxing their *chiaan* into the roots. Raif gazed up at the *widr* leaves that now shivered high above him. Just as he had matured, so had they.

"I don't know if Papa would have been ashamed or proud of me," he said.

Zanari squeezed his hand. "He always told us to follow our hearts. You've never had trouble doing that, little brother. He'd be proud."

"And Mama?" he asked.

He'd only seen his mother a handful of times since coming home. Ever since the council meeting when he'd seen the disappointment in her eyes, Fjirla Djan'Urbi had been conspicuously absent whenever he'd been in the common areas of the camp.

"Of course she is," Zanari said softly.

But he heard the lie. Raif caught a faint glow in the distance, candlelight in the windows of what used to be the serf barracks. The bunk beds would still have thin mattresses and blankets that were little more than frayed scraps of cloth. Few jinn would have been able to conjure something better, unless they'd actually seen a real blanket. Most of the overlords had forbidden their jinn to manifest anything. The shackles wouldn't let their serfs manifest, even if they'd tried. Now, free of the overlords, the jinn knew nothing of soft bedding, good clothing. They were good at conjuring sickles to till the fields or nets to fish the sea, but little beyond that. *A comfortable serf is a lazy serf,* Raif's overlord had once said. A dart of pure hatred shot through him at the memory.

"We should get going," Raif said, tugging at Zanari's arm. "Before another Ifrit patrol comes by."

His sister let out a strangled gasp when a burst of bright-green evanescence swirled just in front of them. They'd forgone evanescing so as not to attract attention, but it seemed their presence had already been noted. Raif raised his hands, *chiaan* glowing at his fingertips, but when the smoke cleared, they fell to his sides as he took in the wizened jinni before him.

"Olram?" he said in disbelief.

The jinni gave a mock bow, his eyes twinkling. "At your service, my lord."

Olram had been on the plantation since before Raif himself was a child, nearly eight hundred summers. Raif's father had tried to free him, but Olram had been a slave to the overlord for too long. Dthar Djan'Urbi's magic wasn't powerful enough to break such longstanding bonds.

Raif moved forward and embraced the old man, whose grip was surprisingly strong despite his years.

"We heard you were back," Olram said. "Come to give the empress more trouble, eh?"

Raif smiled. "What other purpose do I serve in life, grandfather?"

Zanari shifted behind him and Olram's eyes landed on her. "Ah, my pretty girl. You look well."

"As do you," she said with a warm smile.

"Liar."

It was true—he was too thin, and his back had begun to hunch over. They embraced and then Olram beckoned for them to follow him down the slope toward the slave cabins.

"How are you holding up here?" Zanari asked.

The old jinni shrugged. "We do the best we can. The young ones scrounge up this and that in the Vein." He patted Raif on the back. "Thank Shirin for me, will you? She made sure we got supplies even when you were gone."

Raif nodded. "I will."

"So what brings you to us?" Olram asked. "Besides the wonderful company, of course."

"Nothing good," Raif said. "I need to speak to everyone—Calar has a new weapon."

Olram nodded, descending the small hill toward the collection of buildings as nimbly as a billy goat. "I heard about the Marid village. May the gods torture her forever."

"We were hoping that you would join us in the forest," Zanari said.

"We're mostly women, children, and the elderly, you know. Not much help to your revolution."

"That's all right," Raif said. "There's space. It's not safe for you here anymore—"

Olram put a hand on Raif's shoulder. "I loved your father, and you know how I feel about you kids. But if you don't win this war, you and your *tavrai* will be sent to Ithkar or killed. These jinn," he said, gesturing to the serf quarters, "just want peace. They want safety. Give them that first. No one—not even you—is free until the fighting stops."

Raif sighed, nodding. There was certainly truth to that—he was freedom's slave, giving everything he had to a lost cause. Calar had taken away the overlords, and yet nothing had changed. The former serfs still lived in squalor, still went hungry at night.

"Maybe after you hear what I have to say, you'll change your mind," he said.

"Just as stubborn as your father, I see," Olram said.

Zanari leaned close to the old jinni, conspiratorial. "More, actually."

Raif laughed softly. Gods, he was going to miss her. Before they reached the serf quarters, Raif gently held Olram back. Zanari waited beside them, curious.

"When I was in the Marid village, I saw something—something I didn't know existed anymore," he said.

Olram raised his eyebrows. "Speak plainly, child."

"A Ghan Aisouri baby."

Olram's eyes became shuttered, closed off. Raif knew his hunch that Olram had information was correct. You didn't live to be his age and not learn a thing or two about survival. Information was the only real currency anymore.

"Are there more?" Raif asked softly. Taz had told him there were, but he couldn't trust an Ifrit general's word. He needed to know from someone who wouldn't lie to him.

Olram shrugged. "Who's to say? They are the daughters of the gods, eh? It is for the gods to decide."

"I wish the Aisouri no harm," Raif said.

Olram snorted. "I've never heard a Djan'Urbi say *that* before."

Zanari stepped forward. "When we were on Earth, we found an Aisouri on the dark caravan. She is Raif's *rohifsa*—and we lost her to the Eye. Grandfather, believe my brother when he says he wishes Aisouri children no harm."

Olram's eyes sought Raif's in the darkness. "She speaks true?"

Raif held the old jinni's eyes. "Yes."

Olram stared at him. "This changes . . . everything."

"Are they safe?" Raif asked. "That's all I want to know."

The old jinni hesitated, his eyes on Raif's. "Safe as they can be," he finally said.

"But their eyes—" Zanari started. Olram waved his hand, silencing her.

"There are still mages who know how to change eye and *chiaan* color."

"How many Aisouri are there?" Raif asked.

"More than my fingers can count."

Was that possible? Aisouri were born once every several years. There had only been forty-six of them when the Ifrit destroyed their line.

"The gods must be trying to bring them back," Zanari said. "Make up for the loss."

"And the Ifrit know this?" Raif asked.

Olram nodded. "The mothers who try to hide their daughters without getting help . . . the Ifrit usually find them before those who would help them do. You cannot hide those eyes for long. This is what happened in your Marid village. Someone told the Ifrit—maybe a jinni with a family member in prison, maybe someone just tired of being hungry. This was why that village suffered as it did."

Of course. Calar wouldn't want anyone challenging her for the throne.

"How can I help?" Raif asked.

Saving Aisouri children—he'd never thought he'd want that. But Nalia had changed so much in him; her influence was seismic.

"Don't breathe a word of this to your *tavrai*, that's how you can help," Olram said. "Your soldiers are . . . not so open-minded as I would like."

There was a time when Raif would have bristled at the comment, but not anymore. The *tavrai* had begun to worry him. A lot. He wasn't sure he'd be able to keep them in line much longer.

Raif nodded his head once. "I will guard this secret with my life."

Zanari and Raif spent just a few moments with the serfs. It was quickly evident that none of them wanted to be under the protection of the *tavrai*, just as Olram had explained. They were even willing to take their chances with Calar's shadows.

"So, that went well," Zanari muttered as they made their way to a clearing they could evanesce out of.

Raif tried to tamp down his anger. It was hard to fight for people who didn't want to be saved.

Maybe Zanari was right. Maybe there was no hope for Arjinna or the jinn. If the portals ever opened again, maybe they should all get the hell out.

The phoenix brought its beak down on the skin covering Nalia's heart, bare now from where the ghoul had torn at her garment in their fight to the death.

She cried out as the beak broke into her flesh and her heart began to burn, a fire inside her. The pain, at least, was very real. This was no dream.

Nalia turned her head away from the creature and sobbed, her tears mixing with the gray dust of the Eye. What had been the point of it all?

Nalia screamed into the ground beneath her, cursing it, this land that had imprisoned her more than the bottle ever could. Her mouth filled with dust and she didn't care that her death would be undignified—she breathed it in, great, heaving gulps. If the gods were going to let her die, then they would see just what she thought about it.

The last Ghan Aisouri. Yes, Calar had done her job quite well.

Except: she wasn't dead yet. They were punishing her, these loveless gods. They wanted to draw her last moments out, make her see just how much she'd failed. Just how much she'd lost.

The phoenix began to sing again and she glared at it. The gods' messenger. He—she? Yes, she, Nalia was certain—loomed over her, roughly the size of a swan. Her long tail feathers dragged on the dusty floor of the Eye like the train of a bridal gown, yet the dust never settled on the bird's pristine coat. Nalia cocked her head to the side, observing just as intently as she was being observed. The feathers reminded her of an opal, a shimmery faint rainbow glaze over downy white. Eyes the color of a blazing sunset, eyes that were more human than animal. Intelligent, all-knowing.

Nalia hated the godsdamn thing.

"You can go now," she snapped at her as she struggled to her feet. "Go pester another soul. I'll go to the godlands when I'm good and ready. And I'm *not* ready."

The bird continued to sing as she swayed, and Nalia's eyesight began to go in and out. It'd been ages since she'd had food or water. Still, she wasn't going to just hand over her soul to the first pretty bird that came to visit her. Nalia reached down and grabbed a fistful of dust, but before she could chuck it at the phoenix, she recognized the melody.

Awake, awake, the dawn is yet to come.

She stared, frozen, her fist of dust still clutched in her hand. Was it possible that instead of ushering her into death, the gods had answered her prayers for aid?

"Are you here to—to help me?" she whispered.

In answer, the phoenix changed her tune to another familiar song. It was a temple hymn Nalia had learned as a little girl.

The gods do look upon the brave with favor and delight.

The phoenix continued to sing, lifting herself into the air. She was like a small moon that lit a path just for Nalia. She began to fly at shoulder height, hovering above the Eye's plains, her wings gently flapping. She looked back to make sure Nalia was following.

"They'll see you, you know," she said to the creature as she began to move her feet. She stumbled, legs weak. If she didn't eat soon, she'd die, mystical bird or no.

The phoenix didn't seem to care, so Nalia wouldn't either. She followed the phoenix for hours, each step faltering. She tried to stamp down the hope that was beginning to grow in her chest. She was afraid she'd die of despair if the thing disappeared— unless the bird killed her first.

Please, *she begged the gods.* I will be and do whatever you want, just please get me home to Raif, to my land.

The thought of him threatened to crush her entirely. He had to be going mad after seeing her collapse. Had he seen the phoenix, too?

The bird stopped, flapping her wings in the air to stay aloft. "Now what?" *Nalia asked.*

She was so grateful for the company. Even if it was a mythical harbinger of death. The phoenix chirped—again, a temple song from her childhood.

Nectar of the gods, eat and never be hungry.

The song had never made sense to Nalia. She'd assumed it had to do with chiaan. *The phoenix dipped her head and Nalia followed the line of her beak to the ground below. There, glinting in the diamond light, was a small bush with thick, heart-shaped leaves—palest green, rimmed in lavender. Nalia had never seen such a plant before.*

Nalia drew closer to it. The leaves shone, their undersides velvety. When she touched it, the plant's energy pulsed against her skin. She glanced at the phoenix—gods, was she nodding *at her?*

Nalia broke a leaf off the cluster and tore it in half. A milky white substance that released a faint anise scent oozed over her palm. For a moment, she could picture Malek standing before a goblet filled with absinthe and she scolded her heart for missing him, just the tiniest bit. If he were here, he'd be snatching the leaf out of her hand, his arm around her, holding her up. Hayati, no, *he'd say.* We're not as desperate as all that. *Then he'd light a cigarette and curse the darkness.* To hell with this place, *he'd say.* We're going home.

Nalia's stomach growled.

She stared at the plant, considering. The empresses had woken her up. The phoenix had led her here. If she didn't eat or drink something within the next few hours, she'd pass out again and never wake up. Risking poisoning herself was her best option.

Nalia opened her mouth and set the leaf on her tongue. Warmth immediately spread through her. Nalia's skin tingled, as though she could feel every grain of dust coating her arms and face. It was a lovely feeling, like being dipped in a pool of pure chiaan.

The leaf was down Nalia's throat before she realized that this might be the way the gods had decided for her to die—a poisonous plant, a quick, painless end.

Her heart sped up, her breathing growing more shallow as the darkness writhed and swirled before her, suddenly full of pulsing life.

"Wait," she gasped as the plant's blood sped through her. "Not yet—please!"

The phoenix's light dimmed until the gods' messenger was nothing but a pinprick of light in the night that swaddled Nalia in its arms.

"I'm not—I'm—"

A burst of light.

Her body, convulsing, head spinning.

Not ready—not ready—not—

20

KESMIR WAITED IN THE SHADOWS OF THE CRUMBLING plantation as night stole over the land, his scimitar drawn. He was alone but for one large black bird that occasionally roamed over the fields, then flew away in the direction of the Forest of Sighs. It wasn't meeting the handsome Shaitan commander again that had set Kes on edge. No, it was Raif Djan'Urbi Kesmir couldn't trust. The revolutionary commander was fearless, an elegantly brutal fighter who'd cut down some of Kes's best jinn. Kes had tried to give the *tavrai* leader an opportunity to take Calar before she released her shadows, but he wasn't sure if his intent had been clear. No doubt Djan'Urbi had thought it was a trap. Though the battle at the Marid village had been over for nearly two days, a haze of burial smoke still hovered over the forest and the Ifrit barracks, the dead of both sides burning continually. There were so many souls to usher into the godlands. Too many. He suspected the *tavrai* wouldn't be in the best frame of mind when they arrived, and certainly not in a mood to negotiate. Except for Tazlim. He seemed honorable. Good.

Kes's mind had wandered to Tazlim so many times since they'd met. He'd spent the past day since that conversation with the Shaitan commander trying to keep him out of his mind, terrified that Calar would decide to barge into Kes's thoughts before he'd had a chance to properly stow Tazlim into the darkest recesses of his memory. He had a room in his mind, one he'd spent the past few days learning how to build with the gryphon, then training to keep the door to that room barred—and invisible. If Calar knew he was hiding something, it was as good as her discovering the secret. In her increasing paranoia, she would assume the worst, which, in Kes's case, was true. He was betraying her, every day now, in thought, word, and deed. Just this morning he'd gained the trust of one of the jinn Calar relied on to help her govern, a jinni more than capable of creating a post-coup strategy that would keep order in the land.

By virtue of even thinking about dethroning Calar, Kes had constructed a house of cards that was certain to collapse at any moment. It didn't matter that he trained his mind with Thatur, that he was careful. There were too many people involved now, and those people were not trained, though he tried to pass on what he'd learned when he could.

He would die, and soon. The question was only whether or not his death would mean a damn thing at all.

Kes sighed, kicking at the debris near his feet. The plantation was in shambles, the family, he imagined, likely killed in one of Calar's purges. The only Shaitan who'd been able to maintain their holdings were Calar's lackeys at the palace: mages, scholars, and overlords who hadn't fought the new regime. Kes couldn't deny that it gave him pleasure to see the disrepair of the home, nothing but a rotting mansion full of useless trinkets, manifested over thousands of years and passed down through generations of oppressor Shaitan. The rooms had been filled with nothing but broken ceramics, delicate cups and plates with a repeating floral pattern, destroyed paintings that hung cockeyed on the walls or had fallen to the floor, and rugs that were little more than shredded pieces of string. After a life spent on Ithkar's merciless lava plains, Kes had no sympathy for the former owners of this home.

Now he settled on the front porch, where he'd have the best vantage point should the *tavrai* simply decide to surround and kill him. Kes looked up at the sound of a faint, familiar whoosh of wings. Seconds later, Thatur landed, hardly disrupting the dust beneath his feet.

"You look nervous," Thatur said, by way of greeting.

"I am," Kes admitted.

"Do you think he'll come?"

Kes nodded, grim. "I'm not sure what his intentions are, but, yes, he'll come."

They gazed in silence at the sky, Kes careful to keep up the blocks in his mind. He wouldn't be surprised if Thatur were testing him right now.

Better, Thatur said. *Not up to snuff, but acceptable for the time we've spent working.*

Kes suppressed a smile. He doubted he would ever be "up to snuff."

"You say my mistress planned to help him?" Thatur asked, his voice doubtful.

Kes wondered how much to tell the gryphon. Best to let Djan'Urbi open that can of worms. Calar had told Kes of what she'd seen in Djan'Urbi's mind when she'd attacked him the other day: intimate moments that were not her right to see, let alone share. Kes knew how Raif must be feeling—*violated* was too soft a word. There was no doubt, though, that Raif loved Nalia something fierce, and she him. Kes wasn't sure how Thatur would react to discovering that not only had Nalia joined forces with Raif, he'd become her *rohifsa* as well.

"Yes" was all Kes said. "They'd formed . . . an alliance of sorts."

Thatur snorted. "Well, when she returns we'll see about that."

Kes kept his eyes averted. Thatur was still convinced that his Aisouri would return, triumphant and ready to govern. But she was dead—everyone but Thatur seemed to accept that.

The air shifted, just long enough for Kes to call up his *chiaan*. Thatur slipped into the shadows—they'd already decided not to bring him out until it was absolutely necessary. No use letting the *tavrai* know Kes had a gryphon on his side unless they too were on Kes's side.

Five swirls of evanescence touched down: three Djan, one Ifrit, and one Shaitan. He recognized Raif and Tazlim, of course. And, yes, there was Shirin Djan'Khar, the thorn in Calar's side while Raif was on Earth, and the Djan'Urbi girl—Zanari. He didn't recognize the large Ifrit with the orange stripe down his long hair, though—perhaps he was one of the jinn from Earth who'd traveled through the Eye.

"Now might be a good time to put your weapon down" was the first thing Raif said to him.

Kes gripped the scimitar tighter. The jinni had murder in his eyes—and a hollow deadness more frightening than anything else. Djan'Urbi was known for his passion, his short temper. But a cold, seemingly heartless jinni stood before him now. Everything in Kes told him this was a mistake; he should never have agreed to this meeting.

"I don't plan on making it easy for you to kill me," Kes said evenly.

Raif grinned, dangerous. "It's no fun if it's easy."

"Raif," Tazlim murmured, "you promised to hear him out."

"I'm not very good at keeping promises," Raif said, his voice edged and bitter.

Tazlim glanced at Kes, his eyes imploring. Kes sighed and set his scimitar on the ground, but kept his hands at the ready, his Ifrit *chiaan* bubbling inside him. He didn't have time for this. Calar would be looking for him, wanting to know why he hadn't come to bed yet. And what if Yasri had a nightmare? Kes was the only one who could calm her down.

"Kesmir, this is Noqril," Tazlim said, gesturing to the jinni with the orange stripe of hair, "and I'm sure you recognize Shirin Djan'Khar—"

Shirin made a rude gesture and Kes forced himself not to return the greeting, instead giving her a curt nod.

"And this is Zanari Djan'Urbi," Tazlim finished.

Raif's sister had dozens of small braids covering her head, and her green eyes had the weary look Kes saw in so many of his own soldiers. She didn't acknowledge him so much as stare him down.

"If we join forces," Kes said, "how do I know you won't turn on my soldiers?"

"Guess you'll have to find out," Raif said with a heartless smirk. Maybe he was just as crazy as Calar.

"But you're getting ahead of yourself," Raif added. "Why don't we start by you telling me what kind of 'resistance' you actually have."

"You just want me to give you our military secrets with no promise of anything in return?" Kes said.

"Pretty much, yeah." Raif shrugged, then took a step back, evanescence already beginning to pool at his feet. "We can just go right now, too—forget this meeting ever happened."

Tazlim grabbed Raif's arm. "Raif."

Kes narrowed his eyes. "It takes more than a handful of seconds to establish trust, Raif Djan'Urbi—I'm sure you know that."

Raif pointed to his face. "Does it look like I care whether you trust me or not?"

This, Kes realized, was what happened when someone lost their *rohifsa*.

More smoke pooled around Raif's feet. Kes had seconds to decide. "No?" Raif said. "Then I'll see you on the battlefield."

Let him win this, Thatur said in his mind.

"Wait," Kes said.

His eyes moved to Tazlim's and it was only that *something*

in them that Kes couldn't quite put his finger on that made him willing to stay there and deal with Djan'Urbi's sullen aggression.

"Please," Kes bit out. "I'll tell you what you need to know."

The evanescence blew away in a gust of wind and Raif crossed his arms, eyes hard.

"I'm waiting," he said.

This was it: the moment Kes truly turned traitor, not just on Calar, but on his own army.

"We're going to clean out the plantations. Send the remaining serfs to Ithkar. Or . . . kill them," Kes said. "I'll try to keep as many alive as I can. You should begin evacuations tonight."

Shirin cursed. "Why are we even talking to this *skag*, Raif? Clean out the plantations? Those jinn are not your enemies," she yelled, turning to Kes. "What have they ever done to your gods-forsaken race?"

Raif didn't look at Shirin. Instead, he met Kesmir's eyes and for a long moment they took the measure of one another.

"As I explained to Tazlim," Kes began, "I'm here because I'd like to join the revolution. I want my people to be free—I want your people to be free, too. This old hatred must end. We can't go on like this."

Shirin turned to Raif. "This is a trap, another one of Calar's games."

"Maybe," Raif said. But he was looking at Kes thoughtfully, the exhaustion in his eyes reflected in Kes's own. "I, for one, agree with Shirin. My guess is you're a lying son of a bitch and that Calar's waiting at home for you to tell her all about our little meeting, but our Brass commander here disagrees with me."

"I'm here, aren't I?" Kes snapped. "Do you see any Ifrit? If this were a trap, you'd all be dead by now."

"I don't know about that," Shirin said. Her eyes glinted—there was no doubt that she would relish the chance to slit Kes's throat with the scimitar in her hand.

Kes clamped down the surge of annoyance. This *tavrai* posturing was part of the game; he knew that.

"See, this is the problem," Raif said, taking a step closer. "Calar can read minds. You go home to the palace you stole, sleep in the bed that rightfully belongs to my *rohifsa*—" He stopped, looking down at his feet for a moment.

What? Thatur raged. Kes winced—this was not going to end well. Maybe it had been a mistake to bring the gryphon. He was executing remarkable self-control by not ripping off Raif's head yet. Once Thatur made his presence known, though, all bets were off.

Raif straightened and, rather than look angry, all emotion drained from his face.

"What am I doing here?" he said, as if to himself. He looked at Kes, hatred written in his eyes. "You were there all along. The coup—okay, I understand that. I would have done the same before I met Nalia. But Haran—you knew about him. You knew what he was going to do to her."

It had been a slim chance, Raif agreeing to work together. Kes saw that disappearing now.

"Yes," he said heavily.

Raif took a step closer. "And Bashil?"

"I told Calar not to kill the child—"

"But you didn't tell her not to use him to trick Nalia, did you?"

Kes shook his head. "No." Anger surged through him. "You forget what was done to my family. Murdered by Aisouri—"

"Did Nalia murder them?" Raif said.

Kesmir, walk away. Now.

Kes knew Thatur was right, but he wouldn't back down. Not when so much was at stake.

"Not to my knowledge," Kes said.

Raif nodded. "That's because she *didn't* kill them. You condoned the dark caravan—made Nalia a slave—authorized a slave trade of thousands of jinn, an arms trade that brought human weapons into Arjinna. You set a ghoul on Nalia that wanted to *eat her*. You stood by while Calar butchered her brother. You closed the portal between our worlds just to keep her out, no matter how much it hurt the jinn on either side of it. Am I right so far?"

Kes swallowed. "Yes."

"And you want me to *help* you?"

Kes sighed. *It was too much to expect,* he said to Thatur.

"This was obviously a mistake," Kes said.

"You're damn right it was a mistake." Raif's green eyes went dark and his lips turned up in a cold smile. He turned to Tazlim. "I tried, sorry."

Without warning, Raif launched himself at Kes, and as they fell, they crashed into one of the manor house's decaying walls, going clear through the rotting wood and into the abandoned house. Dust rained down on them as they grappled with each other on the floor. The crystals in the chandelier above them shook, the gentle sound a strange background to the brutal sound of fists hitting skin. There was no magic in this fight, no grace.

Just ribs cracking beneath knuckles and the taste of blood in his mouth.

The front door burst open, and in the second Kes turned, distracted, Raif's fist punched deep into his stomach. Kes cried out, struggling for breath. He was dimly aware of the others as they entered the room—there was shouting, then hands gripping his limbs, trying to pull Raif off him. Then a roar that could only be Thatur.

"Holy gods and monsters," Shirin said, her scimitar slipping out of her hand and clattering to the floor. Kes couldn't see out of his swollen eye, but he assumed she was referring to Thatur.

"Let him go before I make one of you my dinner," Thatur growled.

Someone grabbed Kes's bare hand and he was flooded with the jinni's *chiaan*: a curious, bright thing that rushed through him like a summer breeze. He looked up, the eye he could open landing on Tazlim's golden ones. The other jinni stared at him, eyes wide, as their *chiaan* traveled back and forth between their palms.

"Taz! A little help here," Zanari snapped.

Tazlim let go of Kes's hand, but his *chiaan* lingered inside him a few seconds more. "Are you all right?" the Shaitan asked softly.

Kes nodded. Then shook his head—ouch. It was a complicated question, wasn't it? "I don't know," he finally said. He was having trouble breathing.

There was a sharp pain in his spine as a heavy boot made contact with his back and Kes toppled forward. He couldn't keep his head on straight with Tazlim around.

"Gods, Raif, cut it out," Zanari shouted. "Do you not see . . . *this*?" she asked, pointing at Thatur.

Raif turned, his face suddenly ashen. Though he didn't say a word, it was clear that the presence of an Aisouri gryphon only filled him with more grief.

"I don't know, I think he's got the right idea," Shirin said, picking up her scimitar where she'd dropped it and turning her back on Thatur, her momentary surprise at the gryphon's presence evaporating. She crossed to where Kes sat huddled on the ground. She was grinning, her arms crossed, thoroughly entertained. "I kinda like seeing this one in agony."

"And that," he heard Raif gasp behind him, "is why Shirin is my second."

"Hurt this boy again and you will see why I was chosen to train the greatest fighters in our realm," Thatur said, raising a menacing claw.

Tazlim placed his arm around Kes's shoulders. "On three, all right?" he said.

Kes grunted his assent and he let the other jinni hoist him into a standing position.

"You gonna lick his wounds for him, too?" Shirin said.

Tazlim glanced at her, his voice withering. "This jinni is risking his life by meeting with us." He nodded to where Shirin's arms wrapped around Raif. "And I could ask the same of you, sister."

Shirin's face reddened and she said something crude about Tazlim's mother under her breath. But she let go of Raif.

"This jinni is responsible for hundreds of *tavrai* deaths," Raif said. He leaned against what once must have been an elegant banister. He turned his head and spit blood onto the dusty floor.

"I won't deny it," Kes said. Each breath he took was murder— it felt as if Raif had broken every rib in his body. "This is war," he gasped. "Jinn die."

"That's right," Raif said softly, "they do."

"I say we put him out of his misery," Shirin said. "And roast the bird." Her teeth glinted in the light: Raif's *raiga*, they called her. Kes could see why.

"The *what*?" Thatur growled.

"You heard me," Shirin said. "*Bird*."

Tazlim scowled. "Knock Kesmir around any more, and Calar's gonna want to know what he's been up to."

This was true. Kes was already trying to figure out what he'd tell Calar. He'd have to find a discreet healer to fix him up before he returned to her rooms.

Raif rested his hands on his knees. "So why in all hells should we trust you?" he asked. Then he pointed to Thatur. "Or him."

"You shouldn't," Kes said. "But you don't have a choice. And neither do I. Calar must be stopped. So we do what we have to." He straightened up, one hand gingerly pressed against his side. "I've done horrible things. I'm not proud of any of them, though some I would do again if I had to," Kes said. "I'm the general of an army full of jinn who've been told time and again that they're worthless. They're angry about that, and so am I. That being said, how can I alleviate your fears that I'm lying to you? How can I convince you to put this behind us, at least for the time being?"

"Tell us how to get into the prison camp in Ithkar," Raif said.

Kes raised his eyebrows. "I can assure you that none of the jinn there are in any shape to join your army."

"And whose fault is that?" said Noqril. "I came here to bring my people back to Earth, not fight this godsforsaken war. Your empress killed our leader, enslaved our brothers and sisters. The devil take your realm. I just want to go home."

Earth—home? Kes had heard of these Dhoma. Strange, that they should feel nothing for the land of their ancestors.

"If you try to break into it now, you're never going to make it," he said bluntly. "It's heavily fortified and as soon as you show up, Calar will have the full strength of our army there. Even if you do manage to get inside, the prisoners won't make it out alive."

"Then what the hell is your help worth?" Zanari growled.

Kes turned to Thatur, and the gryphon nodded. "If I were to assassinate Calar and take the palace, the army would be sufficiently distracted. It'd buy you some time, anyway."

"All right, what are we waiting for?" Shirin said.

"I'm training him to protect his mind from Calar. He needs time to build his powers," Thatur said.

"How much time?" Raif asked.

"We don't know," Kes said. He heard Thatur snort softly behind him. "A lot of time, according to him." He gestured to Thatur.

Kes hesitated, then turned to Raif. "We have a Shaitan mage sympathetic to our cause. When the time is right, he'll be able to help you. He'd lift the *bisahm* off the prison—whatever you needed. And you should know . . . the Shaitan who's helping us is Ajwar Shai'Dzar." Raif gave him a blank look. Kes sighed. "Nalia's father."

Raif went still. Thatur watched him closely, weighing this new Raif, Kes guessed, against the one he'd taught his Aisouri to fight. For a moment, Kes couldn't help but feel sorry for Raif. The love and grief he felt for the Aisouri was painful to see.

"I'd like to speak with him," Raif finally said.

"Of course. I'll arrange a meeting."

"And you," Raif said, turning to Thatur. "Will you help us, too?"

"That depends on many things," Thatur said.

"Such as . . . ?" Raif asked.

"Your relationship with my mistress, for one."

Raif furrowed his brow. "Your miss—" Understanding dawned on his face. "You're Thatur."

The gryphon bowed his head. "Yes."

Raif looked away, overcome. No one spoke. After a moment, Raif motioned to Thatur to follow him outside. The jinn were silent until they left the room.

"The gods suck," Zanari muttered.

Shirin furrowed her brow. "*Suck?* What does that even mean?"

Zanari sighed. "Human thing. Never mind."

For the next few minutes they waited in wary silence. Raif's and Thatur's voices were too low to hear what they were saying, but at one point Thatur let out an earsplitting caw and Zanari and Shirin rushed out. Raif waved them away.

"Can gryphons *cry?*" Zanari asked, when they came back in.

"If they learn their mistress is dead, yes," Kes said, "I believe they can."

Raif came through the doorway then, hands shoved into his pockets. He turned to Thatur, who stood behind him. "Can he do it? Can he defeat Calar?"

The gryphon's eyes met Kes's and something like satisfaction flickered in them. "Yes," Thatur said, turning to Raif. "In time, he'll be able to do it."

"What about her shadows?" Shirin asked. "We'll all be dead before Calar's whore is finally ready to fight."

"Enough, Shirin," Tazlim said, his voice edged.

She whirled on him. "You don't get to tell me what to do," she growled. "The last Shaitan who tried got stabbed in the heart by Dthar Djan'Urbi."

"Shir," Raif said, tired. "Cool it."

Shirin's eyes flashed. "I'm done with this." She stormed past Raif and out into the burned field.

Raif turned to Kes. "What you did when that soldier of yours tried to hurt the Marid woman . . . it's the only reason I'm here tonight. If you can do that to Calar, I'll wait."

Kes swallowed. Nodded. "I know what must be done."

"Better get training then," Raif said.

He turned and left the house without another word. The others followed him outside, including Thatur, but Tazlim lingered for a moment.

"I'm sorry about all that," Tazlim said. "Raif got some . . . particularly bad news since last I saw you. He's . . . unwell."

"His anger is justified." Kes smiled, wincing at the pain that shot up his cheekbone, then became a dagger behind his eye. Raif Djan'Urbi meant business when he punched someone in the face. "You did warn me he might not take meeting me well."

Tazlim nodded. "That I did." His eyes slid to Kes's. "When last you and I spoke, you said you had a better reason for ending Calar's reign than simply your own survival. What is that reason?"

Kes wasn't ready to tell him what his daughter was, but there was no harm in telling him he had one.

"I have a daughter," he said softly. "I want to make sure she inherits a future free of bloodshed and terror."

Tazlim stared. "But you're so young."

Kes smiled, sad. "Yes. But Calar and I were anxious to have the world we'd dreamed up. A child was a big part of that. Yasri came . . . sooner than we thought she would."

"A chance at a new beginning?" Taz asked.

Kes nodded. "Something like that."

They stood there in the darkness of the abandoned home, lit by a few spheres of golden light Tazlim had thrown into the air, his *chiaan*, the color of the sun.

"Were you an overlord?" Kes asked. "Before you went to Earth?"

Tazlim shook his head. "That was the last thing I wanted to be. I left before I got the chance to be anything but an overlord's son and a soldier."

The dim light in the room played on Tazlim's face, flickering like a candle. "What would you have been instead?" Kes asked. "A palace scholar?"

Tazlim shook his head. "A *pajai*."

Kes's eyes widened. "You wanted to be a temple priest?"

Tazlim smiled at Kes's surprise. "My jinn call me the Mystic."

"The priests are . . . celibate, no?"

"Yes." He flushed, a lovely pink glow—so young despite his thousands of years imprisoned in a bottle. "Now I think . . ." Taz shook his head. "Never mind."

Kes's heart skipped one beat, two. "What?" he breathed. "What were you going to say?"

"Mystic" came Shirin's harsh voice from outside. "Kill the *skag* and let's get a move on."

Tazlim moved toward the door. "Good luck with Calar."

Kes waited until Tazlim left, then slid to the floor, closing his eyes. He could smell the Shaitan's cinnamon-scented evanescence from here and a small smile played on his lips.

Foolish. What utter and complete foolishness. There was a war on and his life was in shambles. What was wrong with him? Kesmir threw his head into his hands. As if he didn't have enough to hide from Calar.

A shadow covered the floor and Kes looked up, to where Thatur towered above him, eyes full.

"The Djan'Urbi boy saw the white phoenix with Nalia. In a vision." He ground his claws into the rotting wood. "I was so certain . . ."

"*Hif la'azi vi,*" Kes whispered. *My heart breaks for you.*

"She loved him," Thatur said, as if to himself. Wonder and confusion swirled in his eyes, which were more colors than Kes could count or name.

Kes nodded. "That gives me hope."

Thatur glanced at him, considering. "She always was different from the others," he said, his voice a soft rumble, like a far-off thunderstorm.

"Their love will change everything," Kes said. "It already has."

PART TWO

I love you as the earth loves rain
Without you I will die
—Djan field song

Destruction leads to life anew.
—Godsnight prophecy, the *Sadranishta*

21

ONE YEAR LATER

RAIF STOOD ON A CLIFF OVERLOOKING THE BEACH BELOW, arms crossed, frowning. He ran his hand across his face, fingers skimming the dark hair of his beard.

A memory came then, a swift stab to his heart, unexpected and brutal as it always was: this time, Nalia was running a razor over his skin.

"You look like your father with this beard." She takes the razor from his hand and gently shaves his face. He watches her, breathless. He's never loved anyone so much in his life.

Tomorrow, she'd have been gone a year and a day. At dawn, he would be expected to end his mourning. A year and a day: the time always marked the end of one journey, the beginning of another. The beginning of a life without Nalia. Every time Raif thought of her, he had to wrap his mind around the fact that she was gone, had to force himself to remember the white phoenix. *Godsdamn that bird.*

Except: some nights, he'd wake up from a troubled, dreamless sleep and hear her calling to him: *Raif. I love you. I love you.* He'd heard those words, haunting, spoken from the godlands. He never saw her, but he could feel her, smell her. *Nalia.* Her name was a silent, anguished cry, the only prayer he ever said. There were no more dreams of her, no more unexpected kisses, or love-drenched conversations in the middle of his sleep. Just that faint voice calling out to him, or nothing. Most of the time, he didn't sleep. Unless there was a bottle of *savri* nearby or a sleeping tonic he'd snuck from the healers' stores, sleep was as intangible as Nalia herself.

There was a roar on the sand below—Thatur was leading the soldiers in *Sha'a Rho*, screaming at anyone who forgot their pose, hitting them with a stick when their positions weren't perfect. They'd be impressive if Raif had never seen Nalia go through the exercises. Next to her, they were bumbling elephants. And here, too, she was present: her gryphon, leading his troops. Her father, helping his rebellion. Pieces of her that lived on, painful because they made it so he couldn't forget.

"What do you think?" Shirin asked, coming to stand beside him.

"I think Calar's gonna beat the shit out of us, as usual."

A coordinated attack with Kesmir and his resistance had required months of painstaking planning. Though Kesmir had been able to shield his thoughts from Calar for a long time, it wasn't until recently he'd been able to resist psychic attacks. And now Kes was ready.

"Are you certain he's good to go?" Shirin asked. "Because he only has one chance to kill Calar, you know that."

Gods knew what she would do to him if Kesmir tried and failed.

Raif was sick of this war, sick of his life, sick down to his bones. Ready or not, he wanted out.

"I made a promise to Samar," he said. "To his people. I'm not waiting any longer."

There was this, too: with both Samar and Nalia gone, Taz's army had begun to grumble. They didn't feel like they belonged anywhere—Arjinna or Earth. Without an empress, the soldiers were no longer certain why they were fighting. Calar had destroyed the realm to the extent that it was nearly uninhabitable. She'd given her monsters free reign to leach all the *chiaan* out of it. The shadows stayed away from fire and water—everything else was fair game. Other than the forest, which was protected by its own enigmatic power, the rest of the land resembled a desert—parched, not a bit of color. The only place the Djan could replenish their *chiaan* was in the forest itself. The Shaitan were having the most trouble accessing their *chiaan*, since the air had been soiled by the shadows' evanescence. The Marid still had the ocean, but many of the streams and ponds had dried up.

Raif understood how the Brass Army felt: there was nothing left to fight for.

He was almost glad Nalia wasn't alive to witness the horror

that had unleashed itself upon Arjinna since he'd returned with the Brass Army. He shook his head slightly, as though she could tumble out of his mind. Thoughts of Nalia were forbidden, something he only indulged in late at night, once he was alone. Pushing her away was how he could be of any use to the *tavrai*.

"Hey," Shirin said, her voice soft.

He turned, the ice inside him cracking just a little at the warmth in her eyes. *I can't give you what you want.* He'd told her that in so many ways and yet she remained, his *raiga*, baring her teeth at his enemies, loyal to a fault. He could feel her winning him over, day by day. *Never* had become *maybe*, and the fact that there was even the possibility of feeling something for Shirin somehow widened the raw, gaping wound Nalia's loss had left inside him. *Maybe* he could love her, in a hundred years and with only a fraction of what he'd felt for Nalia. Maybe that would be enough for her. Maybe that would be enough for him—a shadow love, a shadow life. Maybe.

But probably not.

He tried to smile. "At least if we die, we'll go out swinging."

The plan was simple: every jinni in the Forest of Sighs would evanesce to the entrance of the prison in Ithkar. They'd fight. They'd die. And maybe in the process they'd free the Dhoma and other innocent jinn Calar had imprisoned. Meanwhile, Kesmir would overthrow Calar with the Ifrit he'd recruited.

"And if we don't die?" she asked, her eyes on his, refusing to look away.

"Shirin . . ." *I can't give you what you want.*

She leaned closer and then her lips brushed his cheek, warm

and soft. "See you down there."

Raif watched her walk away, a small part of him—the lonely part that spent his nights sitting by the Gate of the Eye with Touma, who still refused to end his vigil—wishing he could return what she felt for him. He rubbed a finger across the crescent-shaped scar on the inside of his wrist, there since he and Nalia had promised to help one another on a rooftop in Los Angeles. It was all he had of her, except her jade dagger and his memories. He was starting to forget things—the exact shape of the birthmark on her cheek, the angle of her nose.

"She's not coming back, Raif." Zanari sits beside him on a sand dune, watching the sun set just as Raif and his father did so many years ago. Nalia has been gone for six months.

"I know."

Zanari places her palm on his knee. "It's time to move on. To be happy."

She nods to where Shirin and Taz are building a bonfire on the sand, preparing for the evening meal. Because the shadows fear water, the resistance has taken to training on the beach, since the Forest of Sighs has become so crowded with refugees. The evening ritual of fishing and bonfires has become oddly comforting to him.

"How can you say that?" Raif turns to her, eyes fierce. "You, of all people. Do you hear me telling you to get over Phara?"

"Phara's alive," she says, her voice trembling. "Once the portal opens—"

"The portal." He snorts. Nalia's father has been clear—closing

a portal is far easier than opening one. Kesmir's insisted that the Ash Crones could help Calar open it—but she refuses to.

"Your hope is as pointless as mine," he says. Zanari's eyes glisten, and he curses himself for putting that sadness in her eyes. "I'm sorry," he says. "I just . . . I can't think about Shirin, about any of it."

"Little brother, you've been saying that for months."

Zanari stands and gently runs a hand through his hair. "Nalia would be heartbroken if she saw you like this. She'd never wish this loneliness on you."

He doesn't say anything as Zanari leaves, doesn't say the one thing that gives him hope: there is a way to be with Nalia again—he just has to die to do it.

22

KES WAITED FOR TAZ IN THE TINY CAVE THAT HAD
become their favorite meeting place over the past several months.
It was far enough from the waves that lapped on the shore that
it remained dry all day and night, but close enough to the water
that Calar's shadows wouldn't come near. Farther down the
beach, the *tavrai* trained and the Marid prepared their fishing
boats, but the cave was tucked away in seclusion. The glittering
black sand had been covered by thick cushions and blankets.
If they met at night, Kes or Taz would manifest lanterns that
couldn't be spotted from land. It wasn't a deep cave, more like a
small cavern ending in a wall of rock. It was warm and cozy and
theirs.

The late-afternoon sun had spread over the land, sharing
its wealth of light like a generous aristocrat. Kes could feel Taz

before he saw him. The wind seemed to blow a bit harder, its scent sweetened with cinnamon. And then he was there, and when he saw Kes he grinned.

"Gods, I've missed you," Taz said, pulling off his armor. His lips fell onto Kes's and they didn't bother with words for a good long while.

Taz was everything Calar had never been: slow and gentle, with lips that kissed away pain, never inflicted it. Theirs was not a love that scorched; their lovemaking didn't leave marks, didn't require a hungry, bottomless passion, a passion that didn't care who it hurt. Instead, it was the soft glow of candlelight, the flames of a campfire. It was Taz's fingers unbuttoning Kes's *sawala* and his hands tracing scars. It was Kes drawing him closer as he reached for Taz's leather belt, his lips against his lover's bare shoulder, his neck.

Kes had been so certain that Calar was his *rohifsa*, and yet how could that be, when this jinni took his breath away time and again, when hearing his name in Taz's mouth left him shaking, the love that pulsed inside him like a second heart, almost unbearable? With Taz he felt known, not in the way he did with Calar while she read his mind—that, he now saw, was far too easy. The real feat was how Taz was able to understand exactly what Kes was feeling without him ever saying a word. Kes would stare at something beautiful that had been denied him in his life in Ithkar—a field of flowers, the way moonlight caught and held the silver in *widr* leaves—and Taz would simply reach over, take Kes's hand, and gently squeeze. He knew exactly what was needed at any given moment and he gave of himself with abandon—there were no strings attached to his love, no underlying current of fear. There wasn't an imbalance of power, a history sullied with lies and demands. There was just the certainty that this was right, that they needed each other—had *always* needed each other.

It seemed as though he and Taz had each been made for the express purpose of loving the other well: the way their bodies fit perfectly together, the way Taz always knew exactly how to elicit those gasps and moans that echoed softly in the cave. Kes was able to get beneath the calm facade Taz always showed his soldiers, beyond the mystic who contemplated the vastness of the universe. He'd hold Taz while he cried in frustration because everyone he'd loved had died long before he'd been rescued from his bottle. He'd listen with his whole body as Taz shared about the bottle—the fear and rage and helplessness. Kes discovered the precise spot where Taz was most ticklish, this stoic commander who led armies as easily as he prayed to his gods. Taz's peals of laughter would bounce around the cave and he wouldn't be able to stop until Kes kissed him.

And so it was on this afternoon. It wasn't until they were tangled up in each other's arms, content in their exhaustion and covered in each other's sweat, that Kes allowed himself to think about what he had to say.

Taz wouldn't like it.

"You have that look," Taz murmured, tracing the furrows in Kes's brow.

"What look?"

"The one where you're going to tell me something that will make me sad." He leaned closer to Kes. "Don't," he whispered, "make me sad today." Taz gently bit Kes's lower lip and that was sufficiently distracting to quiet him for the next several minutes.

Taz tasted like mint and sugarberries and salty sweat. Kes gave in to that kiss, knowing these moments were numbered. If he failed at his task, he would never have this again. So he pressed against him as though they could fuse together, his *chiaan* surging into Taz so fast that his lover gasped.

But eventually Kes forced himself to gently pull away. Taz sighed. "I know what you're going to say."

"You do? Don't tell me you can suddenly read minds," Kes said. He tried to make it a joke, to keep his tone light, but Taz caught the terror, the deep, deep sadness he was trying to hold back.

"No mind reading. I just know you," Taz said softly.

He ran his hand through Kes's hair, longer now because Taz liked it that way and it was one of the few things Kes could do for him. Anything else would risk Calar's discovering that her consort was absolutely, completely in love with the commander of the Brass Army.

"I know you're ready," Taz said. "Raif told me."

Kes nodded, twining his fingers through Taz's. "Thatur couldn't get inside my head. I thought of every vile thought that would have made him claw my face off if he'd heard—replayed scenes from the coup, every last detail I remembered—but he couldn't get in. He never knew what I was thinking about. He tried to inflict pain once I was tired from keeping him out, but he failed each time. He doesn't quite have Calar's gift, but he said he couldn't even sense that I'd built a wall up. Which means that, if I do this right, she'll be gone before she even knew I wanted it that way."

Taz leaned against the cave wall, a thick pillow propped up between his back and the rock. He held out his arms and Kes crawled into them, resting his head on Taz's chest. Gods, it felt good to be taken care of.

"How about keeping your face away from Thatur's claws, hmm?" Taz said, teasing, his voice tight beneath the lighthearted tone. "As a personal favor to me. I rather like this face of yours, you know."

Kes could feel the blood rush to his cheeks, the smile that refused to stay hidden. "You're the most dangerous thing Calar could ever see in my mind," he said, wrapping his arms tighter around Taz. A surge of Shaitan *chiaan* flew into his veins, as invigorating as a cool breeze on a hot day.

Taz rested his cheek on the top of Kes's head. "I know."

For months they'd managed to pretend they were nothing more than unlikely conspirators, but that had all stopped after the night Calar nearly killed Kes.

Calar pushes her palms against Kes's temples, her eyes filled with rage. "How dare you go behind my back!"

She'd caught him setting a group of prisoners free. He couldn't bear seeing one more soul ripped out by the shadows.

"Calar, look what you've become," he says. "This isn't what we're fighting for—"

White-hot pain, blinding. He hears the agonized cries of a tortured animal bouncing off the stones in the throne room and then Kes realizes it's him, he's the one making that terrible sound.

Kes lies unconscious for a week, waking up on the dungeon's cold stone floor. Calar comes to visit him and he plays the repentant lover. The first place Kes goes after Calar restores him to his post is the Djan temple in the Forest of Sighs, Taz's favorite haunt. Hidden deep in the forest, the temple is a ruin left over from the days before the Aisouri, ancient stone overgrown with moss, vixen roses snaking through crevices in the walls that surround it. The temple's gate is formed by the branches of a grove of unusually large widrs that encircle the entire structure. The long branches of the widr have been magicked into decorative accents, resembling a wrought-iron gate bordered by stone pillars. Through the elaborate patterns Kes catches a glimpse of the temple ruins.

A hush lies over this part of the forest. There is no sound save for the rustling of the wind through the trees. Here, the forest seems to watch him, seems to pulse with more life than usual. Taz once explained that the trees were there to protect the temple and it would not do well to displease them. Kes hopes an Ifrit with Djan blood on his hands will be welcomed. The forest itself has been letting him cross its borders since the night Raif agreed to work with him.

Kes lays his palm against the wooden gate, just as Taz showed him a few months ago, and the branches writhe, then twist away like well-trained serpents, leaving a keyhole arch for Kes to step through. Large tree roots cover the top of the temple walls and buildings, giants climbing over stone arches, using roofs as chairs. Their branches are fused above the whole temple, creating a

canopy that sunlight filters through like drops of golden rain. Kes
ventures into the small clearing, blanketed by a carpet of leaves
that never fade or dry. The temple is filled with their spicy scent.
He slips off his shoes, as is customary in the Djan places of wor-
ship, where earth is the honored element. The leaves tingle, and
though Kes cannot draw chiaan *from them, he feels their power*
nevertheless.

Kes sees Taz before the other jinni realizes he's no longer alone.
He is sitting on a low stone wall, legs dangling, eyes closed. A soft
smile plays on his face, which is tilted toward the sunlight that
rains down on him. Kes's breath catches and that feeling—an
aching certainty that keeps him up most nights—washes over him.

Other than Yasri, Taz is the most beautiful thing he's ever
seen.

Kes suddenly feels shy, uncertain. He's intruding on a private
moment. He should leave the mystic to his prayers, find him
later—

Taz's eyes open and he turns toward Kes, relief and joy flood-
ing his face. He jumps up, and rather than continue the charade
they've been keeping up for months, he flings his arms around Kes
and pulls him close.

"I thought I'd lost you," Taz says, his voice trembling.

Kissing the Brass Army's commander isn't a conscious choice.
It is a primal need, like food or sleep.

He can't do without it any longer.

In the cave it was almost hard to believe they hadn't always
been this way: Taz and Kes, one coin, two sides. They kept their

love a secret, though a handful of their closest friends knew. They'd been surprisingly supportive.

Zanari had even rolled her eyes. "Finally," she said. "Raif and I were taking bets on which one of you would give in first."

Over the course of many months, they'd all made their peace with one another, due in large part to Taz's lobbying. They were all almost . . . friends.

"Who'd you bet on?" Taz asked, genuinely curious.

"You," Zanari said. "But only because I caught you mooning over him more times than I can count." She nodded to Kes. "This one at least knows how to keep a secret."

Raif had smiled, that sadness that was always in his eyes a little more pronounced. He'd nodded, as if to himself. "Love changes everything."

Now Kes sat up, reluctant to leave Taz's arms. He had to get back to the palace and he wanted this last part over with.

"Taz," he said, placing a hand on his lover's knee. "Will you promise me something?"

Taz swallowed, his eyes already misting. "Don't," he whispered. "You're going to be fine, I know it. And when it's all over—"

Kes reached out and gently placed his fingers over Taz's mouth. "I have every intention of spending the rest of my life with you," he murmured. "But if I don't make it, I need to know that Yasri will be okay."

His little jinni—*Papa, look at me! Papa, tell me a story. Papa, I love you.* He ground his teeth at the mere possibility of her losing him. He was the center of her world. And she his. It was a testament to how much he trusted Taz that his lover already knew about Yasri, knew about her purple eyes and the power she was already beginning to come into. The other day he'd caught her morphing into a pool in the palace garden, her Marid side taking over. If anyone had seen her . . . It was a secret that couldn't be kept for long. Taz was the only person other than Calar and Thatur who knew his daughter was a Ghan Aisouri, but soon everyone would know. Yasri was three summers old—she'd yet to realize the whole realm would hate her.

"Thatur has agreed to help me get her out of the palace without Calar knowing," Kes said. "He can get through the *bisahm*. Ri doesn't now how to evanesce yet. It's adorable really. . . ." He sighed and looked away for a moment. Gods, there was so much at stake. "I wouldn't have her go to the forest alone, anyway."

"Kes—" Taz's voice broke, the sound everything Kes was feeling inside.

"Will you be her guardian?" he asked, his eyes meeting Taz's. It was so much to ask. "Will you . . . be a father to her, if it comes to that?"

"I would be anyway," Taz said. "You know that."

They'd spoken only once of the future, in whispers, too scared to let the gods hear their plans. They dreamed of a wedding, of a home where a little Ghan Aisouri would be safe and well loved—cared for by two papas and an ornery gryphon.

Kes leaned his forehead against Taz's. "I know." He gripped Taz's hand, sending his energy into him, all his love, that fire Calar had yet to stamp out.

Taz tilted Kes's chin up. "Your daughter will always have a home with me—as will you."

Our daughter, Kes wanted to say—someday. He was too scared to voice that hope now. How could he dream of it: a life with a Shaitan, both of them caring for a Ghan Aisouri, raising her not as a daughter of the gods but as a girl who could choose whatever future she wished?

Kes stood up, his eyes on Taz. "I have to go. Thatur will . . . he'll be in touch if . . ." He shook his head. He wouldn't say it. *I'm going to get through this. I'm going to live. I'm going to raise my daughter with this jinni.*

Taz bolted up and pulled Kes to him. He didn't say a word, didn't have to. He could feel it all in Taz's *chiaan*: *Don't die, don't make me live my years without you.*

Kes pulled back, his eyes roving over Taz's face. "I love you," he murmured.

"And I you."

His lips brushed Taz's cheek and then Kes forced himself to walk out of the cave, onto the black-sand beach where the foam from the surf slid over his bare feet. When he looked back, Taz was watching him, a wistful smile on his face.

Kes let himself imagine a home tucked away in the Qaf Mountains, or maybe right here, next to their cave. A garden, a swing for Yasri. A shrine for Taz to pray to the gods he so loved. That was the talisman Kes would carry with him into battle.

That was what would keep him alive.

23

MORGHISI WAS THE UGLIEST LIVING CREATURE KES HAD ever seen. He would have expected nothing less from the leader of the Ash Crones. Ever since his first encounter with the ancient dark mage, he'd had no doubt her outer form was a reflection of her *chiaan*, of the damage it could do and the horror it would wreak upon the land. The few times he'd seen the witch use her *chiaan*, he hadn't been surprised to see that it bled out of her, black as the obsidian that covered Ithkar's plains. Kes made no effort to hide his disdain for her work with Mora, goddess of death, and had pleaded with Calar to run, crawl if she must, away from the crone's guidance. But she had laughed at him, tried to kiss away his fears, and, finally, ignored him and continued under the tutelage of Morghisi and her sisters.

There was no love lost between Kes and the crone Calar

affectionately called Mother. Though they were not of the same blood, Calar had been raised by the crones, and it was true that Morghisi had given birth to the evil that had taken root in Calar's heart.

"Mora will be satisfied with our offering," Morghisi said from her place behind what Kes had come to think of as the Butcher's Block. "But I still think it's too small."

The flat slab of rock deep in the crones' volcanic stronghold was slick with blood and the rocky walls still echoed with the cries of those sacrificed today, a faint hum that seemed thunderous to Kes. Calar stood beside Morghisi, silent. To Kes, the crones had, for a time, been a necessary evil: their magic combined with Calar's ruthlessness was what had allowed the Ifrit to stage a coup in the first place. It was the power that had placed the shackles around the jinn on the dark caravan so that the jinn could be traded for the weapons the Ifrit needed to defeat the Aisouri. But Calar had never thought the magic evil, and therein lay the problem.

"This is a small offering?" Kes said, his voice fierce. He was godsdamn *sick* of it all. "Then Mora is a greedy *skag*."

Calar gasped, but Morghisi merely settled her eyes on him, two black orbs, like dried blood. Her forked tongue darted out of her mouth, a thin gray bit of flesh stolen from an ancient magical snake that she'd killed for Mora. It was no legend: he'd seen the preserved corpse of the creature in the entryway to her chambers. As a result of her hunter's trophy, Morghisi spoke with a slight hiss, as though she would eat you for the afternoon meal if she were hungry enough. He knew that at this moment, the crone could see what Calar refused to: he was no longer a willing soldier in this war.

"Death wants her due," Morghisi said. "You will learn that yourself one day soon, I think."

Kes crossed his arms. "As will you."

Morghisi smiled, each of her pearl-white teeth sharp as a Ghan Aisouri dagger. He'd seen her tear jinn flesh with those teeth, blood coating them like glaze on a cake as she chanted to Mora and filled herself with her victims' power. He'd seen her convince Calar to do the same.

"Kes . . ." Calar threw him a pleading look. The *yaghin* around her neck gave off a faint glow as the black swirl of shadows moved beneath the enchanted necklace's smooth surface. "I need to reopen the portal. This is the only way."

They'd discussed it at length the night before. The Ifrit weapons stores were dwindling. *Let's end this, once and for all,* she'd said. Since she'd only closed the portal to keep Nalia out in the first place, there was no reason to be cut off from Earth now that the Ghan Aisouri was dead. She'd been trying since learning of Nalia's death, but reopening a doorway between two worlds proved to be more challenging than she'd expected. She and Morghisi had been storing up power through death for nearly a year.

He'd always told Calar that closing the portal was a rash decision, that the very cost of it, and eventually reopening it, would offend the gods. Hundreds of lives had been lost in the process, sacrificed on the Butcher's Block.

He turned to Morghisi. "Plants die. Animals die. Why can't we use that energy?"

The Ash Crone gave him a scathing look of contempt. "You think flowers and animal hearts are enough to open a doorway between the realms?"

They should never have closed the portal in the first place. The Shaitan mages had said it couldn't be done. But the power harnessed from the dead Aisouri had created Calar's shadows *and* been strong enough to close the portal, the energy encased in the altar itself until Calar made use of it. But there were no more Aisouri to kill—Calar had found most of the ones who had been born since the coup, ending their lives on the very rock Kes now stood before. Calar's unprecedented store of power had dwindled until there was hardly any left.

Which was why he'd just been forced to witness the slaughter of a hundred prisoners—a massacre that, combined with the energy Calar and the crones had been amassing, would allow the dark caravan to begin again by opening the portal with Mora's energy. Kes was only now beginning to realize the extent to which he'd been hypnotized by Calar all these years. How could he have thought the caravan was justified, that it was somehow okay to sell jinn lives in exchange for human weapons? Most of them hadn't even been *bad* jinn, guilty of crimes against the Ifrit.

Calar placed a hand on his arm, attempting to comfort him. "They were just prisoners, my love."

He stared at her, incredulous. "*Just*—?" Kes bit off his retort and turned toward the archway that opened onto the balcony. "Come find me when you're done," he said.

He didn't need to turn around to see Morghisi's triumphant sneer—he'd seen it often enough to know it was there. Kes had always been willing to kill when it was necessary—and when he was only killing his enemies. He'd always drawn the line at enemies, refusing to see all the ways in which Calar stepped over that line herself. For so long Kes thought it would stop, thought that once Calar had gained control of the realm, she wouldn't need to kill innocents. He'd been wrong, of course.

The balcony encircled the entire middle of the active volcano and looked out onto the sea of lava that had turned the fiery mountain into an island. The crones had lived there for centuries, claiming that their proximity to death at all times was what kept them Mora's favored servants. The volcano had erupted three times since the crones had taken up residence in the caves that split off from the balcony, and yet the crones always escaped before the tunnels within the caves flowed with lava. No one knew how old they were; they seemed to be as much a part of Ithkar as the jackals that prowled its barren plains and the lava that flowed like a demon's tears.

Kes leaned on the railing and looked down into the lava below, a brilliant electric crimson against the lengthening dusk. For a brief moment he considered diving into the swirling, molten mass, his despair suddenly overwhelming. He had to clutch at the railing to keep his body from throwing itself off the volcano. There were Yasri and Taz to think of—reasons enough for living. He hadn't thought that things could get worse, and yet they had. He'd lost his cool back there, put the lives of every jinni fighting with him against Calar at risk. Angering Morghisi and arousing her suspicion had left the door open for Calar to suspect him.

After many long minutes, there was a rustle of silk behind

him and Kes turned. Calar stood in the archway, her skin so pale it was nearly translucent, bright against the black *sawala* she wore. She swung her traveling cloak over her shoulders, a swath of bloody crimson.

"Come," she said, holding out her hand. "It's time to open the portal."

Kes didn't allow himself the hesitation he felt. He took Calar's hand, interlacing his fingers with hers. Her *chiaan* rushed into him, scattered and scalding, like it always was now. He knew she'd pick up his frustration, his sadness.

"You're not going to reprimand me?" he asked, an edge to his voice.

"You're entitled to your opinion," she said with a wry smile. "You're awfully cute when you're angry, you know."

Ah, so this was how she was going to play it. Evade, evade. *Fine,* he thought, *I can do that, too.*

He pulled her closer. She smelled like blood, and as he looked into her eyes, Kes found himself wishing they were gold. He forced his thoughts away from Tazlim—he had to focus.

"Forget the portal," he murmured, frantically pushing the sound of Taz gasping against Kes's skin behind an old memory of a skirmish. He felt it slide away, just as he'd practiced with Thatur. "Let's go somewhere you can make me angry."

He pressed his lips against her neck and she leaned into him the slightest bit before pulling away.

Calar laughed, a mirthless trill. "Oh, there's plenty of time to make you angry, Kes."

Crimson smoke began to pool under her feet and he added

his campfire smoke to hers. Just as they began to evanesce, he saw two glittering eyes gazing out at him from the room beyond. Morghisi smiled, a sinister, knowing look on her face. Kes gave in to the evanescence, grateful to be away from the crones and the stink of death.

Moments later, he was standing beside Calar at the location where the portal had once been. Without the usual rip between earth and sky, it was simply a cliff with a sheer drop, facing nothing but the next range of mountains. The twilight painted the sky in large, glowing swaths of color: pink, green, orange, yellow. Because the portal had been closed for some time, Calar and Kes were alone. There was no need for guards—there was no one and nothing to keep watch over.

"Do you remember how we used to come up here?" Kes asked softly.

Years ago, they'd hiked up the Ifrit side of the Qaf Mountains, too afraid to evanesce for fear of detection by the Ghan Aisouri or their army of conscripted serfs. They'd find an isolated nook and watch day turn to night over Arjinna, where the moons didn't bleed and the sky wasn't brown. These were some of his happiest memories, huddled against the rock, holding Calar. Dreaming. Hoping.

Kes turned—Calar hadn't heard him. She'd let go of his hand, walking the few steps to the edge of the cliff. The wind was strong here and her cloak whipped around her so that she seemed to be swirling in place, a priestess in her temple.

Push her, an urgent voice inside him whispered. *Do it before she unleashes this magic, do it before she can hurt anyone else.* But the portal needed to be open—Arjinna was barely habitable. Earth could be a fresh start for him and Taz and Yasri—all of them—if they needed it.

She turned around and flashed him a triumphant smile, and her radiance seemed to spark the air around her. Calar raised her hands to the sky and a furious burst of wind gusted over the cliff. Her hair swirled, pulled by the wind's greedy fingers. She chanted the words Morghisi had given her, words from the old tongue that sounded like the end of things. The wind blew harder and she stumbled toward the cliff's edge. Kes ran to her, though it was the last thing he wanted to do. He held on to Calar with one hand while she crushed a glass bottle under her foot, releasing the *chiaan* of her victims, heedless of him. A musty scent filled the air, slightly sour, like the sulphur swamps in the north of Ithkar. Calar fell to her knees, the ancient words now being torn from her, as though some unseen being were torturing a confession from the depths of her soul. Terror filled Kes. They were on the edge of an abyss, a point of no return. He let go of her, prayed she would fall as soon as the portal opened.

"Mora, Mora!" Calar cried the death goddess's name, longing flooding her voice.

The gray magic bled into the air and the aurora swirled, a pinwheel moving faster and faster, dazzling, blinding. Then: a rush of air followed by a low sonic *boom*. The swirl of colors mushroomed as a shockwave pulsed in the air, so intense it threw Kes off his feet. He landed on his back, hard, gaping as the gray *chiaan* Calar had released tore the sky, ripping the aurora as though it were a colorful piece of fabric. A hole formed—small at first, then pushing outward, its edges foaming, waves of color and magic.

Through the widening space before him, Kes could see an endless desert flooded with moonlight. Instead of the sheer drop that had occupied the space before the cliff, a gaping doorway had materialized. It wasn't nearly as large as the old portal—that one had been more like a border than a single passage—but it would do the trick.

Calar crossed to the very edge of the cliff. She lifted her foot, then tilted forward. Her heeled slipper sank into Earth's sand. She gave a cry of delight, then jumped through the portal. Kes stayed where he was, watching. She turned her eyes on him, incandescent in her victory.

Calar in one world, Kes in another. It was an apt metaphor for what they had become.

24

RAIF FOLLOWED SHIRIN THROUGH THE CROWDED streets of the Ghaz, the hood of his cloak pulled over his head, trying his best to avoid eye contact. There was a certain thrill to walking among the jinn, right under the noses of the Ifrit who patrolled the cobblestoned streets. Evading death filled Raif with grim satisfaction, one of the few pleasures left him. How many times had the Ifrit and Ghan Aisouri tried to kill him? And yet here he was, a free jinni. For the most part, Raif had had few occasions to come to the market. The *tavrai* had always insisted that he was too valuable, that it would be easier for Calar to capture him there, with so many spies mingling among the shoppers and merchants. But Yurik's message had been clear: Raif needed to come, in person. He could have evanesced to the bartender's rooms in the Third Wish, of course, but Raif was tired of skulking around. He needed to be among the people, in the thick of life. He needed to remember what he was fighting for, what tonight was all about.

Though evening approached, the streets were full of a bustling trade. They passed a bakery smelling of *kees*, flat loaves of bread dusted with sugar and spices. Steaming pots of *chal* sat atop tables where jinn sat and talked animatedly with one another while smoking rose-scented tobacco from water pipes. A toothless tiger ambled down the street, pulled along by a jinni not more than seven summers old. Strapped to its back was a crate of sugarberries.

"Wal'kai, wal'kai," the boy called, hawking his fruit in a lilting voice.

A beggar playing a *zhifir* leaned against a wall, a small brass bowl hovering in the air beside him. Only a few passerby threw in a *niba*—most had none to spare. The song tugged at Raif, the memory of the last time he'd heard it tearing him open: staring across the fire at Nalia while Noqril played the song deep in the cave beneath the Sahara. He'd caught her eye and she'd looked away, then stood up and walked deeper into the cave. He'd followed her, down a long, dark tunnel, coming out into a cavern filled with glow worms.

" . . . Raif?"

He started, disoriented as he fell out of the past.

"What? Sorry."

Shirin shook her head. "Never mind."

He dug into his pocket and threw a *niba* into the bowl. The musician nodded his head in thanks as he continued to play.

Soon enough, they were turning into the Vein. Raif could have found it with his eyes closed, so bad was the stench. Other than that, it wasn't entirely unlike the jinn souk in Morocco—he could see why the jinn on Earth had chosen Marrakech as the hub of their life in exile.

"You think Yurik knows what just happened?" he asked Shirin as the Third Wish's sign came into view.

That sound, like a human bomb without an explosion. The earth shook and yet the jolt had come from the sky, not the earth. The aurora had begun to undulate, then whirl, like water in a fast-moving current. His scouts had been just as confused as Raif. Nobody knew what it was, though he was certain Calar was behind it somehow, probably creating another horror in her dungeons at the Cauldron. He hoped Yurik had answers. Usually Shirin handled everything between the *tavrai* and the jack-of-all-trades bartender. Pouring drinks was only a small bit of what Yurik did on a daily basis—Raif knew that. The Ifrit left Yurik alone because they relied on the Wish for information just as much as everyone else. It was the hub of Arjinnan social life, the jewel of the Ghaz, the beating heart of the Vein. Raif wasn't happy with how much Shirin had come to depend on Yurik since he'd gone to Earth. He didn't trust the jinni, not entirely. Yurik worked alone, which meant he had no code to follow, no allegiance to guide his decisions and transactions. No counsel. This was dangerous and unpredictable and it made Raif wary.

And yet. Taz had told him that Yurik was the one helping Aisouri infants to escape detection. And that he'd once been on the dark caravan. Nalia would have liked him for those two reasons alone. Which was why Raif was willing to work with him now, trusting Yurik to be part of their plans for Calar, the prison—all of it.

Shirin pushed open the door to the Wish. The place was packed with patrons sipping from goblets of *savri*, their conversation a din that filled the room. A few looked up as Raif and Shirin crossed the threshold, but it was only a quick glance. Customers at the Wish knew never to look at anyone too closely.

The area behind the bar was empty, but moments later, Yurik pushed through the swinging door that led to the kitchen, carrying a tray with plates of steaming food and a pot of *chal*. He served the food to his customers, then nodded toward the stairs. Without a word, Raif and Shirin followed the bartender to his room.

"What's going on?" Raif asked as he closed the door behind him, waving away the cup of tea Yurik offered. "The sky—"

"The portal's open," Yurik said. He smiled, but there was a deep sadness there—which didn't make sense. This was the best news Raif had heard in a year.

"You're not smiling," Shirin said, watching Yurik. "Why? Isn't this what you wanted—what we've all wanted?"

The magic, the *power* such an act would have required . . . and then Raif understood why Yurik looked so unhappy.

"What did Calar do to open the portal?"

His stomach twisted. Anything involving Calar always came with a high price—one she rarely seemed to pay herself.

"A hundred prisoners from Ithkar were taken away early this morning by a regiment of Ifrit," Yurik said. "No one knows what happened to them, but then the portal opened. . . ."

"Fire and blood," Shirin cursed. "Just one more day and we would have . . ." She turned away from them, hands on her hips. Those were prisoners who were supposed to be freed tonight.

Yurik watched her, silent. Not for the first time, Raif wondered what was going on between these two.

A burst of red evanescence filled the room and Shirin cried out, drawing her scimitar while emerald *chiaan* immediately began to spill from Raif's fingertips.

"Wait!" Yurik yelled, stepping into Raif's line of fire, palms out.

"It's me," said a familiar voice in the smoke. Then a body, a face with a scar across its cheek. Exhausted eyes.

Kesmir.

"Godsdammit, Kes." Raif's heart was racing—he'd been so convinced for that split second that Yurik had conspired against them. An ambush, death above a tavern, not on the battlefield.

"Apologies," Kes said.

Shirin glared at Yurik, her fierce eyes full of hurt. "Since when are you friendly with the Ifrit?"

Shirin had never accepted Kes, though Raif had long ago, against his own will at first and then, gradually, because he'd come to respect him.

Yurik calmly poured himself a cup of *chal*. "We have a mutual concern," he said as a silent, heavy look passed between Kesmir and himself.

Raif looked from one jinni to the other. "Somebody better start explaining. About the portal, about whatever *mutual concerns* you two have. Now."

"I already told them about the portal," Yurik said.

"What happened to those prisoners?" Raif asked.

Kesmir crossed to the fire roaring in the stone fireplace and placed his palms against the flames to replenish his *chiaan*. As he spoke, his voice was heavy. "She killed them," Kes said. "Sacrificed them to Mora."

"So you just let them die?" Shirin growled.

Kes narrowed his eyes. "Everything I do is to dethrone her, to bide my time until I can kill her. I take no pleasure in the loss of life, and being in that room was . . ." He trailed off, the horror in his eyes saying everything. "I know you don't like me," Kes said to her. "And, frankly, I don't like you. But please do me the service of *shutting the fuck up*. I'm doing the best I can."

Raif had to bite back his smile. How many times had he wanted to say that himself to Shirin? Yurik, though, stiffened.

"Careful there, brother," he said softly.

Yes, Raif thought, there was definitely something between the tavern owner and Shirin. He wished she could see it.

Kes sighed, frustrated. "I don't have much time," he said. "There's a lot to discuss."

"I believe, now that the portal has reopened, I can be of service to you," Yurik said.

Raif nodded. "The tunnel."

"Precisely," Yurik agreed.

For years Yurik had been the gatekeeper of a secret tunnel that began beneath the Wish and ended at the portal. Countless serfs had escaped their masters this way, running from their plantations in the dead of night. Raif himself had used it once or twice. It was an incredible feat, hundreds of miles of dirt that had to be moved with magic and sweat. It had been there since before Yurik's time, a secret he'd inherited from the jinni who'd owned the Wish long before him.

"Calar wants to act as quickly as possible," Kes said. "She's transporting jinn from the prison to Earth to sell in exchange for arms."

Fire and blood. The dark caravan would be up and running once again—of course.

"It's not going to work," Raif said, remembering the blur of events in Los Angeles, when Nalia had been trying to steal her bottle from Malek. "The main supplier for your guns is no longer in the business."

It was one of the things Nalia had insisted on doing before she left Earth. She'd refused to go back to Arjinna until she'd done all she could to end the caravan. Convincing Sergei, the human wishmaker who controlled the human arms trade, to stop working with the Ifrit had been a start.

Kesmir smiled, sad. "Yes, we know this. Unfortunately, there are many humans who are interested in the business arrangement the Ifrit offer."

Nalia had worked so hard to stop the caravan—there was no way it was growing under Raif's watch. He had to find a way to keep the prisoners from being sent to Earth.

"How is she getting the jinn for the dark caravan to Earth—bottles?" Raif asked.

"Yes," Kes said. "Calar has already put half the prisoners into bottles. Not all the prisoners in Ithkar—just the ones she thinks are most likely to fetch a good . . . price." At least, Raif thought, Kes had the good grace to be ashamed. He doubted he'd always been, though. Raif had grown friendly with the Ifrit general, but he'd never forgotten all the ways Kes had turned a blind eye to— or assisted in—Calar's evil schemes. "She's having the traders transport them—tonight," Kes continued.

"She doesn't waste time, does she?" Shirin muttered.

"We need to get those bottles before the traders get their hands on them," Raif said. "There's no way I'm letting Calar start the caravan again."

There were already hundreds of jinn trapped with their masters on Earth who still needed to be freed. Maybe that was what Raif could do after the war—leave this realm behind him, do Nalia's work for her. His heart lifted a little for the first time in a year.

"Agreed." Shirin sat on the edge of the small room's only table, a thoughtful expression on her face. "What if we let Calar transport the jinn out of the prison—do the hard work for us— then intercept the traders on Earth's side of the portal?" she asked. "We could send any *tavrai* we can spare through the portal in the next few hours."

Raif grinned. "*Raiga*, you're brilliant! Yes. That's what we'll do."

Shirin blushed and Yurik fixed Raif with a scowl. "That's a pretty big risk. The traders aren't easy prey," he said. "And you'd be fighting three separate battles: one on Earth, one at the prison, and one at the castle."

"Then it's a good thing I have two armies at my disposal," Raif said, "and an Ifrit rebellion to take care of the palace. I think we can handle a few *skag* traders. The prison—well, that's another matter."

"What time are the traders taking the jinn through?" Yurik asked.

"Not for several more hours," Kes said. "We have time, but we'll have to be quick."

Shirin turned to Kes. "Is the portal heavily guarded?"

"Yes, I'm afraid so."

"That needs to change," Raif said. He crossed to the tray of *chal* and poured himself a cup. "I'll need the portal free of guards, so I can send some *tavrai* through in the next few hours. We'll need your help on this side when the traders go through. Guards sympathetic to the cause who will kill any traders who come back sounding an alarm. Can you make that happen?"

Kes hesitated, then nodded. "The traders used to always go through around midnight. Even though we'll have friendly guards, I wouldn't have your *tavrai* evanesce there—lookouts on the Qaf will see your smoke."

"Hence, the tunnel," Yurik said.

Kes glanced out the window. "I need to get back to the palace before Calar realizes I'm gone. I'll fill in my soldiers, find the right guards for the portal—we'll be ready."

"One more thing." Raif glanced at Yurik. "Are you up for a little more traffic in your tunnel tonight?"

"What do you have in mind?"

"The Dhoma aren't the only jinn who want to leave the realm," he said. Zanari would get what she wanted, after all. A new life on Earth, at Phara's side, living with the Dhoma. The thought made him happy and relieved. She would be out of range of Calar's shadows. She'd have a chance at a life with her *rohifsa*. "I'd like my sister to guide anyone who wants to leave through the tunnel: the elderly, children—whoever. We can put them in bottles, just like the traders do. Then we'd only need a few jinn to make the crossing. They'll carry the bottles, just like we did for the Brass Army in the cave on Earth."

Yurik frowned. "Do we have to do this tonight? There's so much else—"

"If things don't go as we hope," Raif said, "we won't have another chance to get anyone through the portal."

Because we'll all be dead, he thought.

"Wait. Let me get this straight," Shirin said, her voice shaking. "You're saying that we'll help anyone who wants to go, even if they can fight?"

Raif nodded. "Yes."

"Raif. That's crazy. We need all the help we can get—"

"We're fighting for freedom—that includes the freedom to choose the battles we fight."

"Raif—"

"*Vi fazla ra'ahim,*" he said softly. *You are a sword. Nothing more.*

They looked at each other for a long moment; then she placed her hand over her heart in the *tavrai* salute, eyes hard. "As you wish, Commander." She spit out the words—a bad taste in her mouth—before throwing another angry look Kes's way. She stalked out of the room and as soon as she slammed the door behind her, the air seemed to lighten.

"You've got your work cut out for you," Yurik said to Raif.

"Don't give up on her," Raif said softly.

He hoped Yurik understood the sentiment behind the words: *You love her in a way I never can.*

Yurik threw a yearning glance at the door, then shook his head. "Gods be with you in the battle, Raif."

He grabbed the tea tray and waited for Shirin's stomping on the stairs to end, then swept out of the room. Raif moved to follow, but Kes stopped him, a hand on his arm. He shut the door behind Yurik, then stepped closer to Raif.

"There's something you need to know," Kesmir said. "I wanted to wait until the last minute to tell you and it seems that last minute has arrived."

What else could he possibly be hiding? "Out with it, Kes."

"I have a daughter."

Raif's eyes widened. It was hard to imagine the Ifrit commander as a father. Not just because he was so young. Raif couldn't picture a baby in his arms, a child calling him *Papa*. It changed his whole idea of who Kes was.

"With Calar?" Raif asked.

Kesmir nodded.

"Better you than me, brother," Raif said.

"Yes, well . . ." Kes looked away, frowning. He seemed to be fighting a battle with himself.

"Kes. I know that we . . . I guess you could say we got off on the wrong foot last year."

Kes's mouth quirked up. "To put it mildly."

"Yes." Raif rested his hand on the Ifrit general's shoulder.

"What I'm saying is, you can trust me."

"I know. It's just . . . my child is unlike most children."

"She messing with minds, too?" Gods, another Calar.

Kes shook his head. "She's . . ." He pitched his voice even lower, and when his eyes met Raif's they were fearful. "She's a Ghan Aisouri."

Raif stared. "What did you just say?" he breathed.

"My daughter is a Ghan Aisouri."

There were no words.

"That was my reaction, too, when the healer placed her in my arms."

Raif shook his head, ran his hands over his face. "Just . . . give me a minute, brother."

There were so many thoughts, so many questions and feelings going through him, Raif didn't know where to start. He stood, pacing. Kes watched him, silent.

"What does Calar . . . think . . . about her daughter being what she is?" Raif asked. "I would have thought . . ."

"That she'd kill her?" Kes finished. Raif nodded. "I know. I considered taking my daughter and just running. I can't explain it, but the *feeling* I had when I saw her—I'd known her for a few seconds and I was already willing to do anything for her." Kes swallowed. "Anything. But there was no time—Calar was already sitting up, holding out her arms."

"And?"

"Calar got this look on her face. . . ." Kes shook his head, and his lips turned up in a soft smile. "What I mean is, I saw her fall in love with our daughter in a matter of seconds. She loved her from the moment she saw her. *Purple* was all she said. Then she looked at the healer and she didn't need to say a word. No one could know but us. So I killed the jinni right then, fast, before she knew what was happening. Before she could feel it. And then we had a mage come in to glamour our daughter's eyes and *chiaan*. I killed him, too."

His confession was wrought with sadness, but no regret. There hadn't really been another option; Raif could see that himself. And he knew if he'd been in Kes's position; if that had been his child, Nalia's—he would have done the same. No question.

"What's her name?" Raif asked.

"Yasri."

A perfect name for a Ghan Aisouri—*yasri* were hearty wildflowers that bloomed in the heights of the Qaf, their petals a shimmering purple.

The love in Kes's voice when he said his daughter's name broke Raif's heart. He and Nalia would never have those children he'd dreamed up in the story he'd liked to tell her, time and again, when they imagined their future together. He'd never watch her belly grow, never see her hold their child in her arms.

Kes sighed. "I worried about what would happen when Ri got older, of course—when she came more fully into her power."

Raif nodded. He didn't need Kesmir to tell him what Calar would likely do to anyone—even her own child—who tried to take the throne from her.

"But then I met Thatur. And . . . and Taz," Kes continued. "For the first time, I feel like there's a way out, whether or not Calar dies."

"Why tell me this?" Raif asked.

"Because you loved a Ghan Aisouri. Because you grieved that dead child in the Marid village. Tazlim will be her guardian should anything happen to me—he's the only other person who knows about Yasri, other than Thatur and Yurik."

"Thatur will train her," Raif said.

"Yes. And I told Yurik because he's risked his life countless times to save Aisouri and I wanted to know that there was one person outside the *tavrai* who would be there should Yasri need help."

"Of course."

"I'm also telling you," Kesmir added, "because if Shirin or any other *tavrai* discover what Yasri is—and she can only hide her power for so long—they will want to kill her. To *murder* her just as I murdered my daughter's ancestors. And I need to know you won't let them."

"There's no question, Kes. I would never let them hurt her." He clapped a hand on his shoulder. "But you'll be around to take care of her, I'm sure of it."

"That's the plan," Kes said.

"Next time I see you, the gods willing, the war will be over."

Kes nodded. "There's one more thing."

Raif raised his eyebrows. What else could Kes possibly be hiding?

"There's a boy who works at the Dragon's Lair—do you know this place?"

Raif nodded—an Ifrit granter's shop.

"Quan is an orphan I took in. If I can't . . . care for him, will you keep an eye on him, make sure he's provided for?"

"Of course. We should bring him to the forest, anyway. When you get back, we'll get him together."

"Yes. When I get back." Kes placed his hand over his heart, relief softening the tightness of his mouth. *"Jahal'alund."*

As crimson evanescence filled the room, Raif returned the salute. *"Kajastriya revlim,"* he murmured.

25

ZANARI'S EYES FILLED WITH RARE TEARS AS SHE THREW her arms around her brother. "I'd almost given up hope," she whispered.

Raif hugged her tighter. "I knew you'd find your way back to Phara somehow," he said.

Not only was she going back to Earth, she finally had a chance to lead—Raif had just asked her to take over the *tavrai* on Earth and the mission to intercept the slave traders with their bottles.

"Come with me," she said, her face buried against his chest. They were on the banks of the River Sorrow and night was creeping in. "You don't have to stay, little brother."

He tightened his arms around her. "Yes I do," he said quietly.

Zanari pulled away. "What about the Brass Army? You only stand a chance if they stay."

"They'll stay," Raif said. "Taz assured me. Those who want to go back to Earth will leave after the war is over."

"Noqril?"

Raif was counting on Noqril's *fawzel* form to give Raif a bird's-eye view of all Ifrit troop movements.

"He's going to help you on Earth, then come back and fight with us," he said. "When it's all over, Yurik will help him through the tunnel, along with the Dhoma from the prison."

"Do you remember when we were on Earth you said that any jinni unwilling to fight for Arjinna wasn't allowed to come back?" she asked.

He squeezed her hand. "You're always welcome here, Zan. No matter what." His eyes fell to the River Sorrow, a salt river born of ancient tears. "There's no shame in wanting to leave—I know that now. I'd go in a second if . . . I were in your place. I used to think the highest honor was death. There's nothing wrong with deciding not to fight a battle you're likely to lose. It's okay to choose life instead of going out in a blaze of glory."

"That's just what Nalia would have said," Zanari said softly.

Raif smiled a little. "Guess she rubbed off on me."

"A year and a day," Zanari said, squeezing his hand. "You gonna be okay?"

"Nah. I'll never be okay—you know that."

They sat in silence a few minutes, Zanari's arm slung around his shoulder.

"You sure you don't want me to stay until you've done the ritual?" she asked, breaking the silence.

Touma was still waiting by the gate, but he refused to sing

the songs or light the elder pine fires. Not until Raif was ready. But he'd never be ready to see Nalia's spirit off. He told himself he would do the ritual after the battle was over. In truth, he waited because maybe he wouldn't have to do it at all. If he died in the battle, the last thing Raif wanted was Nalia's spirit to think he'd given up on her. He didn't want to sing those songs of farewell. Singing them would mean tearing her from his life for good. There was magic in the songs and the fires: they made those who grieved accept the jinni's death. They allowed you to move on— to fall in love again, to build a life without that person. And Raif didn't want to do that.

"I'll do it . . . soon," Raif said. "I've got too much on my mind right now. And if I go there tonight, it'll just mess me up."

This was all true, too: he had to stay focused. There were too many lives to save tonight.

"But you'll say good-bye to her after the battle?" she asked, real worry in her voice.

He shrugged. "Maybe. And I know what you're going to say, but can we not do this now?"

He knew Zanari thought he should move on. But that wasn't an option for him.

She sighed. "Okay."

He squeezed her shoulder. "Good."

The *widr* trees along the bank swayed in the wintry breeze, their willowlike branches skimming the surface of the water. Raif watched them, forcing his mind away from Nalia, away from his sister's departure. If he focused on the coming battle instead, this would all be easier, hurt less. He wondered how Kes was holding up in the palace, awaiting his chance to kill Calar. He could picture Yurik readying the tunnel, Taz organizing regiments, going over the plans with Jaqar and Shirin.

"Ready?" he asked as the stars above winked at him, too cheerful for what this night would bring.

"I've been ready to go home for a long time, little brother."

Earth was home to her now, but it didn't upset him as it once would have. He'd come to realize that there were things more important than the revolution, more important than making your dead father proud.

"Then we'd better get you there," he said.

He took her hand and, together, they evanesced to the Wish. They'd both been to the tunnel before, which was located through a trapdoor in the Wish's cellar. Zanari stood to the side while Raif opened the cellar door. He threw a ball of emerald light into the darkness and started down the stairs.

"I'm getting tired of all these dark journeys," Zanari muttered.

Raif smiled. "This should be the last one for a while yet." He froze as a blade glinted in the darkness. A pair of mismatched eyes narrowed.

"Better tell me who you are before I slit your throat," the jinni said. It was so dark, Raif could only make out the jinni's form. But few jinn had those *hagiz* eyes.

"It's Raif Djan'Urbi, Yurik."

The knife disappeared and a lantern turned on, the warm glow filling the cellar with dim light.

Yurik grinned. "Can't be too careful."

Onions and garlic-filled baskets dangled from the rafters, and the walls were lined with dusty bottles of *savri*. Barrels filled with potatoes and salted meat were stacked in one corner beside a canvas sack heavy with an assortment of weapons.

Yurik turned to Zanari. "You ready for this?"

"I've been ready since the minute I set foot on Arjinnan soil."

Yurik smiled, a sadness in the depths of his eyes. "Been thinking about heading back to Earth myself."

"Even though you were once on the dark caravan?" Raif asked, surprised.

"I'd like a chance to . . . start over," Yurik said.

Shirin. Why did she have to be so pigheaded?

"The more the merrier," Zanari said. She looked around, brow furrowing. "Where is everyone?"

"They're on their way," Yurik said. "I staggered the meeting times so no one would get suspicious. Not everyone's evanescing— no need to alert the Ifrit on patrol. There's . . . something else you need to know about."

Yurik gestured toward a dark corner of the room, and Raif went still as he took in a small group of jinn, each holding a sleeping child. Most of the children were babies, some not much older than three summers—

He turned to Yurik. "Are these . . . ?"

Yurik nodded. "All glamoured, just in case."

The Aisouri children.

"Holy gods and monsters," Zanari breathed. There were over a dozen of them.

Raif nodded to the families, who stared at him in terror. He knew what they were thinking: he was Raif Djan'Urbi, enemy of all Ghan Aisouri.

He placed a hand to his heart. "My *rohifsa* was an Aisouri. We will protect your children with our lives."

Their relief was palpable.

There was a shift in the air and the room suddenly filled with a dozen jinn—Brass soldiers and *tavrai*.

Yurik nodded to them in greeting. "You told them every ten minutes?" he asked a soldier.

The jinni nodded. "The next group will be here shortly."

Raif threw *chiaan* into the tunnel as he spoke. "Zan. When you get a chance, go find Saranya. Let her know we haven't forgotten about the dark caravan."

Raif hadn't been with Zanari and Nalia when they'd gone to visit Malek's sister-in-law, but they'd told him about the leader of the underground caravan.

"Good idea," Zanari said. "She'll be able to get the word out to the free jinn on Earth—maybe they'll help us." She frowned. "I'm not sure if I'm dreading telling her that Malek's dead or not."

"It sure as hell comforted me," he said.

Malek. The bottle. The ring. It all seemed so long ago.

"What's the plan?" another soldier asked.

Raif pointed to his sister. "Zanari will lead the charge when the slave traders enter through the tunnel. Kill them, take the bottles, then head for the Dhoma camp." It was time for him to go. *"Jahal'alund."*

"Jahal'alund," a chorus of voices answered.

"Good luck out there tonight," Yurik said.

Raif nodded. "You too. We'll all need it." He glanced once more at the Aisouri children. He wished Nalia could see this. "Guard them with your lives," he said to the soldiers in the room.

Before he left, Raif grabbed Zanari in a fierce hug. "I love you, Zan," he whispered.

"I love you, too, little brother." Her arms tightened around him. "Don't be a stranger, okay? Come visit us sometimes."

He pretended that was possible. Pretended he'd still be alive when the smoke cleared. "Sure. Give Phara a hug for me."

He kept his eyes on Zanari's until his evanescence took him away. Raif couldn't help but wonder if this was the last time he'd see his sister.

26

KES SLIPPED INTO HIS DAUGHTER'S ROOM AND WATCHED her sleep for several minutes, memorizing her.

Yasri lay in the middle of the bed, limbs splayed out, a thumb in her mouth. The nursery was warm—a small fire kept out the winter chill. Balls of dim red *chiaan* hung midair, providing just enough light for Yasri or the nanny to see without keeping her awake.

In one corner of the nursery sat a collection of dolls and toys. Kes would often sit with Yasri, watching her play, joining when she wanted him to. A thick rug with a pink rose pattern covered the whole floor. It was the room of a girl well loved.

A shadow formed behind the glass doors that led to Yasri's balcony, silent. Waiting. Kes moved forward and sat on the edge of Yasri's bed. He set down the dram that would keep her sleeping for several hours: he'd made sure it tasted like her favorite ice—sugarberry and vanilla.

Yasri sighed in her sleep and Kes reached down and picked her up, holding her against him. It was for her that he risked his life—tonight and all the nights before it—so that she could live in a world where darkness didn't reign.

"Wake up, *gharoof*," he said softly into the pink shell of her ear. He moved back the hair on her face with gentle fingers, pressed his lips against her rosy cheeks. "Yasri. Time to wake up, sweet one."

She stirred, her eyes opening slowly. Dark crimson, like vixen roses—no one would know she was an Aisouri, at least not for a good long while.

"Papa?" she said, her voice heavy with sleep.

"You know your papa loves you, right?"

She nodded as she reached up and put her hands around his neck.

"Do I get a kiss?" he asked.

She pressed damp lips to his cheek. "I'm tired, Papa."

"I know," he whispered. He reached for the dram. "I brought you a treat."

Her eyes opened wider at that. "What is it?"

"Magic," he said. "Drink this and you'll get to go on an adventure. Would you like that?"

She nodded, more awake now, eager.

He took the stopper off and held it to Yasri's lips with a shaking hand. "Drink it all up, little one."

She smacked her lips when the bottle was empty. "Where will

we go on our adventure?" she asked.

"You're going to see some good friends of mine. They know all about you. They're going to take care of you while Papa's working."

She frowned. "You're not coming with me?"

"I'll . . . I'll see you soon," he said. He had to stay alive for her—Kes couldn't bear for this to be their last moment.

It won't be, he reminded himself. He had let Calar take everything from him, but he'd be damned if she took this too.

He pressed his lips to her hair as Yasri's eyes grew heavy.

"Be a good girl, yes?"

She nodded.

"Papa loves you," he whispered once more, as her eyes closed and her body went slack.

He put the bottle in his pocket and, holding Yasri in one arm, made up the bed to look as though she were still in it, should the nanny look in. He wrapped Yasri in a soft blanket made of sea silk and wool. Then he grabbed the rucksack he'd filled with her favorite toys and some clothes.

He stood still, listening. He had to be quick. Kes opened the glass door. Thatur crouched on the balcony, Taz already sitting astride him. They'd been able to get through the *bisahm* because it didn't protect against gryphons. No one had sounded the alarm because the sentries on duty had been handpicked by Kes, all his own trusted soldiers who would be helping secure the palace once he killed Calar.

Taz's eyes lit up when he saw Yasri, and Thatur bowed low—of course. She was royalty, perhaps the next empress, if the Ghan

Aisouri were ever allowed to reign again.

Not likely, Kes thought. He and Taz had already decided that after the war, they would live as far away from the palace as possible.

"She's beautiful, Kes," Taz whispered as he held out his arms. It looked a bit like love at first sight, the way Taz gazed at her. "She looks just like you."

"Thank the gods," Thatur grumbled. "I never wish to see Calar again."

Kes planted a kiss on his daughter's forehead and then tilted his head to look up at Taz.

"I'll see you soon," Kes whispered against his lips.

"Yes," Taz agreed, "soon." He leaned forward, and his kiss was sweet and soft and held the promise of more and more and more.

"I love you," Taz said, so softly Kes might have imagined it, were it not for the look in his eyes.

Kes squeezed Taz's hand, then turned to Thatur. The only reason any of this was possible was because this gryphon had helped him—despite Kes being one of the Ifrit who had ruined his life.

"You're carrying everyone I love," Kes said. "I am forever in your debt."

Thatur met Kes's eyes.

If you don't show up to claim them, I'll be very angry with you, boy. I hope for your sake you do not have to see my wrath. It's terrible to behold.

Then Thatur winked. Kes smiled, shaking his head.

I shall do my best not to disappoint you, Kes thought in return.

Thatur gently placed one of his claws on Kes's shoulder. *The gods keep you.*

Taz held Yasri tight against him, his cheek resting on top of her head. With one flap of his wings, the gryphon rose into the sky, blending into the dark clouds. Kes knew it would be this image that would give him the courage to do what he had to do tonight: his daughter and the jinni he loved, flying to safety.

Kes watched them until they were little more than a speck, and then he watched a great deal longer.

Hours later, Kesmir lay awake beside Calar, afraid to breathe lest she awaken from her restless sleep. Several times his hand had reached for the dagger beneath his pillow, but he was certain, time and again, that she was still half awake. He didn't want her to know he'd been the one to kill her. She deserved that mercy.

It was well past midnight and Kes knew the bottles were being transported as he lay there waiting to kill the jinni who'd once been his best friend, who he'd thought was his *rohifsa*. The *tavrai* and the Dhoma would be fighting on Earth now, cutting down the slave traders. Kes hadn't been awakened by the guards, so he had to assume his plan had worked, and the jinn who were going through the portal to fight on the other side had made it through without detection. Taz, he knew, was waiting for Kes's signal—sparks of white *chiaan* above the palace. This would be the Brass Army's signal to charge the prison and take it over, freeing the remaining jinn.

He whispered her name—if she didn't respond, he would do it. He would kill her.

"Calar."

He could hear the terror in his voice, might as well have announced his intentions. She mumbled something incoherent and turned over.

Do it now, he said to himself.

He closed his eyes, saw Taz's golden ones. Saw him holding Yasri. Failure wasn't an option.

Kes sat up and slipped the dagger out from under his pillow. The metal glinted in the light from the flame that burned continually in the corner. He could see his reflection in it, misery and terror written all over his face.

He eased onto his knees, looking down at her. Calar's hair was splayed across the pillow, her face relaxed, innocent. Cold and beautiful, skin and lips and eyes he'd once covered with gentle kisses. The face that had saved him.

"Hello," the little girl says, her gloved hand outstretched. Her ruby eyes seem to take the full measure of him in one glance.

Behind her, his village burns, the dead slaughtered outside their homes, left there to rot. The wind still carries the cries of his family. He doesn't take her hand, just stares at her. The wound the Aisouri have given him pulses with pain—it is the only thing he feels.

"Come," she says, beckoning. "I want to show you something."

He takes her hand and she leads him down to the fire lake.

Its surface is still, the lava shimmering in the late-afternoon sun.

"Look," she whispers.

There, in the center of the lake, blooms a lotus, its delicate petals open to the sky. Impossible that it should live or grow here, but there it is.

Something passes over the boy's face, a fleeting joy, but then it's gone.

"I have a special power," the girl says. Her voice is soft and gentle. Later, he will realize she is only soft and gentle with him. "I can see inside minds. I know you can't talk right now, but my father is the shirva and he needs to know what happened. He will avenge your family. Your friends."

The boy simply looks at her. She is beautiful, shining against this stark background of death and destruction.

The girl slips off her gloves. Later, she will tell him how her hands ached to touch him then. She couldn't say why, except that he was beautiful and his sadness tore at her heart, a heart she didn't even know existed until right then.

"May I?" she asks.

He nods slightly, curious.

The girl reaches up and gently places her fingertips on his temples. He gasps as their chiaan merges.

"This doesn't hurt, does it?" she asks, anxious. "I'm still learning."

His eyes meet hers and he shakes his head. He wants her to touch him forever. For a moment, he can't look away. Her eyes are like dark rubies, with flecks of amber. He allows her chiaan to seep into him. He can feel the twisted bits inside her, the secret shames. She is the mind reader, but for a moment it feels like he has the power. The boy reaches up his hands and places his palms over hers. Now it is her turn to gasp as he floods into her. His energy is dark, like hers, but laced with a gentle calm. To her, she later tells him, he will always be the lotus in the fire lake: fragile and yet strong enough to survive.

This is what the girl sees when she enters his mind: Blood. Everywhere. Screams, the kind only animals make. Purple chiaan and the calm cold of the Aisouri on their gryphons as they cut down everything in their path. A baby sliced down the middle with a scimitar. Fire and mud and the stench of death.

The girl shudders and the boy grips her hands.

He feels her go deeper. He is a pool and she pushes down, down.

The scimitar, slicing into his face.

The girl goes deeper.

The boy, younger now, running with a friend. "Kesmir, come back!" Alesh yells.

Kesmir stops and turns, grinning.

Behind him is the village, whole and unburned. Lava spurts into the sky from the nearby volcano, but it's an unusually sunny day in Ithkar and the landscape's fierce beauty is softened by the appearance of the sun.

The boy grips the girl's hands harder, the memory suffocating. His body begins to shake and he feels her pull away, closer to the surface of his mind. There: a body on the hard-packed dirt as the fires rage. Alesh.

The girl opens her eyes. Tears roll down the boy's face and she *brings her lips closer, kissing each tear as it slips out of his eyes. His hands slide up her arms, into her hair, and he buries his face in her neck. She wraps her arms around him and holds him close to her and he somehow knows she is home now and she will never leave him. How can this—this—come from something so horrible?*

Kes gripped the dagger harder. The blade was now inches from her heart. His eyes filled and he let the tears slide down his face without shame, just like on the banks of his village's fire lake so long ago. They fell on Calar's face like rain. Her eyes snapped open and Kes froze, the blade suspended above her heart, his mind going blank with fear. She took in the dagger, his face, uncomprehending. He saw the moment when Calar understood what was about to happen: it swept across her face like a storm, a desperate unfathomable sadness giving way to instinct.

Now.

Kes drove the dagger into the space between them, but she was faster, rolling out from under him as the blade plunged into the mattress.

He leaped up, grabbing her arm roughly as she tried to run from him. She had the power, he had the strength. He pressed her back against his chest and brought the blade toward her throat.

Don't think about it, don't think about it—

"Yasri," she gasped, her voice filled with pain.

That was all the time she needed. In the split second that Kes faltered at the sound of his daughter's name, Calar let out a tortured scream, as though her soul were being ripped apart. She didn't bother to run from him or wrest the dagger out of his hand. She didn't need to.

He resisted her with everything he had, pushing his psychic energy against hers. He could feel her frustration, her anger at not being able to hurt him. It was the first time his mind had been locked to her. He strained against the onslaught of her power, every second of his training being brought to bear on this moment. She pushed against his consciousness like a battering ram. He held out for nearly five minutes—an infinite amount of time—and then she broke through. His head exploded with pain immediately—his skull bashing against rocks, his brain ground underfoot, knives carving him open. No amount of training could have prepared him for this. Kes's eyes rolled into the back of his head and his body seized up and dropped heavily to the floor as thick, dark blood poured from his nose, eyes, ears, and mouth. He forgot about the dagger, about the war, about everything, because all that existed now was agony.

He could feel himself letting go, his mind desperate to separate itself from the awareness of pain in his body. Dimly, he heard Calar sobbing one word over and over: *why, why, WHY?* His eyes were little more than two slits, enough to see her on her knees, her face ravaged by rage and grief. She reached out and pulled something off his chest—the *yaghin* meant to protect him from her shadows—and threw it across the room. Then she held up the *yaghin* at her neck and brought the stone to her lips, hands shaking, tears streaming down her face.

You and Ri are the one good thing.

Just as Kes began to go, to fade into that shadowy land that was pulling him into its embrace, he heard the most terrifying sound in the world:

"Sahai."

His fingers twitched against the marble floor. Once, twice, and then they were still. A last, agonized gasp escaped his lips and crimson *chiaan* slipped out of his skin, hovering over Kes as the first of Calar's shadows descended on him.

27

ZANARI CROUCHED BEHIND A LOW SAND DUNE, HER EYES glued to the portal. It was nearly impossible for her to remain silent, to sit still. She felt as though she'd been swimming in a sea of emotion for the past ten hours. Joy and adrenaline and guilt and fear and fury roiled within her. She'd lost her brother but gained Phara. She was leaving Arjinna behind—maybe forever— and now all of Earth was hers to explore.

But first, she had to kill a few slave traders.

She leaned forward as several figures emerged from the shimmering cut between the realms that bled *chiaan* like a wound. Zanari turned to the rows of Brass soldiers who stood in a shallow valley of sand behind her, waiting for her signal to ambush the traders. A shadow crossed over the moonlit sand and she looked up: Noqril, returning from his reconnaissance. He landed before evanescing behind a large dune, so that the smoke wouldn't be visible; then he made his way to her, crouched low.

"How many?" Zanari whispered as he came to join her.

"Ten traders, but they're being guarded by a battalion of Ifrit," Noqril said, breathing heavily. He'd been in the air for hours, going between Earth and Arjinna to keep track of the traders.

"Godsdammit," she muttered. "What do you think?"

"We'll likely suffer casualties, but we'll get the bottles in the end," he said. "It's your call."

How many times had Zanari seen her brother in this exact situation? Weighing the balance of lives lost to lives saved. It had never been easy for him—it kept him up nights—but she'd had no idea how heavy that burden felt. It was a physical weight on her heart. She glanced at the jinn behind her. How many would lose their lives tonight?

"All right," she said. "We have to do it."

Noqril nodded. "I agree."

Zanari stood, her *chiaan* pulsing inside her, and sent sparks from her fingertips—the signal to charge. A cloud of jade evanescence swirled beneath her feet. Behind her, she could see the evanescence of her fellow soldiers, every caste represented. This— right here—this was why she'd finally had to leave Arjinna. The *tavrai* saw the Ifrit and Shaitan in their midst as necessary evils, but to Zanari and the Dhoma, they were equal and their sacrifices honorable.

The evanescence took her, and seconds later, Zanari was at the portal and launching herself at the nearest slave trader, an Ifrit in expensive leathers and with teeth made of gold. He cried out, dropping his sack of bottles in the sand as he scrambled away from her.

"Not so fast, brother," she called.

Zanari threw laser-sharp daggers of *chiaan* at his back and he fell to the sand, the wind knocked out of him. She slit his throat and had already turned to the next trader before his body went still.

Zanari became a maelstrom, a frenzy of blood and sand and cries of rage. *You are a sword, nothing more,* she chanted to herself, again and again. The thought of dying so close to Phara, without the healer even knowing she was there, was too horrible to contemplate. She had to make it through this.

Blood coated her hands and her clothes. This gore—the stink of death all around her—was what Raif had been trying to save her from all those times he'd forbidden her to join in his skirmishes with the Ifrit.

A ball of fiery *chiaan* hit her in the back and Zanari fell to the sand face-first, excruciating pain racing down her spine. She gasped and it was as if she'd drawn half the desert into her mouth with that one breath. Zanari gagged, rolling onto her back just as a scimitar came down onto the sand, barely missing her body. The trader stood above her, eyes full of fury.

Screw honor, she thought. She rolled once more and her body flew down the nearest dune. Running away—rolling away—wasn't what Raif would have done, but Zanari wasn't her brother. She wanted to stay alive more than she wanted to win the love of the jinn she commanded. There was a shout and Zanari looked up from where she lay at the bottom of the dune. Noqril had returned to his *fawzel* form and had pecked out the eyes of the trader, and a Brass soldier finished him off, blasting the Ifrit with his *chiaan*. Noqril flew down to where Zanari lay. He evanesced in midair, landing nimbly on his feet, a regular jinni once more.

"You gonna bite my head off if I pick you up?" he asked.

Ever since they'd met on the *Sun Chaser*, the sand ship that had brought Zanari and Raif to the Dhoma camp over a summer ago, he'd been trying to bed Zanari. She'd rebuffed his advances with narrowed eyes, scoffing, and cutting remarks.

She smiled now, grateful for this oaf of a jinni who had saved her life. "Just don't grab my ass," she said.

Noqril laughed as he leaned down and gently picked her up. Pain shot through her as grains of sand settled into her wound.

"Looks like we need to get you to a healer," he said, once more flashing his wicked, lascivious grin.

She smiled back at him. "Looks like it."

It wasn't how she'd planned to surprise Phara, but Zanari would take what she could get.

By the time Noqril made his way back up the dune, the roar of battle had died down and there was no one left to kill. The sand was littered with the dead of both sides, large sacks of bottles sitting between them like treasure. The few Ifrit left had retreated back through the portal, where they would be cut down by Kes's jinn who waited there for them. It was over. Zanari had won the first battle she'd ever commanded, lacerated back and all.

The sky had lightened to the soft gray of the rabbits that raced through the Forest of Sighs, velvet wisps of dawn. The remains of her little army were already gathering the sacks of bottles.

"Who has first watch?" Noqril asked.

Zanari had promised Raif that there would always be a small company of soldiers near the portal to help refugees as they made the crossing, as well as to intercept any slave traders.

"We'll keep a squad of Brass soldiers here for now," Zanari said.

Noqril nodded. "When we get to the camp, I'll organize shifts for the *fawzel* before we head back to Arjinna." They would need their bird's-eye view for security now more than ever.

Zanari's stomach turned as she thought of her brother, waiting to fight his own battle. She wasn't much for praying, but she'd gotten down on her knees to Tirgan for hours, begging him to protect Raif. She wouldn't be able to rest until the battle for the prison was over and she knew he'd made it out.

Noqril looked down at her, his eyes soft. "Ready to go home?" he asked.

"Yeah, I am," Zanari said.

She glanced through the portal as Noqril's evanescence pooled beneath his feet. Through the thin membrane between the worlds she caught a glimpse of moonlight, though she couldn't see the Widows themselves. Somewhere over that range, Raif would soon be fighting for the Dhoma, fighting for the land he belonged to. Zanari didn't stop looking until Noqril's evanescence took her away.

In the year since they'd left the Dhoma lands to travel across the Eye and fight a losing battle in Arjinna, Phara had been busy.

Zanari, still propped up in Noqril's arms, stared at the camp. There was no sign of the Ifrit destruction from a year earlier, when the homes of the Dhoma had been reduced to nothing more than scattered articles on the desert floor.

Towering sand dunes that formed a natural valley bordered the camp and a large lake sat on its eastern boundary. Improbably high tents of several stories squatted in the sand, with Moroccan lamps of colored glass and lacy metalwork shining from poles planted in the sand before each family's doorway. The light spilled across the sand, the colors reminding her of the aurora. A large bonfire burned continuously in the center. Zanari had fond memories of sitting among the Dhoma and listening to their stories and songs. The last bonfire, though, had been fraught with conflict and fear. Nalia, insisting they could make it through the Eye; Yezhud, Samar's wife, blaming the Aisouri for the loss of so many Dhoma during the search for the sigil.

The anticipation of finally seeing Phara again was dimmed by the loss of Samar and the grief his wife would carry on her heart.

"How do we want to tell Yezhud about Samar?" she asked Noqril.

He sighed. "I'll do it. But first, let's get you to the healer's tent."

Zanari nodded, guilty for feeling so relieved. Her back felt as though it were on fire, and it was only the desire to reach the Dhoma camp that had kept her going. Sweat had broken out on her forehead and Noqril looked down in concern as she began to shiver.

"Better hurry, brother," she gasped.

He started down the dune they'd been standing on, heading toward the center of camp, followed by the Brass soldiers who'd begun evanescing all around them, many carrying large sacks filled with bottles. It was slow going as Noqril made his way down the dune. Every step seemed to vibrate through her, and Zanari bit her lip to keep the screams inside. She whimpered, pressing her forehead against his chest.

"Almost there, sister."

When Noqril stood at the bottom of the dune, Zanari's eyes moved toward the farthest corner of the camp, where a small tent stood on its own, a lamp in the shape of a red star swinging from the pole in front of its flap, which was open. *Finally,* she thought. *Finally.*

Noqril hurried toward the tent, and when he reached its entrance, she took a ragged breath, suddenly nervous. What if Phara had moved on, given up on her? It'd been a year. What if they were just too different—Zanari, temperamental as the wind, Phara as calm as a still lake. A soft humming came from inside and she could hear the sounds of someone moving about in an unhurried late-night routine.

You just crossed through a portal and fought a battle to get here, she thought. *If she doesn't love you for that, then there's nothing else you can do.*

Noqril ducked inside. The tent had been re-created so that it looked just as Zanari remembered it. Warm candlelight, the scent of herbs hanging out to dry, a slight medicinal tang. Thick rugs, two beds: one for Phara, another for patients. The humming stopped and the room began to spin and darken around the edges. There was a soft gasp and the thud of something falling to the floor. Then Zanari saw her: golden Shaitan eyes wide, a wooden bowl of sage at her feet, the leaves scattered on the rug. Her dark hair lay over her shoulders, longer now. The white healer's robes she always wore outlined the soft swell of her breasts, the gentle hourglass of her hips. Phara was the most beautiful thing Zanari had ever seen.

Before Zanari could get a word out, Phara was across the room. She stood beside her, tears streaming down her face. Every fear that she'd made the wrong decision swept out of Zanari as Phara grabbed her hand and the healer's *chiaan* collided with her own. That was all she needed. She smiled.

"Hey," Zanari whispered.

The darkness on the edges of her vision took over and the last thing she saw was Phara's lips, saying her name.

Zanari woke to the sounds of early morning in the Dhoma camp: the clank of pots and pans for breakfast, the laughter of children, morning greetings as jinn passed the healer's tent.

She was lying on her stomach, her cheek against a pillow that smelled of lavender and sage. The pain in her back had all but disappeared, the agonizing burn now a cool tingle.

She heard a soft rattle and her eyes traveled to the other side of the tent, where Phara, her back turned, was brewing a pot of tea.

"Good morning," Zanari whispered.

Phara whirled around and a smile broke over her face as she rushed across the room and knelt beside Zanari's bed. The sight of her was too much: Zanari's eyes pooled over and Phara reached out, wiping her tears away with the back of her finger, then leaned closer, so close their lips were nearly touching. She smelled just as she always had: roses, the desert—whatever starlight smelled like. How many times had Zanari tried to conjure that scent on lonely nights in Arjinna? She'd been so scared of forgetting it.

"Don't ever leave me again," Phara said, the words tumbling out of her. "If you need me to go back with you, I will. I swear it. The moment you went into the Eye, I realized how stupid I'd been and I screamed your name, but you'd all evanesced at once and I was . . . standing in the middle of the desert. You were gone, just . . . gone."

Zanari shifted into a sitting position and pressed her lips against Phara's because she couldn't wait even a second longer. They were warm and soft and sweet.

"I'm staying," Zanari whispered. "Here. With you." She reached out and ran her hand through Phara's lustrous black hair, down her neck, stopping at the top button of her *rohifsa*'s dress. As soon as her back was healed, Zanari would take that dress off and pull Phara into the bed and they wouldn't get out for days and days and days. "I'm not going anywhere you're not," she said.

The change that came over Phara's face was instantaneous— startled joy, like a child seeing Arjinna's aurora for the first time.

It felt as though a flock of birds had scattered and taken flight inside Zanari's chest, soaring.

"You won't miss your home too much?" Phara asked, voice trembling.

Zanari's jade eyes met Phara's golden ones. "How can I miss my home when I'm here already?"

Nalia didn't know how long she'd been following the phoenix through the Eye, but it'd been a long time. Every now and then she'd call out to Raif, hoping he would come back, hoping he would rescue her this time. But he never did.

The nectar of the heart plant burned through her, a scorching river that turned the universe inside out, stars below, sea above. Despite her longing for Raif, she was somehow filled with a sense of well-being, cradled in the palm of a god's hand. Her spirit flew outside her body, dancing, leaping beyond the borders of self, connected to the source of chiaan, her very essence infused with the breath of the universe, all time and space flowing through her; she was infinite.

Bright lights that undulated like a storm-tossed sea suddenly appeared before her, thrown into the Eye like confetti. Rainbow prisms shot out of the dead earth. Sweet delirium. She began to spin, faster and faster, a whirling dervish, her arms outstretched, welcoming the shower of light. This was different. Not her usual day in the Eye.

A road appeared, the gray floor of the Eye dissolving, those awful clouds of hopelessness blowing away, revealing the underneath: a soft, tissue-like substance, flesh of the worlds, raw and pulsing. The white phoenix settled on her shoulder, a delicate weight despite her size, and together they floated down the road, wingless flight. The phoenix's light surrounded Nalia, as though she were in the center of a crystal that shimmered, a torch.

The phoenix sang the old songs, her trill manna from the gods. They traveled for days and days, not stopping to rest for long periods of time, as they usually did. Though Nalia was still wrapped in the warm arms of the heart plant, the phoenix placed more leaves on her tongue. Nalia could feel the evil on the other side of the Eye more strongly with each passing day: Arjinna, crying out to her, a wordless call that settled deep inside her, a burning heaviness that grew and grew.

Home, she would say to the phoenix.

Not yet. This reply would always be in the form of a song, sometimes familiar, sometimes not.

Nalia began to grow feverish: something was changing—she could feel the shift in their journey. She was hot, then cold, and once her heart stopped altogether. Sometimes there was music— old serf tunes played by an invisible musician.

Sometimes Nalia sang along. Three widows weeping all the night, three widows lost their hearts. Three widows mourn the suns that died, their once and only loves.

She thought she saw Arjinna's three moons and she ran, gray dust kicking up all around her, Nalia's hands reaching out and up, only to see them suddenly disappear. She stared in the direction they'd gone, her heart cracking and breaking because Raif Raif Raif.

"Raif," she said out loud, the sound of her voice strange— faint and shattered.

For so long Nalia had stopped when the phoenix stopped, and when the bird rested, she rested. She'd lost all sense of time.

After several days or months or years, she didn't know, the dead empresses of Arjinna joined her on the road, a silent caravan of souls.

One by one they approached her from the darkness, the Amethyst Crown gleaming on each of their heads, shimmering diadems that helped light the way. Each regarded Nalia as silently as the phoenix. Nalia recognized them from her years of study, engravings in the stone of the palace come to life.

Then: a beam of light that shot up so high Nalia couldn't see where it ended. Faint at first, then brighter. Far away, high on a blackened hill, a tree hovered above the earth, suspended in midair, white light pooling beneath and above it. Its branches twisted and curved like thick vines, and each of its many leaves hung like golden fruit.

Tree of life, tree of wisdom, tree of untold power, *sang the phoenix.*

"B'alai Lote," *Nalia breathed. The Great Lote, yet another legend come to life.*

Despite the incredible things she'd seen and done, this was perhaps the most impossible of them all. The old stories spoke of a lote tree with leaves made of pure gold, a tree that gave those who found it wisdom. It held the secret of existence in its very branches, and its sap was capable of healing all ailments. She had seen it countless times, but only as a symbol: its likeness was carved into the wall behind the Ghan Aisouri throne.

Nalia followed the phoenix, and when she settled beneath the branches on a patch of soft, black sand, Nalia did the same. The tree glowed all around her, emitting a constant, almost indiscernible sigh. Nalia rested her palm against its smooth bark. It was warm, and beneath it, she could feel the unmistakable pulse of a beating heart.

As each empress approached her, Nalia sat, cross-legged, a silent initiate in the mysteries of power. One by one the empresses placed an index finger against the space between her eyes—the third eye. Each time, she felt a tingling, burning sensation and then she would fall deep into whatever memory the spirit before her wished to pass down to Arjinna's next empress.

Eila, the first Aisouri empress, looks out over a wide plain in the Djan Valley, her eyes full of violet fire. Dark smoke rises up from the Qaf Mountains. Below, the castes fight one another, brutal tribal conflicts over grains of wheat and bits of rock.

"We are the only ones who can stop this," Eila says to the Aisouri. "Why else would we be given such vast power? It is the will of the gods that we bring peace to this land. We are their daughters." She turned to the violet-eyed soldiers behind her. "It is time to take our inheritance."

Hazal stands before the Ifrit shirza, a jade dagger in her hand. The throne gleams behind her, the Amethyst Crown glitters on her head. "Trespass on our land again and I will not be so kind."

She slits the throat of the woman beside the shirza, and he howls with grief as his rohifsa's blood spills across the marble floor.

Gisaem stands before a young Aisouri. Nalia would recognize the girl anywhere. "Antharoe, you must get that ring. Hide it where it will never be found."

Luxel, weeping over the body of a beaten serf. "This must stop," she says to the gryphon beside her.

"It is the only way to control them, My Empress."

They came, fifteen in all, young and old, all radiating an ancient, deadly power. The memories of their rule flowed through Nalia, filling her with grief and revulsion, awe and terror. The past lay before her, a living thing. Malleable.

The last empress knelt before Nalia and took her hands in her own. Nalia gasped when she saw her face. Antharoe did not speak, though her eyes were fixed on Nalia's. She leaned forward, kissing each of Nalia's palms, then twined her fingers through Nalia's so that their palms pressed against one another. Antharoe's chiaan pulsed through her, a power so vast that Nalia was certain she wouldn't survive the exchange. Her Aisouri tattoos began to glow and as they did Antharoe leaned forward, her lips touching Nalia's, filling her with breath. And Nalia understood: this was a coronation, a passing of the torch.

"It was never supposed to be me!" she cried. "I was the only one to survive. I wasn't chosen, I'm not worthy."

Who would have ruled if the Ghan Aisouri had not been slaughtered that night over three summers ago?

No matter: one by one the empresses fell to their knees and bowed their heads. Before Nalia could say another word, they disappeared, leaving nothing behind but the faint scent of amber.

The phoenix rose into the air, hovering. Nalia stood.

"What?" she yelled. "What do you want from me?"

Wisdom favors the humble, *she sang.* Wisdom favors the brave.

Nalia stared at the lote tree, helpless. The phoenix drew closer; then her beak darted toward Nalia's wrist. Nalia cried out as a sharp pain shot up her arm and blood dripped from her wrist onto the tree's roots. The lote shivered, a conscious creature that beckoned her closer as a sudden gust of wind pushed her from behind.

Her forehead fell against one of the tree's thick roots that dangled toward the sand. Darkness overtook Nalia, but this sleep was an awakening. She could feel herself growing, expanding, stretching beyond all limits of existence. Suddenly she was the tree, roots pushing deep into the center of the worlds, floating upon a river of light. As Nalia peered into the clear waters of the river's undulating waves, she saw her life, droplets of water in a fast-moving current: the past, the present, the future all roiling together, Arjinna hanging in the balance. The Three Widows, each one full and blazing. A wall of water stretching over the land. Shadows and death and an end if she was not its beginning. An obsidian palace and rivers of fire. Ash and blood. She saw herself planting a seed with Raif by her side. The seed became a tree, its roots extending in all directions, traveling deep under Arjinna. Nalia felt the burn of a new set of shackles encircling her wrists, the weight of a crown on her head.

Daughter of the gods, awake.

She bolted upright with a gasp. Suspended in the air above her was a single golden seed. Nalia reached out and plucked it from the air. It glowed on her palm, pulsing with life. She studied it for a long moment. As she went to secure the lote tree's gift in the small pouch at her waist, she paused, staring at the transformation she had undergone while under the lote's spell. Gone were her bloodied rags that smelled of evil filth. Nalia now wore the purple sawala of the Aisouri, palace clothing made of gossamer sea silk.

She looked up. The phoenix sat on a branch of the tree, waiting. Nalia frowned, the dream still inside her, more than memory. She bent her forehead to the tree in thanks, and its chiaan flowed into her, gifting Nalia with its wisdom. She once again saw herself planting the seed, feeling the rush of chiaan and the weight of the crown on her head, the bite of shackles as they braceleted her wrists.

The tree.

The crown.

The shackles.

What did it mean? Then she felt a tug, so like Malek's summons that it was uncanny.

Arjinna.

Arjinna.

Arjinna.

Nalia rested her hand on her stomach. The tug became stronger, like an excited child pulling her hand. It was impossible, unbelievable. But soon there was no doubt.

Arjinna was summoning her.

28

SHIRIN STOOD ON A THIN LEDGE ON THE NORTH SIDE OF
the Qaf range, her hair blowing behind her in the gust of sulphuric
wind that howled past. To the west lay the prison compound that
held the Dhoma and countless other innocent jinn. In a matter of
minutes, Shirin would be evanescing to its stone gate. Her *chiaan*
skittered through her, ready for the rush of a fight.

The clouds covering the moons finally drifted away and Shirin stared at the sky, open-mouthed. Each of the Three Widows
was full, like overripe fruit that dangled from invisible branches.

"Holy gods and monsters," she breathed.

The Godsnight. An ancient prophecy no one ever thought
would come true was somehow unfolding tonight, of all nights.
Shirin wasn't sure if it was perfect timing or the end of all time.
She'd grown up with the stories of how someday the gods would

return to Arjinna, their messenger the Widows themselves. Not in all of jinn history had the three been full on the same night, so there was no mistaking the sign.

A shiver crawled over Shirin's skin. Had Calar brought this upon them with her abominations? The *Sadranishta* made it clear that whatever the gods had in store for them was going to be bad. The jinn holy book did tend to exaggerate, but even a tamer version of "destruction leads to life anew" didn't bode well for any of them. The prophecy had come from a seer over a hundred thousand years ago. The Godsnight, according to the seer, would be a night of magic unlike any the realm had ever seen, disaster and potential wrought from the phenomenon of all three moons being full at the same time. But the holy book hadn't been written by the gods, it'd been written by jinn, so who knew what was actually going to happen? Perhaps the whole thing was just a *pajai* taking artistic license. The temple priests weren't known for their literal interpretations of the universe. Then again, *plagues will tear the land asunder* was another part of the prophecy that, if not true, was unnecessarily overdramatic. If the seer who'd seen the Godsnight in a vision all those centuries ago had interpreted his vision correctly, then the realm—and everyone in it—was screwed.

The *tavrai* were always superstitious before a battle—this did them no favors. Shirin needed her soldiers to be focused, to be swords themselves. She was always telling them not to over-think, to stay out of their heads and in their bodies, aware of every breath, every muscle's movement, how they held their scimitars, how they replenished their *chiaan*. But all the training in the worlds wasn't going to make her soldiers suddenly forget the gods might be smiting them at any moment.

She scanned the scene below. The Brass Army waited in the shadows on the Ithkar side—just over a thousand jinn, all that was left after a year of living among Calar's shadows. Behind her, on the Arjinnan side, stood another thousand jinn—*tavrai* and any other jinni who could stand on two legs and wanted to fight.

To the east, she could just make out the spires of the Cauldron in the moons' bloody, sulphur-tinged light. Raif was a fool for thinking Arjinna could be one big happy jinn family. The Ifrit weren't suddenly going to become just and good because Calar was gone. They'd spent centuries killing the Djan, the Marid. And they hated the Shaitan just as much as Shirin did. Raif kept saying that this—tonight—would be the last battle of the war. But Shirin knew better. It would be the last battle of *this* war. The next war would start tomorrow, when the Ifrit decided they still wanted to be in power.

But who would Raif be if not an idealist?

Raif. How many times had she prayed to the gods to take away her love? Though he'd certainly warmed up to her, even allowed, in recent months, the few times she'd dared to be affectionate, she knew he was far from giving her his heart. But she didn't need his whole heart, much as she wanted it. Shirin wished she had the guts to tell Raif that even if he could only ever give her a tiny fraction of the love he felt for his Aisouri, that would be enough. He would never get over Nalia, she knew that. She'd be insane to think otherwise. But Nalia was gone and Shirin was here. She held on to the memory of what had happened last month—briefly perfect and endlessly painful and something that still gave her hope, even when it shouldn't.

She'd come upon Raif sitting against a tree deep in the forest. For once, he looked at peace. Green swirls of *chiaan* crawled up his arms and he was gazing at the bit of moonlight that slipped past the thick branches of the elder pines. Shirin drew closer and he looked up, really *looked* at her for once. He smiled and patted the thick carpet of moss he was sitting on. They sat like that for a long time, silent. She breathed deeply of his earthy, sandalwood scent. Felt wisps of his *chiaan* on her skin as his palms sat against the moss, replenishing his magic. A breeze blew past, carrying the soft cry of a *lasa* bird. It was said that when two jinn heard the *lasa*, they would fall in love. Just a story, but right then, she let herself believe it.

Shirin turned to him and gently tilted his face toward hers, just the tips of her fingers on his chin. His eyes were glassy, warring between his love for Nalia and the comfort of Shirin. She didn't pretend he loved her now. But she knew she could ease his pain, be the one he found shelter in. He didn't move away as she leaned in and pressed her lips to his. Instead of breaking off the kiss as she assumed he would, Raif's lips parted, tentative at first, then more certain. His hands reached up, his fingers tangling in her hair. Joy like she had never known pulsed through her and she let herself move closer to him, to taste the mint leaves he must have been chewing before she arrived, her tongue against his, her arms around his neck. She didn't mind the beard, the way it scratched her chin, because it meant he'd been there, so close, so real. His lips were soft and hungry, and when she pulled him down on top of her, he met her urgency, his hand snaking up her shirt, gently gripping her ribs, and for a moment, Shirin was the happiest jinni who had ever lived.

Until he whispered, "Nalia."

They both froze and he pushed himself off her, scrambling back as though she were one of the forest's nighttime predators. And it was only then that she realized she hadn't felt his *chiaan* as he kissed her. She'd let herself open up to him, had given him all that longing and love and desire, but he hadn't given her that energy of his that her blood craved. She'd only felt the echo that always happened when two jinn touched each other.

"Shir, I'm sorry," he said, shaking his head, as though coming out of a dream. A nightmare. "I . . . can't. I'm sorry, but I can't."

She lay there on the moss, chest heaving, and covered her eyes with her hands. "Go," she whispered. "Just go."

Once she heard him walk away, she curled into the moss, her hot tears slipping into it. The moss thickened, pushing itself up so that she was lost in the crevice of a soft series of mounds. *Jolip*, a plant that brought healing to the brokenhearted. That, she realized, was why Raif had been sitting there. Why he'd even, for a moment, allowed her to kiss him. It hadn't been him, but the moss, trying to stitch their shredded hearts. Shirin sobbed until, exhausted, she fell asleep, cradled in those soft emerald arms.

Now, as her eyes traveled over Ithkar, preparing herself for battle, she held one thought in her mind: the fact that Raif had even sought out the moss told her he was trying to move on. And she'd be there waiting when he finally did.

A swirl of golden evanescence appeared beside her: Taz, back from inspecting his troops.

"Can you believe this shit?" she asked, when his smoke cleared. She gestured toward the offending sky. The aurora, for once, paled in comparison to the moons, the colors muted by the blazing light.

Taz's eyes shifted upward, his face filled with a momentary rapture. "It's amazing. I never thought I'd live to see a prophecy come true. Then again, I wasn't expecting to live for quite so long."

"This isn't amazing! It could, I don't know, kill all of us, destroy the realm—who knows? You spent way too much time meditating in that bottle, Mystic."

Taz smiled at the nickname the Brass Army had given him. "It's the only way I survived."

Shirin would never understand how Taz could still believe in the gods' benevolence when everything pointed against it.

"Are we good at the palace?" she asked.

"Kesmir said he'll do it when she's sleeping. Should be any time now." The worry was plain in Taz's voice.

"What about his soldiers?" she asked.

"They're in place," he said. "As soon as we see the signal, we go. Thatur is staying close to the palace to assist Kesmir—no doubt he'll be in for a fight once word gets out about Calar."

"And if we don't see the signal?" she asked.

Shirin was only half confident that Kesmir would succeed in killing Calar. More likely, she'd take him down and then where would they be? She'd never thought this was a good plan, but it was the one Raif was stubbornly sticking to, so she was here, awaiting his orders.

"We're to wait until dawn," Taz said. "If Kes doesn't . . . if he can't . . ." He swallowed, his eyes shifting behind him, to where the palace overlooked the Infinite Lake. "We still go with the plan." He pointed to the sky. "Unless, of course, they have anything to say about it."

"And I'm sure they do," she muttered. "You seen Raif anywhere?" He should have been here by now, preparing to advance.

As if on cue, a burst of green evanescence shot out of the air—Raif, finally.

"You good?" she asked as he strode toward them.

"Define *good*." Raif gave them a grim smile as he pulled out his scimitar, his eyes scanning the desolate landscape of Ithkar. He seemed to be purposely ignoring the moons above.

"*Good* is we pull off the greatest prison break in the history of jinn and live to tell about it," she said.

"Then I'm good." Raif glanced at her. "Godsnight or no, we're going in there."

She nodded. "Understood."

This was why Raif was always the best soldier on the field: he didn't care about anything but the fight. Even ancient prophecies and the threat of plagues from the gods didn't distract him from the task at hand.

Raif gently clapped Taz on the back. "He'll be okay. We're gonna see that sign over the palace any minute now."

Taz nodded. "I hope so."

In the distance, Shirin could make out Noqril in his *fawzel* form. He'd returned from the skirmish with the slave traders on Earth and would remain here until the battle was over. His birds-eye vantage point on what went down on the earth below gave the *tavrai* a slight edge over the Ifrit. She envied him his flight, the wind under his wings, no longer burdened by his body. He could leave and nothing here would hold him back or make him want to return.

Must be nice.

Raif began walking away, then hesitated, turning back to them. "Nalia's brother was imprisoned here. Her plan had been to set him free as soon as we got the ring, but Calar found him and . . . well. It feels right, doing this. It's what she would have wanted. And the Dhoma inside—she and I both owe them a blood debt." His voice grew heavy. "It's the least I can do for Samar."

Shirin watched the grief settle over Raif. Losing Nalia, losing Samar. Shirin wasn't sure Raif could take any more. He made his way toward his troops, shoulders hunched, body tense.

Taz leaned toward her, quiet. "Keep an eye on him out there. I've never seen a jinni so eager to die."

She'd watched Raif mingle among the troops, fooling them with his confident smile and his hand on their shoulders—they'd never know anything was wrong.

Raif turned and caught her eye. She stuck out her tongue and a small smile dusted his face. *I did that,* she thought. Her heart filled with a longing so fierce, a love so brutal, she couldn't say a word.

"You know," Taz said, "it takes time."

"What does?"

"For the heart to love again. My *rohifsa* has been dead for over three thousand summers and not a morning goes by that I don't think of him."

"And yet you've moved on," she said. It was the closest they'd come to acknowledging the relationship between Taz and Kes.

"In one sense, yes, I have," he said. "That's the funny thing about the heart: it can hold two people in it at the same time." He shrugged. "Raif is pure passion and drive. If he lives long enough, he won't be able to help falling in love again." He patted her arm. "You're good to him—you're good *for* him. He knows that."

Shirin was tired of competing with a ghost. *You win,* she told Nalia. Raif would always love Nalia best. But dead girls couldn't kiss or hold the boys who loved them.

"Thanks, brother," she said softly.

Taz nodded, his eyes back on the palace. "Anytime."

Shirin willed her body to evanesce. She wasn't going to let Raif out of her sight tonight, because she loved him, yes, and because maybe, just maybe, there was hope.

If he lives long enough, he won't be able to help falling in love again.

Shirin wanted to be there when he did.

29

TAZ GAZED AT THE MOONS, FULL OF WONDER. THOUGH he worried for Kes and and every soldier who would be fighting tonight, he couldn't drown the excitement thrumming through him. The Godsnight. It hadn't escaped Taz's notice that he was able to experience the most important night in the history of jinn faith only because of his long imprisonment. What would happen tonight? If it was indeed the gods' night, their sense of time was not the same as that of the jinn. A night could be a few minutes or a million years. What songs and stories would be composed about the coming hours—the full moons, whatever happened in the palace with Kes and his soldiers, the battle at the prison, the journeys through the portal? The very air felt charged with importance.

He looked away from the moons and returned to his vigil,

eyes back on the palace just across the range. By now the sun should be rising over the Arjinnan Sea, yet the sky remained dark, the moons burning brighter with every passing minute. Perhaps dawn would never come again in his lifetime.

Taz had been here for hours now, nervousness turning to terror as he waited for Kes's signal. Calar should have been dead long ago, with Kes's troops taking over the palace and Kes himself throwing shards of white *chiaan* into the air. Instead, there was only this eerie quiet and the darkness above the palace.

"I'm sorry, brother," Raif said softly as he came to stand beside Taz, his emerald evanescence slipping down the side of the mountain.

Taz shook his head. "I know him—Kes will wait to the last minute. Calar sleeps fitfully, he'll be afraid to . . . afraid to wake her."

Every muscle in his body was tense as he forced himself to stay on this mountaintop and not evanesce to the palace. He wouldn't let himself accept that Kes was dead, or good as dead. The gods couldn't be so cruel, to take away both of the jinn he loved. Not after Taz's centuries of devotion, not after those years in the bottle spent in meditation and worship.

Taz moved away from Raif, overcome as the first of the dawn prayers sounded over the land. Tears slid down Taz's face as the lament filled his ears, calling on his Shaitan goddess, begging her for the one thing Kes would need now more than ever: grace.

Restless goddess of the skies, send us your spirit on the wind. O Grathali, fill us with the power of your ever-changing, ever-shifting grace.

Taz wiped his eyes with the back of his hand, angry swipes that he knew Raif pretended not to see. The *tavrai* commander kept a respectful distance, silent as the prayers continued. Taz thought of Yasri, sleeping in Thatur's nest, unaware of the dangers her papa faced. The thought of her warmed Taz's heart, the one bright spot in the night's terror. In the time it'd taken Thatur to fly them to his nest, Taz had felt a connection to the child he hadn't believed was possible to experience so quickly. She was not of his blood and yet he loved her. He loved the parts of Kes that were in her face, loved her glorious Ghan Aisouri *chiaan*, loved how she curled into him as though she knew she was safe.

Please, Kes. Please be alive.

A cascade of rocks slid down the mountainside just as the Marid call to prayer began. He was dimly aware of Shirin's voice as she came up to them: "Raif, Taz. We can't wait any longer. Let's do this."

Shirin was right: it was time. He and Raif had agreed that if they didn't see the sign by the final changing of the guard, which took place just after the dawn prayers, the Brass Army and *tavrai* would storm the prison anyway. The hope was that even if Kes failed in his assassination attempt, his Ifrit comrades would still be able to take the palace. If Kes had failed, then Calar might have read his mind. It was possible they were walking into a trap, but none of Taz's scouts had reported any movement from the palace toward Ithkar. Their road to the prison was clear.

Everything in Taz strained toward the palace, toward that boy with the garnet eyes, toward the bravest jinni he'd ever known.

Brave as Nalia herself had been. From where he stood, Taz could make out the palace's domes and columns, the elegant arches, the waterfall that shot toward the Infinite Lake. Somewhere inside those walls, Taz's future happiness lay under the knife of Calar's magic, dependent on a mercy she didn't possess. It didn't matter that she loved Kes—she would only see him as her would-be murderer now.

He turned to Raif. "You still want to go through with the plan?" Taz asked, anxiety taking over sense.

"Of *course* we still want to go through with the godsdamned plan," Shirin snapped.

Raif threw a glare at her before leaning closer to Taz, his voice pitched low. "I know just how you feel, brother," he said. "I know all you want to do is go to that palace and find him. But your soldiers are depending on you. This is our best chance to rescue the Dhoma. If Calar has caught Kesmir, we won't have an opportunity like this again."

He motioned for Shirin to follow him and together they scrambled down the mountainside. Taz watched them for a moment, facing the prison just as the faint shimmer of the *bisahm* above it shuddered, then disappeared. Taz couldn't see the Shaitan *tavrai* mages who worked their magic against Calar's defenses, but he knew they were down there—if it weren't for their ability to destroy the shield above the prison, there'd be no hope for their plan.

An ear-splitting caw came up the range behind Taz, followed by the sound of furiously flapping wings. Taz turned just as Thatur skidded to a stop, sending a shower of rocks his way.

"Kesmir?" Taz asked. *Something's happened to him, gods, no, please—*

Thatur's wings flapped, agitated, and worry shot through his rumbling voice. "I waited at our meeting place and he never showed." The gryphon's eyes full of sorrow, he growled and began to pace in a circle.

Taz had noticed the grudging affection that had developed between Kes and the formidable gryphon. It occurred to Taz that the creature might be nearly as beside himself with fear for Kes as Taz was.

"He's alive—he has to be," Taz said, as much to comfort himself as anything else. Thatur's only answer was another rumbling growl.

"Take me to the palace," Taz said, desperate. "We have to help him."

The gryphon just looked at him.

"Thatur, *please.*" Taz was begging and he didn't care, he didn't care because Kes had to be alive, he had to, *he had to.*

"Calar could be on her way right now with her shadows," Thatur said, his voice cold. All it would take was one of the prison guards evanescing to the palace with the news that the *tavrai* were bombarding the prison. "And you would abandon your soldiers who have pledged their blood to you? Abandon those prisoners?"

Taz's face warmed with shame. "You're right," he said, voice heavy. "I know you're right. But—"

"You are the commander of the Brass Army," Thatur growled. "Now get down there and act like it—before I throw you off this mountain myself."

Taz nodded wordlessly. Kes would be furious if—*when*—he found out Taz had considered leaving the battle for him. Golden evanescence began to swirl around his feet. He scanned the battlefield below, searching for Raif. They were already surging toward the prison, with Raif at the very front. Hoping, Taz well knew, to die. And here he was, letting it happen.

"I'll see you down there," Taz said.

Thatur nodded, suddenly distracted. The moons began pulsing with bright, shimmering light—a beacon. Taz felt a slight shift in the air, but he couldn't place it. The land seemed to hold its breath, the calm before the storm.

"Thatur?"

The gryphon didn't seem to hear him as he turned toward the Arjinnan side of the range, his eagle's head cocked to one side, as though listening to a faraway whisper. His body went still and tense, then he leaped into the air, wild-eyed.

"What is it?" Taz shouted.

Just as Taz's body began its shift from flesh to smoke, Thatur shouted his answer from the sky above. Whatever he'd said to Taz was lost in the roar of the battle beginning below them, and Taz had no choice but to give himself over to the magic that would throw him in the thick of it.

30

DARKNESS, ENGULFING. UNENDING.

Nalia trudged on, her bones aching, weary, but she wasn't stopping, couldn't rest. The summons from Arjinna was a magnet, dragging her across the Eye. She couldn't ignore it if she tried. A high-pitched keening sounded far behind her—a ghoul that had been tracking her for days.

Nalia picked up speed. She had to make it. They'd come so far.

Raif. Arjinna. Raif. Arjinna.

Then: a glimmer of light. Nalia blinked. Stared. This was not the phoenix's clear diamond light but rich, creamy beams of moonlight. Familiar. A shape, indistinct at first, shrugged off the Eye's endless night, with spires reaching for the sky. Metal bars. A gate.

Arjinna.

Nalia began to run, her feet flying over the dust. The phoenix kept pace, singing a wordless song, a gorgeous melody Nalia had never heard before, a song that evoked the terrible beauty of her land and those who dwelled in it.

Just as Nalia neared the Gate of the Eye—it was the gate, she could see the familiar copse of trees behind it—the phoenix whirled around, her great wings pushing a breeze into the airless void. The song faded away, already a memory, and Nalia's companion hovered before her, fixing her with the intense gaze Nalia had come to know so well. Her breath caught and she was seized by something between grief and elation. Words weren't needed. Nalia knew what the phoenix was telling her.

This was good-bye.

Nalia's eyes filled and she reached out her hand, her heart burning already with the loss.

"Please don't leave me," she whispered.

The phoenix drew closer and allowed Nalia to rest her palm atop her head. The creature's energy was ancient and strange, all-knowing, all-seeing. It flowed into Nalia, mixing with her own *chiaan*: powerful, deadly, wise. The phoenix's opal feathers shimmered, growing brighter and brighter. She opened her pearlescent beak for one last song.

Sing, for the night has gone. Dance, for the sun will rise.

The final note was a pure trill that encompassed all of creation—the beginning, the past, the present, and the distant, unknowable end. As the note reached an ecstatic height, the phoenix burst into flames, gold and white and silver tongues of fire that engulfed the bird completely. Nalia cried out, falling to her knees before her friend. A shower of ash rained down, covering Nalia, a baptism.

A single white feather floated among the ash and Nalia held out her hand, catching it on her palm. As soon as it hit her skin, strands of pure gold swirled around the feather: a delicate chain that the feather now dangled from, its sharp stem encased in a golden ring attached to the necklace.

"*Shundai,*" Nalia whispered. *Thank you.*

The feather would be useful later on—now she remembered seeing it in the vision from the lote tree, one thread in the thousands of strands that encompassed all time.

Nalia stood, then slowly, reverently, walked the last few steps to the gate. The phoenix's power filled her as her own *chiaan* sang through her skin, mixing with that of Antharoe's and all the empresses who had accompanied her on the last leg of this dark journey. Nalia raised her palms in seeming surrender, then called forth the lightning within her, summoning the land's power to her. The gate blew apart in a blaze of violet *chiaan*.

Nalia stood on the threshold of her realm, gazing up at the sky, shielding her eyes against the sudden light and the clarity of shape and form that had been denied her in the Eye. The Three Widows blazed, each one perfectly full and as bright as the sun, just as she had seen in her vision at the lote tree: the Godsnight. As though aware of her eyes on them, the moons began to shimmer, bright and throbbing like a beating heart.

The tree had told her it would happen, but Nalia had assumed it was a symbol, a metaphor for the change that would be wrought in Arjinna once Nalia claimed the throne. But no—it was really happening, this ancient, horrible prophecy. She could still recall the fear she'd felt during her vision: nothing good would come of this night. A new wave of hopelessness threatened to drown her and Nalia looked away from the moons, focusing on the familiar stars. They winked at her from above, the color of Malek's absinthe: Piquir's sword. Jandessa and Rahim. The Great Cauldron, *B'alai Om*—Bashil's favorite. All against a backdrop of lime, magenta, and plum swaths of color, the Arjinnan aurora blazing like a Welcome Home sign.

She pressed her palms together and held them to her heart, this heart that mourned and loved and fought and hoped and hadn't stopped, no matter how much it went through.

Nalia stepped through the gate and set foot on her land.

"My Empress!"

Nalia started, nearly falling over as a bundle of black rags threw itself at her.

"Oh, My Empress! I knew it, I knew you were alive! I knew the gods would not give up on you!"

Nalia stepped back. The jinni was tall, covered in mourning rags, his crimson eyes bright.

"Touma?" Her voice came out as little more than a croak.

She'd often spoken to the phoenix, but *often* in the Eye meant perhaps once every few days. The sound of her voice in the dark had been more terrifying than the silence, a confirmation of just how alone she was.

The Ifrit fell to his knees, sobbing. "A year and a day you were gone." He pointed to the sky. "They sent you to save us from whatever the Godsnight will bring."

Nalia stared. "I've been in the Eye for *a year and a day*?"

Her time in the Eye had been like her time in the bottle, where minutes felt like years and months felt like seconds. But she'd never imagined . . . A year. Raif had thought her dead for *a year*. Nalia had been so certain that he was still alive, that the *tavrai* continued their fight. But what if she was wrong? What if they'd been annihilated long ago?

"Touma, is Raif, is he . . . ?" Her voice caught with wanting. *Please be alive. Please.* So much could happen in a year.

"Alive and well, My Empress," he said, beaming. "He hasn't done the mourning rituals yet. I think a part of him knew you were coming back."

For a moment, the scene before her undulated, a wave of light, and she swayed, suddenly lightheaded with relief. Hunger raged through her—when was the last time she'd sipped the heart plant's nectar? She couldn't remember having anything to eat in all this time—just the milk from the plant, for a year. How had it kept her alive? Touma rushed to support Nalia, gripping her elbow firmly.

He drew her to the wall and had her sit against it while he

manifested food: warm *kees*—the bread she'd fantasized about during her hungriest moments in the Eye—soft cheese, sugarberries, a steaming cup of *chal*.

Nalia stared at the food, ravenous, overwhelmed. Her voice caught as she picked up a sugarberry. "Thank you, Touma."

Touma's eyes filled with tears again. "An empress, and yet you eat the food of the poorest jinn as thought it were a banquet of the gods."

She smiled. "This is the first food I've had in a year, Touma. It's . . ." She ate the berry and its juices spread across her tongue, sweet and tart. "Delicious."

He cried even harder. "Oh, My Empress," he wailed.

She ate a few bites of the bread and cheese, then sipped on her *chal* as Touma went through handkerchief after handkerchief, manifesting them in quick succession. Suddenly he stopped, choking on his own tears as his eyes fell on Solomon's sigil, which still hung from Nalia's neck by a leather cord.

"*Khatem l-hekma,*" he whispered, using the Moroccan name: ring of wisdom. "We thought it had surely been lost forever."

His eyes grew fearful and Nalia knew Touma was reliving those years when he'd been forced to be a slave to a human king, then punished for the rebellion Tazlim had led. Three thousand summers in a bottle, and he'd spent his first free year sitting by this gate, honoring her. How could she ever reward such devotion?

"Hide it," he whispered, gesturing to the ring. "Don't let them see."

The way he said *them* sent a shiver down her spine. Were the *tavrai* that awful?

Nalia placed her palm on Touma's cheek. "Everything will be all right. The tree told me."

Touma frowned. "Yes, we most certainly need to get you to a healer, My Empress."

Nalia sighed. How could she ever explain the journey she'd undergone and the riches it had bestowed upon her? And she didn't need a healer, she needed her *rohifsa*.

A white light burst into the air, beyond the ridge of the Qaf range, just over Ithkar.

Raif.

"What are the *tavrai* doing in Ithkar?" she asked, fear replacing the joy of her arrival. She had to get there right away—to help Raif, to keep him alive.

Touma told her of all that she'd missed in a quiet voice as they made their way toward the Forest of Sighs on foot for fear an Ifrit patrol would catch sight of her violet evanescence and warn Calar of Nalia's return. The journey was long, too long. Every second when she wasn't with Raif was torture.

"An alliance with the Ifrit?" Nalia said, worry spiking in her voice. She placed her hand on Touma's arm as she caught the red of his eyes. "No offense. You know what I mean."

"None taken, My Empress. I don't like these brutes any more than you do. We may have the same color eyes, but that's where our resemblance ends."

"I know."

Nalia's mind reeled. Zanari was leading a battle on the other side of the portal, Raif and Taz were storming the prison, and Calar had manifested monsters that seemed unkillable.

"Touma, we have to go to Ithkar—"

"You must see a healer first," he said firmly. "My Empress, I say this with all respect: you are not looking like you can fight a battle right now."

Maybe he was right. But waiting . . . knowing Raif was so close . . .

It was slow going, moving from shadow to shadow. The light from the Three Widows made Nalia feel exposed, even more so because she was unaccustomed to anything but the impenetrable darkness of the Eye. Her eyes ached, blinded, and she held up her hand, shielding herself from the moons. The land was unusually quiet, the villages deserted, the Forest of Sighs dark and impenetrable. The more they walked, the better Nalia felt: she was ancient and newborn, a vessel for all that was of her land and all that would be. Past and present and future resided beneath her skin and yet a growing horror took root in Nalia. Something was deeply wrong, an evil that she felt in the very marrow of her land. In the time Nalia had been gone, Arjinna had become diseased, dying all around her. Gone was the luster of its vegetation, gone was the energy that thrummed through the dirt, the air, the water. The *chiaan* had been sucked dry from the land, leaving her world half dead.

As if he could read her thoughts, Touma sighed. "It is a bad time, very bad time. I have to go to Ithkar to restore my *chiaan*—I am one of the few lucky ones who can do so. The shadows do not go there. The Djan?" He gestured to the barren countryside. "Where can they find *chiaan*? It's a bad time, My Empress," he said again, "a very bad time." Then he smiled, his eyes shining as he gazed at her. "But not anymore!"

There was a caw in the air then, a furious flapping of wings. The skin on the back of Nalia's neck prickled, the sensation so familiar, it was like slipping on her old battle leathers.

Nalia-jai.

She heard his voice in her head at the same time she realized what—*who*—was in the air. She turned, crying out as her gryphon sped across the sky, straight for her. As soon as the creature landed, he bowed deeply.

My Empress.

It was too much to hope for, impossible, and yet . . . Nalia stared at the luminescent eyes that looked back at her: aquiline and somehow all-knowing, every color that existed swirling inside them. And then she saw the blue feathers that rimmed those eyes. Only one of the Aisouri gryphons had those.

"Thatur," she whispered.

"Welcome home, child." Then he growled, a sound that was all too familiar. Unfortunately. "You have a lot of explaining to do, young lady."

She laughed and placed a hand on Thatur's flank, sending her *chiaan* into him. He vibrated with pleasure, the closest to purring a gryphon could get, and she leaned her head against his warm body, tears slipping down her cheeks. How was it possible? The last time she'd seen Thatur was the night of the coup. He'd been tearing the limbs off the Ifrit around her, guarding Nalia with his wings, his beak. But the palace was swarming with Ifrit and there were guns, so many guns, shooting all the time, everywhere. The floor had been slick with blood—it'd been hard to keep her footing. A bullet had sliced through Thatur's wing, and as he roared in pain and rage, Haran dragged Nalia down a set of stairs, one hand over her mouth to shut off her screams. Then he'd thrown her in the basement room and forced her to stand against the wall with the other Aisouri. Just before the guns opened on them, Nalia's mother began whispering the prayer of the dead.

All these years Nalia had assumed he'd died along with the other gryphons. She'd asked around at Habibi, the underground jinn club in Los Angeles where she'd once danced with Raif, and it seemed she'd been correct: no one had seen a Ghan Aisouri gryphon since their mistresses had been cut down by the Ifrit. He'd been the only comfort in her childhood, save for Bashil. The one voice she'd learned to trust in that palace of lies.

"They said you were all dead," Nalia whispered, her voice trembling. "It's not possible . . . how are . . . oh my gods. *Thatur.*"

A sob broke out and Nalia turned, worried, but Touma waved away her concern. "Tears of joy, My Empress."

Thatur let Nalia cling to him for a moment and then, in customary Thatur fashion, her gryphon gently disentangled himself.

"My Empress. A bit of decorum, if you will," he said, his voice gruff. His eyes fell on the white feather around her neck. "Raif Djan'Urbi told me he saw you in a vision with the white phoenix. But that isn't . . . it's not—"

"It was the phoenix who kept me alive all year. She guided me, taught me things, protected me. She left me this one last thing before her Burning." It had been less than an hour since her phoenix's feather fell among the ashes and yet it felt like days ago. "She was . . . my friend."

"*Hala dkar,*" Touma whispered. *All honor to the gods.*

"It comforts me to know you weren't alone, child," Thatur said.

Nalia nodded. "I wouldn't have made it without her."

I missed you, Nalia-jai. She heard the words in her head, clear and strong, the connection with her gryphon unbroken after all this time.

I missed you, too, she thought to him. *I missed you every day.*

She felt the rumble of his purr where her hand rested against his flank, the vibrations running through her.

I still require a full accounting of your whereabouts these past four summers, he added.

I know, she thought.

And I don't approve of this Djan'Urbi, you should know that right away.

Nalia's eyes widened. How did he know about her and Raif?

Oh yes, he said, noting her surprise, *I've heard all about it. And I have . . . opinions, My Empress. Strong ones.*

You'll come around, she thought, grinning.

Thatur humphed, a combination growl/caw. *We'll see about that.*

"How are you feeling?" Thatur asked, out loud, for Touma's benefit.

Nalia took stock. Now that she'd eaten a bit and gotten some fresh air, she felt wonderfully restored. Her *chiaan* thrummed through her, more powerful than ever before, thanks to the empresses in the Eye.

"I know I don't look it," she said, glancing at Touma, "but I feel . . . good. Really good."

"Then I have a request." Thatur took in her thin frame and frowned. "But perhaps it isn't a wise course of action."

"What is it?" she asked.

"Tonight Raif and the *tavrai* are breaking into the prison in Ithkar," he began.

"I know," she said. "Touma already told me everything."

Thatur nodded, then turned to the Ifrit beside Nalia. "Kesmir never gave the signal."

Who was Kesmir?

Touma's eyes grew wide. "Is he . . . ?"

"I don't know," Thatur said, his voice heavy.

Touma noticed Nalia's confusion. "Kesmir is the Ifrit I spoke of—Calar's lover. Former lover. He is now Tazlim's *rohifsa*."

"Tazlim's *what*?"

Thatur nodded his head. "Much has happened since you've been gone, My Empress."

Clearly.

"How can we rescue this Kesmir?" she asked.

"That will require more soldiers on our end, I'm afraid. It will have to wait. Now, what I'm about to request is a lot to ask—I know you must be tired from your . . . journey. But there is a way you can be useful during tonight's battle. If you were to go to the palace—"

"The *palace*?" Touma nearly shouted. "Are you out of your mind?"

Thatur gave the Ifrit a withering look. "As I was saying, if you were to go to the palace and alert Calar of your presence—she might hold back her troops. It would buy the *tavrai* time to get the prisoners out."

Nalia's heart sank. She'd have to wait even longer to be reunited with Raif. And yet she'd waited a year—what were a few more hours? Her land needed her, and if going to the palace would protect Raif, then there was no question of what she would do. Distracting Calar might save his life and countless others. Nalia glanced once more at the moons. How long did she have before the plagues of the Godsnight started? It might be impossible to find Raif in the chaos.

"Of course," she said.

"My Empress," Touma said, "I must object. You're unwell—"

"I'm fine. Truly." The gods hadn't kept her alive just so that she could die as soon as she walked through the Gate of the Eye.

"Are you, child?" Thatur asked.

He wouldn't have made the request if he'd thought she couldn't do it. Thatur had always known her limits, always required that she reach them—and then go a little further. He'd felt her *chiaan* just now, he knew what she was capable of. But for the first time in her life, Thatur was giving Nalia a choice. He was still her teacher, still her battle companion—but he was now her subject and she his empress.

That would take some getting used to.

"I'm fine," she repeated. "Now, what did you have in mind?"

"There are dead to burn," Thatur began. "It would be wise to ensure your caste is sent to the godlands before Calar hides them."

The swaying skeletons of her Aisouri sisters. She'd never seen them hanging before the palace gate, but she'd pictured it more than once. Thatur was right: once Calar learned that Nalia was in Arjinna, the first thing she'd do was hide those skeletons, just to spite her. And, if she were honest, Nalia wanted to make sure Calar knew that she'd returned and that the Ifrit empress's days on the throne were numbered.

Nalia was desperate to go straight to where Raif fought in Ithkar. She wanted to find him, kiss him, never let him go, and kill anyone who dared to hurt him. But she'd made a promise in the Eye—to herself and to the empresses. She had to burn her dead. Her caste needed to be set free, not roaming the in-between, forever locked out of the godlands. From her time in the Eye, Nalia knew there could be no worse fate. And Thatur's battle strategy was a brilliant one: Calar wouldn't be able to resist turning her troops on Nalia. It could be the difference in the *tavrai* winning or losing the battle.

Touma placed his hand on his scimitar and nodded briskly. "If you insist on this, I shall accompany you and—"

"Touma, it's too dangerous," she said.

"I have sat by this gate night and day, My Empress, waiting for you," he said. "I am sorry, but you are stuck with me. And also this: Raif Djan'Urbi would kill me if I let you out of my sight before you were returned safely to him."

Nalia frowned. This was an unexpected complication. "All right. But I'm warning you, Touma, you're risking your life."

"Being alive in Arjinna at all is risking one's life," he said softly. "I serve at the pleasure of the Empress."

"And I serve at the pleasure of the land." She turned to Thatur. "Take me home."

She and Touma climbed on Thatur's back and she grabbed the feathers near his neck. Her gryphon vaulted into the sky, setting his course for the palace.

31

RAIF SPRINTED TOWARD THE PRISON, HIS FEET SKIM-
ming over the shards of obsidian that covered Ithkar's floor,
jet-black daggers that he kicked into the sky as he raced toward
the death he'd prayed the gods would give him. Tazlim was by
his side, in charge of the right flank of soldiers, while Raif led the
vanguard and Shirin covered the left flank.

A horn sounded on the ramparts and a swarm of scarlet evanescence hurtled toward him from the prison gate. Raif grinned,
high off the blood pumping through his veins, the adrenaline
that screamed *yes yes yes*.

Beside him, Shirin laughed as the first Ifrit materialized
before them, launching herself at the guard with feral joy. The
Brass Army roared behind him, and Raif was nothing but his
hands that bled *chiaan* and the blade of his scimitar. He hoped

Nalia could see him now, hoped she knew that he was going to burn this prison to the ground.

The moat was in his sight now, red-hot liquid that the Ifrit on the prison's ramparts manipulated. Monsters not unlike the sand army Raif had fought in Morocco reared up from the lava, stepping out of the fire and hurtling toward Raif and his soldiers, fireballs in the shape of bodies. The Ifrit in the Brass Army fought fire with fire, blasting the monsters back into the moat with the strength of their *chiaan*.

Scalding rain drenched Raif's advancing army and he was soon surrounded by the cries of the *tavrai* and Brass soldiers as the fire hit their skin. He nearly dropped his scimitar as the deluge seared his own skin, exposing the bone on his forearm. He followed his Ifrit soldiers, who were strengthened by the inferno and pushed through the fiery assault, absorbing the flames before they could reach Raif. They directed their *chiaan* toward the moat, pulling the fire away so that the path to the gate was clear.

Raif grinned at the Ifrit Brass soldier closest to him, nodding his thanks, then led the charge to the gate and, together with Taz, blasted it open, a volley of emerald and gold *chiaan* surging against the gate like a broken dam. A roar sounded behind Raif as his soldiers advanced. He guessed they had a matter of minutes before Calar descended with her army of shadows.

As the bodies of the prison guards fell to the ground, Raif bolted through the gate. He was immediately hit with the stench of disease and unwashed bodies, death and despair. Emaciated figures looked out from the doorways of the low barracks that spread across the rough terrain, eyes bright with fever or dull from impending death, most of them children and the elderly.

"Gods and monsters," he breathed.

Bashil had been *here*? He knew it had been bad, but this was worse than anything Raif could have imagined.

The air shifted around him and he turned as Taz evanesced, golden smoke spilling around him. "What's the plan, brother?"

"We'll focus on getting these jinn out before Calar comes— our army seems to have the Ifrit covered. Can you lead the ones who are too weak to evanesce back to the forest while the rest of us take care of the guards?"

Taz nodded and Raif rushed toward the prisoners, grabbing the jinni closest to him, a male Marid. "We're here to help, grandfather," Raif said. "My jinn will lead you to safety. Can you help gather the prisoners?"

The jinni placed his fist over his heart in the *tavrai* salute. "It would be my honor, Raif Djan'Urbi."

Raif bowed. "The honor's all mine."

Most of the prisoners wouldn't be able to evanesce, even though the *bisahm* over the prison had been destroyed and its gates flung wide open. These jinn were on the brink of death— most of them clearly did not have access to their *chiaan*—and it was obvious that the shadows had also been here, ravaging the land. There was the telltale black dust they left behind when they'd sucked the *chiaan* in an area dry.

Raif shielded his eyes as he looked up. Noqril was pecking out the eyes of the Ifrit in quick succession, blood dripping from his beak. Raif knew it must lonely up there without Samar; he hoped the Dhoma leader could see them from the godlands.

There was a battle cry behind him and Raif whirled around, throwing the dagger strapped to his belt at an advancing guard. The Ifrit fell and Raif threw his *chiaan* into the jinni's heart, killing him instantly. Another guard sprinted toward him and Raif jumped to the side. He swung his scimitar in an elegant arc, the blade flashing in the moonlight. It connected with Ifrit flesh and the jinni's head flew off.

"Nice," Shirin said appreciatively. Her blade dripped with blood and her eyes were bright with battle lust.

Raif grinned. "All in a day's work." His father would have approved, happy that all the sword-fighting lessons he'd given Raif throughout his childhood had paid off.

For what felt like an hour but was likely only a matter of minutes, Raif cut through the bodies of Ifrit, sometimes with his scimitar but most often with perfectly aimed shots of *chiaan*. Raif was a machine as he made his way through the prison, a god of death, Mora incarnate. He had no thought except where he would next direct his energies. *Blood, bone, and breath to a master bound.* That's what it had said on the shackles Malek had forced Nalia to wear. Now he too had a master, and Raif was bound to its deathly commands: *kill, kill, kill.*

A high keening pierced the air and Raif cursed as lightning-fast figures vaulted from the high wall surrounding the prison, their gaping maws filled with needle-sharp teeth: ghouls. He darted to the side as one of the creatures reached for him, its claw catching on his tunic. White-hot pain shot down his arm, and Raif turned to face the ghoul. Out of the corner of his eye, he could see Taz already leading a long line of prisoners out a side gate.

Raif shifted into a defensive position, his eyes on the ghoul's. He wanted a hard fight—blood and bones breaking. No magic, no blades. He wanted the fight of his life.

"Hungry?" Raif dropped his scimitar and held out his arms as he faced the ghoul, grinning.

There was a howl to his left, and before Raif could turn he was thrown to the ground, Shirin's body on top of his. Behind her, the ghoul cried out as a barrage of *chiaan* hit his chest from a nearby Brass soldier. The monster fell heavily to the ground, dead.

"If I weren't trying to save your life, I'd kill you right now, you bastard," Shirin said. And then she was shaking, her eyes filling, her body wracked with sobs.

It took him a moment to realize that Shirin—*Shirin*—was crying. Raif put his arms around her, dazed and feeling a little cheated as he lay in the mud holding the wrong jinni. He'd been so ready to die. *Fool.* Nalia would be furious if she knew what he'd been about to do. But it hadn't been a conscious choice. It was instinct now, this desire to die. What was happening to him?

A trumpet sounded and Shirin pulled away as a burst of red evanescence tumbled over the ridge: the Ifrit army, Calar and her shadows no doubt not far behind.

"Fire and blood," Shirin muttered. "I was hoping we'd have a little more time."

Raif scrambled to his feet, suddenly exhausted, bone-tired. *I'm done,* he thought.

The realization hit him, clear and final. This was the last battle he'd command for the *tavrai*. The last time he would lead them. It suddenly occurred to Raif that Zanari was right—it was time to go. There was nothing here worth fighting for, worth dying for, now that the prisoners had been freed and the portal opened.

A ball of fire arced over the sky from the westernmost ridge of the Qaf, where a small Ifrit outpost looked over the prison. It hit the ground, a thunderous blast that threw Raif off his feet. Shards of obsidian rained down and Raif covered his head as their sharp points lacerated his skin. Another ball of fire, this time so strong that the ground leaped up. For a moment Raif was suspended in midair, riding the wave of the blast until he fell back to earth, the ground coming up hard and fast. Pain exploded in Raif's side as bone connected with rock. He heard the groans of the others around him.

"What the—" Raif looked toward the mountains and went cold at the sight: a legion of Ifrit soldiers had evanesced into the prison grounds, twice the size of the Brass Army, fresh and ready for battle.

A burst of golden evanescence engulfed him—Taz. "The prisoners are safe. I've got them manifesting tents over by—" He choked on his words, staring at the newly arrived Ifrit. "Oh, for gods' sakes." He pulled out his scimitar. "Here we go again."

Shirin put her hand on his arm. "Wait. They're not fighting us."

"What?" Taz took a few steps forward, Raif behind him.

It was true. The Ifrit who'd arrived weren't fighting the *tavrai*—they were taking down what remained of the prison's security forces and the ghouls.

"Kesmir," Taz whispered. "These are his jinn." He turned, grinning. "All is not lost."

Shirin hurried to spread the word, but Taz waited with Raif, the need to know what had happened to Kes pressing against his heart. Had they helped him escape? It was too much to hope for, but Taz couldn't help fanning that flame. He'd never been one to give up, to lose heart. Even the loss of Lokahm and all those years in the bottle hadn't been able to crush him.

He turned to Raif. "How do you want to proceed?"

"You should talk to them," Raif said.

Taz cocked his head to the side. "I think it would be best if you—"

Raif shook his head. "It wouldn't be best."

Defeat—no, *surrender*—had settled around Raif's eyes. He placed a hand on Taz's shoulder. "I'm not my father. And I'm done trying to be. You and Kesmir's Ifrit," he said, nodding toward the approaching jinn, "will change this realm for the better. Unless the gods have other plans, which, judging from the sky tonight, they do." Taz opened his mouth, but Raif held up his hand. "This isn't my fight anymore. I'm done, Taz. I'll fight until Calar is dead, but then I'm going back to Earth to do what Nalia wanted more than anything else—I'm going to unbind every jinni on the dark caravan. And when I'm done . . ."

He didn't finish, but Taz could see in his eyes exactly what Raif planned to do when he was finished liberating the jinn enslaved on Earth.

"Go," Raif said softly, before turning away and grabbing a burning torch from its place on the inside wall of the prison. Taz watched as Raif touched the fire to one of the wooden barracks. The flames licked the wood, devouring a wall before Taz turned away.

He crossed the yard, one hand still holding his scimitar. These might have been Kes's jinn, but they weren't Taz's, not yet anyway.

"Jahal'alund," said a female Ifrit dressed in battle leathers. Her eyes blazed crimson and her red hair fell to her waist, shimmering strands that glowed in the moonlight: Fazhad, the Ifrit Kes trusted most, his right hand in the rebellion.

Behind her stood three other Ifrit soldiers: Halem, Xala, and Urum. Taz had only had occasion to speak with them a handful of times over the past year, coordinating attacks, passing along information. Just behind them stood Ajwar, Nalia's father, his eyes heavy with exhaustion.

"Fazhad," Taz said, his voice barely a whisper. "How is he?"

She shook her head, her eyes going to the moons: the second-most powerful jinni in the Ifrit army was trying not to cry. And Taz knew, he knew, and he held out his hands, as though the air could hold him up but it couldn't and he was on his knees *Kes Kes Kes.*

It didn't matter that he was the commander of the Brass Army or that these jinn would never respect him again. It didn't matter. Nothing mattered. This was what it was like in those first weeks in the bottle, a gaping hole inside him, the loss unbearable, darkness and nothing, nothing but this dagger point of grief slicing into his heart. This would be the blow that would kill him.

"Tell me," a voice beside him growled: Raif.

Fazhad took in a shuddering breath. "He's gone. Calar . . . it wasn't pretty."

Taz fell forward, his head against the shards of rock, and they cut into him and he wanted to gouge out his eyes, slice his throat. He gripped the shards, let them break the skin on his hands.

Then he heard Raif's voice in his ear—calm and soft. "Think of Yasri, Taz. She needs you—you're all she's got. You're her father now, do you understand me?"

Yasri.

Oh, gods, that little girl. Taz squeezed the obsidian in his fists harder.

He called on his last reserves of strength, then nodded, suddenly numb. "Okay," he whispered.

Raif helped him stand and Taz looked at the jinn before him. He'd always felt things deeply: the gods, his lovers, life itself. It was a weakness he could not overcome.

He gave a small bow. "Forgive me," he murmured.

Kes. Kes.

"There is nothing to forgive," Fazhad said. "You honor him with your grief."

Raif turned to Fazhad. "What's happening at the palace?"

"When Kesmir . . . when we realized Calar was still alive, we fought as planned," Fazhad said. "She didn't release her shadows, but it was impossible to get into her room."

"Then how do you know Kesmir is—" Raif began, but Fazhad held up her hand.

"A servant girl went into Calar's room when she heard the empress screaming. Calar was on her balcony—she didn't see the girl. Kes was already gone. He had the look of—" Fazhad glanced at Taz.

"Say it," Taz said.

"She used her shadows on him," Fazhad said, her voice soft.

Taz turned away, fist in his mouth. It was the very worst thing he could have heard. As the minutes passed, only a small part of him was aware of the conversation that took place around him.

"Need a plan—" Raif was saying.

"Room for us in the forest—"

"Shadows any second now—"

There was more talking, just a distant blur of voices to Taz, and then Raif was leading him away. "We've gotta evanesce, brother. Grab my hand."

"What's happening?" Taz mumbled as he felt Raif's fingers close around his own.

Taz's training was only now beginning to kick in through his fog of grief. Focus on the task at hand, bottle everything else up. Be like the *tavrai*: *You are a sword, nothing more.*

"Our army just got a whole lot bigger," Raif said. As evanescence pooled around them, he tugged on Taz's hand. "Look at me, Taz." Taz looked. "We're going to destroy Calar. For Kes. For Nalia. For all of us."

Taz nodded. "Okay," he said, as if to himself. "Okay."

His *rohifsa* was gone, but there was still a war to fight for the Arjinna Kes had been willing to die for. And a little girl who'd be waking up soon, asking for her papa.

32

ARJINNA LAY BENEATH NALIA, A DISTANT CANVAS OF burned fields and spilled blood. She gave herself over to the sensation of the world falling out from under her. The feeling tugged on her memory: late-night patrols high over the Qaf range, swooping into Ithkar in search of Ifrit, joyrides over the Arjinnan Sea on sleepless nights. Each memory was filled with the exact sensation of speed and weightlessness that coursed through her now. Flying on Thatur's back was one of her earliest memories. Aisouri were matched with their gryphons at age three, thrust into the sky whether they were ready or not. That first time had been terrifying—her whole world growing smaller and smaller until it disappeared entirely. Thatur had been a gentle teacher: firm, yet warm. So different from her mother. Her happiest moments were spent skimming the sky above her land, closer to the stars and far from the palace.

The Three Widows shone like a torch lighting Nalia's way to the home of her childhood. She held on to Thatur by squeezing her knees against his sides, fingers gripping the thick feathers at the nape of his neck. Nalia could feel the flap of the great wings in her own skin, the rhythm thrumming through her. Despite her exhaustion and the horror of this homecoming, she felt the familiar thrill of the sky, the delicious dance of wind and cloud on her skin.

Touma sat behind Nalia, holding her so tightly that his fingers dug into her ribs. He cried out every time Thatur dove through a cloud or swooped closer to the earth.

"Oh, gods," he gasped as Thatur plunged into another cloud. "Does he really have to do that?"

Nalia let go of Thatur and spread her arms, trailing her fingers through the swaths of mist. It was like holding a god's hand. She laughed, tasting the sky on her tongue.

"Are we there yet?" Touma gasped, his eyes squeezed shut.

"Almost," she said as the palace came into view. It loomed over the Infinite Lake, the moonlight outlining the mother-of-pearl domes, the towers and spires of her youth.

Every window glowed—clearly Calar had discovered what was happening in Ithkar.

Hurry, Thatur.

Perched atop her gryphon's back, Nalia could see the fire that leaped into the sky across the Qaf, devouring the prison where Bashil had been held captive for so long. It was what she would have done herself—erase it from the realm. Make it as if it had never been. Nalia took in a shuddering breath. Knowing Raif was down there, knowing she could simply ask Thatur to change course and she'd be in her *rohifsa*'s arms, was one of the hardest tests of her will that the gods could give her. Yet if there was one thing Nalia had learned as a Ghan Aisouri, it was that what she wanted did not matter. Could not matter. This was how she would help Raif most. And she had to burn her dead. If Calar hid them, Nalia would never forgive herself.

"I'm coming for you," she whispered into the wind.

She didn't know who she was speaking to: Calar, Raif, or the Aisouri who had been slain in the coup.

Maybe all of them.

They drew closer to the palace, Thatur's body casting a broadwinged shadow on the Infinite Lake below. The palace rose above it, glittering lapis lazuli and lavender marble, with a shimmering *bisahm* covering it like an impenetrable soap bubble. Of course. Why hadn't she thought of that?

"Thatur," she said, her voice urgent, "I can't get through—"

"As long as you're with me, you can."

She'd forgotten that *bisahms* only prevented jinn from breaking through them. Since she and Touma were *on* Thatur, they would also be able to get through.

The home she'd grown up in lay before her, the mosaics on its domes catching the moonlight. The courtyard below was empty, a vast swath of intricately tiled ground that stood before the palace gate. But there was something that had not been in the courtyard before. She'd noticed a flickering light in front of the palace as she'd been flying—this was its source. Nalia pointed to the cauldron of fire.

"What is that?" she asked Touma. "Is it just to replenish *chiaan*?"

Touma shook his head. "Calar uses it to burn her victims. It is lined with iron—horrible."

It seemed there was no limit to what Calar could do: working with the Ash Crones, ripping the *chiaan* right out of the land, and these tortures she seemed to gain so much pleasure from.

We have to stop her, Thatur, she thought to him.

We will, My Empress. Now that you're here, her time is limited. Very limited indeed.

Nalia started as a plume of crimson evanesence swirled past the palace's front gate, then disappeared. They were so high up, the guard hadn't noticed them.

They would soon enough. It'd been over a year since she'd been in a fight, since she'd had proper nourishment. But everything in Nalia thrummed like a well-oiled engine. She was ready for this fight. And the next. And the next.

"My Empress," Touma pleaded, "I beg of you, please reconsider. You can come back some other time, with your army and Raif. . . ."

She turned her head, her violet eyes meeting his crimson ones. "The reason that made you wait outside the Eye for me all this time," she said, "is the same reason I must do this tonight."

Now that she was here, Nalia couldn't leave without burning her dead. Couldn't leave without letting Calar know that she was back and that Nalia had every intention of destroying her.

After a moment, Touma nodded. "I understand."

Ready? Thatur asked.

"Touma, hold on." Nalia gripped her gryphon's feathers.

Ready.

They crashed through the *bisahm*, the magic stinging her skin like a thousand bees. Behind her, Touma cried out, cursing Calar and her entire lineage. The *bisahm* shuddered as they left it behind, then resumed its shape. A thick, honeylike substance briefly coated her skin. It shimmered, then disappeared as quickly as it had come.

"Drop us off on that ledge," she said, pointing to a small outcropping of rock just beneath the lip of rock the palace was built on.

Antharoe Falls crashed into the lake below, throwing mist over them as Thatur descended. After he landed, Nalia had to pry Touma's fingers from around her waist before slipping off the gryphon. When his feet touched solid earth, Touma knelt and kissed the rock. Thatur rolled his eyes.

"I'll make sure no one gets to you," Thatur said. "As soon as I see that all the Aisouri are burning, I'll pick you both up. Yes?"

Nalia nodded. *"Salaa'khim,"* she whispered.

Victory or death. It was what the Aisouri always said to one another before a battle.

Salaa'khim, My Empress.

Thatur launched himself back into the sky. She turned to Touma. "Are you all right?" she whispered.

He nodded, still looking a bit green. "My blood is yours." He motioned to the set of stairs cut into the side of the mountain. "After you, My Empress."

As she climbed the narrow staircase, the carvings that covered the palace walls began to emerge from the mountain's face. The images told the story of the realm's history, of how the Ghan Aisouri had vanquished the Ifrit and enslaved the rest of the castes. That was how Nalia understood it now. Growing up, she'd been taught that the Aisouri had liberated the castes from a hard life of tribal warfare. She ran her fingers along a carving of Eila, the first Ghan Aisouri empress. Images such as this one were how Nalia had been able to recognize the empresses when they'd visited her in the Eye. It was eerie, seeing them carved into stone, long dead yet so alive to her.

Nalia braced her hands against the rock, drawing *chiaan* from it. She needed the earth's calming energy as much as the additional strength. She frowned, pressing harder. For so many summers she'd longed for the power of Arjinnan *chiaan*, but this energy was little more than a trickle, like the faint strain of a lone violin where once there had been the bombast of a full orchestra.

Gods, what has she done? Nalia thought, murderous.

Touma nodded as he watched her. "This is what I am talking about, My Empress."

Nalia went still, holding an arm to stay Touma as an Ifrit guard shuffled by on the tiered ledge above her. She waited until he'd passed, then ascended the last of the stairs and forced her eyes to look up.

The firelight from the massive torches beside the gate and the flames in the cauldron made it easy to see the forms that swung in the breeze.

All those bodies, on top of her, crushing Nalia until she can barely breathe. The scent of blood, bullets ripping into flesh—

She drew in a ragged breath and moved closer to the gate, Touma at her heels. They ducked behind the cauldron as another guard came rushing past.

"What in all hells is going on in Ithkar?" he growled at his companion. "As if we don't have enough problems *here*."

"A godsdamned mess, that's what," replied a gruff voice. Nalia froze, listening. "Sentry came by and said the *tavrai* broke into the prison. 'Spect we'll be headed that way soon."

Seconds later, there was the sound of a flurry of wings and vicious caws: Thatur.

It begins, she thought.

Nalia waited while the guards sprinted toward where Thatur hovered in the air, dodging the guards' bolts of *chiaan*. The guards wore armor, but nothing she couldn't pierce through with her *chiaan*. And the armor was little more than paper when one of Thatur's claws was pressed against it. Nalia sprinted toward the gate of her ancestors, several feet away from the cauldron.

"Hey—" one of the guards called.

Nalia's *chiaan* shot out, a stream of beautiful violet daggers that instantly found their aim. The guard fell heavily to the stone floor, unconscious. She sent a churning sphere of *chiaan* at the other guard before he could react, and he tipped over the cliff's edge with a bloodcurdling scream. She scanned the perimeter— so far, they were the only two guards on duty.

Now, Thatur thought to her.

Nalia threw back the hood of her cloak, then raised her hands as her eyes focused on the figures swaying in the breeze. The sight made her reel, the horror of it all washing over her. She was the last, the only one. Forever alone.

It would be impossible for Nalia to tell which one belonged to her mother or the empress—all that was left of the Ghan Aisouri were bleached bones with scraps of fabric clinging to them.

A bell began to ring behind the gate. Soon, she'd be running for her life.

I am Ghan Aisouri.

While Touma stood behind her, ready to cut down the next guard who crossed their path, Nalia directed her *chiaan* toward the massive cauldron of fire, drawing the flames to her, then throwing it at the bodies of her caste in a wide arc, a burning slash of paint across the night sky. She sprinted across the vast length of the gate, fire trailing from her fingers. As the flames caught the figures that hung from iron chains, the air filled with smoke and the crackle of an inferno. A stream of Ifrit *chiaan* cut across the outdoor pavilion—a guard, charging toward her from his post near the mountain's edge. Nalia flipped over the poisonous barrage of magic, never breaking her concentration from the task at hand. She flew across the palace courtyard, dodging the guards who barreled toward her from a small barracks. They cried out as Touma and Thatur attacked. She recited the prayer of the dead over and over as she drew more fire to the corpses above her.

"*Hala shaktai mundeer,*" she screamed. "*Ashanai sokha vidim. Ishna capoula orgai. Hala shaktai mundeer.*"

Gods receive our souls. Fill them with grace and light. Grant entrance to your eternal temples. Gods receive our souls.

A hulking figure blocked her path, an Ifrit soldier wielding an abnormally large scimitar. Touma and Thatur were both engaged in their own furious battles—this Ifrit was all for Nalia. He grinned as he advanced on her.

Nalia smiled back. "It's up to you how you want to die," she said.

The Ifrit laughed. "Nice last words, little jinni."

Nalia gave him a pitying look as she danced past the point of his weapon, a nimble series of steps born of a warrior's grace. The Eye had whittled her down to nothing but bone and hard muscle: a swift predator. After a few useless swipes, the Ifrit gave up on his weapon, tossing it aside as he held up his palm, sending a burst of *chiaan* to her chest. Nalia threw herself to the ground, hand reaching for the gold hilt of his scimitar, but not before the Ifrit's sparks of *chiaan* nicked her skin. Nalia bit down a scream of pain and flipped up as her hand closed around the hilt, plunging the guard's own sword into his stomach in one smooth motion.

Vicious caws pierced the air and Nalia looked up. The sky was swarming with *vashtu*, dark creatures that feasted on flesh. She hadn't seen the monsters since Raif had fought them on the beach in Los Angeles. The vile things scattered as Thatur hurtled through the air. He dove down, drawing the *vashtu* toward the swarm of guards who now spilled from the palace gates. Hundreds of Ifrit barreled toward Nalia and Touma, sending a volley of *chiaan* their way. Touma's *chiaan* found its mark every time, the fearful jinni who'd ridden to the palace with her nowhere to be found. The guards cried out as the *vashtu* descended on them, momentarily diverted by the sharp beaks and talons of Calar's blood-crazed creatures.

"I think we may have overstayed our welcome," Touma gasped, his hands on his knees, but his eyes glued to the guards before them. "May we call it a night, My Empress?"

She looked at the bodies that littered the ground around him, then nodded. "I think we've done enough damage for now."

Thatur pulled back from the fray of guards and *vashtu* and landed at Nalia's feet. Bits of flesh hung from his beak and dark patches of blood stained his chest.

"Thatur!" Nalia stared at the blood, but he shook his head.

"Not mine."

The gryphon faced the Aisouri bodies that burned across the gate, filling the air with a musty scent. He bowed low, whispering the prayer of the dead himself before rising.

Silent tears streamed down Nalia's face.

"We must go, child, " Thatur whispered to her, covering her with a protective wing, as he'd done when she was a little girl.

Nalia took one last look at the Ghan Aisouri. The row of skeletons was awash with amethyst fire. Flakes of ash flew through the air and the remains of Nalia's caste coated her hair, her skin.

Nalia mounted Thatur, then assisted Touma. Just as they were about to take off, she felt a familiar tug on her heart—*hahm'alah*.

"Wait," she said.

Thatur pawed at the ground. "My Emp—"

"Just a minute," she whispered.

The magic of true names was how she'd been able to

communicate with Bashil while he was imprisoned in Arjinna. For one wild second she thought it was him, that he was somehow alive again and trying to get his big sister's attention. But that was impossible. Of course.

She knew who it was.

Nalia held up her hand as a puff of violet smoke swirled from her palm. Pure hatred shot through her when the image crystallized.

Calar.

The Ifrit empress was sitting on the throne in the palace, the Amethyst Crown on her head. The next image was of her opening the balcony doors that stood outside the throne room just above the palace gate.

Nalia raised her eyes to the actual balcony as the door opened and Calar stepped out.

"Fire and blood, is that her?" Touma asked as Calar appeared.

Long white hair, ruby eyes, and that face, that face that had smiled as Bashil lay dying. The last time Nalia had seen Calar, she'd been shooting a bullet at the empress's chest. Nalia's eyes settled on the Amethyst Crown, and a cold rage filled her at what had been done to secure it.

"Yes," she said. "That's her."

Calar was covered in blood—it was on her face, her hands— everywhere. Her eyes shone with a feverish, manic glow.

Kesmir, Thatur thought. Nalia felt the gryphon's grief for the Ifrit general as if it were her own, a deep despair that emanated from her gryphon's core.

She gasped at a sudden pressure against her consciousness,

as though Nalia's mind were a mansion with many rooms that Calar was trying to forcibly enter. Nalia pushed back, stemming the flow of pain Calar was trying to direct at her. She could feel Antharoe's power within her, resisting Calar's evil *chiaan*. The empress gave a cry of rage and leaned against the balcony, her hands gripping the railing as every bit of her concentrated on the Ghan Aisouri below, her features growing increasingly frustrated as Nalia remained unharmed. There was a cry to her left and Nalia's concentration broke as Touma battled with a guard who was charging toward Thatur.

That was all Calar needed. Nalia's head filled with blinding pain, like getting shot, only worse because she couldn't lose consciousness—Calar wouldn't let her. She fell off Thatur, clutching her head in her hands. Thatur tried to shield her, but just as Nalia hadn't been able to protect Bashil from Calar's psychic attacks, so it was the same with Thatur.

A laugh, high and cruel, flitted inside her head, drowning out all other sound. Calar attacked Nalia's mental defenses, her own mind a psychic scimitar that slashed at Nalia's consciousness again and again. Nalia shoved back, using the training from her childhood, drawing on every ounce of strength she had left to fight the Ifrit empress's attack.

Nalia writhed as the pain split her in two, struggling against the presence that had slithered into her mind. As though she were a chef setting out her most prized dish, Calar let her memory of Bashil's death slip into Nalia. She could feel Calar's pleasure at watching Nalia try to save her brother, a sadistic ecstasy that plunged into Bashil's head. There was his *chiaan*, curious and open, and then Calar's euphoric rage as she crushed his mind, obliterating it. Nalia screamed—the Nalia in Calar's memory and the Nalia who lay on the palace floor beside Thatur and Touma. Her heart her heart. Then a whisper, so faint Nalia could barely hear it: cold and sharp, like a dagger drawn in a bedroom.

Welcome home, Nalia.

She felt Calar's satisfaction, but her hold on Nalia was already loosening. It would be gone in moments. Nalia rallied every bit of strength within her and threw Calar from the deepest parts of her mind, away from all that was precious and private to her. Calar held on, though. Nalia could feel her scrambling to maintain her hold while Nalia lay on the mosaic floor, panting. She forced herself to stand, then wiped off the blood that dripped down her nose with the back of her hand.

She fixed her eyes on Calar. *You're wearing my crown.*

Calar grinned. *It's a lovely accessory.*

I'm going to kill you, Calar. And it will hurt like hell. And then I will take that crown and put it on my head. Time's up, bitch.

It was something Malek would have said and it made her smile, pleased at the little bit of bad in her. Nalia called up the strength left in her and severed the connection. Calar staggered back, her palms against her temples.

Touma picked Nalia up and settled her on Thatur before jumping on behind her.

"To the forest, friend," he called to Thatur. He held tightly to her with one hand, the other streaming *chiaan* at the guards below.

Within seconds they were in the air, leaving the palace and its burning dead far behind. Nalia leaned her forehead against Thatur's broad neck, lightheaded and gasping.

You're out of shape was all he said. *Training starts tomorrow.*

Nalia smiled against his feathers. She wouldn't have expected anything less.

Take me to him, she said.

Thatur swerved east, toward the dark patch of land occupied by the Forest of Sighs.

33

RAIF STOOD ON MOUNT ZHIQUI, STARING AT THE PALACE. It was little more than a speck at this distance, but even from here he could see the flames that had begun to spread across the gate, first a spark, then a fiery ball reaching toward the sky.

"What do you think *that's* all about?" Shirin asked. "Wasn't us, right?"

"No, it wasn't us," he said. It looked like a sunset—red and orange, purple, and yellow. "I thought all of Kesmir's Ifrit had gotten out. Guess a couple stayed behind to start a little trouble."

He glanced up at the full moons, frowning. That fire wouldn't be the last strange thing they saw before everything was said and done. He wondered what it meant, that the Godsnight had begun on the first anniversary of Nalia's death. Maybe this was how the gods mourned her loss. It would be a fitting way for them to say good-bye to her.

The whole land seemed to be holding its breath. The expectation in the air was heavy—he could almost feel it on his skin. No one knew what would happen, when the gods would strike. And no one could possibly be ready when they did.

They evanesced back to the forest, Raif parting ways with Shirin as soon as he emerged from his cloud of smoke. He made sure that some of the Brass soldiers kept an eye on Taz and went in search of Thatur. He suspected the sight of Yasri would be a comfort to Taz, if only to give the commander a reason not to throw himself in front of a ghoul, as Raif had. Yasri was still in Thatur's nest with Raif's mother, who'd been tasked with minding her. No one knew how to get there but Thatur himself—where was the damn bird? Raif hadn't seen him once during the battle. It wasn't like him to avoid a chance to rip out Ifrit throats.

Raif walked through the tent city that had sprouted from the Forest of Sighs like a sea of mushrooms. The battle for the prison over, he spent the next few minutes circulating among his soldiers, spreading praise and encouragement. The decision he'd made on the battlefield seemed to have drawn out some of the pressure that had been building within him ever since he'd returned from the Eye. He felt light, as though he already had one foot in the spirit realm. The years stretched out before him, lonely. His future had been spoken for since he was a child. He wasn't sure he knew how to live for anything but the revolution. Or Nalia.

Hundreds—no, *thousands*—of jinn lay scattered and homeless in the forest, their fear and despair latching onto Raif, a foreboding he couldn't shake off. What else would the gods bring them tonight? The moons still hung in the sky, though it was easily past noon, the sun nowhere to be seen. He tried to remember what the priests had said of the Godsnight, but all he knew was that it would be bad. Plagues, death at every turn. There was one thing to be grateful for, though: Calar had never shown up with her shadows.

Raif made his way to where the *tavrai* had gathered in the center of camp. All he wanted was sleep. As he approached, Shirin looked up from where she was crouching near a sizable bonfire, stirring one of several pots of stew. The smell of lamb and nutmeg reached him, and Raif's stomach growled. He was tempted to grab a bowl, but that would mean being alone with Shirin and he wasn't ready to acknowledge what had happened on the battlefield. Instead, he raised his hand in greeting and crossed to where Kesmir's Ifrit were deep in discussion. After a few moments of pretending to listen to the debate over what the next course of action should be, Raif felt a hand on his arm. He knew before he turned that it was Shirin. Her *chiaan* was like standing in the middle of a dark forest or gazing into a well—solid and quiet. So different from Nalia's.

"Eat, Raif," she said.

He took the clay bowl of soup she offered him and her hand lingered on his. Her eyes asked a question but he looked away, refusing to give the answer she hoped for. *I can't give you what you want.*

"Thanks, Shir."

She nodded, her lips twisting as she tried—and failed—to mask her disappointment.

That kiss lingered between them, and it would never go away. Raif still didn't understand why he'd let her press her lips to his or how he could have forgotten Nalia for even a moment. He just remembered this overwhelming need to feel something beyond his heartbreak, to feel alive again—wasn't that why he'd rested on the *jolip* moss in the first place? When Nalia's name came out of his lips, it was like coming up for air. He couldn't believe he'd betrayed her memory like that. And he felt terrible for hurting Shirin. What a way to repay her loyalty.

Shirin started back toward the fire but then stopped, looking toward the sky as a familiar caw sounded above. Raif turned toward the sound, shading his eyes against the brightness of the Three Widows as Thatur approached. He hoped the gryphon had a good reason for sitting out the battle. A sudden hush fell over the camp. Something about the way he flew—urgent, focused—demanded attention. Raif could just make out the silhouettes of two riders perched on Thatur's back. One was tall, clearly male. The first rider was likely female—slight, nearly dwarfed by the jinni who rode behind her. She was too far for Raif to see her face, but she sat astride the gryphon with ease.

"Is that your mom with the kid?" Shirin asked.

Raif shook his head. "I don't see a child. But I don't know who—"

The words caught in Raif's throat as Thatur began his descent. He still couldn't see the female jinni's face, but there was something . . . he couldn't quite . . . it was almost as if . . .

Raif's *chiaan* sparked inside him, pulling him toward Thatur, and the bowl Shirin had pressed into his hands slipped from his grasp as he started forward, stumbling like a man dying of thirst toward an oasis. He heard Shirin call his name, but her voice sounded far away, as though he were underwater.

It was impossible. He knew that. But the hope that had deserted him returned in full force and Raif teetered on the edge of sanity, gazing up at the approaching gryphon as a worshipper to a god. With each passing second, his certainty grew. He wanted to run, to shout with joy, to scream, but all Raif could do was stand there, stunned.

Impossible, impossible.

Thatur drew closer, and he'd barely touched down before the smaller of the two jinn he carried slid to the ground and sprinted toward Raif. Her eyes, bright and violet, her lips forming his name.

Nalia. Nalia. NALIA.

He shouted, an unintelligible exclamation of joy, as Nalia vaulted into his arms. She sobbed, her body shuddering against his, and he held her tightly to him, murmuring her name over and over. He squeezed his eyes shut tight and breathed her in: amber and the Eye—a smell like cold wind. He had to enjoy this while he could, this dream, this break with sanity—whatever was happening to him—he didn't care because it felt so real, so real, maybe he'd died in the battle and thank gods he had. *Nalia, Nalia*—

She pulled back, just enough to see his face, the tips of their noses touching. He smiled and her fingers brushed away the tears that streamed down his cheeks.

"I don't want to wake up," he whispered. "Please don't let me wake up this time."

"I'm here," she said against his lips. Her voice—gods, that voice—low, intoxicating. Her breath in his mouth, her *chiaan* flooding into him. "Raif, I'm here. I'm really here."

She pressed her lips to his and Nalia's *chiaan* swept through him, so much and so quickly that he nearly fell over. Her fingers in his hair, her body pressed against him, and as she whispered *I love you, I love you* against his lips, he let himself believe it was real. Either way, he was never waking up from this. He picked her up and spun her around and she laughed, her eyes bright, flooded with tears.

"Took you long enough," he murmured, setting her down again, as his fingers traced the lines of her face.

Her lips—her beautiful, perfect lips that he'd dreamed about night after night—turned up. "I was on the scenic route."

"Scenic route?"

"Human thing," she whispered, kissing him again.

He pulled back, staring at her. "This is real. This is happening."

Nalia nodded, her eyes drinking him in.

"Oh my gods," he said, crushing her against him, dazed.

Alive, alive—

Raif was only dimly aware of the jinn surrounding them, of Thatur softly growling his disapproval at their displays of affection.

He caught the scent of smoke in her hair, as though she'd been near a—

Fire.

He knew exactly why a Ghan Aisouri would be setting fire to the palace gate.

"You burned them," he said.

She nodded. "I wanted to see you first, but I had to."

"What if Calar—"

"I had to," she said simply. "Thatur said it would help you," she added. "We were trying to distract Calar. That's why I went to the palace before I came here."

"You've been in the Eye for a year and the first thing you did was go into battle for me?"

She leaned her forehead against his. "You're the first reason for why I do anything."

Raif's hands shook as they coiled her hair around his fingers. The last time he'd seen her, Nalia's hair had been nearly shorter than his and she'd been dying on the floor of the Eye. Now she was alive, her hair as long as when he'd first met her, falling around her shoulders in waves. She smiled softly as she rested her palm against his beard.

"I thought you didn't want to look like your father."

"You weren't here to shave me."

He turned his head and pressed his lips to her palm, gasping a little as her *chiaan* slipped past his lips. He could feel the change in her, not just her power but something else—something limitless and vast, ancient and wise that was now a part of Nalia, as much as her heart or the lungs inside her chest.

She no longer belonged just to him anymore.

Raif stepped back and let his hands fall to his sides. They

stood there for a long moment, staring at each other. Her eyes begged him to understand.

He did. There was no question what needed to happen—now, before the jinn around them acted.

The leader of the *tavrai*, son of Dthar Djan'Urbi, unsheathed his scimitar, dropped to one knee, and bowed his head as he placed it at her feet. After a moment, Raif raised his head, his eyes meeting Nalia's.

"My Empress," he said, loud enough for the surrounding jinn to hear, "my sword is yours. I pledge my blood to you."

34

BEING STABBED, GUTTED, BURNED ALIVE—ANYTHING was preferable to this.

Shirin stared, the weight of her unhappiness crushing. *Let this kill me,* she begged the gods, *let me be free.*

Violet eyes. Tattoos snaking up her arms. Even after spending a year trudging through the Eye, Raif's Ghan Aisouri was beautiful. Shirin had been expecting that. But the love in her eyes, the gentleness with which this Ghan Aisouri was looking at a Djan boy: Shirin could never have imagined. To see how much they loved each other was a very different thing from hearing about it for a year.

Nalia was too thin and her hair and clothes were coated in the same fine, gray dust that had been on all the other jinn who'd traveled through the Eye. But there was a fierceness to her, a regal authority. It radiated, like an aura. Though Nalia was small, she seemed to take up more space than the jinn around her.

The moment Raif fell to his knees, Shirin knew it was over. What little hope she'd had that they might one day be together fled and it would never come back. Raif Djan'Urbi would never love her. His words sliced Shirin open—couldn't everyone see her bleeding to death?

"My Empress," he said, his voice trembling with emotion— love, *adoration*—"my sword is yours. I pledge my blood to you."

How could this boy worshipping at the feet of a Ghan Aisouri be the Raif Djan'Urbi who'd coolly sentenced traitors to death and carried out the punishment himself? How could those lips that never left that *salfit*'s skin be the same ones that had shouted with joy after all the Aisouri had been slain?

That night, Raif had picked Shirin up and spun her around. They'd fallen to the grass, crying and laughing in each other's arms. *They're gone! They're fucking GONE!* he kept saying, over and over. And now . . .

Nalia knelt before him and pulled something off her neck. Raif's eyes widened as she took his hand and placed whatever it was on his palm, her lips grazing his fingers as she said, "And I to you."

As Raif looked down at his hand, Shirin caught a glimpse of what Nalia had given him: A ring. She'd given him a ring.

Solomon's sigil. It had to be. Gods, Shirin thought it couldn't get any worse. Nalia's lips brushed Raif's ear, and whatever she'd whispered to him was enough for Raif to pull her against him once more.

Rohifsa, he said to her.

"This needs to stop right now," said a voice beside Shirin.

Jaqar. His words woke Shirin from the miserable trance she'd fallen under and she took a breath, shoving the parts of her that had just died far away, where she'd never have to see them again.

"Agreed," Shirin said, surprised at the cold detachment in her voice. She turned to the jinn behind her, speaking to the *tavrai.* "*Tavrai* Djan'Urbi has just publicly denounced all we fight for. As such, he's a traitor and will be held accountable." She caught the eyes of her strongest fighters. *I'm dying, dying, breaking into a thousand pieces and he'll never know, he'll never know.*

"Put him in chains," Shirin said. The jinn hesitated and Shirin growled, *"Now."*

A flash of violet light seared the air and a translucent, indestructible barrier went up between Raif and the jinn.

"Touch one hair on Raif Djan'Urbi's head and I will make you sorely regret it," the Aisouri said, her eyes burning. Actually burning—Shirin could have sworn she saw amethyst flames in them.

Nalia's voice was low and soft, with the cadences of the aristocracy, yet there was no question it belonged to a jinni who would order an execution or start a war, if need be. She had a slight accent, acquired, no doubt, during her time on Earth. There wasn't a trace of cruelty in her voice or delivery, just a firm resolve backed by the ability to follow though with her threat.

"I think you'll find it difficult," Tazlim said, stepping in front of Shirin and the *tavrai* who had come to her side, "to fight the Empress *and* her army—as well as the leader of your own."

Tazlim glanced at Nalia and inclined his head, his eyes heavy with grief. "My Empress."

Though most of the Brass Army was at the camp in the clearing deeper in the forest, those near Tazlim hurried to flank him.

Nalia broke into a smile, the warmth of which surprised Shirin. She returned his small bow. "*Jahal'alund,* Tazlim."

Tazlim walked toward the gryphon and when the bird saw the Brass commander's face, he closed his eyes and his head fell forward. He clawed once at the ground, tearing a gash into the earth as he mourned for Kesmir.

The Ifrit jinni who'd accompanied Nalia on her ride to the forest hurried toward Raif. Shirin couldn't remember his name—some fool who'd refused to leave the Gate of the Eye for the past year.

"She needs a healer, sir. Food, rest. Not . . . *this.*" He gestured to Shirin and Jaqar with a look of contempt.

Raif nodded, then stood slightly in front of Nalia, his eyes on Shirin's. "You don't have the authority to sentence me—not yet." He turned to the jinn assembled. "You fought a battle today, and fought it well. We have dead to burn, mourning songs to sing. There will be a council meeting after the first meal tomorrow, at which time we'll discuss our next steps."

He looked at Shirin again and the past year swam between them—his grief, the late nights she'd stayed up with him, fighting side by side, that kiss.

"There is no *our* where you're concerned, Raif." She gestured toward Nalia. "You bowed down to an Aisouri and called her Empress. For fuck's sake, Djan'Urbi—there's nothing to discuss!"

Nalia calmly studied Shirin, and the pity Shirin recognized in those eyes unraveled her, the hatred unspooling into a tangle of knots. She could hardly breathe for the rage that crawled up her throat, settled in her lungs. Shirin curled her fists, lest anyone see the *chiaan* that was sneaking out of her fingertips. She couldn't let this *salfit* rattle her.

Shirin took a step toward the barrier, fury radiating from every pore in her body. "I hope you aren't expecting the rest of us to bow and scrape before you." Her hand slid to the hilt of her scimitar.

Raif stiffened, but Nalia merely smiled, wary. Like a snake eyeing its prey. The skin on Shirin's neck prickled.

"You must be Shirin," she said.

Shirin tightened her hold on the hilt of her scimitar. She felt exposed, as though the Aisouri could see every wish for Raif she'd made inside her heart.

"I wonder what else the dear leader of our revolution has told you," Shirin sneered. "Perhaps every military secret of the *tavrai*?"

Hurt lashed across Raif's face. *Stop,* a voice inside Shirin yelled. But Shirin couldn't stop, not now, not after the nightmare she'd just witnessed, the battle she'd just fought. She was so gods-damned *angry* and sad and so, so tired, the weariness weighing her down. She couldn't deal with a Ghan Aisouri on top of it all.

Raif stepped forward. "Fire and blood, Shirin. Can't you just—"

But he stopped as Nalia did the unexpected. She bowed, with one hand to her heart. It was a courtly bow, the kind the empress might have given to one of her Shaitan overlords. At least, that was what Shirin imagined. She'd never seen the empress up close.

"Thank you for taking care of my people," the Ghan Aisouri said. "I am forever in your debt."

Shirin drew in a sharp breath. *My people.* Like she owned them. Shirin turned to Raif and he sighed.

"Tell me you did not just hear that?" she said, her voice edged.

Raif ignored her, shouting at the jinn who stood around them, silent witnesses to the demise of the only successful revolution the jinn had ever had.

"This is not a performance for your amusement," he said. "Go and find something useful to do."

But none of them left. Nobody knew who was in charge anymore, least of all Shirin. And the respect Raif had enjoyed for a lifetime was crumbling right before her eyes. There was no coming back from this—Raif had turned traitor, whether he'd admit it or not.

"You want them to leave so you can try to bully us into accepting this piece of trash?" Jaqar said, gesturing to Nalia.

"That's it," Raif growled, murder in his eyes.

Nalia put her hand on his arm. *"Rohifsa,"* she whispered. "Those are just words, no?"

After a moment, he nodded and stood down. Submissive, her little pet already.

Nalia turned and addressed Shirin and Jaqar, including the jinn who surrounded them with one glance around the clearing.

"I know there is little love for me in this forest," Nalia said. "And I will not force myself upon you. But before you banish me, before you give up the possibility of us working together to rid this land of Calar, let me tell you what I saw in the Eye, what I learned. It might change your minds. You may always hate me—you certainly have every right to. But please, let me prove you wrong. Let me earn my crown, and if I am not worthy, I'll go. I will leave Arjinna and you will never see me again. I only want to help our people, and if I cannot do that, I won't cause discord with my presence."

"*Your* crown?" Shirin said. "You say you want to help change Arjinna and yet you still insist on the old ways—a crown for your pretty little head, a palace to live in. It's only been four years since your kind beat us and killed us. *Four years.*" Shirin turned to the *tavrai.* "What if one of us wants a crown, eh? What if we don't want any crowns at all?"

The *tavrai* nodded their assent, some cheering,

"I don't want to rule," Nalia said. "But the gods have decided otherwise."

"The gods," Shirin scoffed. She pointed at the moons. "You mean those assholes? The ones who plan to stamp us all out in, I don't know, the next few minutes? If the prophecies are true, you won't have a land to rule anyway."

"Then what the hell are we fighting for?" Raif growled. "She's been in the Eye for a year. She survived that hell and she comes home and the *first thing* she does is go to the palace to help us, to keep Calar from sending more soldiers over the Qaf." He turned to Nalia. "You need to rest. We'll continue this tomorrow."

Before they could turn away, Shirin stepped closer. "What about Solomon's sigil?" she asked, her voice pitched low so that only Jaqar, Raif, Nalia, and Tazlim could hear.

"I saw her give it to you." Shirin turned to Nalia. "So which one of you will force all of us to do your bidding? Somehow I'm guessing it won't be him."

"You have no idea what the hell you're talking about, Shirin," Raif said.

Nalia's eyes fell on Shirin's. "I was a slave too," she said. "And I think that ring is the most evil thing that has ever been created."

"Which is why neither of us will be using the sigil," Raif added. "I've told you before—the ring would only give us another, more powerful master. It would make everything we've fought for pointless."

Raif looked at Shirin. Not a glance, but a real look that took the measure of her. Did he find her wanting? Hadn't he always?

"What you saw at the prison—me and the ghoul," Raif said softly. "Remember?"

How could she forget? It was a few *hours* ago. She shouldn't have saved him. But almost as soon as she had the thought, Shirin regretted it. No matter what he did to her, she would always save him.

"Lucky for her I didn't let you kill yourself," she said. Shirin spit on the ground, the highest form of contempt she could think of. "It would have been better if you'd died."

Nalia turned to Raif, real fear written on her face, and he pressed closer to her. "I'll explain later," he said softly.

His eyes drank her in, as though she was an elixir, a tonic, the only thing he wanted. As if he hadn't heard a word Shirin had just said. It was so horribly obvious that he'd enslaved himself to her, whether he realized it or not.

How could he? *How could he?*

Raif turned to Shirin. "The reason why I'm calling a council meeting is not because I want to lead us. It's because I don't. And this has nothing to do with Nalia. I made the decision earlier today. You can ask Tazlim if you don't believe me."

The words were thorns that wound their way through her insides.

"I'm your second," she said, her words almost a whisper. "I'm . . . and you . . . what the hell, Raif?"

This was more than betrayal. More than rejection. She'd loved Raif enough to be willing to die for him. She'd kept him alive in his darkest hours, she'd been his shoulder to cry on, his punching bag, and now he was telling her none of it had meant a thing to him, not a thing. She thought of Yurik: *From the moment I met you, all I've ever wanted to do is make you happy.* Raif would never say something like that to her. How could she have been so blind? She'd pushed away the only jinni who had ever given a shit about her—and for what?

"I pledged my blood to you," she said, her voice finally breaking. She pointed to Nalia. "She and her kind stood by while my overlord raped and killed my mother *in front of me*, then did *despicable* things to me. Again and again." Raif stared, his face going pale. The shock in his eyes gave her a savage satisfaction.

He reached for her and she stepped back, growling. "Don't you fucking touch me."

"I had no idea," Raif said, his voice pained. "Shir—"

"Why else would a little girl stop speaking for over two years?" The tears were falling now and she didn't care, she didn't give a damn. "If you knew, would it change anything? Would you kill her now like you should?"

"No." He didn't hesitate, not even for a moment. "Nalia was a child when the overlords owned us—we all were. This is not her fault. I . . ." He sighed. "Shir. Look at me."

She couldn't. She didn't want his pity—that wasn't why she'd said those things. And now his Aisouri was there feeling sorry for her, gods, why had she said any of that—

"I wish we'd rescued you before any of that happened."

She glared at him. "Well you didn't."

Raif's eyes fixed on hers. "Don't make an enemy of me, Shirin," he said softly. "Don't push me away. No good will come of that."

"Too late," she said.

Raif sighed. "As you wish." He put his arm around Nalia's shoulders and drew her toward the path that led to his *ludeen*.

There was no way in hell Shirin was letting them walk away like that.

All Raif wanted was to be alone with Nalia. But they were only five steps out of the communal area of the camp and Shirin was already yelling again.

"Aisouri," she called.

Nalia turned around and Raif gripped her shoulder more

tightly. He knew he'd kill the first jinni who tried to do her harm and he really hoped it wouldn't be Shirin.

Nalia simply looked at Raif's second, waiting, betraying none of the fear and fury that Raif knew must be all over his face.

Shirin took a step forward. "You are hereby banished from the Forest of Sighs, by order of the *tavrai* council. You, your army, its commander, and the bird need to get the hell out." Her eyes went to Raif's. "Time to choose, brother."

He stepped forward, Nalia just behind him, so close he could feel the heat of her body. She'd been back from the Eye for mere *minutes* and this—*this*—was how she was welcomed. It shamed him, that the *tavrai* could be so petty, so incapable of seeing the big picture.

"We're to have a meeting," Raif said, his voice even. "But first, we have dead to burn. Do not dishonor them. Prepare the pyres."

Shirin lifted her chin. "No. Not until this *salfit* is out of our forest."

"Fools," Thatur growled.

Raif looked over at him in surprise.

"This Ghan Aisouri carried Solomon's sigil for a year and has returned here to keep her vow. She has been anointed by the gods themselves," Thatur continued. "She wears the white phoenix's feather around her neck—the only jinni to be in its presence without dying—and you dare, *you dare*, to speak of her in such a manner?"

They needed to be alone. *Now.* Raif was starting to hate every jinni who was keeping him from being in his *ludeen* with Nalia.

"With the ring we could end this war *right now*," Shirin

snarled, "and yet they refuse to use it, to stand by while more jinn die."

"On Earth," Nalia said, "the sigil is called *Khatem l-hekma*—the ring of wisdom. By exercising the right *not* to use it, Raif is demonstrating his wisdom. The ring is a threat to Calar, maybe one strong enough to convince her to step down. But even if she doesn't, we have an army more than capable of defeating her forces."

"We don't need an army," Shirin said. "Not when Raif can put that ring on his finger and tell Calar to get the hell out of here." She turned to Raif, her eyes full of fury. He'd seen her look at other jinn like that, but never him. "What are you waiting for?" Shirin gestured to the sky, still dark and glowing with the full Three Widows. "Who knows what the gods will bring next? We need to prepare—"

"You always told me you'd rather die than be a slave again," Raif said quietly. He stepped forward, his hands out, pleading. "Shirin. If I put on that ring, then you're a slave again—*my* slave. Is that what you want? I won't wear the Master King's sigil. Not if there's hope of defeating Calar some other way."

"So we have this amazing weapon," Shirin said, "but we're not going to use it."

Jaqar turned to the *tavrai*, a sneer on his face. "Some kind of battle strategy, eh?"

"Calar doesn't need to know we don't want to use it," Raif said. His patience was wearing thin. "Once she learns we have the ring, she'd be a fool to stay here."

Shirin shook her head. "I can't see her leaving that throne, ring or no."

"If I wear the ring, I'd be choosing *for* Arjinnans," Raif said. "The whole point of this war is that they have the right to make their own decisions. Give the Brass Army a chance. Give Nalia a chance."

"Where is the Raif Djan'Urbi who danced on the tables when he heard the Ghan Aisouri had been killed?" Shirin said. "The one who said he'd rather die than bend the knee? Your father gave up his life so that we could be free of royal rule. No *tavrai* will spill blood for her. I certainly won't."

"I want Arjinnans to choose," Nalia said. "I have no intention of forcing myself upon the realm."

"And what if we choose to execute you for your crimes?" Jaqar said. "I have no doubt you've got a lot of *tavrai* blood on your hands."

"Then you'd better be prepared to string me up right next to her," Raif said.

"Well. I guess there's nothing else to say." Shirin shook her head. "Meeting or no meeting, you're one of them now. See you on the other side of the battlefield." She turned to go.

"The enemy is in the palace, Shirin," he said.

"I don't think so," she said softly, looking back at him. "Not anymore."

Raif took in the *tavrai* standing before him: old, young, some friends of his father's, some too young to remember Dthar Djan'Urbi. He'd never had so much ill will directed toward him.

He saw hatred—*hatred*—in their eyes. Betrayal. They didn't understand. Why couldn't they understand?

"Those of you who wish to join us"—he threw his hand toward the forest floor and a green line of *chiaan* shimmered between them—"cross this line. We believe in an Arjinna where you can love who you want, and a land free of bloodshed."

"One ruled by a Ghan Aisouri empress," said Jaqar. "Don't forget that."

Raif hesitated. He'd bent the knee already, claimed her as his empress. He could no longer call himself a true son of Dthar Djan'Urbi. But that didn't matter as much anymore.

"Yes," Raif said. "One ruled by a Ghan Aisouri empress—*if* that is what the realm desires."

"What if the realm doesn't want that?" Shirin said.

"Then I will serve Arjinna as she wishes me to," Nalia answered, spreading her hands in a show of submission. "The gods showed me in the Eye—I will lead our realm and bring it back from ruin." She glanced at Raif. "But I won't be doing it alone."

The look she gave him lessened the misery of losing his people. She was alive, *here*, and he wasn't alone anymore.

"The choice is yours," Raif said. "I've made mine."

The line glowed, reflected in the eyes of his brothers and sisters.

No one stepped over it.

35

THE *TAVRAI*S REACTION TO NALIA AND TO THE RING WAS a confirmation from the gods: if she didn't lead, the realm would be reduced to packs of snarling dogs, each one fighting for control, spinning the realm into further chaos. Hers was a war with many fronts and she needed time to sort it all out: Calar and her shadows, the divided loyalties of the Ifrit, the *tavrai*, the Brass Army, and all the jinn who were simply trying to stay alive. If she hadn't spent a year with the white phoenix or lain beneath the lote tree, she wouldn't have thought it possible to untangle the mess the realm was in.

She could feel Raif's sadness in his *chiaan* as he stared at the glowing line he'd drawn between him and his family. Nalia hadn't expected any *tavrai* to cross the line and it hurt, seeing his soldiers reject him. She knew how hard it was for Raif when he turned his back on them and began walking away, his shoulders drawn in. The *tavrai* watched, silent. She followed his lead, her hand in his, Taz and Touma and Thatur staying well behind in order to ensure their safety. Their little party was halfway to the clearing where the Brass Army waited when a cry arose from the *tavrai*. Nalia turned just in time to see the hulking jinni who had stood beside Shirin throw another jinni into the dirt and begin pummeling him.

Raif turned, a look of recognition crossing his face. "Aw, hells." He cupped his mouth with his hands and when he spoke, his voice was a furious growl. "Jaqar, stand down!"

The jinni ignored Raif, the sound of his fists hitting flesh echoing in the clearing.

"Who . . ." Nalia's voice died as she caught sight of the jinni's face as he flailed in Jaqar's iron grip. The disfigured flesh could have been anyone's, but his eyes: that particular shade of gold, the almond shape—*Bashil's* eyes. She knew exactly who the jinni was.

"Father!" she cried.

And her world was remade yet again.

Instinct took over and Nalia launched herself at Jaqar, caring little for her stature as the heir to the throne. Empress or no, she was going to save the last surviving member of her family.

Jaqar looked up, a menacing grin crossing his face just as Nalia landed a blow to his jaw. He stumbled back, leaving her father in the dust. She could have used magic, but Nalia wanted to feel his bones give way beneath her flesh, to show Jaqar she could fight him any way she pleased.

Ajwar Shai'Dzar stared at his daughter, tears falling down his ravaged face. A faint smile slipped across his lips before he fell into a coughing fit, blood dripping down his chin. Raif yelled and Nalia turned just as a burst of Jaqar's green *chiaan* hit her in the chest. She stumbled back, gasping. Raif sprinted toward her, but she raised a hand.

"I've got it," she said. Raif stopped, uncertain. "This is my fight." She faced Jaqar, flexing her fingers. "Are you sure you want to do this?"

He pulled out his scimitar, his voice dripping with hatred. "I've been waiting my whole life to kill one of your kind, you worthless bitch."

Thatur roared, stamping his claws against the hard-packed dirt.

"That's it," Raif said. "I'm killing him. I'm killing him right now." Raif moved forward, a dagger in each hand, but Thatur stopped him with one of his powerful wings.

"The empress is the finest warrior in the land. Let them see for themselves what happens when someone dares to cross her," he said. "They won't soon try it again."

Nalia gestured to Touma, who stood a few steps to her right, *chiaan* bleeding from his fingers. "Touma—my father," she said, without taking her eyes away from Jaqar.

Despite her exhaustion and the strain Calar's attack had taken on her, Nalia's adrenaline was coursing through her: she itched for the fight. Nalia hadn't realized how much she'd wanted this—fists and blood, shooting *chiaan* like iron-tipped arrows. If she'd had this in the Eye, it would have reminded her she was alive, that the power she'd been born with had not abandoned her. Nalia didn't want the grace of the court. After the massacre of her people and being a slave on Earth, she liked getting her hands dirty. Craved it.

Touma helped Nalia's father to his feet and out of the ring that had instantly developed around Nalia and Jaqar.

She stood still, watching. Waiting.

Jaqar gave a yell and evanesced—faster than she'd ever seen a non-Aisouri twist his body into smoke. He landed beside her just a moment later, but Nalia had already slipped out of his reach, graceful and swift despite her dark year in the Eye. She reached inside for the reserve of *chiaan* that filled her body, and her hands blazed with blinding violet light as she drew the magic to the surface of her skin. Nalia threw her *chiaan* at her opponent, the magic surging over him like a wave. Jaqar flew into the air and landed heavily on his side. She heard a bone crack, his agonized scream.

"Are we done?" she asked.

He spit and she stepped back before it could hit her. "Not nearly," he growled.

Jaqar pushed back to his feet and lurched toward her just as Nalia evanesced, landing directly behind him. She kicked Jaqar's legs out from underneath him, but as he fell, the blade of his scimitar swiped across her middle. The metal found its mark, the pain a bloom that spread across her abdomen.

"Nalia!" Raif started into the ring, but halted as Nalia reached her hand up, her eyes on the sky above.

A bolt of lightning flashed, a blinding cobra of light, followed by an earth-shattering clap of thunder that sounded directly above the forest. As a second bolt sped toward them, Nalia reached out her hand, halting it with her *chiaan* just before it pierced Jaqar's chest. The air sizzled as the lightning remained suspended between flesh and sky. Nalia drew its energy into her, the Ifrit side of her magic gorging on the electric blade's energy. It rushed into her, filling Nalia with its scalding power. It tasted like the sky, like the beginning of the worlds, like spicy peppers. She stood over Jaqar, her eyes locked on his, straining against the power of the bolt. For the first time, the hatred in his eyes was replaced with fear, a terror so deep his body shook.

"I will never force you to bend the knee," she said, loud enough for all the *tavrai* to hear, "but touch one of my people again and it will be the last thing you do."

She threw the bolt into the ground and it stabbed the green line Raif had drawn, scorching the earth so that the line disappeared, the *tavrai* crying out as they moved back as one.

"Together, we can defeat Calar and heal our realm," she said to the jinn assembled as she backed away from the circle. "There is no *us* or *them*—just *we*. This fighting brings us no closer to our freedom. And it ends tonight."

Nalia turned her back without another word and rushed to her father's side, leaving Jaqar panting in the dust. Ajwar Shai'Dzar's eyes fluttered open. He smiled, weak, and lifted a hand to his daughter's cheek.

"My beautiful Empress."

He slumped against Touma, unconscious. A jinni in white robes rushed to him with her bag of supplies. Nalia stiffened.

Could she trust a *tavrai* healer to care for a former Shaitan over-lord?

The jinni looked up, her deep blue eyes kind. "I do not take sides in these conflicts. I only fight disease and pain. Your father is safe with me."

Strong arms encircled her as Raif helped her to her feet. "Nice trick with the lightning," he said, brushing his lips against her hair.

He went in and out of focus. "Nalia?"

Darkness.

"You know we have to kill her, right?"

Shirin turned at the sound of Jaqar's rough voice. His face was ashen and he rested his hands on his knees, breathing heavily. Nalia had really done a number on him. The fact that he was even walking pointed to the healer's abilities more than to his strength.

After seeing what Nalia had done with the lightning, Shirin had turned and run blindly into the forest, only stopping on the banks of a small pond once she was too tired to go on.

"*We?*" she said.

"You want to kill the *salfit* just as much as I do—don't pretend otherwise." Jaqar massaged his cheek, which was already sporting a sizable bruise from where Nalia had punched him.

"You're right, I do," she said. "But she's apparently all-powerful and Raif has the ring. We're screwed."

Jaqar's eyes flashed, bright in the moonlight that filtered

through the treetops. "So what, after everything that's happened to us, we're just going to . . . give in? Shirin, if we let this go on, we might as well return to the plantations and kiss our overlords' rings."

His voice trembled with emotion on that last word, reminding Shirin that behind his tough exterior, Jaqar had endured his fair share of loss, humiliation, and pain. Everything he did was to ensure none of them had to live the life they'd been born into ever again. His posturing was all armor. Now, he'd finally let her see beneath it. They'd come a long way from their frenzied, rough lovemaking in the forest.

"Jaqar, there's no way in all hells we'll be able to kill an Aisouri. She made it through the Eye—lived there for a whole godsdamn year! You saw what she could do . . . that lightning."

Jaqar smiled. "You're absolutely right. We'd be fools to fight her."

She threw up her hands. "Then what are we arguing about this for?"

"I didn't say we shouldn't kill her—I said we shouldn't *fight* her. You know what I thought was interesting?"

Shirin said nothing, only raised her eyebrows. There was plenty she'd found interesting.

"The first thing she did was run straight to Djan'Urbi. The look on her face—tell me she wouldn't do anything to protect him."

"She doesn't need to protect him. Raif has the ring," she said.

"I don't think he does."

"What do you mean? We saw her give it to him—"

"Do you remember what Raif said at that first council meeting after he came back from Earth?" Jaqar said. "The Aisouri was obligated by a vow to give him the ring, but he'd chosen to have her carry it because it was safest with her."

"What's your point, Jaqar?" Shirin snapped.

"I think he'll have the Aisouri keep the ring again. As you said—she's apparently all-powerful. Why would he keep the ring on him if he doesn't want to use it?"

"Well, great, it'll be even *harder* to get—" Shirin's stomach gave a sickening turn. "You want to use Raif as bait."

Jaqar nodded. "Give the Aisouri a choice—the ring or his life."

"She'll call our bluff. Keep the ring, kick our asses, and save Raif. We'll be back at square one—and that's *if* she doesn't kill us."

Shirin didn't have many standards, but this was one of them: you don't kill the people you love. There was no way, in any universe or situation, in which she would kill Raif.

Jaqar leaned against a tree, a thoughtful expression on his face. "She doesn't know you wouldn't be willing to kill Raif—she doesn't know the first thing about you. Or me, for that matter. Raif's shat on everything we believe in, betrayed all the *tavrai* who've pledged their blood to him. That's as good a reason to kill a jinni as I've ever heard."

She pushed past him. "This is ridiculous—"

He grabbed her arm before she could leave, his grip painful. "We need to act soon, Shirin. We have a window of opportunity while they're still in the camp. We don't do this now, it's over."

She wished there was another battle to fight right now so she could kill everything in sight.

"You know I'm right," he said softly, letting go of her arm. "We have to get that ring. And the Aisouri has to die."

If Nalia died after a year of his grieving her, Raif would be dead, too. But what other choice did they have? Nalia was back; there were more Aisouri children popping up than ever before. The caste was rebuilding itself and everything would just go back to how it was.

Shirin ran a hand through her hair. "Let's just say, for argument's sake, that she takes her chances and fights us? Then we've gained . . . nothing."

"She knows guns are faster than *chiaan*."

Oh.

"And if Raif has the ring?"

"We outnumber him, take it, then command the Aisouri to leave the realm—or command her to kill herself. Whatever. Simple as that."

Whatever. Like killing Raif's *rohifsa* was all in a day's work.

Shirin shook her head. "I can't, Jaqar. This isn't who we are. We have to find another way—"

"There is no other way, Shirin!" he shouted, finally losing his temper. "If we don't kill her and get that ring as far away from her as possible, then the Ghan Aisouri will be in power once again. And, this time, they'll have a ring that can enslave us all."

"Raif would never let that happen," she said.

Jaqar gave her a pitying look and her face warmed. "It's no secret that you want to bed the commander, sister. I, for one, don't care what you do in your free time, so long as it's not letting traitors go free." He sighed. "You disappoint me, Shirin—I thought you had the instincts to lead us. Maybe I was wrong."

Shirin shoved Jaqar up against a tree, her lips nearly touching his. "Do not make the mistake of thinking you can use that against me. After what he pulled today, I want to see Raif hang just as much as you do." She could taste the lie, bitter and numbing. "But we're not going to do it like this, in secret, like thugs. We'll have a council meeting and a vote."

"A *raiga* without teeth is no *raiga* at all," Jaqar said.

Shirin pushed off him and crossed to the pond, shaking. She stared at the still water as the rage and love and hurt tumbled through her. She could never kill Raif. And everyone knew it. She was such a godsdamn fool.

"You can't save the life of a tyrant just to keep one man's heart from breaking," Jaqar said.

The words burrowed into her, deep. She felt the horrible truth of them in her bones.

Nalia had to die. And if it killed Raif to see her gone, then so be it. This was war—none of them had expected to live through it, anyway. And this—this would kill Shirin, too. Whatever made Shirin *Shirin* shattered into a thousand pieces as she made the decision to destroy Raif's life.

"All right," she said. "What do you have in mind?"

36

RAIF HAD HAD NO CHOICE BUT TO LEAVE NALIA IN THE healer's *ludeen*, which was located in the hollow of an improbably large *widr* tree. He'd posted Thatur, Touma, and a regiment of Brass soldiers outside while he helped to burn the prison battle's dead. Nalia only learned all this after she awoke from dreamless sleep several hours later, panicked and lost.

"Raif," she gasped.

Nalia looked around for her *rohifsa*, the white phoenix, anything familiar.

"He'll be back soon," said a quiet voice from a corner of the *ludeen*. The healer Nalia had briefly spoken to in the clearing smiled, her hands full of fragrant herbs.

"I'm Aisha," she said, handing Nalia a warm cup of *chal* after she sat up.

She reminded her so much of Phara, Zanari's sweet healer who'd patched up Nalia more than once. But, instead of being a Shaitan, as most healers were, Aisha had sapphire eyes. A Marid.

"Thank you," Nalia said as she accepted the thick clay mug. "I know it must be hard to help someone your people hate."

Aisha shrugged. "The *tavrai* have only ever known sorrow. They were fed it at their mother's breast. You terrify them—your power, how you've changed our commander. They can already feel the shackles returning."

"And you?"

"A Djan loving a Ghan Aisouri gives me hope. And hope is a rare thing these days. We need more of it."

Aisha mixed a compound with a mortar and pestle, then crossed the *ludeen*. "May I?" she said, gesturing to Nalia's tunic.

Nalia nodded and Aisha gently lifted the long shirt. The ugly gash across her abdomen was now only a faint red line.

"Wow," Nalia said. "Those are some herbs."

Aisha smiled. "The Forest of Sighs has many secrets."

The healer rubbed a dark-blue paste over the wound and a tingling coolness spread through Nalia. Then she held a small bottle up to Nalia's lips.

"Just a healing tonic," she said at Nalia's questioning glance. It tasted of rosemary and cloves with a slight medicinal bitterness.

Nalia lay back against the pillows, almost crying at the feel of a mattress beneath her body and soft sheets against her skin. She sank into its warmth, the first bed she'd lain in for over a year. And light that banished the darkness—candlelight and lanterns filled with wisps of *chiaan* the color of a calm tropical sea. The healer's room had been carved out of the velvety wood of a *widr* and carried the tree's faint, familiar scent. Nalia breathed deeply. She was home. Alive. It was so unexpected, so wonderful, that she laughed softly, turning her head into the pillow.

"Maybe I gave you too much of that tonic," Aisha said.

Nalia shook her head. "No, no. I just . . . the Eye . . ." She shivered, pulling the blankets closer to her, joy giving way to a deep, aching exhaustion.

Aisha placed a hand on Nalia's shoulder. "Rest, Empress. You'll need your strength."

Nalia looked up in surprise. "I thought healers didn't take sides?"

Aisha bit back a smile. "I lied."

This kindness, the hope that some of Arjinna's people were willing to change, filled Nalia with an overwhelming gratitude. She blinked back tears, laughing again.

"I'm sorry," she said.

"It's to be expected—you've been through a lot."

Aisha stood and blew out the candles so that only the lanterns filled with *chiaan* lit the room. Nalia closed her eyes, a darkness that she could finally welcome.

Raif returned several hours later, face haggard, smelling of elder-pine smoke from the burnings. Aisha stepped out of the *ludeen* and Nalia reached out her arms. He fell into them, his face buried in the crook of her neck.

"I'm sorry I smell like death," he murmured.

"I'm sorry I smell like the Eye."

He laughed softly. "Aren't we a pair?"

He pulled something out of his pocket and handed it to her. A familiar jeweled hilt, a blade fashioned from enchanted jade that caught and held the room's light. Her Aisouri dagger, the only thing left from her childhood.

Nalia bit her lip as tears threatened. "You found it in the Eye?"

She imagined him being alone in his room with nothing of hers but that dagger. He nodded and as her tears fell, he held her against him. They rested, wordless, just holding each other, until the healer returned.

After Aisha examined Nalia once more, she released her into Raif's care. "Rest and food," the healer said. Nalia's wound had already healed. "That's what she needs now."

A hush stole over the camp as snow began to fall, the tiny flakes swirling around them before carpeting the ground. Nalia shivered and Raif pulled her close as he led her deeper into the forest. She gripped his hand, afraid he would disappear again. Eyes, most of them hostile, stared at them from the *ludeens* they passed on their way to Raif's home. Raif didn't seem to notice or care. He looked at her and smiled, boyish and sweet. It was almost impossible for them to hide their eagerness to be alone, to say and do all the things they'd imagined while she'd been trapped in the Eye.

"We're almost there," he said, squeezing her hand.

Behind her, Touma and several members of the Brass Army followed. Nalia didn't need to ask why such a large guard was necessary. She breathed deeply, relishing the scent of the forest. The sharp sweetness of the pines, the rich, damp earth. The trees seemed to watch them, bearing witness to this miracle—Nalia and Raif, alive, holding hands. It was nearing evening now, but there was no sunset: the moons continued their otherworldly glow. She wouldn't let herself think of the Godsnight, not now. *Just some time, please,* she begged the gods. *Let me rest. Let me be with him.*

All around her was the rustling of life: birds chirping, animals slinking through the underbrush. In the Eye, the only sound Nalia had ever heard were the cries of hunting ghouls or the sound of her own voice, the phoenix's song.

Raif's tree house was set apart from the others, nestled in the branches of a sturdy *widr*, fused to the wood as though the *ludeen* had grown from it. Bottle-glass windows were scattered all over the walls, like the windows of a ship. Impossible to see through, they reflected the warm glow inside, scattering the thin blanket of snow on the ground with the pinks, greens, and blues of the glass. A stream gurgled nearby and the wind sighed through the *widr*'s silver leaves, which seemed to catch and hold the moonlight so that each leaf shimmered. A spiral staircase curved up from the ground to the rounded doorway, ending in a small porch. It was just as Raif had once described it to her.

Nalia gripped his arm. "It's perfect," she whispered.

"*Batai vita sonouq,*" Raif said, his eyes never leaving her face. *My home is yours.*

The words were a different kind of tonic from the one Aisha had given her, a warmth that stole through her whole body.

Once inside, away from the eyes of everyone in the camp, Raif picked her up and carried her to the bed.

"I'm filthy," she protested.

"We'll manifest new sheets," he said. "I'm sure these aren't up to your standards, anyway." He grinned and she thought of the silk sheets she'd manifested in their tent in the Dhoma camp.

"This feels like the height of luxury to me," she said.

Without warning, she burst into fresh tears and Raif held her to him. "It's over," he whispered. "It's over."

But it wasn't. Calar still ruled the realm and the *tavrai* wanted Nalia to hang. The horrors of the past years were far from over.

They lay on their sides, gazing at each other for hours. Marveling.

"I still think I'm going to wake up," Raif said, gripping her hands as though she would float away. He was wearing the same expression he'd had after she'd nearly drowned in the Pacific, trapped under Haran's body—love and fear mixed with a fierce resolve.

"Me too," she whispered.

Nalia knew she must look a sight, but she hadn't been prepared for the shock of seeing Raif so transformed. He seemed much older, harder. The beard gave him a ferocious look. But his eyes—they shone with joy, tracing the lines of her face, over and over.

"How?" he whispered. "How are you here? How are you even alive?"

She told him as much as she could put into words: the phoenix, the heart plant, the vision at the lote tree, the empresses. He fingered the white feather around her neck.

"Do you remember the times we were together while you were gone?" he asked. "Malek's mansion—"

"The City of Brass," she finished. "I kept wishing for more." She brought his fingers up to her lips. "And that last time in the Eye, when the phoenix came . . ."

Raif leaned his forehead against hers. "I thought you were dead, Nal. I prayed to the gods for a sign and they took me there, to the Eye. I thought they were giving me a chance to save you—" His voice caught and she pulled him against her, murmuring all the things she'd wanted to say for so long.

"I gave up on you," he said, his voice anguished.

"No, you didn't." Nalia rested her palms on either side of his face. "I felt you the whole time I was there. You helped me through. You always do."

"Gods, I'm such a coward." He told her of the ghoul he'd almost allowed to kill him, of his choice to step down as leader. "You were up against so much more and you never gave up."

"I had you to get home to. Knowing you were out there, fighting . . . how could I stop? If I'd thought you were dead . . . I would have looked for the first ghoul that would eat me, myself."

He shook his head. "The gods wouldn't have let you."

The gods. Why did they only intervene at the last moment? She shifted and her eye caught his scimitar propped against the bedside table, within easy reach. Who knew what the *tavrai* would try to do tonight?

Raif pressed his lips to her forehead. "I almost lost this chance," he murmured against her skin. "If it weren't for Shirin . . ."

She shuddered and he held her closer, his body warm and real and safe. What would she have done if he'd been dead when she walked into that camp?

She'd had an immediate dislike of Shirin, but Nalia would be forever grateful for how she'd saved Raif. Grateful that Shirin loved him enough. It'd been impossible not to feel sorry for her, watching the girl's heart shatter.

"You pledged your blood to me," Nalia said, awed. Raif Djan'Urbi, leader of the revolution—her former enemy she'd been commanded to kill, taught to hate—loved her, *served* her.

"I pledge everything of myself to you." He said those words so matter-of-factly. The sun is yellow, spring comes after winter, *I pledge everything*. The tip of his nose brushed against hers. "My Empress." The *my* was proprietary in the best kind of way.

"But the *tavrai*—"

"They'll have to decide for themselves what or who they'll fight for. If they choose to fight against you, then so be it." His voice was laced with sadness.

She shifted, propping herself up on an elbow. "Raif, I can't let you fight against your friends, your family."

"*You're* my family."

Family. Such a simple word, but it meant the world to hear him call her that.

She sat bolt upright. Family: where was Zanari? Nalia hadn't seen her in the clearing, and no one had mentioned her. It was as if she were—

"Where's Zanari?" Her voice went high with panic. *Not Zan, not her too. Please, please*. "Raif, please tell me she's not—"

"Shhh, it's okay. She's fine. She's on Earth." Raif drew her against him. She sank into his arms, relieved. "Zan's gonna be so happy to find out you're home." He smiled, wistful. "She's one of the Dhoma now."

"Zanari's with Phara, then?"

It was hard for Nalia to imagine Zanari ever leaving her brother's side, but, as she well knew, love made you do unexpected things.

Raif nodded. "Of course. Did you really think they'd be apart for long?"

Nalia shook her head. "No." Her smile faded a little. "So she's gone—for good?"

"Yeah." He sighed. "And many others before this is all over." He twisted a strand of her hair around his finger. "What happened at the palace?"

She told him to the best of her ability, and by the time she'd finished, a look of horror had crossed his face.

"She could have killed you," he said. "She almost killed *me* that way."

She put a hand on his arm. "I'm stronger than she is. I know I am. And we have an army. And whatever the Godsnight brings. Who knows how that will work in our favor?"

"The Godsnight," Raif muttered. "Perfect timing." He shook his head. "I wish we could just . . . go."

"Leave the war to fight itself?" she asked, shivering as his fingertips trailed over her collarbone.

"Yes. We'd just run. Wherever Calar's mind couldn't follow." He sighed. "We'd go back to our tent in the Sahara."

A soft smile played on Nalia's face as she pressed her hand

against the sheets. Instantly, they became the slippery silk that she'd manifested for their last night in Morocco. Raif stared down at the shimmery fabric.

"Close your eyes," she whispered.

The wooden walls of Raif's *ludeen* turned into the animal hide of the Dhoma tents. An intricate Moroccan lamp dangled in the center of the tent, throwing rose light in lacy patterns all over the roof and floor. The room filled with the scent of amber and sandalwood and the faint tinge of a campfire.

Nalia leaned over Raif, her lips against his ear. "Your wish is my command."

He opened his eyes, taking in the changed surroundings. "How did you . . ." He shook his head. "Show-off."

She grinned and threw an embroidered pillow at him, the magic so real that grains of sand coated its delicate designs.

"Oh, now you're asking for it," he said.

Nalia squealed as Raif gently tackled her, laughing as his fingers found her most ticklish spots. When his body shifted on top of hers, she pulled him closer, hungry. Raif's hands moved down her arms and gripped her waist. She nodded at the question in his eyes, her fingers already undoing the buttons of his tunic.

"Are you sure?" he murmured. "You're not too tired or—"

She stopped him with a hard kiss, one that obliterated all thought and turned them into a tangle of limbs, their clothes thrown in every direction. The sheets turned gray from the Eye's dust and the ash of the burnings. The grit on their skin had trails running through it of sweat, kisses, tongues, teeth. Nalia held on to him and didn't let go, didn't look away. *I am yours yours yours.*

Raif pulled her close, gentle, then ravenous, and nothing, *nothing* would ever separate them again.

No one would write a song about the feel of Raif's *chiaan* flooding her, the way it made Nalia suck in her breath and arch her back as he held her, marveling. The stories would not speak of the way he gasped when she touched him, the way she moaned softly against his ear, her hands gripping his hair as his lips fell against her breasts. The great poets could only imagine the desire that carried them that night, the empress and her Djan revolutionary who would transform their land and the hearts of their people with this ecstatic, all-consuming love that refused to die.

37

THERE WAS A KNOCK AT THE DOOR AND THEY BOTH jumped, roused from exhausted, blissful sleep. Raif slid off the bed, alert, tense. He reached for his scimitar.

"Raif?" came a woman's voice through the door.

His shoulders relaxed and he turned to where Nalia lay, naked and perfect despite being absolutely filthy from a year in the Eye. "My mother," he said. "Is it okay . . . ?"

Nalia sat up, biting her lip. Despite everything that had happened tonight, it was the first time he'd seen her look nervous. "All right," she said, quiet.

"Hey." He reached out, trailing the tips of his fingers through her hair. "I love you."

He pressed his lips to her bare shoulder before pulling on some pants. Nalia threw on one of his tunics that littered the floor and the pair of *sawala* pants she'd been wearing as he walked to the door, shirtless.

"*Raif.*" She gestured to his bare chest. "Can you at least pretend we haven't—you know. It's your *mother.*"

"Nal, I think she knows what we've been doing." He laughed as Nalia buried her face in her hands.

Raif opened the door and his mother stepped into the *ludeen*, her long lavender-gray hair shimmering in the candlelight. She looked around the room in confusion and Raif bit back a smile—they'd forgotten all about their Moroccan decor. Her eyes found Nalia immediately and his mother stared at his *rohifsa* for a long, agonizing moment, her lips a thin line.

She hates her, Raif realized. *She hates her but she loves me too much to say it.*

A Ghan Aisouri, in her son's bed. A Ghan Aisouri who her son had just pledged his blood to, as his sovereign. His mother hadn't been there to see it, and he suddenly remembered why: she'd been with Kesmir's—now Taz's—daughter. His friend's loss was a despair Raif couldn't think of right now. He needed these few hours to himself, to be happy, to smile.

He would attend to Taz first thing tomorrow, see what he could do to help his friend through the hell of losing his *rohifsa*. He wanted Taz to be the one to tell Nalia about Yasri, to introduce them, to share stories of the girl's extraordinary father.

He watched as Nalia's eyes traced his mother's face: he had her eyes, the same stubborn tilt to her chin. The rest of him was his father. It grieved him to know Dthar would never know Nalia, nor she him. They would have liked each other, he was certain.

"I love your son," Nalia said, the first to speak.

His lips turned up—he'd always admired how direct Nalia was. Never coy—she didn't play games. And he loved that those were the first words she said to his mother. To her credit, his mother's eyes widened slightly and her frown lessened.

"I love him more than anything or anyone in the realms," Nalia continued. "I can't make up for what my caste has done, I know that. And I don't want this power. But I have it and it's my duty to the gods and Arjinna to serve the realm." She glanced at Raif. "I choose him. I always choose him. I have no wish to hinder or dishonor the work the *tavrai* do or to dishonor your husband's memory." She gestured to Raif. "Or his legacy."

"Then why does my son call you *Empress?* Because that is very much hindering our work and—" She turned to Raif. "It dishonors his father and all he stood for."

Raif had given his whole life to the revolution. Couldn't she see that? Couldn't she be happy for him?

"Your son calls me Empress because I *am* the empress." Hearing those words said out loud was not as hard as Raif expected it to be. He swallowed as his mother's face darkened. "But I choose to be a servant, not a tyrant. The gods spoke to me in the Eye—"

His mother snorted. "The gods. Ogres in the sky who care little for our problems, I think." She turned to Raif. "What would your father say? In one second you threw everything he died for away. Love her, fine. Bow down to her? Pledge your blood?" Her eyes filled. "For shame, son. For shame."

He wasn't angry, not anymore. Just disappointed in her.

"Papa told me he fought for us," he said. "Not the *tavrai*, not the realm. For his family." Raif came to Nalia's side and drew her against him. "She's part of this family now, Mama." The words sent goosebumps over his skin. "Will you give us your blessing?"

His mother sighed, one long breath of discontent. "I can't. I'm sorry, Raif, but I can't."

He'd expected as much. And still it hurt. A lot.

"I'm sorry, too," he said softly.

She glanced at Nalia. "Are you in need of a healer?"

"Thank you. No. I'm . . . I'll be fine." Her words came out in one breath, her agitation at the exchange obvious. She was feeling guilty, he could see that. Nalia thought she was breaking apart his family. This was no way to start a life together.

There won't be a life together if you don't fight for one.

"I'll let you . . . rest then." His mother glanced pointedly at Raif's bare chest, then gestured behind her as she stepped outside. "There's also the matter of—"

"Of *me*," growled a familiar voice behind her.

Thatur poked his head inside the *ludeen*. His beak snapped as he bit out his words, taking Raif's room in with one sharp-eyed glance. "My Empress. This arrangement is highly inappropriate. I'm sure Djan'Urbi here would be more than happy to manifest a suitable *ludeen* for you, seeing as he pledged his blood *to the empress*, who should not be sleeping in the quarters of a common soldier."

"Thatur—" she started, but he held up a wing to silence her as though it were a hand.

"By ancient law and divine right, you are the sovereign of this realm. And"—his eyes flicked to Raif, then the bed—"I humbly suggest you conduct yourself as such."

Thatur's timing couldn't have been worse. Raif's mother bristled and he gently shook his head at her. Raif, unlike his mother, was well accustomed to the gryphon's gruff superiority.

"Thatur, now's not the time," Raif said. "You can boss her around some other day."

"Her place is on the throne," Thatur growled. "My job is to keep her alive until she can get there. If you haven't noticed, there are hundreds of jinn in this camp who wish to see her dead, and you two . . ." He cleared his throat. "You two *together* is only fanning the flames. It's not safe here."

Raif frowned. "There's nowhere else to go."

"I know a place," Thatur said. "My nest is—"

"I'm not leaving Raif," Nalia said.

Ever, he thought. He never wanted to let her out of his sight again.

"And if I leave this camp tonight, I'm telling the *tavrai* I'm afraid of them, and I'm not," she said. "If there's any way to salvage a partnership, I need to do that. We stay until a decision is made at the council meeting tomorrow morning."

Her tone brooked no argument, and Thatur gave a frustrated growl before backing out of the *ludeen*. "Stubborn as ever, I see. I'll take my leave—under duress." He bowed. "*Sleep* well, My Empress."

Raif rolled his eyes at the emphasis on *sleep*. He and Nalia hadn't seen each other in a year—what did they possibly expect of them? But Thatur was right: it looked bad. And Nalia was right, too: if they truly wanted to work with the *tavrai*, they shouldn't give them a reason to be angrier than they already were.

"I missed you, too, Thatur." Nalia smiled at her gryphon as he launched into the sky with an angry flap of his wings. Raif bade his mother good night, then closed the door.

He leaned against it, arms crossed, watching Nalia from across the room.

"He's right, Nal. You're . . . we shouldn't . . . *gods* . . . If you want to fix things with the *tavrai*, maybe it's better if we—" He shook his head. What was he saying? "No. I thought you were dead for a whole year. Fuck them."

He was across the room in two strides and he pulled her against him, his kiss incinerating every breath of space between them.

"I choose you," she whispered. "The *tavrai*—the whole realm—will just have to deal with that."

They talked well into the night, holding each other as they tried to make up for a year's worth of words and kisses and *chiaan*.

Finally, she pulled away. "I love you, but we both smell terrible. What should we do about it?"

"I smell as good as a vixen rose, but yes, you really do need to clean up," he teased.

She gave him a playful shove and as he manifested a bath for her, she slipped out of her clothes. He watched her, admiring the lines of her body, the swell of her breasts, the Ghan Aisouri tattoos that swirled over her hands and arms. Nalia stepped inside the tub, sighing as she submerged her whole body underwater. She looked so happy when she came up for air and stuck her head over the lip of the tub that he laughed out loud.

"Other than being in bed with you, this bath is the most amazing thing that has ever happened to me," she said.

"More amazing than manifesting lightning?" he asked, grinning.

"Oh, yes. Yes, yes, yes." She laughed, splashing the water like a child. "I'm alive, you're alive, and soon I'll be clean—everything is perfect."

With a simple swirl of her finger, she changed the water every few minutes when it became gray with dirt. He washed her with a cloth and his hands, marveling the whole time. To touch her—to hear her voice and see her—it was as if every wild dream he'd ever had had suddenly come true. Raif no longer kept expecting to wake up from a dream or discover that he was dead, that he was in the godlands. He didn't look over his shoulder to see if Malek and Bashil were nearby. This was real. *Real.*

Slowly, the filth of the Eye disappeared from Nalia's limbs. Once she was clean, she pulled him in with her, clothes and all, and they held each other in the warm water, scented with the jasmine soap that Nalia manifested—one of the few things from Earth she loved. He laughed as she helped him take off his sopping wet uniform, closed his eyes, and smiled as she scrubbed the battle off his skin, washed the hopelessness right out of him. When she was finished, she changed the water once more, then leaned against him, her back curled against his chest.

"Tell me our story," Nalia said as she lifted her foot out of the water, her slender leg coated with iridescent bubbles.

"I have to change it, I think," he said, holding her tighter. "An empress can't live with a farmer."

She went quiet, still. Raif had been joking, but now it dawned on him that it was true—no matter how much he changed the realm, he was no partner fit for someone like her. He could barely read and yet he was in love with a jinni who spoke the old language and could manifest anything under the sun. A jinni beloved by the gods, who'd saved her time and time again.

"Nal?"

"What about with an emperor?"

He froze. "What?"

Nalia turned, facing him, unashamed of her naked beauty. Thick strands of hair tumbled over her shoulders, framing her face, which glowed from the heat and the scrubbing she'd given it. Opalescent bubbles were scattered across her skin like pearls. It hurt to look at her.

"Can an empress live with an emperor?" she said.

Was she saying what he thought she was saying? Because that was . . . it was . . .

Raif shook his head. "*Rohifsa*, I'm not . . . I could never . . . I—"

"Will you marry me?"

He gripped the edges of the tub, staring at her. Nalia cocked her head to the side, waiting. A birdlike gesture he now realized she must have picked up from Thatur in childhood. There was no jinni worthy of her, least of all Raif. And no jinni could possibly rule by her side. There was no one in the realm who—

Tazlim, a voice inside him whispered. *Tazlim is worthy.* The realization threatened to crush Raif. Gods, why hadn't he thought of it before, how perfect they'd be? His courtly elegance, his ferocity on the battlefield . . . With Kesmir gone, the way was clear for Nalia—Taz was already devoted to her, though it would take him centuries to fall in love again. No matter. Royal marriages weren't about love—they were a partnership forged to govern a people well. Raif had demonstrated his inability to lead three times in this day alone: near suicide during the battle, giving up his position leading the *tavrai* so he could wallow in his grief, and drawing a line that not one of his soldiers was willing to cross. No, he couldn't govern by her side.

Raif had lived through her death: knowing she was alive was all that mattered now. This would be one more thing he'd sacrifice for the realm. For her future happiness. Wasn't he used to that?

There was a gentle splash of water as Nalia raised her hand and tilted his chin up. Her eyes were ancient and strange and devastatingly familiar.

"Will you marry me?" she asked again.

"No," he said softly. It was the hardest thing he'd ever said.

Nalia's eyes widened in shock, her voice drowned in hurt. *"No?"*

Why did that one word feel like he'd reached into his chest and ripped out his own heart?

"You need to rest. We can talk about this later." He manifested a towel and handed it to her, turning away because the pain on her face was too much to bear. Gods, he was so confused. He loved her so much, what was he saying, where were these thoughts coming from? It was insane, the idea of him being an emperor. He didn't even like his soldiers to call him *sir*—how could he bear being called *My Emperor?*

Nalia grabbed the towel he held out to her and threw it to the floor. "Later? No, you don't get to tell me you won't marry me and then just go back to sleep. Why, *why* would you do this?" Her voice broke and he watched his stubborn, strong girl force the tears in her eyes to keep from falling. It made him fall even harder for her.

"I'm no emperor," he said, meeting her furious gaze. He put his hands on her shoulders. "I love you. I love you with every breath I will ever take, I will serve you until my dying day. But me on a throne beside you? No. Tazlim, maybe—"

"*Tazlim?* What are you— Raif."

She closed her eyes and took a breath. Then she slid forward and pulled him **against** her. She was strong—stronger than he imagined a jinni living off nothing but hallucinogenic leaves for a year could be. The shock of her against him, with not a single layer between them, was too much. There was no resisting this, her. He'd been a fool to think it possible, even for a minute.

"You once told me," she said, her voice no louder than a sigh, "that I could belong to someone without them owning me."

He remembered: the cave full of glowworms, making love on a carpet of moss.

"We belong to each other," she whispered against his lips.

He couldn't concentrate, not with her pressed against him like that. It'd been so long since he'd felt *anything*. Since she'd returned, all those months of suspended desire had been rushing through him, making up for lost time. He gasped as she pressed her palm against his heart, unprepared, as usual, by the intensity of her *chiaan*. It was dipped in lightning, a new magic forged in the desert sands of Morocco, sharpened by grief in the Eye and the tutelage of a mythical creature. He was a godsdamn fool for even considering a life that wasn't by her side. The real sacrifice, he realized, wasn't giving up the position of power she offered him. It was being willing to go against everything he believed in, to wear a crown on his head, if it meant he could have her for himself. If it meant he could serve the realm in a better way, however unexpected it was.

"Stubborn as ever, I see," he said, repeating Thatur's words.

"So I'm told." She grinned—she'd won and she knew it. Nalia moved her lips to his ear. "Marry me," she whispered.

He kissed her shoulder, then her neck, her chin, her forehead. His emerald Djan eyes met her violet Aisouri ones.

A soft smile played on his face. "As you wish."

Her entire face lit up. "That's a yes. Yes?"

He laughed and pulled her deeper into the warmth of the water. "Yes, Nalia. I'll marry you."

38

Nalia stands at the top of Mount Zhiqui, gazing to the north. In one hand, she holds the Amethyst Crown, its gems sparkling in the moonlight. In the other, her fingers grip her Aisouri dagger. The Ifrit territory lies before her, a patchwork of gray, black, and red. Volcanoes spit fire into the sky and the smoke and ash that lie like a blanket covering the peaks and valleys have turned the Three Widows crimson—open sores that bleed over the land.

The smoke suddenly clears and Ithkar comes into impossible focus. Deep inland, a castle made entirely of volcanic rock looms above the landscape, the specter of what an Arjinna ruled by the Ifrit would look like. Its sharp angles give it the appearance of a Gothic cathedral. This, Nalia knows, is the Cauldron— Calar's former seat of power. She's heard stories of it many times, described to her by the older Aisouri who've flown above it on their gryphons during late-night raids and surprise attacks.

Certainty settles over Nalia as she gazes at the land. She will build her kingdom from the ashes. Set this realm on fire.

"It begins here," she says.

The moons flicker in response.

Nalia awoke, eyes wide. *It begins here.*

In Ithkar, of all places. The Brass Army wasn't going to like this at all.

The candles in Raif's *ludeen* had burned out, but the moonlight beamed through the bottle-glass windows that had been fashioned into all four walls of the *ludeen*, bathing the room in a colorful display of light. Raif lay beside her on his stomach, one arm flung over her middle. He was clean-shaven now, once again resembling the Raif she'd fallen in love with. Their clothing littered the floor and the bathtub stood in the middle of the room, the water long gone cold.

The *ludeen* creaked in the wind, like a ship at sea, and the branches of the *widr* tree it was nestled in swayed like the gentle lapping of waves.

Raif opened his eyes, a soft smile spreading across his face. "You're still here," he said.

She brought her lips to his forehead. "I'm still here."

He tilted his chin up and kissed the tip of her nose. "And we're getting married."

"Oh, good, I was afraid you'd change your mind," she teased.

He shifted onto his back. "You're never going to let me live that down, are you?"

She crawled on top of him and rested her head on his chest. "Not a chance."

Nalia had known from Raif's hesitation after those words left her mouth—*Will you marry me?*—that he was fighting a war inside. Love versus Duty. Self versus Sacrifice. Not once did she imagine he didn't love her enough to say yes. Which was why there'd been no way she was getting out of that bathtub until she knew Raif Djan'Urbi was going to be her husband.

"Raif?"

"Hmmmm?" He was still half asleep, drawing lazy circles on her back.

"It offends the *tavrai* to see me here. This is the only part of Arjinna they call their own and they've fought hard for it." She propped her chin up so she could see him better. "I won't deny them their sovereignty. There will be no more fighting between us, no more death. We'll form a kingdom in exile. Calar took my throne . . . so I'll take hers."

There was a momentary heavy silence.

"You want us to go to *Ithkar*," Raif said, going still.

Nalia nodded. *I will build my kingdom from the ashes.*

"You're kidding, right?" he said. "That place is a wasteland."

"Exactly," Nalia said. She slid off Raif and sat up. "There's plenty of space. A castle for us to set up in. And the best part—Calar won't be expecting it."

"That's . . ." Raif paused, considering. She could tell he was working it out, all the pros and cons, as though it were a battle.

Coming up with a strategy, logistics. Finally, he nodded. "That's actually kind of brilliant—even if it is hot as all hells there. And if this meeting with the *tavrai* goes as badly as I think it will, we'll have a place to go." He held up a finger. "Which reminds me."

Raif opened a small drawer in the bedside table and handed her the sigil. "I need you to keep this on you, Nal."

"Raif, I carried it for a year so I could give it to you."

"Think of it as . . . an engagement present," he said.

She snorted. "I don't want it. Give me something pretty. Give me nothing at all."

"There was a reason I put it in your safekeeping to begin with," he said. She started to speak, but he gently put his fingers over her mouth. "Before you say it—I'm glad I didn't have it while you were in the Eye. I probably would have used it and gotten all of us killed in the process. And if you can manage to keep hold of it in the homeland of the ghouls, I'd say you're the best candidate for the job, wouldn't you?"

"If the *tavrai* find out, they'll be furious."

"They already *are* furious."

She sighed. "There's no other choice?" Nalia didn't want it against her skin anymore. It felt cold, evil.

"You're the one who can grab bolts of lightning from the sky," Raif said, planting a kiss on her head. "I think it will always be safest with you. And hopefully someday soon, we can get rid of it."

He was right. Nalia reached up and took the leather strand the ring hung from and once again placed it around her neck. The ring rested beside the white feather, burnished gold against snow white.

Raif ran his fingertips along the feather. "Why do you think the phoenix gave this to you?"

"I don't know. But she never did anything without a reason." Nalia hadn't had time to think of the why—she'd been grateful for the reminder of the creature who'd saved her life, and a reminder of all that she'd seen in her visions.

"We should talk to your father. Maybe he'll know something about it," Raif said.

She nodded. Her father was one of the most learned scholars in the land. If he didn't know what the feather meant, then no one did.

A knock sounded on the door and he groaned.

"Is it always like this?" she asked. "People knocking on your door at all hours?"

"Pretty much, yeah." He smiled, rueful. "No one's exactly used to me having company."

Nalia burrowed farther into the warm bed. "I'm not getting out this time."

He slipped out of bed and pulled the blankets up to her chin. "I wouldn't let you even if you wanted to."

He threw on some clothes and then crossed to the door, taking one more longing look at her before heading out. She heard voices, but they were too quiet for her to recognize them.

"What's going on?" she asked sleepily as Raif came back in. He tugged on his boots and tied the laces before coming over to sit on the edge of the bed.

"Shirin's finally calmed down, thank gods," Raif said. "It's been years since I've seen her that angry. We're gonna try to talk everything through before the meeting."

"Talk it through? Raif, she wanted to *hang* you." Nalia sat up. "Let me come with you, at least."

Raif gently pushed her back against the pillows. "This is how Shirin is. I've known her since I was ten summers old. She loses her temper, tries to cut down everyone around her; then she cools off and we pick up where we left off."

"I don't know . . . ," Nalia said, doubtful.

"Shirin knows the *tavrai* can't fight Calar *and* the Brass Army. She's a good leader. She knows that in order not to destroy her army, she has to accept ours."

"What about me being the empress?"

Raif sighed. "I'll try to explain about what you saw in the Eye. That might help. But . . . yeah, she's never gonna be okay with that."

"It's just you two?" she asked.

"Yeah." He smiled and kissed her gently. "I'll be fine, *rohifsa*. Now go back to sleep."

After a few minutes it was quiet again on the porch. Raif didn't come back and she soon fell asleep, seduced by the softness of the bed, the clean sheets.

Nalia awoke to the door bursting open. She sat bolt upright, forgetting her lack of clothing. Thatur immediately covered his eyes with a wing. "For the love of the gods, child!" he growled, forgetting his courtly manners.

"What happened?" Nalia asked, panicked. She reached out a hand and a tunic lying on the floor hurtled toward her.

"It's Raif," he said. "I think he's being ambushed."

"*What?*"

"He went into the woods for a talk with Shirin and then I noticed that Jaqar fellow—"

"Take me to him," she said. "Now."

Shirin couldn't look Raif in the eye. It was the first time she'd ever been truly ashamed of herself.

What am I doing? she thought. In what universe was it okay for her to hold a gun to Raif Djan'Urbi's head?

She'd been hoping it wouldn't come to this, that Raif would be in possession of the ring and that he'd simply be outnumbered, without any choice but to give up the sigil. But in her heart she knew that Jaqar's plan would play out. Nalia had the ring. Nalia would die. Shirin knew it would feel bad, but actually being here, doing this to him . . .

"She won't give you the ring," Raif said quietly.

He hadn't bothered to fight her. That had been the worst part. Raif had been so eager to make up, so quick to believe Shirin wanted to mend their rift, that he'd agreed to take a walk, had gone so far as to tell Thatur, who'd been guarding his *ludeen*, that he'd be fine. The relief on his face when Shirin said she was sorry, that she'd lost her temper and of course she wouldn't have him hanged, had made her sick to her stomach. Making things right mattered so much to him—*she* mattered so much to him. Why couldn't she see that before?

Shirin had even produced a few tears. Those, she was certain, had sealed the deal. Shirin Djan'Khar did not cry easily. He'd believed her because she'd always given him every reason to trust her. He'd believed her because she knew that the last thing he wanted was to lose the ragtag family of soldiers he'd grown up with. And he'd believed her because he knew she loved him. Perhaps that was his biggest mistake, thinking that love wouldn't make someone do horrible, desperate things to the person who didn't love them back.

Raif had always fought with his heart, not his head.

She'd taken him to the small, secluded clearing where they'd once trained together in the early mornings. Shirin had come to think of it as their space and no one else's. The hurt, the shock in his eyes when Jaqar and the others took hold of Raif, the way she could see the jinni she loved realize what a fool he'd been, that he'd tied his own noose—she'd rather die than see that again.

"I think she'll give us the ring," Shirin said. "And I think you know that, too."

This awful plan would work, if only because if she were Nalia, if *she* had something that would keep Raif alive, she'd give it away in a heartbeat. But there was no point in telling Raif that. This betrayal, there was no coming back from it.

"Would you really kill me?" he asked.

The uncertainty in his voice hurt. He didn't know if he could trust Shirin with his life anymore. By turning on him, by conspiring against Raif, she was already breaking her blood pledge. Her word, it meant nothing now. It was as if all those days and nights of fighting side by side had amounted to nothing. One choice had wiped everything they had away.

No, she wanted to say. *Of course I'm not going to kill you. But Nalia doesn't need to know that.* Jaqar had only been able to convince her this plan would work because when Nalia looked at Raif, Shirin could see the ferocious, undying love that she herself felt for him. The kind of love that nothing, not even the gods, could take away. That jinni would do anything for him. It was the only reason Shirin had agreed to Jaqar's plan in the first place.

But now that she was here, all Shirin could see was how she'd been played, how stupid she'd been. This time *she'd* acted with her heart, not her head. They were going about this the wrong way. This was how the Ifrit did things.

Would you really kill me, he'd asked her.

"How many traitors have you seen me execute, Raif?" she said.

"I'm not a traitor, Shirin. Everything I do is for the realm."

"No, everything you do is for *her.*"

"It's the *same thing,*" he said.

"That's the problem, Raif: it's *not* the same thing."

There was a commotion in the stand of trees across from where Shirin stood with Raif and, a moment later, Nalia burst into the clearing, followed by Taz, Thatur, and Touma.

"Raif!" His name was a strangled cry that broke from her lips.

He smiled, soft. "I'm sorry, *rohifsa.*"

It was the calm certainty that radiated from him that was Shirin's first clue that none of this would play out as she and Jaqar had expected. Raif had already fought whatever battle had been coming—Shirin just wasn't certain what the outcome of it was.

Nalia and Raif stared at each other, silent.

Jaqar sauntered toward Nalia, a smug smile on his face. He was followed by a dozen of his toughest fighters, each holding a semiautomatic weapon stolen from the Ifrit. "As you can see," he said to Nalia, "we aren't so easily dismissed."

"You were never dismissed," she said, her eyes glued to the gun pressed against Raif's temple.

"That," Jaqar said, crossing to stand beside Raif and Shirin, "is a matter of opinion. It's very simple: give me the ring or Raif dies."

"Your logic is faulty," Thatur growled. "If that boy dies, Nalia will kill each and every one of you and *still* be in possession of the ring. You'll lose everything."

Violet *chiaan* seeped out of Nalia's clenched fists and Jaqar pointed his gun at her. "She may be the most powerful jinni in the realms, but she's just a pile of skin, blood, and bones if one of these things has its fill of her. No jinni is as fast as a human gun. She knows this. She saw that with her own eyes in the palace. And if he dies, she loses everything, too." He smiled at Nalia. "Don't you?"

Uncertainty pooled in Shirin's stomach. She'd assumed Nalia would bargain and yet she just stood there in silent conversation with Raif.

For the first time since Nalia had walked into the Forest of Sighs, Shirin realized just how much she'd let her broken heart take over: *What am I doing?*

Did Shirin want Jaqar to have the ring? Did she want it? *No.* She'd been so angry at Raif, so jealous of Nalia, that she hadn't been able to see straight, to think any of this through. She'd never once thought about what would happen to the ring after it was in Jaqar's hands. Shirin's eyes swept over the jinn gathered at the temple. Nalia and her guard were outnumbered three to one. Jaqar's forces had guns; Nalia had none. Formidable as her power was, it wouldn't be enough. That was what Shirin and Jaqar had counted on. The chances of both Raif and Nalia coming out of this alive were slim. The chances of *either* of them coming out of this alive were slim.

What have I done? What have I done? It was as though a fog had finally lifted from Shirin's head.

Jaqar raised his gun and pointed it at Raif. *Gods, gods.* She could tell from the look on Jaqar's face that he would shoot, he would. But that wasn't . . . wasn't what they'd discussed. She'd said— *Oh, gods.* How could she have been so *stupid*?

She'll call our bluff. Keep the ring, kick our asses, and save Raif. That's what Shirin had said last night. But it wasn't until right now that she understood what Jaqar had said:

She doesn't know you wouldn't be willing to kill Raif—she doesn't know the first thing about you.

Jaqar had never once said *he* wouldn't be willing to kill Raif.

"I've got it, brother," Shirin said, keeping her voice steady. If she shot Jaqar, the other jinn would immediately shoot Raif for him. That was a risk Shirin wasn't willing to take. Maybe she could buy the Aisouri time. But how?

"No, I don't think you do, Shirin," Jaqar said. "You'd never kill him. You told me that already. Drop the gun."

"This isn't what we agreed to." Panic drenched her, a wave, she was drowning in it. She turned to Nalia. "Give us the godsdamned ring, you stupid girl!"

She felt Raif's head move just slightly. He was shaking it, telling Nalia no.

"Jaqar will kill you," she growled to Raif. "Tell her to give him the ring."

"*Drop the gun*, Shirin," Jaqar said.

It fell from her fingers, thudding in the dirt below her. She bared her teeth at Jaqar, Raif's *raiga* once more. If she lived through this, she'd kill him with her bare hands.

"I told the gods that if I could just see you once more," Raif said to Nalia, "that I could die happy. They upheld their end of the bargain. Do not give them that ring, Nal."

Out of the corner of her eye, Shirin saw Taz shift into a more defensive position. Shots rang out, bright sparks of light bursting from a gun to Shirin's right—one of Jaqar's jinn. Taz fell to the ground with a cry—alive, but badly wounded. Nalia didn't turn around, didn't even flinch. Every bit of her was focused on Raif.

"The ring, Aisouri," Jaqar growled. He clicked the gun's safety off.

Nalia's eyes bored into Raif's, their gaze so intense that it was if they were alone.

"I love you," Shirin heard Raif whisper, his eyes on Nalia. Her own lips formed the words.

Nalia reached her hands up to her neck, skimming the leather cord that the sigil dangled from.

"Nalia." Raif said her name as a command. She shook her head, defiant. "*Nal.*"

"Raif," Shirin begged. "Let her." He ignored Shirin, his eyes on Nalia. He was saying good-bye.

"Jaqar," Shirin yelled, "stand down. Give them a godsdamned chance to think!"

Without moving his head Jaqar spoke to his soldiers who surrounded them. "Watch Shirin. Kill her if she tries to save him. In fact, when you get a chance, kill her for *wanting* to save him."

Shirin began to shake then, her whole body trembling. It was like that night in her overlord's room, when she'd tried so hard to cut off her hand, terrified he would come in and do all the horrible things he'd done to her mother. Stupid girl. Stupid, stupid girl.

Jaqar had deceived her just as much as she'd deceived Raif. This wasn't just about trying to protect the realm from Nalia. Jaqar wanted the ring. And he would kill anyone in his path to get it.

"If you give it to him," Raif said to Nalia, ignoring Jaqar, "he'll put it on and kill both of us anyway." His voice was soft, resolute. "He'll be worse than Calar—look how much he enjoys power already. Don't condemn the realm to more suffering."

No one said a word. Wind rustled through the trees, eerie and ominous, the sigh of a ghost. Silent tears poured down Nalia's face, but her eyes glittered, bright and fearsome.

"What's your choice, *salfit*?" Jaqar asked.

He fired his gun just a breath above Raif's head. Shirin cried out, but Raif didn't so much as flinch, didn't look away. Neither did Nalia.

He was ready to die. Shirin gripped his arm. "Raif, please," she said.

Nalia pulled the leather cord that held the ring off her necks and the sigil slipped onto her palm.

"No," Raif whispered, then louder. "Nalia, *no.*"

"He's left me no choice," she said, her eyes begging him to understand.

The Aisouri raised the ring—

Took one step toward Jaqar—

—then slipped it onto her finger.

Everything happened at once.

Shackles slid around Shirin's wrists—every jinni's wrists. Thatur reared up, slicing the jinn closest to him in two with his claws. Nalia threw herself at Jaqar, commanding him to stand down, but not before he let out a volley of shots at Raif. Shirin didn't think—she threw her body in front of Raif's, and as the bullets sliced into her, as metal bit flesh, the weight Shirin had carried with her all her life disappeared. The pain, the end—it was a gift. Why had she fought so long against it?

Death was a mercy she hadn't seen coming.

All around her a battle raged, perhaps the most important one of the war: the *rat-a-tat* of the guns, the bitter scent of magic, the cries of rage and pain and triumph. And then it faded to a dull roar as two familiar green eyes stared down at her. She looked and looked, drank in the sight of them until she'd had her fill.

Raif screamed her name and his arms went around her, holding her body against his.

It was enough.

Shirin was dying in his arms.

Her eyes were open, dark as elder pines, the light inside them fading. Raif was covered in her blood.

I can't give you what you want.

"Shir, I've got you. You're okay. I've got you."

"Sor . . . sorry," she gasped. "I didn't think—"

"It's okay," he murmured. "Just stay with me."

How had everything gone so horribly wrong? The silence that had engulfed him the moment she went down fell away and he was surprised to hear only a bit of scuffling before the clearing itself went silent.

Nalia.

Raif's head whipped up, his eyes searching for her. She'd taken the gun from Jaqar and was pointing it at his head. Nearly all of Jaqar's accomplices lay dead on the temple floor, made short work of by Thatur and Touma. The gryphon's beak was red with blood. The rest of Jaqar's soldiers sat paralyzed, no doubt under Nalia's command. They all were—he could feel the shackles around his wrists, two gold bands. The ring on Nalia's finger caught the moonlight and glimmered.

Raif held on to Shirin even though everything in him wanted to go to Nalia, to stop her from doing something she'd regret. She didn't look at Raif once. Her entire being was focused on the jinni in front of her.

"I can't tell you how very tired I am of guns being pointed at me and the people I love," Nalia said, her voice cold and calm.

Raif's wrists burned and his stomach tingled, the ring's magic a tangible thing in his skin. He could feel her power, knew without a doubt that he would do whatever she asked of him, whether he wanted to or not.

"Get on your knees," Nalia said to Jaqar. There was no mercy in her tone, no indecision in her eyes.

He obeyed. The fool had no choice, not with that ring on Nalia's finger.

Jaqar glared at her. "So you're—"

"Shut up," Nalia said. His voice cracked and he opened and closed his mouth, shock registering on his face. "Last words are a kindness and I am not feeling kind."

Raif went very still—he didn't even realize he was holding his breath. Jaqar closed his eyes, his lips moving in silent prayer.

"Open your eyes," Nalia said.

He did. An empress stared at her subject.

Nalia pulled the trigger.

The bullet hit Jaqar square in the forehead. He was dead before he fell to the ground. Raif stared at her, shocked. It was what he would have done. But Nalia never did what he would have done.

Nalia threw the gun down and turned to Raif, shaking. There she was—there was his *rohifsa*. Touma was beside him in a moment.

"Go to her," he said quietly, taking Shirin from his arms.

Shirin nodded. "Go."

Raif stood and crossed to Nalia in three long strides, then gathered her in his arms. Nalia didn't say a word, just held on to him. He could feel her fear for his life in the *chiaan* screaming through her, the horror over what she'd just done.

"I thought you were going to die," she whispered over and over. "I thought you were going to die."

"I'm okay," he said. "We're okay."

It had been a gamble, what she did. They might have waited too long, but she'd trusted her instincts, and his warrior empress was rarely wrong.

Raif looked over her shoulder, toward Thatur. The gryphon's claws were poised over the head of the traitor *tavrai* closest to him. Raif nodded at the unspoken question that glimmered in Thatur's eyes. This was something Nalia wouldn't do, but it was well within his moral code. They'd tried to kill her. They'd nearly killed Shirin and Taz, who was propped up against a tree, his face gray. They'd betrayed their blood oaths to their commander. There was no choice about what needed to happen.

He held tighter to Nalia, made sure she wouldn't be able to turn around. Thatur slit the throats of Jaqar's three remaining soldiers with terrifying ease, each kill so quick that only an exhale escaped their throats before they fell down. Nalia tried to look, but he didn't let go of her until it was over. Her body suddenly went slack against his: she knew. When Nalia finally did turn, her body shuddered as she took in the gore.

"It had to be done," he murmured in her ear. "I'm still the commander of the *tavrai* and it's within my right to punish them as I see fit."

He wasn't noble, or good. Noble and good would have gotten him killed long ago.

Nalia turned to him, placing her hands on his chest. "We can't be this, Raif. What I did, what you did—we can't."

He ran the backs of his fingers across her cheeks. "Then let's make a world where we don't have to."

She nodded and wrapped her arms around his neck. "I was so scared," she whispered. "When Jaqar fired that gun at you, I—I—"

"I'm here," he said, crushing her to him. "I'm here."

After a long moment, Nalia pulled away and held out her hand. Though Solomon's sigil was far too big for her, it had somehow shrunk in size and now fit perfectly on her index finger. It glowed, shimmering in the darkness. He ran his fingers over the metal. It was warm to the touch, as though it were a living thing.

"How does it feel?" he asked.

"Good," she admitted. "Too good."

Nalia reached down and pulled the ring.

And pulled again.

"Raif," she said, panicked, her voice barely above a whisper. She looked up at him, sheer terror crossing her face. "It won't come off."

PART THREE

The revolution is inside all of us.
— Nalia Aisouri'Taifyeh

39

THE CAMP WAS UTTERLY SILENT WHEN THE COUNCIL members walked out of the meeting house. The darkness that had settled over the land since the rise of the Godsnight moons added to the despair in Raif's heart. There was no way to prepare for whatever horrors the gods would unleash upon them. Nalia had told him about the human stories of a god who sent locusts, killed the firstborn of every family—what would the jinn gods do? How much worse could it possibly get?

Every jinni in the land now wore shackles, bound to Nalia and the ring. The council refused to believe that this hadn't been the plan all along. Refused to believe she'd had no choice but to put it on. Everything his father had worked for was falling apart, and Raif couldn't help but feel that it was his fault. Even if parting ways with the *tavrai* and bending the knee before Nalia had been the right thing to do.

Just minutes before, the council had left the meeting house as one after Raif recounted what had happened in the clearing and told them of the plan to move to Ithkar.

Traitor, more than one of them had said.

Murderer.

Liar.

It was as he'd expected, but the cut was deep. Alone with Nalia in the place where he'd planned so many battles with his father—and then in his father's place, with Shirin and Kir and Zanari at his side—was too much. Raif crossed his arms and rested his head on the table, devastated.

Nalia ran her fingers through his hair, silent. Nothing could lessen his gratitude for her presence by his side, for the blood that pumped through her veins, for the air in her lungs. He wished they could see what he saw in Nalia. He wished they weren't so quick to discard him.

After a few minutes Nalia stood and grasped his hand. "Come," she said. "This is a battle you've won, not lost. Let your soldiers see you. Let the *tavrai* know you can't be broken." She pressed her lips to his cheek. "You'll be emperor soon. They need to see your strength."

Emperor. He'd never been more undeserving of a title.

Raif was the first to walk out of the meeting house, Nalia waiting to join him until he'd had a moment to get his bearings. He knew she was afraid they would think this was all her influence—and she wouldn't be wrong. But that wasn't necessarily a bad thing.

Thatur padded along behind them as they crossed through the camp, his eyes scanning the premises. Touma flanked Nalia's side, scimitar out. Before and behind was a squad of Brass Army soldiers, now promoted to Nalia's personal guard, each one handpicked by Thatur. Touma was captain of that guard, a position he'd more than earned. It saddened Raif that all this protection was necessary, that he was trying to save his *rohifsa* not from Calar, but from the jinn he'd grown up with, his family.

You're my family now, he'd said to Nalia the night before, after she'd finally come out of the Eye—and he meant it. *Wife.* The word settled inside him, warm and right.

This is what you were born for, Dthar Djan'Urbi had told his son, not long before he died. Born for what, exactly? To lead the *tavrai*? To marry the empress of Arjinna? To be *emperor*?

As they neared the healer's *ludeen,* where Taz and Shirin lay recovering from their wounds, Raif stopped, cursing under his breath. The council members were standing in a line, with the rest of the *tavrai* assembled behind them, in defensive positions, his mother front and center. He could see the regret in her eyes, the disappointment that her son was on the other side of the fight. Where just a few hours ago the clearing behind the healers' *ludeen* at the far end of the camp had been filled with the Brass Army's tents, now Raif could see only the soldiers themselves, dutifully lined up. Waiting.

If there were bloodshed here today it would be a victory for Calar, no one else.

"Morning exercises?" Raif asked, his tense voice betraying his concern.

Raif had tried to explain to the council why it had been just to execute Jaqar and the others, but they'd been unwilling to hear his side of things. He'd killed *tavrai*—that was all they needed to know. Raif flexed his fingers in anticipation of the fight to come. He could feel his *chiaan* inside him, a coiled rope waiting to snap free. Beside him, Nalia tensed.

"Leave," his mother said, her gaze unflinching as she stared down her son.

Just one word, but it tore his heart in two.

"Please," he said. "It doesn't have to be this way."

"No," a voice behind him said, "it doesn't."

Raif turned and a bad day suddenly got much, much better: *Zanari*.

The first thing she did was throw her arms around Nalia. "Gods, sister, don't ever do that to us again," Zanari said, crying in that messy way of hers.

Nalia clutched Zanari, kissing her cheek again and again, heedless of the *tavrai*. "You did it," Nalia said. "You got them through. You kept him alive."

Zanari grinned. "*Nalia and Her Blind Seer?*" she said.

Nalia wiped her eyes. "No. *Zanari and Her Blind Aisouri*."

Zanari turned to Raif and hugged her brother fiercely. "Yurik told me Nalia was back. I came as soon as I could."

"I don't know if this is terrible or perfect timing," he murmured. "Did you hear about Jaqar?"

She nodded. "I ran into Aisha. She told me everything." Zanari glanced from him to Nalia. "Whatever you decide, I'm with you."

Their mother stepped forward, hand against her heart. "Zanari-jai, you have no idea what's been happening—"

"Mama, I love you," Zanari said. "I respect and admire you. But Nalia is your daughter now, too, whether you like it or not. And she's my sister." She wrapped one arm around Nalia's waist, the other around Raif's. "I'm standing with my family. We're strongest when we're together—isn't that what Papa always said?"

"I can't dishonor him this way," his mother said. "I can't. *Ma'aj yaqif-la.*" *I wash my hands of it.*

The light went out of his mother's eyes and she turned, walking into the darkness.

Zanari glanced at Raif. "She'll come around."

"I don't know, Zan," he said softly. It was one of the saddest things he'd ever seen: the silhouette of his widowed mother as she turned her back on the only family she had left.

Raif raised his hands in surrender and faced the *tavrai* council. "We'll be gone within the hour. *Kajastriya vidim.*"

The council, then the *tavrai*, left without a word. They knew the Brass Army outnumbered them. They'd seen Nalia call forth lightning from the sky, seen the ring on her finger, felt the shackles around their wrists. If there was one thing he'd taught the *tavrai*, it was to know which battles to fight.

"Well, that's a bummer," Zanari said as they watched them go. "I don't know about you two, but I could use a glass of *savri*."

Zanari manifested a bottle of the spiced wine so loved by the jinn and they passed it around. Nalia moaned as the wine touched her tongue, her first taste of it since Morocco. Raif laughed softly, twining his fingers through hers.

"How are the Dhoma?" Nalia asked.

Zanari tilted her hand back and forth: so-so. "Phara's got her work cut out for her. The prisoners who came in from Ithkar were in pretty bad shape. It's been tough without Samar, too."

Nalia nodded. Raif had told her about his death—one more person she cared about who Calar had taken.

"It must be nice, though," Nalia said with a small smile, "being with Phara."

Zanari sighed, content. "You two know how that is."

Raif nodded, pulling Nalia a little closer.

"I still can't believe it, sister," Zanari said. "The Eye, the phoenix. All of it. Amazing. This one"—she pointed to Raif—"was in bad shape. I mean, *bad*—"

Raif smacked her arm. "She gets it."

"Thanks for taking care of him," Nalia said. She lifted Raif's hand and pressed her lips to it before taking another long swig of *savri*.

Someday she and Raif would have the time to really talk about the year apart, but for now, Nalia was just trying to enjoy every second that he was beside her.

"He's kind of high maintenance," Zanari said with a wink. "Good luck with that, sister."

Raif laughed. "I wish I could say you were lying."

"Does it feel weird being back?" Nalia asked.

"Technically I've only been gone a little over a day," she said. "But I'm definitely Dhoma now. It's kind of nice, not having to take sides."

"If the gods would let me have it any other way," Nalia said, "I might be right there with you."

"No you wouldn't," Zanari said. "You two—you love this land. You wouldn't be able to stay away for long. It would kill you."

Nalia heard the truth in that and Raif nodded. "Now we just need to get rid of Calar," she said.

"No big deal, right?" Zanari said.

Raif snorted. "Right. No big deal."

Zanari pointed to the ring on Nalia's finger. "So . . . when are we going to talk about that?"

Nalia sighed. "Gods."

"Not gonna lie, I got the scare of my life when I stepped through the portal and felt these suddenly slide around my wrists," she said, holding up her hands, now shackled. "And seeing those moons. That scared the shit out of me, too."

"Why didn't you run back through the portal?" Raif asked.

"The Godsnight stuff—I just decided to hope my luck held out. There was no way I wasn't going to see Nalia. Yurik was in the tunnel and he explained about the ring—word gets around fast, by the way—and I figured Nalia wouldn't be *such* a terrible mistress. . . ."

"I don't know," Raif said, lightly bumping his shoulder against Nalia's. "She's awfully demanding. . . ."

Nalia tried to smile. "I know you guys are trying to make me feel better. But . . . other than Raif dying, this is my worst nightmare."

Zanari patted her knee. "You lived through the Eye. As the humans say, *this too shall pass.*"

"One day back on Earth and she's already speaking human," Raif said.

Though their banter was comforting and Nalia appreciated the effort they were making, she couldn't feel anything but hopelessly depressed that Solomon's sigil had fused itself to her skin, a parasite.

They were quiet for a bit then, each lost in their own thoughts. Zanari manifested another bottle of *savri* and passed it to her brother.

"I'm sorry," Nalia said, her voice soft, "about your mother."

"She'll change her mind," Zanari said, slinging an arm around Nalia's shoulder. "I got my temper from her. Remember how stubborn I was about being mad at you in the cave?"

Nalia nodded. Zanari had been furious with Nalia, and for good reason: Nalia had killed Raif's best friend. Though Nalia had been forced to do it, the act was unforgivable. And yet both Djan'Urbis had managed to forgive her. If the *tavrai* had ever found out, though . . .

"She's trying to do right by our father, and I get that," Zanari continued. "I just hope she realizes the mistake she made sooner rather than later."

Raif took a large swig of the spiced wine. "There's something else you should know, Zan. Something Yurik probably didn't know or he would have told you." His voice trembled slightly. "Kesmir didn't make it."

Zanari stared. "He . . . oh, gods." Her head fell into her hands. "I hate this war."

"Wait," Nalia said, gripping Raif's hand. "Taz's *rohifsa*—are you certain? Thatur thought maybe Calar had thrown him in the dungeon. . . ."

Raif shook his head and ran a hand through his hair in agitation, eyes heavy with exhaustion.

"I wish you could have known him, Nal," he said. "Kes was . . . well . . . gods, I don't even know where to start."

They told her, each jumping in when the other trailed off. It was one of the most heartbreaking stories Nalia had ever heard.

"Gods," she said, when they were finished. "And Taz—he was willing to help us fight today. If I'd known . . ."

Raif placed his hand over hers, warm and reassuring. "It's what he needed. When I thought I'd lost you, I could only function when there was a fight to be had. You did him a service." He looked at their intertwined hands. "Kesmir had . . . a daughter," Raif said. "With Calar. He named Taz her guardian."

"Holy shit," Zanari said.

Raif smiled a little. "That was my reaction too."

Nalia shook her head. It seemed as though Arjinna was a land of orphans. "How old is she?"

"Three summers," he said.

"Is she still at the palace?" Nalia asked.

"She doesn't know . . . all of it?" Thatur's voice was a low rumble as he made his way to them from where he and Touma had been sorting out last-minute details with Nalia's guard.

Nalia looked from Raif to Thatur. "All of it?"

"I think we need to let Taz explain the rest," Raif said. "It's his story to tell." He gestured toward the healer's *ludeen* and Nalia followed, uneasy.

Aisha opened the door to them, smiling at Nalia. "You look well, My Empress."

Raif raised his eyebrows. "I thought you didn't take sides?"

She and Nalia exchanged a smile. "Things change," Aisha said. She took Nalia's elbow and led her into the room. "I assume you have need of a healer in Ithkar?" she asked.

Nalia nodded. "Yes, of course."

Aisha gestured to several leather bags. "I'm happy to serve, if you'll have me."

Nalia bowed, palms pressed against her heart. "It would be . . . wonderful. Aisha, thank you so much." She turned to Raif. "See? All is not lost."

"Thank you," he said to Aisha. "You have no idea how much that means to us."

"Where's Shirin?" Raif asked, looking around the room.

"She said she'd be more comfortable in her *ludeen*," Aisha said. "One of the other healers is with her."

He sighed. "I guess I won't be able to see her before we go."

Aisha nodded. "That might be for the best. She's . . . very upset right now."

"If you need to go to her . . . ," Nalia said.

Raif shook his head. "I know Shirin. She'll want some space right now."

The jinni had held a gun to Raif's head just hours before, and yet, somehow, Nalia's heart hurt for her. She knew how devastating loving someone that much could be. How it could make you do crazy things.

Nalia crossed the room to where Taz lay on a bed, his head turned toward them. His face was drawn, eyes deeply sad. A small child sat on the end of the bed, smoothing the hair of a doll. Nalia crouched down beside the bed and took Taz's hand into her own.

"I'm so sorry," she whispered, careful not to speak too loudly in front of the child.

"They told you about Kesmir?" he said. She nodded.

"They told you everything?" Taz's eyes went to Raif's. He shook his head.

"You saved me this happiness," Taz said to him. "I'm grateful."

"We could all use something to smile about tonight, brother." Raif said.

"You and your secrets, all of you," Nalia said. "What is it?"

"Yasri?" Taz called to the little jinni. He held out his hand and she moved closer, taking it.

Calar's daughter, she reminded herself. Crimson eyes, the same high cheekbones and white hair. *She's just a child,* Nalia thought.

"I want you to meet my friend," Taz said. "Her name is Nalia."

"Hello," Nalia said.

Yasri stared at Nalia's eyes, transfixed. "Pretty eyes," she said, tilting her head. "Purple."

Taz laughed softly. "Yes, that's right."

The room seemed full of electricity, expectation. Nalia had no idea what was going on.

"Aisha," Taz called. "Could you . . ."

The healer came over and reached out her hands. "Yasri, can I see your pretty fingers?" Someone had painted her nails a light pink.

Yasri put her hands in Aisha's and giggled as the healer's blue *chiaan* swirled over their hands. Nalia smiled. The sight of a child did her good. And if she was Kesmir's daughter as much as Calar's, there was no doubt she'd turn out fine, especially with Taz as her papa now.

And then—

Nalia gasped, staring at the child's eyes. It was like looking into a mirror: purple as her own, but a darker shade, like the *yasri* flowers in the mountains.

Tears slid down Nalia's cheeks as she reached out a trembling hand and gently stroked Yasri's cheek.

"You," Nalia whispered, "are so beautiful."

Yasri reached out a hand and wiped the tears off Nalia's cheeks. "Don't cry, Nah-la." She reached out her arms and Nalia picked her up and twirled her around, their laughter bouncing off the walls until every face in the room except for Yasri's was bathed in tears.

Nalia turned to Raif and the smile she gave him was full of joy and sorrow and a wonder she had never known.

He grinned, not even bothering to wipe away his tears. "See why we wanted to surprise you?"

She nodded. A Ghan Aisouri. A *Ghan Aisouri*. Just when she was getting ready to hate the gods, they pulled something like this.

The door opened and Thatur ducked in, barely fitting through the slim doorway.

"Bird!" Yasri cried.

Nalia laughed at the expression on Thatur's face.

"He doesn't like that," she whispered to Yasri. "But if he makes you mad—and he will, all the time—you go ahead and say it."

"Nalia-jai, don't put any ideas in the child's head," Thatur grumbled.

She laughed. "I hope you enjoyed your freedom, Yasri—now you'll have to deal with him every day for the rest of your life." She gave Thatur a wink.

"I think you'll agree that your training paid off," he huffed.

Nalia smiled. "It did indeed."

"Yasri doesn't know yet," Taz said quietly from the bed. "I thought maybe you could be the one to show her."

Nalia turned to him, still holding Yasri. "Are you sure?"

"It would honor her—and Kes," he said.

"It honors me, too," she whispered.

Taz gave a slight bow of his head. "My Empress."

Nalia took Yasri to an oval mirror ringed in sea glass that hung from the wall. "Yasri, look." Nalia pointed to the mirror.

The little jinni's eyes slid to the glass, her dark purple beside Nalia's bright amethyst. Calar's daughter gasped, clapping her hands in delight.

"Purple!" she cried, pointing at the mirror. She giggled and her small, chubby fingers reached for her reflection.

Nalia kissed her head. "We're not alone anymore, little one," she said.

"Nal," Raif said, his voice soft. She turned. "You're not the only ones."

40

NALIA HAD NEVER IMAGINED SHE'D REIGN OVER A KING-
dom of ash and fire.

Nor that she would come to love its savage, unapologetic
beauty. Ithkar's air was thick with volcanic smoke, pouring into
her lungs, seeping into her skin. By all accounts, she should hate
it just as much as everyone else in her court and army. But the
region was a wonder of undiscovered gems. In the week since setting up her kingdom-in-exile, Nalia had taken to traipsing across
Ithkar's vast mist- and steam-shrouded plains, solitary treks that
helped her make sense of all that had happened to her: the Eye,
reuniting with Raif, the ring, setting up a kingdom. It had been
a long, devastating year, and even the joy of falling asleep beside
Raif and waking up to him every morning was not enough to
dispel her unease, to lessen the weight of this ravaged land.

The lava lakes, the power of the volcanoes, the rare tree or lotus—all of these things reignited her wonder, helped Nalia forget, if only for a moment, the sigil that refused to come off her finger. It alienated her, this ring of power. It set her apart in ways she abhorred. She could see the fear in the eyes of the jinn who served her, the way their shoulders hunched forward waiting for a command. The shackles they'd fought so hard to lose fused to their wrists. She herself hadn't given them a reason to feel this way, but of course they did—she would have, too. It would be like Malek returning from the dead and putting her back in the bottle.

And there was nothing she could do about it.

So she walked and walked, or rode Thatur, skimming the clouds high above Ithkar, up where the air was fresh and sweet. The view of the volcanoes from above and the constant moonlight made the lava even more electric, set against that dark backdrop. And though the moons seemed to bleed, she loved them, too. Something about this dark, fearsome land called to her. She was, after all, part Ifrit—the fire of Ithkar ran through her veins. Though she explored as much of the barren territory as she could, Nalia steered clear of the Ash Crones. They were a fight for another day, an ancient evil who would take much more of her time than Nalia currently had to uproot from their cave deep in Ithkar. She could only fight so many wars. For now, Nalia had to focus on her people, on her training. She would have to face Calar, and soon. The Ifrit empress knew of the ring by now—she would be wearing her own set of shackles—yet she didn't show the slightest inclination toward abdicating the Aisouri throne.

She hadn't used her shadows, though—for one reason and one reason only: Yasri. Nalia would never harm a child—but Calar didn't need to know that.

It seemed they were at an impasse: Calar would not leave, and Nalia refused to wrest her crown from Calar's head through the use of a human master's ring. It was hard to explain to her soldiers—even to Raif—why she would not command Calar to step down or to give Nalia control of the shadows. It wasn't just her visions from the lote tree that convinced Nalia such a path could only lead the realm into even more despair. She was quick to admit that the visions played no small part in her governing, but that her main reason was that she needed to win the hearts of her people.

"If I use the ring to dethrone Calar, what have I shown of myself, how have I earned the right to lead?" she'd said to Raif and the others who counseled her just this morning. Taz, Touma, Thatur, and Aisha sat at a large table set low to the ground, sitting the Ifrit way on thick cushions atop woven rugs. Zanari would have agreed with her, but she was already back with the Dhoma.

Nalia begged them to understand. "Every jinni in the realm will see yet another Ghan Aisouri whose power keeps her above the fray. They need to see me defeat Calar because I am better than her, because I refuse to resort to evil means to get what I want. I want to fight her on my own terms, risking my very life for this land. Anything else would be a sham and I would not be worthy of the Amethyst Crown."

As the others left the room, Raif had gently drawn her to him. "No one thinks you're afraid to fight her, *rohifsa*. Using the ring would save countless lives—I tell you that as a commander in this army of yours. You know I stand by whatever you choose—but are you willing to take the risk that there will be unnecessary dead?"

"I am. Is that wrong?" She'd looked at him with pleading eyes. Both of them so, so tired.

He shook his head. "No. I had to make the same kinds of choices too, with the *tavrai*. It's never easy. I just . . . wish you wouldn't go up against her again. I'm tired of seeing you almost-dying."

Later that afternoon, a lone Ifrit messenger presented himself at one of the Brass Army checkpoints high in the Qaf Mountains. After thoroughly interrogating him and inspecting the parchment on which a message was written to Nalia in a scrawling hand, he was finally brought to the Cauldron's throne room.

The soldier, little more than a boy, handed the parchment to Nalia with a shaking hand. When Nalia opened it, a small smile flitted across her face:

I want my daughter.

Nalia manifested a pen and inkwell, then wrote in her elegant cursive:

I want my throne.

"Take it back and give it to the jinni who calls herself an empress," Nalia said. She manifested bread, cheese, and a bottle of *savri* and handed it to the messenger. "For your trouble," she added.

The Ifrit's eyes widened and he took the parcel, then bowed. "Many thanks, My Empress," he said.

At Nalia's obvious surprise, he bowed once more. "You have friends in the palace" was all he said before turning on his heel and marching out of the room.

"Well, that was unexpected," Taz said.

He and Raif had just come from a meeting with their commanders, Taz reporting to Nalia while Raif traveled to the camps below the Cauldron to help train the soldiers.

"It was," she said, thoughtful. Maybe there were more jinn on her side than she thought.

"What are you thinking?" Taz asked.

Nalia leaned back against the uncomfortable throne made of slippery onyx. "Calar keeps her shadows at bay for fear they'll hurt Yasri. We need to attack before she becomes impatient. Before she stops caring if Yasri gets hurt."

"Agreed."

It was time to end this war, time to build, and heal, and grow, but Nalia couldn't do that until she was ready to face Calar. Though Calar had refrained from using her shadows, she'd employed a different strategy, one that wore Nalia down as surely as any battle could: *hahm'alah*, the magic of true names.

She hadn't been surprised when Calar began using the ancient form of communication between jinn. Usually only a jinni's parents, siblings, children, and spouse ever knew a given jinni's name, but Calar had stolen Nalia's true name out of Bashil's head—it was how she'd been able to trick Nalia while in Morocco, using the name to lure Nalia to a secluded location deep in Marrakech's souk. She used it now to torture Nalia day and night, a barrage of hateful images Nalia could never return because she herself did not know Calar's true name. Nalia would feel a slight tug on her heart and have no choice but to see whatever Calar sent her.

Bashil, convulsing on the ground.

A pile of dead Aisouri, after the coup.

Calar, torturing a *tavrai* messenger.

On and on they came. They kept her up at night so that she was forced to roam the onyx halls of the Cauldron, the very walls of which seemed to bleed evil energy. The torches on the wall cast sinister shadows and the heat suffocated her, mist from the volcano slipping through the windows, coating the walls with moisture so that they constantly sweated. There were rooms Nalia avoided, either because the energy was too dark or what was inside them too vile. Raif always found her at some point, drawing her back to bed, staying up with her until she fell asleep.

She was absolutely exhausted. The fight with the *tavrai*, the move across the realm—it had taken more out of Nalia than she wanted Raif or anyone else to know. The Ifrit stronghold was full of jinn: Kesmir's recruits who'd defected from the Ifrit army, Brass soldiers running messages, Nalia's advisers. She couldn't walk down the hall without being consulted on one matter or another.

And then, of course, there was the ring. Nalia rested her forehead in her hand, elbow propped up on the throne.

"Are you ill, My Empress?" Taz asked with concern.

"I don't know. Tired, I guess." She placed a hand on Taz's arm. "How's Yasri?"

Taz had recently tried to explain death to her, what it meant that her father was in the godlands.

"She's doing as well as can be expected. She misses Kes something terrible." He looked down at his hands, his mouth tightening. "As do I."

"It won't get better," Nalia said, "not for a long time. But he gave you a gift in her, I think."

"She makes me laugh." Taz shook his head, wondering. "Even when I'm in the worst place, worrying that Kes wasn't burned . . . She's a sweet girl. Sometimes . . ." He hesitated. "Sometimes it hurts to look at her. She's so like him."

"And her mother?"

"That I don't know. Yasri asks after her sometimes, but not too often." He smiled at Nalia. "She keeps pointing to her eyes, asking about you: *Nah-la. Nah-la.*"

Nalia laughed. It was adorable how her little Ghan Aisouri sister couldn't quite say Nalia's name. "Bring her to me sometimes, will you?"

"Of course."

"And the boy—are they getting along?"

Taz had told her about a child who had been of great assistance to Kesmir—Quan. He'd been brought to Ithkar not long after Kesmir's death and was now in Taz's care.

He nodded. "He's like a big brother to her. I'm grateful for them both." Taz stood and bowed. "Anything else I can do?"

"Oh, Taz, you've done so much. No, thank you. I'm fine." He raised his eyebrows. "Really, I am."

"I have it on good authority that Thatur won't have time to train you today. Every now and then, I believe an empress is allowed to take a nap."

"You know what? That's a good idea."

He spread his hands. "My job is to provide wise counsel, is it not?"

She followed him out of the throne room and headed down the hallway to the rooms set aside for her and Raif. She'd magicked them to look like their tent in Morocco, the only comfort they had in the nightmarish palace. Few jinn had skills like Nalia's. The ability to create and maintain an illusion such as this was something learned from Shaitan mages, most of whom Calar had killed. There were still so many jinn who were unable to manifest some of the most basic necessities, though Nalia was trying to fix that. Small classes were now being held, taught by the few Shaitan in their ranks. There was also a healthy bartering market, the jinn trading wishes to suit their needs.

Nalia crawled onto the bed, curling up into a ball in its center. The sigil pulsed against her skin, keeping her awake. An incessant tapping. It wanted to be used and did not like being ignored. After a half hour of tossing and turning, unable to rid herself of the aching weariness because the godsdamn ring wouldn't shut up, Nalia sat up in bed and pulled her Aisouri dagger from where she'd left it on a small table.

"Enough," she said into the empty room, to the ring, to Calar.

Nalia held the dagger against her skin. One quick slice— maybe two, she wasn't sure if she'd be able to get through the bone the first time.

They'd tried everything to get the damned thing off her finger and now she was alone, reduced to tears, an unwilling master who was hated and feared by all but a handful of supporters and the Brass Army.

It was as though she'd harnessed every jinni in the realm, turning them into beasts of burden she could move at will. She was terrified to say a word, fearful she'd accidentally force someone to obey a command. It was a curse, being a master. She didn't want this power, wanted the ring off—lost at the bottom of the sea, melting in a volcano. It was sucking on her *chiaan*, this terrible leech of hers.

Just as she began to press the razor-sharp blade against her index finger, the door to her quarters opened. "Nal, your father's ready to—" Raif stopped, his eyes traveling from Nalia's tear-stained face to the dagger in her hand. Then he went very, very still. "Look at me," he said, gentle. "Sweet one, look at me."

She did. "I have to get it off, Raif. I can feel it, all the time, it'll make me bad, it'll make me like her—"

"*Rohifsa*. I love you so much. I love every single bit of you, and if you cut off your finger, that will break my heart. Okay?" He moved toward her with tentative steps. She gripped the knife, paralyzed.

Raif knelt down and placed his hand over the ring. His palm was warm and his *chiaan* calmed the terror galloping through her. "We'll find a way," he said "But this isn't it."

He pulled the dagger out of her hand and Nalia fell against him as he gathered her up in his arms.

"This wasn't in the visions, me wearing the ring," she said. She'd been obsessing over this, day and night. How had she diverted from the gods' will? "I must have made a wrong step, I just, I don't know. . . ."

"Yasri wasn't in the visions either, was she?"

She paused, looking up at him. Raif was right—she hadn't thought about that. And a poor role model she'd be for her Ghan Aisouri sister, cutting off her finger because she didn't trust herself, because she was a little bit tired. Because she was embarrassed.

"Nal, who knows what all that stuff in the Eye meant? You did the only thing you could—I'd be dead if you hadn't." Raif kissed her head, then helped her to stand. "First, *savri*. Then your father is going to fix this."

"I'm sorry," she whispered. "I don't know what came over me."

"It's okay," he said, drawing her toward a small table where a bottle of *savri* and glasses sat. "No big deal. I'm just never letting you out of my sight again."

She raised her eyebrows and he gave her a tiny wink. "Sit. Drink."

41

A FEW MINUTES LATER, RAIF WAS GUIDING NALIA PAST the hideous tapestry of Ifrit exploits that lined the main hallway, which Nalia had insisted they keep up as a reminder of the Ghan Aisouri's misuse of power. The small tower where Ajwar Shai'Dzar conducted his experiments was at the back of the castle, far from the fortress's bustle. As one of the foremost scholars in the land still living, he'd set himself the task of learning everything he could about the ring. The steep staircase that led to the tower had a banister made of interlocking bones that had been blackened by soot. Nalia went up the steps slowly, pulling up the long, flowing kaftan she wore. Raif was behind her, one hand on the small of her back. The door at the top of the stairs had a carving of a dragon's gaping mouth.

"Lovely people, the Ifrit *shirzas*," Raif said.

Nalia pushed open the door to the small room. Her father and Taz sat at a long table that held a pot of *chal* and several delicate tea glasses. They stood as she came into the room, respectful. Touma and Thatur remained standing, ever on alert. Despite being in the Cauldron, her father had managed to make it surprisingly comfortable. Colorful lamps he'd no doubt manifested himself hung from the ceiling. Candles, stuck to tables and shelves with their own dripping wax, were scattered throughout the room.

"Ah, My Empress," her father said as Raif shut the door behind them. Awkward and maimed, he motioned for Nalia to take the seat at the head of the table.

My Empress. She was his daughter and yet he wasn't comfortable using her first name, let alone terms of endearment.

"Hello, Father," she said, settling into the leather chair.

She tried not to stare at his face, at what Calar had done to him. He was hardly recognizable. She wondered how excruciating the pain had been, how he'd managed to survive it. There hadn't been much time for discussion, and so for days they'd remained strangers to one another, just as they'd always been. Until they talked about Bashil. They'd cried together over his death and he shared stories of her brother that Nalia had never heard. It had been a sweet hurt, learning of her brother's antics on the plantation her father owned. But when they weren't reminiscing about Bashil, there was little for them to discuss and so they remained formal with each other, as though they were still in the palace, at court.

Nalia had never known quite how to speak with her father. Before the coup, she saw him infrequently, a phantom she shared certain traits with, one who occasionally came to court but spent most of his time at the palace locked in the library with the other scholars. She'd seen his plantation only once, on a routine patrol with the Aisouri. They'd never shown one another affection. Nalia did not love him, nor, she supposed, he her. But she was nevertheless overjoyed that he'd survived Calar's wrath and grateful to Thatur for keeping him alive.

Now she sat across from him, drinking *chal*, the earthiness of the Arjinnan tea a balm. A plate of food sat on the table—fresh fruit her father had manifested, along with warm bread and hard-boiled eggs. A tureen of soup sat steaming beside a stack of bowls—cardamom and rose and lentils, her favorite. Did her father know that? Or was it his favorite too?

Taz stood and began pouring soup into the bowls while Thatur gave Raif a rundown about training and Touma updated him on security. Taz passed a bowl to Nalia, and she sighed in contentment as the fragrant soup slid down her throat.

"Do you know," she said, "I don't think I've eaten anything today."

Touma shook his head as he glanced at her over Raif's shoulder. "This is not good, My Empress."

"He's right," Taz agreed. "You need to keep up your strength."

A smile flitted across Nalia's face. "I *did* manage to survive a year without meals."

Ajwar turned to her. "When there's time, I would love to hear more about this heart plant."

Raif sat down beside her, resting his scimitar on the table. "What do we do about this ring?" he asked, dispensing, as he always did, with small talk. "It's becoming unbearable for her."

"May I?" Ajwar asked, holding out his hand.

Nalia hesitated for a moment, then nodded, reaching toward him. Her father gently took her hand into his own. His *chiaan* was curious and bright, an inquisitive energy that reminded her of Bashil. This moment was one of the few times he'd ever touched her.

Ajwar inspected the ring and her hand for some minutes, mumbling to himself. Seemingly satisfied, he let go of her, adjusting his gold-rimmed spectacles.

"It's astounding magic," he said with the awe of one of Earth's scientists. "As you know, the overlords once had rings with a similar purpose. I myself had one—" He stopped, looking at Raif, apologetic. "A fact which I now greatly regret," he added. "But those rings, they didn't have a fraction of this one's power."

"Can it be destroyed?" Nalia asked. "I mean, without having to cut off my hand."

"No one is cutting off your hand," Raif said, tense.

"If you were to cut off your hand, yes, I suppose you would no longer be able to control jinn with the ring," Ajwar said. "But"— he reached over and lightly patted her hand—"this would not be a wise course of action." He leaned back in his chair, a thoughtful expression on his face. "I don't believe it can be destroyed. I suspect Antharoe might have tried and failed. It would explain why she had to hide it on Earth. There are old diaries of hers I once had the privilege to read. She never said it directly, but her dismay over the existence of the ring leads me to believe that she would have destroyed it if she could. As far as my understanding goes, the ring only ever left Solomon's hand after he'd died. To me, this suggests that the ring will not come off until you . . . well."

Nalia had heard several versions of the story on Earth, one of which described a host of slaves bowing before the Master King for nearly eighty years, following his last command. None of them knew that he'd been dead all that time until the ring slipped off his finger and clattered to the floor of his throne room. They'd had no idea they were free. His last command had been for them to bow before him, and so they had: *for eighty years.*

"So I have to *die?*" she said, her voice high with panic. She could almost hear Malek's voice: *That's absurd. I want a second opinion—someone kill this fool for wasting my time.*

Ajwar leaned forward, his eyes on Nalia's. It hurt to look at them—those were Bashil's eyes. "I'm intrigued by your vision at the lote tree. No jinn in the history of our race has ever been so fortunate. Truly, the gods were with you. Did you see the ring in your vision?"

Nalia shook her head. "No. There was a point at which all I saw was gold light radiating from my hand. And Raif was beside me."

"A thought," Taz said, leaning forward and looking down at the ring himself.

"Of course, Tazlim," her father said.

Nalia knew the two of them spent countless hours studying the old texts together. It was Taz's favorite thing to do, and Ajwar was the only other jinni in Ithkar with the passion—and aptitude—for such tasks.

"We've been focusing on how to destroy the ring or take it off her finger. But what if we . . . separated the power itself from the object?" Taz said.

"Isolate it," Ajwar said to himself..

"Somehow, the power to enslave was placed in the ring," Taz said. "By Solomon's god or a human mage—whoever made it."

"But if something can be put into the ring . . . ," Nalia said, grinning at Taz.

Raif's eyes lit up. "It can be taken out." He leaned back in his chair and ran his hands through his hair, heaving a relieved sigh. "I knew if I got the smartest people in the realm together, you'd figure something out."

"An extraction spell, yes?" Taz said, glancing at Ajwar.

Ajwar studied the ring, his brow furrowed in concentration. "I don't think it'd be possible to take power out—it's treating Nalia as a host, much like a parasite. The ring only works when worn—thus, by fusing with the wearer, it acts in its own self-interest, resisting anything that threatens it. In taking power out of the ring, we may accidentally extract *her* power, which puts her life at risk. However, I may be able to reverse the *direction* of the power."

He gently tapped his forefinger with his chin, deep in thought. Nalia swallowed the lump that formed in her throat—Bashil used to do that. She'd thought it was one of his little quirks, not something he'd picked up from their father.

"What do you mean by 'reverse'?" Raif asked.

"Whoever wears the ring would be enslaved to all the jinn of the realm, rather than be their master," Ajwar said.

"No," Raif immediately said. "We're not doing that."

Yes. Yes, we are. Nalia felt a rush of recognition at her father's words, a rightness. *Of course.* This was what the lote tree had been saying. She knew she'd have to give up her freedom for the realm—she'd just had no idea it would require this.

The room was heavy with silence and Raif looked around, his expression incredulous. "We're *not doing that.* It would kill her. They'd command Nalia to, I don't know, jump into a volcano." He turned to Nalia, eyes pleading. "Don't tell me you're actually considering this? Nal, you could barely handle one *pardjinn* master. This would be thousands of jinn masters, and most of them do not like you very much."

Nalia hated to see his pain, his worry. But Raif's love for her was part of why his council couldn't always be taken into consideration: he refused to put her in danger. As soon as her eyes met his, he cursed under his breath.

Nalia glanced at Ajwar. "Can you do this?"

He hesitated. "You must understand, this is incredibly difficult magic—the most advanced I've ever seen. I'd need time and . . . I honestly agree with Djan'Urbi on this. I don't recommend it."

She felt Raif relax beside her.

"When I was enslaved on Earth," Nalia said, "my master had a painting of the lote tree in his office."

Ajwar raised his eyebrows. "A human knew of *B'alai Lote*?"

"They have a different name for it: the *Sidrat al-Muntaha.* It's located in the seventh heaven—the closest humans can get to Allah. Like us, humans believe that the lote tree is a way to get divine inspiration from their god."

Raif smirked. "So, what, Malek thought he was 'divinely inspired' to enslave you?"

"I thought you weren't religious," Nalia says.

"I'm not." Malek stubs out his cigarette and comes to stand beside her and together they gaze at the painting. His hand slips around her waist and he pulls her closer to him. "I just like to remind myself that it's possible to have God's ear every now and then."

"Why?"

"So I can tell him to get out of my way."

Nalia shook her head. "Malek didn't have a god," she said softly. "He was his own." She leaned forward. "I think the humans are right, though. The lote tree is the voice of the gods, speaking in images and feelings. And I know with everything in me that the gods want Arjinna to be my master. That was clear in the vision. I thought it was symbolic, but the more time I spend here, the more I see that everything they've shown me has been real. No metaphors, no symbols. I saw shackles go around my wrists. If we're to reverse the power of the ring and the jinn become my master, it would explain why I will have those shackles."

Taz leaned forward. "An empress shackled to her people? How could you rule? What would be the limits of the commands they could give you? Is any of this even possible?"

Ajwar shook his head, still deep in thought. "I honestly don't know."

But Nalia knew. This would be the only way an empress

would be unable to hurt the land or her people.

"It *is* possible. It has to be," she said.

"Nalia, you can't be serious!" Raif exploded. "You'd be a puppet on a string. You wouldn't have time to rule—you'd be too busy granting wishes for fishermen and farmers."

She turned to her father. "Would it be like that? In the vision it felt like . . ." She sighed. It was so difficult to put into words what she'd seen in the Eye. "Like destiny."

> *She plants a seed. The seed becomes a tree, its roots extending in all directions, traveling deep under Arjinna. Nalia feels the burn of a new set of shackles encircling her wrists.*

"The gods want me to be enslaved again." *An end,* the lote had shown her, *if she was not its beginning.* "I'm sure they can figure out the details. Just do what you can. Please."

Raif pushed his chair back and it crashed to the stone floor. "I'm going for a walk."

"Raif—" She stood just as he slammed the door behind him.

"Let him go, Nalia," Taz said. "These are hard words to hear, no?"

She knew Raif felt powerless to help her. She knew it killed him to know she would be hurt again.

"He doesn't understand—" she started, but Taz shook his head.

"He does—that's the problem," Taz said. "He knows he can't take you off this course. And, unlike you, he doesn't trust the gods."

"And you still do?" she asked. "After . . . everything?"

Taz inclined his head. "I don't like the choices they make all the time," he said softly. Nalia knew he was thinking of Kesmir, his own bottle, and the love he'd lost to Solomon's enslavement. "But I never would have survived that bottle with my mind intact without them. I spent a lot of time contemplating their nature. They are ineffable, yes, but they gave us *chiaan*." His voice softened, reverent. "Imagine: they gifted us with the very life force of the universe. Our manifestations, our bonding to the elements, the physical feeling of our souls—not a concept, but a tangible living thing inside us. The human god never did that—no gods have ever done that. Even if our *chiaan* was the only gift the gods gave us, they'd be worthy of our worship and respect."

Nalia smiled. "*This* is why I want you to be my spiritual adviser—it's exactly what I'm talking about."

She'd already asked Taz when she'd begun assembling her court. He'd demurred, worried that his grief over Kesmir and his new fatherhood would keep him from adequately serving her, clouding his judgment.

"If I may," Ajwar interjected, "my daughter speaks truth. You are a wise jinni, Tazlim. And she needs your wisdom as much as she needs my magic and Raif's battle expertise."

"It's the best way you can serve Arjinna," she said softly. "And me . . . if that's what you want to do."

"I can't help but feel I've just been tricked," he said with a small smile.

"An empress can never be too cunning," she teased, eyes sparkling. "So . . . yes?"

Taz met her unwavering gaze. "I serve at the pleasure of the empress." He inclined his head. "It would be my honor."

"Excellent—so we have that settled," Nalia said. "Taz will be my spiritual adviser and my father will find a way to reverse the ring's power."

She stood, but Ajwar put a gentle hand on her arm. She stilled at that small, unexpected touch.

"You must understand," he began, "this magic . . . it might not work. And it will take some time. I've never done something like this before."

"It has to work," she said simply.

"What do we do about the war in the meantime?" Thatur asked.

There was a soft knock on the door and Touma moved toward it, scimitar drawn, just in case. "Enter," Ajwar called.

The door swung open and Raif walked inside. His eyes met Nalia's, his expression contrite. "I apologize," he said.

Nalia wondered how many things he'd had to break before he came back. Gods, she loved him.

She smiled and reached for his hand. "You're just in time."

"We're discussing our next steps with Calar," Taz said.

Raif nodded. "I have a few ideas about that. Most of them involve her lying dead on the palace floor."

"Agreed," Nalia said. "So we kill Calar and her shadows, then take back the palace while my father figures out what to do with the ring."

She held up a hand. "And before either of you say it, I refuse to use the ring at all—I did that once already, and you saw what happened."

"Justice is what happened," Thatur sad.

"Death. Death is what happened." She was still haunted by that bullet in Jaqar's head. Nalia didn't regret killing him. She regretted how easy it had been.

She turned to Taz. "So, how do we destroy those shadows?"

It was a discussion they'd had little time for between the move to Ithkar and the reorganization of the Brass Army and its new Ifrit members.

"The only way to do this is to get the *yaghin* Calar wears around her neck," Taz said. "Kes told me it's how she stores and controls the shadows."

"Around her neck, huh?" Nalia said.

The things she'd had to do to get her bottle off Malek's neck. Nalia frowned, her eyes on the moons: pulling him closer in her bed, sitting on his lap in a movie theater, getting him drunk on drugged wine while she endured his kisses, waiting for him to pass out. And, sometimes, she wasn't *enduring* it and that had been the very worst part.

Raif slipped an arm around her shoulder. "We'll figure something out together."

Together. Nalia wasn't sure she'd ever get used to not facing everything alone.

"I draw the line at me having to seduce Calar," she said.

"Yes," Raif said immediately, "I like that line."

Ajwar pushed up his glasses. "I believe I've lost the thread of this conversation."

"It's going to be challenging to get something off Calar's neck," Nalia said.

"Yes, I imagine it will be," Ajwar agreed.

She wondered how this absentminded scholar had caught the eye of Nalia's mother, one of the most vicious Aisouri in the palace. *Opposites attract,* Malek had once said to her. Maybe he was right. Did her father grieve her? Did he long for her late at night? It was hard for Nalia to imagine, and yet Mehndal Aisouri'Taifyeh had had two children by Ajwar and kept him as her lover all of Nalia's life.

"I need a little more time to regain my strength before we put any of our plans into action," Nalia said. "But we can't wait too long."

"And what of the Godsnight?" Taz asked.

The moons remained full to bursting, each night becoming more luminescent. And yet nothing happened. Sometimes, Nalia even caught herself forgetting about the prophecy.

"We just have to hope the gods will be on our side when it happens," Nalia said.

Raif frowned at the moons. "Good luck with that."

Nalia and Taz burst out laughing. It was such a Raif thing to say, so utterly irreverent.

"What?" Raif said.

"Nothing, *rohifsa,*" she said, kissing his cheek. "Nothing at all."

42

THE NEXT DAY, NALIA GOT UP EARLY—AT LEAST, SHE thought it was early. It was difficult to tell time when the sun never rose.

She found Taz in the Ifrit's main temple for Ravnir. It was, perhaps, the most austere of the temples in Arjinna, with its stark, almost violent, beauty. A large open square built in the center of a lava lake, the temple was easily big enough to fit five hundred jinn on their knees in prayer. The volcano that had birthed the lake towered over it, no longer active but imposing nonetheless. As in the Cauldron, thick stilts held the temple above the lava. A wide circle, cut in the center of the onyx tiles, looked down into the liquid fire below. There were no railings or walls to prevent worshippers from falling into the lake. There were no ornaments or altars or symbols of Ravnir. The fire was enough.

Taz was sitting near the center of the temple, alone. His legs were crossed, hands on his knees. Though he was silent, Nalia knew he was in prayer, his head tilted back to look at the moons. This, she thought, was Taz in the highest form of himself. A *pajai* in the making, always in conversation with the gods, always seeking to understand.

But alone. Always, it seemed, alone.

Yasri would ease some of that burden, Nalia was certain of that. The little girl was rarely not at his side. She preferred to be held, rather than walk. She called him *Tazeem*. She patted his cheeks, as though she knew an invisible river of tears flowed there. Though young, she had an old soul.

Sensing her presence, Taz turned. He stood, bowing. "My Empress."

She reached out her hand. "Taz. Do we need the formalities?'"

He took it. "Sometimes they're a good reminder."

"How could I possibly forget I'm the empress?"

He smiled. "How indeed?"

To herself, she'd always be Nalia. But not to anyone else, save Raif.

"What do you need?" he asked.

"Come," she said. "This temple terrifies me."

He laughed. "Where are we going?"

"My favorite place in Ithkar."

He held her hand as she evanesced, picturing the one place in this foreign land that gave her peace. When they arrived, Taz smiled.

"This is my favorite place, too," he said.

She'd come to call it the Mist Lake. The water was light blue, almost white—opaque, like a blind eye—and a permanent cloud of mist lay over it. Here and there broken tree trunks shot up through the water, large sticks with jagged ends. A thick silence lay over the lake like a shroud. It was the eeriest place Nalia had ever been, but something about it drew her. Maybe what she liked about the Mist Lake was that it was unabashedly sad. It didn't pretend at happiness; it wallowed, something she wasn't allowed to do.

They settled on its banks, arms around their knees. "I love the silence here," he said. "I don't miss the bottle at all, of course, but there are days when all the noise, the people—it's too much."

She nodded. "I don't miss the Eye—or my bottle, for that matter—but I know what you mean. It's strange to be alone and then suddenly be surrounded on all sides. All I wanted for the past year was to be around people, to be drenched in light, and yet I find myself wanting to sit in the dark, alone."

"Yes," he said. "Funny how it works out that way."

Nalia reached out a hand and trailed her fingers through the mist. It was cool, deliciously damp. Perhaps the only place in Ithkar where she wasn't sweating. The Ifrit territory—like the Ifrit themselves—seemed to operate only in extremes.

"What do you think about when you're here?" she asked.

"Kesmir," he said softly. "Always Kesmir." He sighed and she reached out, placing a hand on his arm. There were no words she could say, Nalia knew that well enough.

He glanced at her. "What brings you here?"

"I come to think about Calar. It suits her, no?"

"That it does," he said. "What do you think about, if you don't mind me asking?"

"I try to understand what she wants. She's always getting into everyone else's head—but what's in hers? What drives her?"

"Power."

"Maybe. Yet I can't help thinking there's something more." She shook her head. "Raif told me you'd learned that the Ash Crones have been training her since childhood."

Taz nodded. "Yes. Delightful bunch of hags, aren't they?"

Nalia's lips turned up. "Yes, I'm sure we'll be making their acquaintance at some point. It makes me wonder . . . what did they do to her? How could one jinni be so evil?"

"The lure of power warps the soul. Look at Jaqar," Taz said.

Look at Malek.

"What a senseless . . ." She sighed. There was so much that could have been avoided. She turned to Taz. "Enough talk of sad things. I came looking for you for a very important, very happy reason."

He smiled. "Well, we could all certainly use more of those."

For once, the task at hand was a warm glow that filled her up. There was a war and the gods were going to bring chaos to the realm and yet all she cared about was what would happen tonight.

"Taz, when you studied at the temples, did you ever see the priests perform a . . . well . . . a marriage ceremony?"

He gave her a long look. "My Empress, I'm flattered, really, but I just don't think we belong together."

She swatted at him and he laughed, his eyes warm. "Be serious," she said. "This is kind of really important."

He leaned back on his hands. "Yes, I did. But that was thousands of summers ago. I'm sure things have changed. Then again," he added softly, "some things are timeless, aren't they?"

"Yes, they are." She smiled, joy and terror and love threatening to spill out at any second. She imagined Raif, holding the wedding chalice to her lips.

"What does Raif say about all this?"

"I haven't told him. I thought it could be a surprise."

She'd spoken to Zanari about her plan before she'd returned to the Dhoma. Raif's sister would be coming through the portal in just a few hours to help by keeping Raif away from Nalia while she put the finishing touches on the temple she'd chosen.

He smirked. "Pretty confident, aren't you?"

She thought of her proposal, in the bathtub of all places, of his *Yes, Nalia, I'll marry you.* They'd held that in their hearts like a secret, speaking of it in late-night whispers.

"I don't think he'll be opposed."

"You're aware that no Ghan Aisouri has ever married, right?" he asked. Nalia nodded. He looked at her for a long moment, thoughtful. "When you become empress, I don't quite know what that would make Raif."

"Emperor," she said. Taz's eyes widened. "I want him to rule by my side as an equal."

"I . . ." He shook his head, overwhelmed. "That's . . . very unorthodox."

"This kingdom cannot be as it once was," she said. "I want to build it on love. On acceptance and tolerance and understanding. What better way to start than have a Djan and an Aisouri on the throne, ruling together? The gods chose me. The people chose Raif. This way, everyone's happy."

Taz grinned. *"Mahan laudik.* You bless the realm with this decision."

Many favors—yes, this was what a life with Raif would bring. Many favors from the gods. Nalia hoped, anyway.

"So, you'll perform our ceremony?"

Taz bowed slightly. "Yes. When do you wish—"

"Tonight."

"Raif. You're not honestly going to wear that?" Zanari said. She gestured to his faded uniform. "I mean, it's easy enough to manifest something clean. Gods."

Zanari flicked her fingers at him and his uniform switched to the dark-green tunic and tailored pants of a *sawal-hafim,* formal attire worn for special ceremonies.

"Isn't this overdoing it?" he said, looking down at the elaborately embroidered tunic. "Taz said it was just a blessing for the troops."

"Trust me, little brother, you'll be glad not to look like you just rolled off the battlefield. I'm doing you a favor—you can thank me later."

Raif snorted as he headed up the lavender marble steps that led to the temple. He sort of missed being bullied by his sister.

Few jinn knew about the temple located high in the Qaf Mountains. Raif only knew of its existence because Nalia had started going there not long after she returned home. Because the Aisouri could access all elements, it honored every god; and so Nalia had opened it up to all jinn, making it the first temple of its kind. Each day saw more and more jinn coming to the temple, worshipping their gods together. It was a start, but it would take a lot more than a temple to unite Arjinnans.

Though he railed against the gods, Raif had taken comfort in this place. The arch at the entrance to the temple was made entirely of amethysts that sparkled in the moonlight, reminding him of Nalia's eyes, of the crown that she would one day wear on her head. Much like the Djan temple in the Forest of Sighs, it had no roof but the star-studded sky. Colorful prayer flags shivered in the breeze, the fabric covered with the handwritten prayers of the faithful. A *widr* tree suspended in midair honored Tirgan. Though its roots were not packed beneath the earth, it was as alive as any tree in the Forest of Sighs. Flowing over a large section of the stone floor beneath it lay a piece of the Arjinnan Sea that had been plucked out by a *pajai* thousands of years before in honor of Lathor. Raif could hear the gentle rush of its waves, reminding him of the months spent training with the *tavrai* on the black sand beaches. The air that blew over the temple carried the scent of spices and herbs, and whenever Shaitan entered, they were surrounded in a gentle gust as they honored Grathali, goddess of air. And then there was Ravnir: a bolt of lightning caught by Antharoe. No matter the weather, it never went out. Yet instead of reminding him of the Ifrit, of death and destruction, the bolt made Raif think of Nalia. He could still see the lightning strike her over *Erg al-Barq*, the way it had filled her body. Witnessing what had happened to her atop that sand dune in the Sahara had been a turning point for Raif; after that he never questioned that she was a daughter of the gods.

As soon as Raif passed under the temple's amethyst arch that led to the courtyard reserved for prayer, he stopped, blinking as he took in the scene before him. Instead of the soldiers he'd been expecting to pray with, it was empty. Hundreds of candles glimmered around him, nestled in the temple's nooks and arches, wedged between cracks in the walls. Snowflakes drifted from the sky and fell gently to the temple floor or settled on the ancient *widr* tree that took up most of the courtyard. The tiny lights strung across its branches reminded him of a cavern in another land, where he and Nalia had claimed each other for good.

There was a slight scuffling sound and he turned just as Yaṣri looked up at him and giggled. She began skipping toward the *widr*, vixen rose petals falling from her hands. His eyes followed the path of petals that began at his feet and stopped at the tree. Nalia stood beneath the *widr*'s swaying boughs, adorned in a pale lavender kaftan made of sea silk that caught the candlelight in its gossamer folds. She looked so much like she had that first night he'd seen her at the top of Malek's stairs. Her hair lay against her shoulders and a Djan bride's crown of wildflowers encircled her head.

All the air left Raif's chest in one long sigh. Nalia met his eyes, hope and love and joy written all over her face. She wasn't a Ghan Aisouri or an empress. She was just his Nalia. It only took Raif a few seconds to reach her, and he didn't stop until she was in his arms.

It was almost too good to believe that after Malek, Haran, the bottle, Bashil, Calar, the Eye—after everything they'd been through—they could have this. His eyes traveled the lines of her face, adoring, his chest full of this love that was so great it seemed a power all its own, like they could paint the sky with it, if they wanted to.

A slight cough sounded behind him and Raif turned, still holding Nalia in his arms.

"Don't you dare kiss her until you say your vows," said Taz. He wore the ceremonial robes of the Shaitan *pajai*. Because of his studies both inside and outside the bottle, he'd been inducted into the priesthood after he officially became the spiritual adviser of the court.

Are you sure? Raif had asked him. Priests couldn't marry, couldn't have lovers. *Raif, the gods gave me two* rohifsas—*I doubt there's a third out there,* Taz had said. *And, frankly, I couldn't bear loving someone again. This is where I belong.*

And yet despite his horrific loss mere days ago, Taz was truly happy for Raif and Nalia. He looked at peace, standing before them, prepared to lead them through their vows to each other and to the gods.

"I've got my eye on them, Taz," Zanari said, coming up behind Raif with a smirk. "Don't you worry."

"A blessing for the troops?" Raif said, laughing.

"It was the best I could do!"

"She really is a terrible liar," Phara said, joining Zanari. "I can't believe you fell for it."

"Phara! You're—but you—" Raif grinned and walked over to the healer, hugging her. "How long have you been here?"

"Since this morning," she said. "I wouldn't miss this for the worlds."

This would mark Phara's first visit to Arjinna—during the Godsnight, of all times.

Raif turned back to Nalia, reaching for her again. "How long have you been planning this?"

"Officially? Since this morning," she said. "But I talked to Zan about if before she left for Earth last week."

He shook his head. "What other secrets do you have up your sleeve?"

Nalia gave him a wicked grin and he blushed as Zanari burst out laughing, "Welcome to the family, sister."

Nalia leaned into Raif, smiling, while Yasri giggled, hiding behind Taz, then peeking out at Nalia every few moments, her eyes full of wonder.

"Let's get married," Raif murmured to Nalia.

She kissed his nose. "What an excellent idea."

Zanari and Phara took up their places behind them along with Nalia's father and Thatur, who had quietly joined them under the tree, witnesses to the first wedding of a Ghan Aisouri.

Nalia's father stepped forward, gently kissing his daughter on the cheek. "Many blessings, Daughter," he said quietly. Raif knew it was the most affectionate he'd been in her life.

Raif noticed Touma standing guard at the temple entrance, openly weeping.

Zanari rolled her eyes. "Just wait until you start your vows—then he'll really be bawling."

A soft plume of green evanescence filtered through the archway and, a moment later, Fjirla Djan'Urbi appeared. No one made a sound as she crossed to Raif, ducking under the delicate silver *widr* branches that draped over the couple. She stopped, just a few feet from him. Her chin trembled and he went to her, wrapping his arms around her tiny frame. He caught Zanari's eye and nodded to her in thanks. *Told you she'd come around,* her answering smile seemed to say. His mother held tightly to him for a long moment; then she stepped away and crossed to Nalia. Raif watched them, tense.

"Nalia-jai," his mother said, using the suffix reserved for immediate family members. "Thank you for loving my son so well. I hope you'll forgive me for my . . . difficulty with this."

She reached for Nalia's hand and Nalia took it, resting her forehead on the back of Fjirla's hand in a sign of respect.

Raif's eyes filled. He hadn't realized until this moment how desperately sad his mother's rejection of Nalia had made him.

"*Batai ghez sonouq,*" his mother whispered against her hair. *My family is yours.*

The rest of the ceremony was a blur: the wedding chalice, the binding tattoos that appeared on their ring fingers, glowing as they said their vows, then settling into their skin, a shimmering dust of gold that would mark Nalia forever as his beloved, and she his. And, finally, the kiss.

As their lips touched, the others cheered, sending ribbons of *chiaan* around them that burst into stardust. Nalia laughed against his lips, her eyes shining.

"My wife," he whispered against her cheek.

"My husband," she whispered back.

Just days ago she'd been in the Eye, lost to him—it seemed—forever. Now she was here, his wife, *his wife*.

Nalia leaned close and whispered her true name in his ear: *Ashanai*—*Grace*. It was the perfect name for her.

His lips traveled across her cheek. *"Qalif,"* he murmured. *Hope.*

Grace and Hope—yes, they could use that in each other's lives.

Raif turned to Taz and nodded, letting him know that the final act of the ceremony—the exchange of true names—had been completed.

"Mahan laudik," Taz said. *Many favors.*

Their little party of guests erupted into tearful cheers once again and Raif pulled Nalia to him, giving her a far less chaste kiss than the one during the ceremony.

As he pulled away the sky went dark, as though the moons were candles that had been blown out. Raif instinctively stepped in front of Nalia, shielding her body with his.

"Touma," he called, "what is it?"

As the jinni closest to the temple's entrance, he'd be able to tell them what was happening.

"Oh, sir, this is not good," he called back through the darkness, "not good at all."

"That's a little cryptic, Touma," Raif snapped.

Nalia pulled him toward the entryway and he followed.

Despite the candles scattered around the temple, he could hardly see through the inky darkness.

When Raif looked out of the archway, he saw that his army's fires continued to blaze on the northern side of the Qaf range, but the light of the moons had disappeared. Then he saw why. They hadn't disappeared: something was blocking them.

"Fire and blood," Taz breathed.

The Arjinnan Sea had turned into one big wave, so high that even from their vantage point at the top of the Qaf Mountains it seemed as though the moons had drowned. As it began to crest, the Widows winked back into view, their light bleeding onto the land, three waterfalls of lunar lava.

The first plague of the Godsnight had begun.

43

IT DIDN'T MATTER THAT NALIA HAD THE POWER OF ALL four elements. The wave would kill her before she had a chance to absorb herself into it. The water reached its peak, taller than the tallest building she'd seen on Earth. It seemed to hover there, suspended. She stood atop Mount Zhiqui with the Brass Army spread along the Qaf's ridge, staring down in horror as the tsunami crashed onto the shore. It hit the earth with the sound of a whip cracking, wiping out the fishing villages with one punch of its watery fist. In seconds the Marid territory was covered in water.

All along the ridge the jinn who'd traveled to Ithkar with Nalia cried out in helpless terror. Nalia stood, rooted to the ground, too overwhelmed to picture a location to evanesce to that the water wouldn't be covering in a matter of seconds. But she couldn't just stand there—she had to get on the ground, save as many lives as she could.

She looked around for Thatur and spotted him among a group of horrified Brass soldiers.

Thatur, she thought to him. *Come. There's work to do.*

In seconds he was by her side.

"I'm going to warn the jinn farther inland," she said to Raif. "Thatur and I can see what's going on from the sky—we're their best hope."

Raif nodded, wordlessly pulling her to him and kissing her temple.

"Aisha!" Nalia yelled to the healer farther down the ridge.

She held up her bag of medicines. "I'll be ready, My Empress."

"Nalia—the *tavrai,*" Fjirla said, placing a hand on her daughter-in-law's arm.

"I'll warn them," Nalia said. "I promise." It didn't matter that they hated her—they were her people, too, and she wasn't going to let them die.

"They'll try to hurt her—" Raif began, but Nalia was already shaking her head.

"We don't abandon people because they don't like a Ghan Aisouri," she said.

"The ring," Raif said. "What if you used the ring?"

This was how it started, wasn't it? Justify use of the ring for good purposes, until you couldn't tell the good from the bad. Nalia couldn't bear to force anyone's will, and yet, if it would save lives . . .

"Nal, you have to use it," Raif said. "Command everyone to evanesce here. You could—"

"That won't work," said a quiet voice behind them. Ajwar stepped closer. "In order to evanesce, a jinni needs to envision the place they are going, yes?"

Raif nodded. "So can't Nalia just—"

"No," Ajwar said. "She can't get into their minds like Calar can. Commands work differently. The only way she could help these jinn is to use *hahm'alah*—which means she'd have to know the true name of every jinni in the realm in order to show them where to evanesce."

"And even if she could summon them," Taz added, "the danger is too great. The wave could pull them apart midflight."

"Even if we were to risk it, the energy it would take to summon thousands of jinn at once—it could kill her," Ajwar said.

Raif looked like he wanted to argue, but then he nodded, tense. "I'll have the army start manifesting boats," he said. "We'll round up the survivors." He gripped Nalia's hand. "Be careful. No heroics. I don't want to be a widower, do you understand?"

She nodded—he knew her so well. "I love you," she whispered, just before Thatur shot into the sky.

"The Marid," she yelled to Thatur over the howling wind and the deafening sound of the wave destroying everything in its path. Though the villages were gone, jinn had to be down there fighting for their lives.

"Too late!" he said, and though she knew he was right, Nalia stared at the devastation below her, desperate to find drowning jinn to save. The Marid had taken the brunt of the wave. Why would Lathor do this to her own people?

The sea covered the Temple of Lathor entirely, the ancient house of worship annihilated by the wave's force. The moons continued to bleed, shimmering waterfalls of light that spread over the ocean.

Thatur pushed on, toward Djan territory. The water was moving fast, but it seemed as if the jinn who weren't on the coast hadn't seen the wave. The sky should have been full of evanescence as jinn ran for the mountains, and yet . . . nothing.

"Thatur, the *tavrai*—we have to help them."

He ignored her.

Thatur!

She felt him sigh, a rumble that reverberated through her bones.

Nalia-jai, it's not safe. She slanted her body, forcing him to turn toward the forest, and he growled. *They don't deserve it.*

They don't deserve to die. They hated her, but that didn't matter, not now. The enemy was the wave, not each other.

We'll have to agree to disagree, Thatur grumbled as he dove down, speeding toward the trees below them. As soon as he passed through the *bisahm* and into the center of camp, Nalia jumped off his back. The *tavrai* were in the middle of their evening meal, and they stared at her from where they sat at their bonfires, open-mouthed.

The *tavrai* on guard duty ran toward her, scimitars out, but she ignored them, Thatur guarding her as she moved toward the nearest bonfire.

"A wave," she panted, pointing toward the sea. "It just covered

Marid territory—everyone's probably dead—"

One of the guards moved closer to her, eyes full of hatred. "This is just some Aisouri scheme—"

"Listen to me!" Nalia shouted. "You have to evanesce now— before the water comes. Get to the mountains."

A roar sounded on the edges of the forest, as though a giant were walking across it, stomping on every tree he came across. "Please," she begged.

"Nalia—we're leaving. *Now*," Thatur shouted. He hadn't yelled at her like that since she was a child.

"Please," Nalia screamed to the *tavrai* as Thatur pulled her toward him with one of his powerful wings.

Nalia looked around, frantic, as the roar of the wave drew closer.

"Evanesce, *now*. That's an order," said a voice behind Nalia.

Nalia turned and caught Shirin's eyes. The jinni was a few feet from her and Nalia lunged, grabbing Shirin by the arm and pulling her toward Thatur.

"Get behind me," she yelled.

Shirin hesitated. "But—"

"None of it matters, sister," Nalia said, the heaviness of their short history together playing out across Shirin's eyes. "Do you want to live?"

Shirin jumped on, sliding her arms around Nalia's waist.

The sea surged toward them, a filthy brown wave that broke the trees in its path like twigs, flooding the outer perimeter of the camp. All around them the *tavrai* began to evanesce, their *ludeens* above the water line buying them extra seconds, but only until the wave could barrel through the forest.

Thatur took off, speeding toward the Qaf range. He landed and Raif sprinted to them and wrapped his arms around Nalia as soon as she dismounted.

Shirin slid off Thatur's back and Raif finally caught sight of her.

"Shirin," he breathed.

She bit her lip, eyes filling, and he pulled her to him in a wordless hug.

Nalia walked to the edge of the cliff, giving them space, and joined Phara and Zanari.

"Oh, gods," Zanari whispered. The entire forest was covered in water. She turned away, sobbing quietly into Phara's neck.

All around them jinn were evanescing onto the mountain, but there weren't enough—hundreds more *tavrai* were down there.

Nalia glanced at Shirin and Raif, who were watching the people they'd spent their whole life with die right in front of them—and there was nothing they could do about it until the water was calm enough for them to start sending boats down. From what Nalia could see, all that remained of the *tavrai* head-quarters directly beneath them was a dirty lake studded with uprooted *widr* and elder pines.

Raif crossed to his sister and put a hand on her arm. "You both need to go back to the Dhoma."

"But we can help. I'm a healer, I can—" Phara began, but Fjirla stepped in.

"This isn't your fight—either of you. Zanari left for a reason. If you stay, you may never leave," Fjirla said.

"They're right, Zan," Nalia said. "And someone needs to tell the Dhoma there might be a lot of jinn coming through the portal tonight."

Raif gave his sister a hug, holding her tightly "Be well," he whispered.

Taz ran up to Zanari, Yasri crying in his arms, Quan at his side. "Will you—"

Zanari reached for her and Phara took the boy's hand. "Of course."

Taz ruffled Quan's hair, then kissed Yasri on the head. "I'll see you soon, sweet one."

"Tazeem!" she cried, reaching for him as Zanari's jade evanescence surrounded her. Seconds later, they were gone.

Nalia jumped back on Thatur. "What's the plan?" she asked Raif.

"Taz and I will cover the Djan plantations. Nal and Thatur, you get the Ifrit villages."

"I'll go to Yurik," Shirin said, coming up behind him.

Raif nodded. "All right."

Shirin turned to Nalia.

They couldn't have looked more different: Nalia in her shimmering kaftan and bridal crown, Shirin in her worn battle leather, her hair in a tight braid. "Thank you," she said softly.

Nalia nodded. She didn't like Shirin Djan'Khar, but she was glad to have saved her life. *"Jahal'alund,"* Nalia said.

Thatur vaulted into the sky, racing the wave, while the others evanesced around them, the land's only hope.

Shirin evanesced onto the cobblestone lane before the Third Wish. It was the first time she'd been there since the morning before the prison break. Music and loud laughter drifted out through the open door, the patrons oblivious to the watery grave that awaited them. Shirin kicked the door wide open and made her way to the bar, jumping on top of it and letting out one of her piercing whistles. The room immediately went silent.

"The Godsnight has begun. Lathor is smiting the land—a wave is coming," she called, breathless. "Get your families and evanesce to the Qaf—there's no time to spare."

She grabbed the nearest jinni by the scruff of his shirt. "Where's Yurik?"

He pointed toward the stairway leading to Yurik's room. She raced up the stairs and threw open his door as the bar dissolved into pandemonium. Yurik was standing by the window, staring at the Three Widows. He turned.

"Shirin," he said, surprised. He regarded her, wary. "To what do I owe this pleasure?"

She opened her mouth to warn him, but the words wouldn't come. All she could do was stare at Yurik, shocked by the sudden flood of emotion at seeing him. Shirin had thought she'd lost everything the morning she'd held that gun to Raif's head, but she hadn't. Not by a long shot. It had taken the Godsnight for her to realize what had been right in front of her all along.

"Hey," he said, gentle. He walked slowly toward her, as though she were a wild animal in pain. A *raiga*.

And suddenly she didn't want to push him away anymore. Didn't want to deny herself this one good thing.

"I've been so stupid," she said, the words catching in her throat. "I didn't see . . . I couldn't see . . ."

Her eyes filled with tears and they spilled down her cheeks and Yurik's arms were going around her and he was holding her close, his lips brushing her hair. She clung to him, breathing in his scent, like honeysuckle and elder pines. She'd never realized how good he smelled.

"It's okay," he said quietly. "Everything's okay now."

There was the sound of screaming in the street and a crash as the wave made contact with the homes surrounding the Ghaz.

"What—?" Yurik started, but Shirin gripped his hands in hers.

"We have to go—the Godsnight, a wave . . ." Her evanescence swirled around them and she held tightly to him. "You trust me?"

He nodded. "Yeah, actually, I guess I do."

She pictured her favorite spot on the far eastern ridge of the Qaf range. Moments later they were there, standing above the ravaged realm, hand in hand.

"You saved my life," he said, staring at the water-soaked land in horror.

She glanced at him, his face familiar and suddenly so dear. How could she have been so blind? How could she not have understood her own heart, which had tried so hard to pull her toward him all these years?

"I owed you one," she said softly.

They stood there for a few moments, breathing in tandem, their eyes on the destruction below. And, gods help her, she knew there was so much happening right at that very moment that deserved her attention, but all she could think was *Yurik Yurik*.

"I heard about . . ." Yurik frowned as he looked down at their intertwined hands. "What happened. With the Aisouri and Jaqar. And Raif. I'm sorry."

She shook her head. "I'm not."

In the long days of recovery since trying to save Raif's life that final time, Shirin had begun to heal in more ways than one. Letting go had been easier than she'd thought it could be. And it wasn't just Raif she'd let go of as her body mended. It was Arjinna too. Watching Nalia in the clearing—her love for Raif, her choice to put on the ring, the execution of Jaqar—Shirin knew that, in the end, Nalia would be on a throne. And Shirin wanted no part of that. She wasn't quite sure what that meant for her. The revolution was dead without Raif, and the land was destroyed. There was nothing to fight for anymore. If she wanted to, she could walk away from it all without a backward glance, without it being wrong or cowardly. But could she let herself?

"You love him," Yurik said. She could hear the pain he tried to mask for her sake.

"Yes," she said softly. "I think a part of me always will. But he's not the future. Not mine, anyway. And I'm tired of waiting for something I will never have. Tired of being a *raiga.*"

"I'm leaving," Yurik said, letting go of her hand. "Going to Earth. There's . . . there's nothing for me here."

Yes there is, she wanted to say, but the words were lodged in her throat. Her breath caught, the pain swift and unexpected. So she would lose this, too.

"Were you going to say good-bye?"

He reached out a hand and gently ran his fingers along her

jaw, a soft-as-silk touch her body craved.

"I was, yes," he said. "I was hoping . . ." He let his hand drop and a small, sad smile flitted across his face. He shook his head slightly. "I'll miss you."

What would it mean to let him in? To stop fighting this man who wanted nothing but to be good to her? She looked at him, outlined in the moonlight, his hair its usual disheveled mess, his eyes warm despite their pain.

"Do you . . ." She bit her lip, terrified of what his answer might be. "Do you need some company?"

This was the freedom Raif had been talking about. Not endless war, but this choice, this man.

Yurik stared at her, unbelieving. "You would come with me?"

She took a breath, shy, and a little frightened of herself. "If you'll have me."

Disbelief, then joy, flew across Yurik's face. He pulled her to him, his arms wrapping around her, his cheek against the crown of her head.

"Shirin, of course I'll have you. Always. *Always.*"

They moved at the same time. Yurik's kiss was soft and hungry, gentle and all-consuming. It was the end and the beginning, banishing all the fear and loneliness she'd carried around with her ever since she was that little girl on her overlord's plantation.

For the first time in her life, Shirin felt completely safe.

"When can we go?" she asked as he held her close to him.

"I'd say now's as good a time as any," he said.

She nodded. "Then let's say our good-byes and get out of this godsforsaken place."

Thatur landed in the first of many Ifrit villages located in the center of Arjinna.

"Help!" Nalia shouted, running through the streets as soon as Thatur landed.

Cries for help tended to get people's attention. She directed her *chiaan* toward the doors of the little homes, blasting them open as she ran down the small lane between the wooden cottages.

Jinn began pouring into the lane, their screams reaching a crescendo as they caught sight of the approaching wave. They began evanescing, filling the air with crimson smoke. A jinni pushed through the throngs of villagers, a small child in her arms. It was clear from the child's limp body and pale face that he was too ill to evanesce. The jinni screamed for help, but the panicked jinn ignored her cries as they evanesced to higher ground. She fell to her knees, and Nalia grabbed hold of the woman and her child before they were trampled by the mob, dragging them off to the side with the help of Thatur.

"Thatur . . . ," Nalia began, and he nodded, crouching low. Nalia jumped onto her gryphon's back and reached out her arms. "Give me the child," she said. "You can ride behind me."

The woman looked up, her eyes widening as she caught sight of Nalia's purple eyes and the gryphon she rode. She began to back away.

"It's all right," Nalia said, her hand still outstretched. She could hear the water getting closer, battering everything in its path.

"Get on," Thatur snapped. "Or you and your child will die."

The jinni handed over the boy, then scrambled up behind Nalia, clinging to her as they leaped into the sky. Nalia held him close—he wasn't much younger than Bashil. She hugged him to her, this light-as-a-bird boy.

Thatur headed toward a flat cliff where many of the villagers had gathered. Aisha was in the process of setting up an impromptu clinic, and there were already several jinn in need of her care, sustaining all manner of injuries from the flying debris. The jinn stared as Nalia and Thatur landed. Most of them had never seen a Ghan Aisouri and her gryphon before, not unless they were being raided. When Nalia returned the child to his mother, the jinni burst into tears.

"*Shundai,*" she said, over and over again.

"Take your son to the healer," Nalia said softly. She raised a hand in farewell as she and Thatur pushed back into the sky.

In the light of the Three Widows, Nalia could clearly make out the small structures below, nestled in the fields and on the outskirts of the Infinite Lake. If it weren't for the wave of water hurtling toward the jinn who enjoyed the evening meal with their families, unknowing, it would be a peaceful sight. When he touched down, she sent Thatur back into the air without her.

"Go warn the village next to this one. I'll evanesce to the Qaf if you can't make it back to me in time."

"My Empress—"

"We have to split up," she said. "It's the only way."

He roared. "No."

"I am your Empress and I am commanding you to *go to the other village.*"

Thatur fixed her with a look of pure rage and shot back into the sky. Nalia started toward the first home.

"Empress, eh?"

She whirled around. An Ifrit clad in armor stood before her, crimson *chiaan* streaming from his fingers.

Nalia raised her hands, brimming with her own violet *chiaan*. His eyes widened at the royal color and the smirk on his face disappeared. "Yes. Empress."

Before he could attack, Nalia's *chiaan* wrapped around the Ifrit, a glowing rope that was impossible to escape. He struggled against it, cursing. Nalia leaned close to him. He smelled of sulphur and charred meat. She pulled the scimitar from its holster at his waist and he whimpered. She placed the blade against his neck. It was so tempting.

"You tell *your* empress Nalia says hello," she whispered. The jinni nodded, frozen with terror. Nalia slashed at the rope of *chiaan* and waited for him to evanesce before warning the villagers.

Thatur returned before Nalia evanesced, the roar of the approaching wave sending them back into the sky.

"The villagers?" she asked him.

"Safe now—though the sight of a gryphon was, I think, just as terrifying as the water."

For the next hour, they flew through Arjinna, warning the jinn as they touched down in the plantations where serfs had remained, free from their masters and tilling the fields themselves. They flew over the churning mass of water and earth, plucking Djan and Ifrit out of the sea that threatened to drown them. Together, Nalia and her gryphon carried the sick and the elderly, anyone too ill or old to evanesce. By the time the wave had covered all of Arjinna, finally halting at the cliffs of the Shaitan territory with its elegant chateaus and the palace far above the water line, there were thousands of jinn huddled on the cliffs and plateaus of the mountains that separated Arjinna from Ithkar, many of them Ifrit who'd settled the land since Calar's takeover.

Nalia and Thatur aided Raif's rescue boats that carefully navigated the sea in search of survivors. It was nearly impossible to evanesce while submerged in water. The element was too strong, overpowering the body's ability to transform into smoke. It was slow going, pulling half-dead bodies from the water and transferring them to the mountains.

After one more turn around the land, it was clear there was no one left to save. This time, Nalia allowed Thatur to take her back to Ithkar. As they passed over the watery tomb that was her land, she recited the prayer of the dead, her voice falling into the sudden stillness left in the wave's wake.

44

TAZ SAT ON THE EDGE OF A CLIFF, RESTING FROM A NIGHT
of pulling the dead from the water to ensure they'd be burned
and not condemned to an afterlife in the shadowlands. Arjinna
lay below him, almost entirely covered in water. The water ended
just below the palace, sparing the only jinni in the land it should
have wiped out. The sun had yet to rise and the moons continued
to bleed over the land.

"Do you think this is all that's in store for us?" Raif asked,
coming to sit beside him.

Taz had been wondering the same thing. "If it is, only Lathor
got to punish us. Somehow, I can't imagine the others showing
mercy."

Raif sighed heavily. "I don't know how much more we can
all take." He gestured to the refugees. "They've lost everything."

Taz nodded. So much suffering. An endless supply of misery.

"We did the best we could," Taz said softly.

Their search for survivors had confirmed their worst fears: more jinn had drowned than survived.

"We have to tell ourselves that a lot these days," Raif murmured.

Behind them, thousands of refugees had pitched tents in Ithkar and were manifesting what they needed. Wailing filled the air. The *pajai* who'd survived the wave kept their eyes on the sky, their lips moving in silent prayer to the gods.

Taz was no longer filled with wonder for this night. It had begun with such promise: Raif and Nalia, joined together, changing the realm with their love. It had ended with senseless death. What had he been thinking, talking about how *lucky* he was to witness a prophesied event like this? The wave had shaken Taz, threatened his devotion to the gods. It was one thing for him to be condemned to the bottle, it was another to see scores of dead children and families floating facedown all over the realm.

"Where's your mother?" Taz asked.

"As soon as the wave stopped, I took her to the Cauldron. She's looking after the children."

"I suppose there are a lot of orphans now," Taz said quietly.

"After tonight . . . yes."

They sat in heavy silence and then Raif stood, clapping him on the back.

"Come," Raif said. "You need food. There's still a lot of work to be done."

As they made their way to one of the fires, a whistling noise came from the direction of the sea, an eastern wind carrying the scent of salt and the musty dampness of dark, unexplored places. Taz shielded his eyes as dust along the range kicked up, and he had to throw his hands out when a particularly strong gust threatened to push him off the ridge entirely. The darkness made it difficult to get his bearings and he nearly plummeted to the choppy water below. The Shaitan sometimes called their goddess the Trickster. She was so unpredictable, ever-changing. Taz tired of her.

Raif swore as tents began to topple, the sky filling with flying projectiles as the wind picked up speed, bullets in the dark that found their mark in soft flesh. Taz cried out, pain exploding through his head as an oar from one of the rescue boats drew a deep gash on his forehead, nearly knocking him unconscious. Raif shouted something to him, but whatever he said was lost in the wind. The gusts became a roar, and the water covering Arjinna began to pull back into the sea, leaving behind the drowned land.

Taz stumbled about, woozy, colored lights flickering before his eyes. He thought his eyes were playing tricks on him until he realized that the wind had begun pulling *chiaan* from the earth—a rainbow of color that swirled against the darkness, a funnel cloud heading straight for the Qaf range.

He followed Raif, scrambling down the mountain into Ithkar, sliding part of the way, barely hanging on as the wind pushed and pulled his body. The mountains were hundreds of feet tall, but evanescing wasn't an option. Already Taz had seen the few jinn who, in their panic, had tried to evanesce. They'd been torn apart in the gusts, their essence ruptured—instant death.

It was slow going as his fingers, raw and bloody, gripped the rock, and he screamed as he bashed his knee on a jutting rock it was too dark to see. The dust the wind had thrown into the air blasted him in the face so that he had to keep his head tucked into his chest to avoid being blinded. Just as he was certain his muscles were about to fail him, Taz found a crevice in the rock and wedged his body inside as jinn all around him fell over the mountaintop to the obsidian plains below. Raif, he noticed, had found a similar crevice, both of them holding on for dear life.

It wasn't long before Taz was crying out as he lost his grip on the crevice wall. A gust of wind sent him flying into the face of the mountain, his body helpless against the invisible fists that beat him to a pulp. He caught a ledge and held on with both hands. A falling stone grazed his temple, the pain searing, his vision going in and out. And then, suddenly, the wind changed direction. Taz could still hear its roar, but he was no longer being continually backhanded by Grathali.

He reached the bottom of the mountain, raising an arm to shield himself from the flying shards of obsidian that the wind was kicking up from Ithkar's floor.

He blinked.

Stared.

Nalia was standing in the center of the *chiaan*-filled maelstrom, violet *chiaan* beaming from her palms, shooting out from the tips of her fingers like starlight. She'd taken hold of the wind, drawing it to her. Obsidian swirled around her small frame, as though she were controlling an army of ravens.

The Empress of Arjinna was battling with the gods—and winning.

Raif could only stand by, helpless, as Nalia raised her hands and directed the tornado deeper into Ithkar. His ears ached from the strong winds, and the black dust and ash of Ithkar had gotten into his eyes, his nose, his mouth. Once the wind finally left them, Nalia collapsed to the ground and Raif ran to her. He picked her up in his arms and evanesced to the Cauldron, with Taz, Touma, and the rest of her guard not far behind.

"I'm fine," she kept saying, her eyes bright, feverish.

"Have the Brass Army set up stations with healers to help Aisha," Raif said to Taz. He pointed to the deep cut on Taz's forehead. "Have them look at that, too, brother."

"Later," Taz said. "There's work to be done."

"That wasn't a request," Raif said. "Have everyone who has the energy begin manifesting food. Have the Marid supply some freshwater."

The lakes and rivers and wells of Arjinna were now polluted with salt water. This placed the burden of procuring drinkable water on the Marid.

"What should we do about the portal?" Taz asked.

"I'll use *hahm-alah* to contact Zanari," Raif said. "The Dhoma will need to be ready."

Scouts had reported a mass exodus, a stampede leaving dozens of jinn injured or killed. The majority of the jinn were in Ithkar looking alternately dazed and terrified, but many had been willing to risk the horrors of Earth and its wishmaker humans rather than sit around to wait for whatever else the gods had in store for them. Raif didn't blame them. He knew Shirin and Yurik were out there, thankfully gone before the stampeding started. It had been a quick good-bye—forgiveness and moving on. He hoped he'd see her again someday, but he knew wounds like Shirin's could take decades to heal. He was glad—beyond glad—that she had Yurik.

"Taz," Nalia said, her voice strained. "Would I be right in guessing we'll have two more disasters?"

They'd already seen water and wind—earth and fire had yet to make an appearance.

Taz nodded grimly. "I'm afraid so."

"Then we need to start evacuating people," she said. "Send soldiers to the portal to instill order and begin preparing the refugees to leave for Earth in groups, each one accompanied by a regiment of soldiers. Let them know this is just a temporary solution until the sun comes back out."

It would be an enormous burden on the Dhoma, but it was their only option.

Taz gave a slight bow. "As you wish, My Empress."

Raif followed him out into the hall. "Once you're finished, take my mother and the other children to the portal and get out of here," he said.

"I'll escort them and return to—"

"No," Raif said. "Yasri needs you. Nalia needs you. And I sure as hell can't command this army without you. Don't die on me, brother."

"What kind of soldier would I be if I left the fight when you needed me most?" Taz said. "I'll get your mother and the children out, but I'm not leaving."

The corner of Raif's mouth turned up. "Can't say I didn't try."

When Raif returned to Nalia, her father was at her side. "Daughter," he said, "you should leave too. We can set up your court on Earth and you can return once it's safe."

Nalia shook her head, resolute. "I'm not abandoning the realm."

Ajwar gave Raif a pleading look, but he just rested a hand on Nalia's shoulder and sighed. "I serve at the pleasure of the empress."

Nalia placed her hand over his. "Let's go help," she said, looking up at Raif. "I don't want to hide here while everyone below suffers."

Raif turned to Ajwar. "Can you get a restorative tonic from Aisha?" He ran his hand over Nalia's hair. "My wife doesn't know how to rest."

My wife. Saying those words gave him a thrill. He held what had happened in the temple all those hours ago close. No matter what happened next, he'd have that.

After Ajwar left the room, Raif sat on the floor and pulled Nalia onto his lap. She rested her head against his chest, holding tightly to him.

"I know it's horrible to even think about the wedding after everything that's happened," she said, her lower lip trembling, "but I had such a beautiful night planned."

"It *was* a beautiful night." He tilted her chin up. "It was the absolute best moment of my life, marrying you."

She smiled, her eyes filling. "Mine too."

He pressed his lips against hers, letting himself pretend that there weren't any more plagues from the gods and that Nalia wouldn't have to fight Calar or deal with the sigil on her finger. He didn't want much, didn't want a kingdom. All he cared about was having this jinni by his side for the rest of his life.

Nalia rested her head on his shoulder. "I guess you'll just have to take a rain check for our honeymoon."

"Rain check? Honeymoon?" He laughed softly. "Let me guess—human things."

"Mmm-hmmm," she said, yawning.

Within seconds she was asleep. He held her against him, leaning his head against a wall, eyes closed. Ajwar roused them when he returned with the tonic.

"I have an idea," Nalia said. She downed the tonic, her nose wrinkling.

Raif smiled. "Of course you do. And I bet it's dangerous."

"Only a little." She grinned as she turned to her father. "On Earth, I read about carpets that flew in the sky," she said. "In the stories, these carpets had jinn magic. Can you do this?"

"I . . . suppose." Ajwar took off his glasses and rubbed his eyes, clearly exhausted. He'd spent most of his time helping Aisha in the healing room she'd set up in the Cauldron. "But for what purpose?"

"Transportation," she said. "So many of the jinn are too hurt to evanesce, and we need to get them to Earth or to the healing room here in the Cauldron before the next plague hits."

Raif glanced out a large window that looked over the plains. He eyed Ithkar's volcanoes warily. Tirgan and Ravnir had yet to make an appearance. He wondered what the gods of earth and fire had in store for them. It wasn't going to be pretty.

"It might be a good idea to get them off the land too—they'd be safer in the air," he said.

"Clever," Ajwar said approvingly as he rolled up his sleeves. "We'll need—"

There was a flash of violet light and a stack of carpets appeared, then another and another.

"—carpets," he finished, smiling. "The mages at the palace always were excellent teachers. Your manifestation skills are a testament to that."

Ajwar's knowledge was vast—there was so much he could teach Nalia, Yasri, and the other Aisouri. Not just the Aisouri, he suddenly realized: all of them. Nalia was lucky to have such a learned jinni in her court—*their* court, he reminded himself. He couldn't think of himself as an emperor, equal in power to her.

Ajwar held out his hands, mumbling Shaitan spells as his golden *chiaan* shimmered over one of the carpets. It seemed to rustle, then hovered in the air. He placed one palm on it and pushed down. It remained flat as a board. He glanced at Nalia.

"Would you like to try it?"

Nalia nodded eagerly, her eyes alight with curiosity. She climbed onto the carpet, then gestured for Raif to get on, too. He looked at it, wary.

"Scared?" Nalia teased.

"Of course not," he said. He jumped on behind her, marveling at how firm the fabric was—it felt as though he was sitting on the floor. "Okay, a little," he whispered. "Don't kill us."

She laughed and leaned forward, grasping two of the tassels

that dangled from each of the carpet's four corners.

"How do I—" She pulled them and the carpet shot up so fast Raif's ears popped. It was like one of the human elevators he'd been on in Earth, but much, much faster. Nalia's delighted shriek echoed off the black stone in the Cauldron's high ceilings.

"This reminds me of my Maserati," she said, turning to him. At his questioning look, she added. "A car. Malek gave it to me. It was so fast—I used to drive all night sometimes."

Raif wondered if Malek would always find a way to insert himself into their conversations, their life. Her dead master had embedded himself so deeply inside Nalia's psyche that Raif was certain Malek had left a part of himself behind—he'd never had any intention of letting Nalia go.

Stop it, he thought, pulling Nalia against him. She was his wife. There was nothing Malek or his memory could do to change that.

Almost as if Nalia knew what he was thinking, she turned her head and kissed him on the mouth, hard. They were high enough to touch the vaulted ceiling of the Cauldron, high enough that no one could see them.

No one could see them.

Nalia pushed Raif onto his back and climbed on top of him. Without a word, he slid his hands beneath her wedding dress, in tatters now, and she bit her lip as he gripped her hips and drew her closer. She leaned over him, her hair falling around his face so that all he could see in the darkness were her glowing eyes, the contours of her perfect face.

"I heard a rumor," she whispered against his lips, "that if you don't consummate your marriage, it's as if you weren't married at all."

"Well," he said, "we can't have that, now can we?"

She smiled as she brought her lips to his ear. "You might want to remember that this hallway. . . ." She gasped as he pressed against her, his *chiaan* shimmering over her skin like strands of emeralds. "Echoes."

They had to be quick, and maybe it was wrong, to do this when there was so much suffering, when they could be helping people. But what if this was their only chance—what if this was the last night of their lives?

She kept her dress on, the bridal crown of wildflowers still miraculously in her hair. Nalia pulled off his tunic, careful not to let it go flying over the side of the carpet, which, thankfully, was large enough to fit four jinn comfortably.

"Nalia? Raif?" her father called from below. "Everything all right?"

Nalia stifled a laugh against Raif's chest. "Yes," Raif called, biting down a moan as Nalia's lips traveled down his neck, her hands doing things he'd only imagined on late, lonely nights. "Just . . . checking something," he said.

He rolled so that Nalia was beneath him, running his fingers through her hair as he brought her face closer to his. "Everyone is going to know," he murmured.

Not that it would stop him. Even one of the plagues couldn't stop them now.

"Good thing we're married, then—it's less scandalous."

They wrapped themselves around each other, their kissing

frenzied—love at the speed of light. Nalia lay on her back, arms above her head, their hands intertwined. Raif never realized how *tangible* love could be, how you could taste it, hold it. There wasn't enough time, they had to hurry—

Oh, gods. Nalia pressed her palm against his mouth, sucking in her breath at the same time he cried out her name, the sound muffled by her hand. They stared at each other, breathing heavily, eyes glazed.

"I think," Nalia said, her voice so low he could barely hear her, "we're officially married now."

45

THROUGH IT ALL, THE PALACE REMAINED DARK, SILENT. There was not a hint of evanescence above it, no sign that Calar was rallying her troops or sheltering them. Nalia had told Taz that she'd seen most of Calar's army perish in the flood, and those who hadn't seemed to have no intention of fighting Nalia or the other jinn. They stayed in small groups, looking dazed. It occurred to Taz that as of tonight, Calar might no longer have an army to speak of. Were her shadows enough to protect her? He doubted it. Taz relished the thought of her death, of seeing her die in front of him. He hoped he lived long enough to spit on her corpse—but not before he found out what she'd done to Kes. He had to make sure his body was burned.

No one knew what was happening in the palace. With Kes and all his informants gone from the premises, there wasn't anyone to tell the resistance what Calar was planning. Taz hadn't realized how much they'd grown to rely on the luxury of Kes's information until it—and he—were gone.

Taz rested against a mound of Ithkar's dark soil, watching Nalia and Raif as they circulated among the jinn, an empress and emperor of the people. They organized groups, directed healers, manifested medical supplies and food for jinn too injured to do it themselves. Enchanted carpets were passed out to all the jinn, many of them already in the air, families who tried to get as far away from the land as possible. It had been a brilliant idea on Nalia's part. Already there were countless casualties from the wave and the windstorm. No doubt whatever Tirgan and Ravnir threw their way would be just as bad, maybe worse.

As much as Nalia said she didn't want to be empress, there was no doubt that she was made for just such a purpose. Her compassion was real, her sorrow authentic. She got her hands dirty, received blessings from peasant women, and tended the needs of the Ifrit, her supposed enemies. And Raif—he'd given so much in service of the realm and still he gave more. Taz had never known a jinni so selfless, so determined to wipe out evil in his midst. He helped the *tavrai* who, just days ago, had thrown him out of the forest as though he were a piece of trash. He administered tonics to the jinn who'd called for his execution, gave nourishment to their children, sat with them while they cried for those *tavrai* who the wave had taken away. There was no doubt he was just as deserving of sitting on a throne as his wife.

They would have to be crowned soon—Nalia was empress by birth and could already claim the title, but only Taz and Thatur knew that she intended to have Raif be named emperor. They'd gone so far as to abolish caste prefixes to their last names—the first jinn of Arjinna to intermarry. Usually the male's name became the couple's family name or, if the married couple was of the same sex, the older jinni's name. But Nalia and Raif were now the Taifyeh'Urbis. *May they reign with light and power,* he thought, amending the expression of honor to use *they* instead of *she*.

Taz prayed the jinn would see the wisdom of Nalia's choice, how the realm needed Raif just as much as it needed her. Nalia brought out the very best parts of her husband, balanced the dark and light within him. Yet it was his love for her that had given Nalia the courage to enter into her birthright. He was the first jinni to ever call her *My Empress*, the first jinni to recognize who she was and to kneel at her feet. The realm needed his humility, his ability to recognize greatness. Raif's choice to follow her had paved the way for Nalia—without him, Taz very much doubted she would ever have claimed her title. They needed each other to be their best selves.

Taz looked away as a look of pure devotion passed between the newly married couple. Kesmir had looked at him like that once, on their last day together in the little cave by the sea. Taz could live off those stolen afternoons with Kes for the rest of his life, but the memory of them was a poor substitute for Kes himself. Taz hadn't allowed himself to dwell on the loss because if he thought about it for too long he wouldn't be able to care for Yasri, wouldn't be able to breathe. So he'd thrown himself into helping Nalia set up her court, attacked the problem of the ring, helped

Raif plan the coup against Calar that would soon take place. And now he focused on the Godsnight, on keeping as many jinn alive as possible.

The god of earth's plague began as a rumble beneath Taz's feet—the earthquake he'd been dreading. He jumped on the carpet Nalia had given him as the ground began to shake in earnest, the plates beneath Arjinna shifting so that the hard ground became a sea that bucked and swelled. Steam poured down the volcano the Cauldron sat precariously perched above, the stilts that held the Ifrit stronghold to the volcano's rock shaking.

As hundreds of carpets surged into the sky, some with whole families of jinn sitting on top of them, clutching one another, Taz raced to the Cauldron. Aisha, Ajwar, and hundreds of injured jinn were inside, and if he didn't get them out soon, they'd perish. The sound of falling rock was deafening, the roar interspersed with the screams of jinn who became trapped under boulders or fell into chasms that hadn't existed moments before.

Taz ducked as he flew his carpet through the Cauldron's open doors, not stopping until he'd reached the cavernous room the healer had commandeered for the sick.

He spotted Aisha right away, her white robes coated in blood and grit. The healer and Nalia's father were carrying any jinn who couldn't mount a carpet on their own to a long line of carpets that hovered in the air. Taz grabbed one of his Brass soldiers and together they began to help, the Cauldron swaying as though it were a leaf blown by the wind. Onyx tiles began to fall from the ceiling, hitting more than a few jinn. The room filled with frightened cries, but Taz and the others didn't stop until all the injured jinn were on carpets and sailing out of the Cauldron. Taz pulled Aisha over to his carpet, helping her on, while Ajwar scrambled onto the spot beside her. Seconds later they were speeding out of the Cauldron. They'd no sooner made it through the door than the entire structure collapsed into the steaming volcano.

Aisha screamed, holding on to Ajwar as Taz navigated the skies and scanned the plain for Nalia and Raif. Panic overtook him as he squinted his eyes against the moons' light, hoping to see Thatur carrying them in the air. But there were only the undersides of the flying carpets.

"Hold on," he called to Aisha and Ajwar. They nodded, their faces pale, their terror palpable.

He brought his carpet as low to the earth as he dared—he'd already seen several jinn topple off their carpets as the fabric got caught under the avalanche speeding down the side of the Qaf Mountains. The plain became a series of earthen ruptures, the shaking so intense that it was as if the land were in a bottle being thrown by the gods. There was a shrill caw and Taz whipped around. Thatur was screaming at Nalia not far from where Taz flew, the gryphon's words unintelligible in the din. Nalia was bending down, trying to hold the earth together with her *chiaan*. An impossible task, but that had never stopped her before. The earth was not like Grathali's wind, though, and, even from the distance between them, Taz could already see Nalia's *chiaan* diminishing, bright purple fading fast to lavender. Touma stood by, trying to guard her and keep his balance as the earth shattered all around them while Raif was on his knees, grasping Nalia's hands in an attempt to stop her flow of *chiaan*.

"What in all hells is she doing?" Aisha yelled.

"Being Nalia," Taz called back. He shot toward them and jumped off his rug.

"Don't move," he said to Aisha and Ajwar. They nodded as the rug hovered in the air, a few inches from the ground.

"Nalia," Raif was shouting, pulling at her. "So help me gods, if you don't stop right now—"

"No, I can do it, I can—"

"My Empress—you need to get on your gryphon," Taz said, kneeling down so he could lock his eyes onto hers.

"No," she shouted above the din, her voice frantic. "I did it with the wind, just let me—"

"That's it," Raif growled. Her grabbed her around the waist and threw her over his shoulder. He held on tighter as Nalia tried to work her way out of his iron grip.

"Raif! Just give me a minute!" she yelled.

He ignored her. "Touma, get on Taz's rug," Raif said to Nalia's captain of the guard.

The Ifrit stood his ground. "I will when the empress is safely in the air," he said.

"Gods and monsters," Raif muttered.

He bodily forced Nalia onto her gryphon, Thatur nodding his approval. She writhed against his arms, but he had her in an iron grip. Touma and Taz jumped onto the carpet with the others, and they all took to the sky just before the ground they'd been standing on disappeared below the earth's surface, creating a chasm so deep it seemed to go all the way down to the center of the worlds.

"I'm sorry, *rohifsa*. I had to," Taz heard Raif say to Nalia.

She slumped against him, spent. "I know. I'm sorry, too." He smoothed back her hair and gave Taz an exhausted look.

"Well done," he said to Raif. Here again was one more reason why the Taifyeh'Urbis needed one another.

Ajwar leaned toward Taz. "Is my daughter always like this?"

The corner of Taz's mouth turned up. "Always."

Her father frowned. "She must get it from her mother."

From the sky, the disaster below was a distant roar. Taz could hear the flap of the gryphon's wings, the panicked beat of his own heart, Touma's mumbled prayers, Ajwar's labored breaths. Aisha was calmly going through her medicine bag, organizing her supplies. Nalia grasped Raif's hands where they held her around her waist, pulling him closer, and the longing Taz felt then for Kes was so agonizing he had to wrap his elbows around his knees to hold himself together.

The sky was full of flying carpets of every color and size, jinn of all castes watching their realm break, their faces filled with horror. There was no coming back from this devastation—not even Nalia could stitch their world back together. A rush of energy washed over the carpets as a crash echoed throughout the land, so loud Taz had to cover his ears. Screams filled the air as jinn fell off their carpets and plummeted to the earth below, falling too swiftly to evanesce. Aisha cried out as she went over and Taz threw himself across the carpet, grabbing her hand just in time as Touma held on to his waist with one hand and the carpet with the other. Ajwar caught her bag just as it slid over the edge.

"I've got you!" Touma shouted as Aisha continued to scream.

Taz's muscles shook and sweat broke out on his forehead as he strained to lift her. It took a few harrowing seconds, but he finally hoisted her back onto the carpet and she collapsed against him, sobbing.

"Is she okay?" Nalia called, clutching Raif, eyes wide.

Taz waved his hand. "She will be."

The jinn around him began to shout and Taz followed their gaze, staring at the unthinkable. The entire northern ridge of the Qaf range—the mighty mountains that had scraped the sky just moments before—collapsed from the sea to the western ridge. The mountains where Nalia and Raif had just gotten married, where Taz had once fallen in love with a Djan soldier long before going to Earth, were now reduced to dust as the earth's maw opened for the rock, greedy. The only part of the Qaf still standing was the western ridge that held the palace and the portal—a few small mountains that overlooked the Infinite Lake.

Where once mountains had separated Arjinna and Ithkar, there was no longer a border. In mere minutes, the chasm the mountains had fallen into closed up, the land suddenly flat, as though the mountains had never been there. An impossibly high pillar rose out of the earth in their place, perfectly round and smooth, made of the same blue and gold lapis lazuli as the mountains. Its circumference was the size of the small reflecting pool in the Shaitan temple; Taz had no idea what the gods intended it for.

With mountains gone, the land was one, the obsidian plane of Ithkar giving way to the sodden earth of Arjinna and, beyond that, the Gate of the Eye. Raif shouted an incoherent stream of words as he pointed to the gate and the wall that had always separated Arjinna from the Eye. Taz's eyes followed where his finger pointed.

The earth was rumbling toward Arjinna's southern border, a wave of dirt and rock that breached the towering wall, tearing it down in one fell swoop. Taz held his breath as the darkness of the Eye roiled, spinning like a top over the gray dust that coated its floor. The air filled with the keening of thousands of ghouls.

Gods, no, he thought.

They couldn't fight an army of ghouls. They might as well never leave the sky, or fly through the portal and somehow close it behind them, abandoning Arjinna forever, leaving it to the monsters.

Taz reared back as a blinding flash of diamond light shot across the Eye, covering it with a thick membrane of glossy, opal light.

Nalia gasped, her eyes filling with tears as—just for a moment—a white phoenix soared toward the sky, disappearing in the clouds. The earth stilled then, waiting, Taz knew, for the last plague to begin.

46

THIS TIME, THEY HAD MERE SECONDS BEFORE THE NEXT plague hit.

Bolts of lighting stabbed at the jinn in the sky, hundreds of them, each one seeming to aim for its own victim. Thatur dove down, faster than he ever had, holding his wings against his flanks to gather speed. Raif held on tight to Nalia, shielding her with his body. She screamed as the bolts of lightning began shooting toward them from high above, faster and faster, in such quick succession that the sky was filled with a continuous, deafening thunder. Raif had assumed the volcanos would overrun and lava would cover the land—it seemed an appropriate plan of attack for the god of fire. He and Nalia had been fools to think they could outwit both Ravnir and Tirgan with enchanted carpets. Perhaps it was the carpets that had made the god of fire choose lightning, the most terrifying of his weapons.

A bolt sped past them, so close it singed part of Thatur's tail. A pained caw ripped from his throat but he never lost his focus, tilting to the side as he dodged the bullets of lightning that rained down from the sky, swerving expertly so as not to hit the carpets around them. Raif pressed his knees against the gryphon's flanks and Nalia gripped the feathers on his neck, white-knuckled.

There was nowhere for them to go. The Qaf Mountains were gone, the Cauldron had collapsed, and there was no shelter to be found in Arjinna with every structure destroyed by the wave. Dark burn marks crisscrossed the ground where Ravnir's bolts scorched the land.

"Thatur says he knows of some caves, deeper inside Ithkar," Nalia yelled as she turned to him.

He hadn't heard Thatur say a word, but then Raif remembered how the gryphon was able to communicate with Nalia. Raif looked behind him, motioning for Taz and the others on his carpet to follow as Thatur sped farther north, to the wild lands of the jinn. Soon steam blanketed the whole land, the lighting bolts here coming just as fast and thick, but harder to see. It felt as though they were flying through clouds during a terrible storm. Raif continued to keep his body hunched over Nalia's, pushing her head down, even though he knew it was little protection against Ravnir's onslaught.

Thatur navigated the unfamiliar landscape as though he knew it well, and Raif realized that this was where the gryphon must have hidden after the coup, before he built his nest in the

Qaf. Several long, agonizing minutes later, Thatur slowed, waiting for Taz to come alongside him.

"The cave is just ahead," Thatur said, dodging yet another lightning bolt. "Stay right behind me and don't stop."

Thatur shot forward and the clouds of mist parted slightly as a very small opening in a craggy mountain came into view. The gryphon swooped down and Raif's stomach lurched. Within seconds they were inside a cave. Raif held up his hand, throwing emerald balls of light ahead of Thatur as he flew through a low tunnel, slowing just before an arch that led into a cavern large enough for all of them to comfortably rest inside.

Nalia added her own spheres of glowing *chiaan* to Raif's, and the cavern glowed with soft, pulsing light. Raif slid off Thatur, his legs wobbly, and reached up for Nalia. She fell into his arms, hugging him to her.

"Let's stay in this cave forever," she whispered.

"Okay," he said.

She let go and crossed to Thatur, where the gryphon lay on the ground, panting. Raif had never seen the formidable creature so exhausted.

Nalia knelt down and wrapped her arms around Thatur's neck and planted a kiss on his beak. She whispered into his ear and the sound of a soft, lionlike purr echoed in the cave.

Then: "My Empress, kindly release me and behave like the royal leader you are."

Nalia laughed and kissed him on the top of his head before releasing him. "I love you, you crazy bird."

"Gryphon," he growled.

Taz's carpet came through the arch, and once he'd stopped the thing he stumbled to the ground and lay flat on his back.

"Fire and blood," he said. "How are we even alive?"

"The gods are good," Aisha said.

Raif snorted. "That's the most ironic thing I've ever heard."

Raif's father-in-law chuckled quietly and he caught Raif's eye, smiling. It was hard to believe a former Shaitan overlord and a Ghan Aisouri were part of his family now. Raif wondered if his father could see him from the godlands. What would Dthar Djan'Urbi have to say about his wife and her father?

Touma crossed to Nalia and bowed. "Is there any way I can be of service, My Empress?"

"No, Touma, rest—you deserve it."

"Gods, I'm thirsty," Taz said.

"I can help with that." Aisha focused her Marid *chiaan* on the stalactites above them, the rock sweating water.

Nalia manifested several clay cups and jugs just as a stream of water gushed into them.

Taz laughed and raised his cup of cool water to Aisha in thanks. She smiled, sipping at her own.

They decided to stay in the cave until they could no longer hear the thunder. Even Nalia didn't try to go back out and lead more jinn to safety. They all knew it wasn't likely that they'd make it back through the lightning storm a second time.

Raif sat in the mouth of the cave, his turn to listen. The thunder continued for over an hour and then suddenly stopped, replaced with a deafening silence. He waited a few minutes more, trying to see through the mist. There didn't appear to be any more flashes of lightning.

He ran back to the cavern, where the rest lay sleeping.

"It's over," he said, louder than a whisper, quieter than a shout.

Five pairs of eyes snapped open and Touma's head fell into his hands as he wept. Nalia sat up from where she'd fallen asleep propped against Thatur, her eyes meeting Raif's. She smiled at him; he could feel her relief from where he stood.

Nalia and Raif mounted Thatur as the others jumped back on their carpet. The mist from the smoking volcanoes had become thicker and it was slow going, Thatur navigating through the sharp piles of rock that dotted this landscape.

"Nalia . . ."

Raif stiffened. "Did you hear—"

"Yes," she said.

"Nalia . . ."

A whisper in the mist, a voice ancient and strange. No, not one voice, a chorus with a snakelike hiss.

"Ghasai œɲæ."

"Oh, gods," Nalia said. She looked at Taz and her father. Something passed between the three of them, a palpable fear.

"It's the old language," Raif said, "isn't it?" He didn't understand a word, but Raif knew it when he heard it.

Nalia nodded. She felt suddenly cold to the touch and goosebumps covered her arms. He held her close to him. The last time Nalia had come into contact with the old language, she'd tried to kill herself.

"What are they saying?" he asked.

"We want your breath," Nalia whispered.

"Ghasai nëjër. . . ."

"We want your blood," Ajwar said.

Fire and blood. Raif knew exactly who was out there. Now the voices were drawing closer, surrounding them, darting and feinting, swordplay with words. Thatur growled.

"Ghasai zæë. . . ."

"We want your bones," Taz murmured.

Breath, blood, bones. Something tugged at Raif's memory and then his breath caught.

"Breath, blood, and bones to a master bound," Nalia whispered. The words that had been on her shackles from Malek.

Taz turned to Raif. "Are you ready, brother?" Raif's hand went to his scimitar, but Taz shook his head. "That won't be enough."

The mist parted and the Ash Crones stood directly in front of them, naked but for swaths of black rags that were tied around their limbs and torsos, crisscrossing lines that bared their breasts and the gray tufts of hair between their legs. Long black hair fell from their balding heads in greasy strands and their eyes were onyx pits—casteless, as though they belonged to a race all their own.

There was nothing to compare the sight of their horrid bodies to—translucent flesh, bulging veins, yellowed teeth, sharp as daggers. A hot wind gusted through the mist, and their horrific stench wafted over the jinn. Raif gagged, but Nalia reached out her hand, as though to touch them. The crone in the center smiled, a forked tongue darting out of her mouth, hungry. Her eyes flashed with evil intent. This must be their leader, who Kes had spoken of—Morghisi.

"*Death wants her due,*" the dark mages chanted as one. "*Mora, goddess of all that dies, Mora, Mora, Mora.*"

Black *chiaan* streamed from the tips of their fingers as they raised their arms, straight as boards, fingers pointed at Nalia, Raif—all of them.

Not now, he thought. *Not this way.* He and Nalia were going to die someday—soon or in a thousand years—but there was no way in hell they'd give up their spirits in front of these monsters.

Nalia sucked in her breath, as though she were choking, as though the very air in her lungs were being ripped out of her. Raif held out one hand, palm up, the other in a viselike grip around Nalia's waist.

"Be gone, daughters of Mora," he said, his voice thundering in the heavy quiet of the wilds.

Emerald *chiaan* surged toward them, a wave of magic, everything he had in him. It was joined by Taz and Ajwar's golden *chiaan*, Aisha's electric-blue Marid power, and Touma's dark-crimson energy. Nalia clutched at her throat, her breath rattling, blood seeping down her nose, and he closed his eyes, remembering their wedding, making love on a magic carpet. *My wife, my wife.* Raif dug deep inside himself and discovered a store of power he didn't know he had.

There was a cry of rage, a dissonant cacophony of sounds that pummeled his ears, and when Raif opened his eyes, the crones were gone and Nalia was heaving beside him, gulping air.

"What *was* that?" Touma cried.

Nalia leaned her damp forehead against Raif's chest.

"The first battle in a war we don't have time or strength to fight right now," Raif said.

Breath, blood, and bones: not on his watch. Raif wiped the blood off her face with the edge of his sleeve.

"Let's get out of here," she whispered.

Thatur pushed into the still-dark sky as they made their way south.

47

"SO YOU FINALLY MET THE ASH CRONES," AJWAR SAID AS he came to stand beside Nalia.

She glanced at him. "Lovely bunch of ladies."

"Delightful," he agreed, his voice dry.

Nalia could still feel the tendril of blind submission they'd placed inside her through their hypnotizing chant. How had they known the words that had been on her shackles from Malek, the words that were on the shackles of every jinni on the dark caravan?

"Was it their magic that made the slave trade possible?" she asked, glancing at her father.

"I suspect so." He shook his head. "They are as old as this land, capable of the greatest evil—as you yourself have seen. Most dark magic can be traced back to them."

Nalia sighed. "I'll have to deal with them eventually."

"Yes," he said. "But first things first." He pointed to the palace.

"First things first," she agreed.

Kill Calar, take back the throne. Easier said than done.

"The *sadrs* say the Godsnight is intended to purify the land," Ajwar said.

She sat on a low mound of dirt, gazing at her destroyed realm, too exhausted to cry. Hundreds of jinn had been lost in the last plague, too many to count. Arjinna had been ravaged by the gods and yet the moons still hung from the sky. Why didn't the sun return now that the gods had finished their plagues—or had they?

The plagues, the Ash Crones—and she still had to dethrone Calar and rid the realm of her shadows.

"The humans have stories of their god doing the same," she said. "A long time ago, he covered the earth with water—a never-ending storm. All the humans died and all the animals except two of every kind: male and female."

Nalia had often wondered what the humans had done that was so bad as to warrant mass death and destruction. Even after returning from the Eye and seeing the violence done to Arjinna by Calar and the effects of the war between the castes on the land and its people, Nalia still didn't understand what good could come of destroying entire civilizations. Jinn, and humans for that matter, weren't failed experiments or projects. They were intelligent beings who loved and dreamed—who deserved a chance to live, a chance at redemption.

"The humans were forced to start over," Nalia said, "but it didn't change anything. In fact, I think they became even worse."

She thought of the slave trade between the humans and Ifrit—jinn lives in exchange for human weapons. *Build, heal, grow.* That was what Nalia needed to do. And now that there was no longer a barrier between Arjinna and Ithkar, it would be much easier to find peace among the castes in a united Arjinna. *Maybe,* Nalia thought, *as horrible as they are, the gods* do *have a plan.*

"After the human god covered the Earth, what happened?" her father asked. "Where did the water go?"

"A dove carried an olive branch as a sign from their god. It came from a newly grown tree, which meant that there was now land somewhere in the vast ocean. The water disappeared, and they were able to build a new world."

Nalia fingered the seed from the lote tree. It had grown warm since the last plague ended, pulsing against her skin. The vision in the Eye had shown her planting the seed. But where? She was terrified of choosing the wrong place—what if another plague came and destroyed the tree before it had a chance to grow?

She pulled the seed out of her pocket and held it up for her father to see. It shone gold. "I think this is our olive branch. Except I don't know where to plant it."

Ajwar wiped his glasses and looked closer at the seed. "This is from your lote tree, no?"

She nodded. "It's changed since the plagues began. Like it's alive."

"And your vision did not show you where to plant it?"

She shook her head. "I thought it was in the mountains, but"—she gestured toward the flat plain that stretched from the sea to the farthest western range—"most of the Qaf is gone."

Planting it by the palace was too dangerous. What if Calar's shadows sucked the life out of the tree before it had a chance of healing the land?

Nalia heard her name and looked to where Raif was calling her, beckoning toward the lapis lazuli column that stood between Ithkar and Arjinna.

"It's no mountain, but . . ." Ajwar shrugged. "Maybe that is where the seed needs to go."

"But there's no soil."

Ajwar smiled. "Daughter, how do you know that?"

The seed began to glow.

"That is a sign from the gods if I ever saw one," he said.

When they reached the pillar, Raif didn't need to say a word. Carvings were spreading from its base to its top, depicting the history of the jinn, as though an invisible sculptor were cutting into the rock: their beginning, created from smokeless fire. The nomadic days, when the castes lived as tribes. The emergence of the Ghan Aisouri. The war between the castes and the enslavement of the Djan, Marid, and Ifrit. On and on the carvings climbed and though Nalia couldn't see to the top of the pillar, she knew it would show the coup and the Godsnight.

Nalia ran her hand over the carvings, so finely wrought. She turned to Raif. "I think . . . I think I know how to make the sun come out."

Nalia took Raif's hand and, together, they evanesced to the top of the column, followed by Nalia's father, Thatur, Taz, Aisha, and Touma: their court, which included one member of every caste. They landed, Thatur flying around the pillar, keeping watch. Some of the jinn who'd survived the plagues gathered below, dozens from every caste. The rest were still scattered in the temporary camp that had been set up, unaware of Nalia and Raif on the pillar.

The top of the pillar was wide and smooth, perfectly flat. Raif took off the pouch he always wore around his neck and emptied the rich, dark earth of the Forest of Sighs onto the lapis lazuli surface. Nalia took the golden lote seed out of her pocket, and together they knelt, burying it in the earth and watering the soil with their tears. They were tears of joy and sorrow, shed for all that was lost, and all they hoped to gain.

They stood and stepped back, waiting, gripping each other's hands. Slowly, then faster, a bright green shoot appeared. It grew, reaching for the sky—from seed to sapling in mere moments. The trunk thickened and branches sprouted from it, a replica of the lote tree in the Eye, the tree of wisdom. Soon it was full-grown, its thick branches hanging over the top of the pillar, the roots surging toward the ground below. They pushed down, past the bottom of the pillar, then far below Arjinna's surface. The tree's magic spread, covering the realm with golden light. Grass and flowers, gurgling streams and healthy, fragrant trees burst from the earth like jubilant dancers. A sweet breeze blew away the stench of sulphur and death, and Ithkar—*Ithkar*—began to teem with life as well. Trees heavy with fruit covered the once-barren plains, and the lava morphed into surging rivers that brought life to everything it touched.

And the Eye: as the gold of the lote tree met with the phoenix's light, a desert appeared, with dunes that glimmered in the moonlight, stretching as far as Nalia could see. It was as if the Sahara had blown across the worlds and settled where the dust and ash and horror of the Eye had once been. Not a ghoul in sight. Nalia's breath caught and she stared at the realm, her eyes shining.

"Come," she whispered, beckoning for Raif to join her. She placed her palms against the tree, just as she'd done in her vision in the Eye. Raif placed his palms beside hers. The silken wood breathed with life, warm, as though blood, not sap, coursed beneath its bark.

A surge of emotion and power, *chiaan*, and intent filled her. Raif gasped and Nalia knew he was feeling it, too. It was as if they'd tapped into all the lives and energy of the realm, of every sentient being within it. Nalia wasn't just aware of the whole— she could feel the individual strands of every jinni in Arjinna, could feel their desire for peace, an end to the war. Each of them a master, Nalia and Raif their slaves, but in a way that felt right.

These were shackles she was willing to wear. She turned to Raif and he nodded his assent.

Wisdom was a feeling, a gut instinct that grew inside her like the tree itself, its branches twisting around her bones, her heart. It flooded Nalia, filling her with certainty: she and Raif were meant to lead this realm together, hand in hand, a course set upon over twenty summers before by an Aisouri in the palace and two Djan revolutionaries on an overlord's plantation. Nalia glanced at her court, her eyes settling on her father. She held out her hand, Solomon's sigil gleaming in the light of the Widows. Ajwar crossed to her and rested his palm against her own. He looked from Nalia to Raif.

"Are you sure?" he asked.

They both nodded. Other than marrying Raif, Nalia had never been more certain of anything in her life. Her father closed his eyes and began to sing the spell he'd painstakingly created, each word filled with magic and intent. He had a beautiful voice, one that Calar hadn't been able to silence no matter how hard she tried. Nalia's finger began to tingle, then burn. Raif gripped her other hand, his forehead resting against her own.

Just when the pain became unbearable, Solomon's sigil fell from Nalia's finger to the soft carpet of grass that had sprung up at the base of the tree. It glowed, blinding, just as it had when they'd first found it in the cave. The ring rose, then hovered in the air between them, the gold turning into four long, liquid strands. Nalia's skin began to burn once more as the gold twisted around her wrists, then Raif's, forming an infinity pattern, then splitting as the gold braceleted their wrists with thin shackles.

The moons disappeared from the sky and the sun broke through the night, a single beam falling onto Nalia and Raif, a benediction from the gods.

Somewhere, perhaps on some invisible plane of the gods, Nalia heard the faint song of her phoenix.

Rise from the ashes, it sang. *Set this realm on fire.*

Raif sucked in his breath. "Nal, look."

Thousands of jinn had gathered below the pillar Nalia and Raif stood upon while others remained in the air, hovering on their carpets. Slowly, as though a wave were moving through the crowd, the jinn knelt. They were of every caste. Some wore the uniform of the *tavrai*, others wore the armor of the Ifrit or the purple-and-white armbands of the Brass Army. Men, women, children—all gazed up at Nalia and Raif.

"You honor us," Nalia said, bowing, her voice somehow amplified as though she could speak into every jinni's heart. "The land is healing," she said to her people, "but it's not whole. It's only if we work together that we will achieve the peace we all desire. It is the greatest wish of this realm to be free of Calar and her shadows, to be free of our ancient hatred for one another. The revolution isn't fought or won on a battlefield. The revolution is inside all of us, a war we must fight in our own hearts. When I look out, I see jinn of every caste, helping one another after what we've endured together. It's clear to me that we have won, even though there is so much work left to do."

The jinn let out a cheer and Nalia stepped back as Raif moved forward. "*Tavrai*, Ifrit, Marid, Djan, Shaitan"—he turned to Nalia. "Ghan Aisouri. We have spent too many years in darkness, too much time bowing to masters who enslave us to their evil desires. This ends now, today. My father fought for this moment, to see what I see before me—the castes standing side by side, equal, with real hope for the future. I married a Ghan Aisouri because I love her, because I see that it doesn't matter what color your eyes are or who you are taught to hate. In love, we are united. We are your slaves and you—Arjinna—our master. Help us build. Help us grow. Help us heal. Together, we are light to one another, a race united by one wish, one goal: to be free, equal jinn. The future begins here. Now." He placed a fist on his heart. *"Kajastriya Arjinna."*

Amid the cheering a cry pierced the air as Thatur swooped by and Taz, who jumped onto his back, cried out, *"Kajastriya Sula! Kajastriya Sulahim!"*

Light to the Empress. Light to the Emperor.

The jinn took up the cry, and sunlight burst across the realm, covering every inch of darkness—except for one patch of land. The palace lay shrouded in a starless night, waiting for Nalia and Raif to claim the throne that was rightfully theirs.

The Godsnight was over. A new day had dawned.

48

NALIA STOOD ON THE SOFT BLACK SAND, FACING THE Arjinnan Sea. She'd dreamed of this in the Eye: golden light, rich like butter, melting over the turquoise sea, bathing her in its warmth. There were times during the Godsnight when Nalia had never expected to see dawn break over Arjinna again.

Now she filled her lungs with good, clean salt air. The water temple of Lathor stood in the distance, rebuilt by the Marid. The temple-in-the-sea's liquid walls shimmered in the early-morning light, the domes blue against the lavender sky. The wind—so gentle, nothing like the windstorm of the Godsnight—swirled around Nalia, filling her with its *chiaan*, a stronger energy than she'd ever experienced on Earth. She focused on the rough granules of sand beneath her bare feet, the feel of her *chiaan* rushing through her in anticipation of what would come next.

"Begin," Thatur said, his voice a low rumble.

He stood to her right, holding a thick wooden stick in his claws. Nalia knew that wood would be making contact with her skin again and again before their morning training session was through. Thatur was a strict taskmaster: nothing but perfect form would please him. His presence, that stick—it was the past come to life once more, a promise that all was not lost. Her race lived on—here, now. Nalia could feel her dead Aisouri sisters around her, invisible witnesses, guardians who would not let her fail.

This was the weapon that would destroy Calar: not a ring of power but Nalia's stubborn refusal to submit. She'd gone through these poses as a slave on Earth, as a despairing jinni in the Sahara, and now on the land she'd reclaimed, its empress.

Raif sat on a rock, knees pulled up, watching her, his eyes heavy with sleep. He'd spent the past few days with the defectors from Calar's army, the force he and Taz led now vastly larger than whatever soldiers Calar had managed to keep with her in the palace. But—as Taz and Raif had seen time and again in that year when Nalia was gone—Calar's shadows would more than make up for the lack of flesh-and-bone soldiers. Raif glanced more than once at Thatur's stick, frowning. She knew he hated it, but both she and Thatur had been firm: this was the Ghan Aisouri way. Nalia let go of her awareness of Raif and Thatur and retreated inside herself as she raised her hands to the sky in Dawn Greeter—the first of the thousand poses of *Sha'a Rho*.

Despite her year in the Eye, the movement slid through her muscles, familiar. As she moved through the poses, Nalia could feel the difference the phoenix, the heart plant, and the ring had brought to her *chiaan*. Her power had become expansive and at the same time more anchored than ever before. She felt the pull of the land, could feel Raif more acutely. There were parts of him that would always be inside her after their vows to one another, after everything they'd gone through.

Moving through these ancient poses was not just for Nalia's benefit, but for all of them. Nalia could feel the despair, envy, terror, hope, love, hunger—everything that burned in her people's hearts. The collective energy of the jinn coursed through her veins, inserted itself into the very marrow of her being. She *was* Arjinna, its bright, flowing, moving center.

"Focus, child," Thatur said. "You are the trunk of an elder pine rising to the sky."

Nalia heard the wind catch Thatur's stick before she felt it against her leg. Pain shot up her right side and Nalia let it flow through her as she concentrated on the movement.

She adjusted her leg so that it was in the proper alignment, her lips turning up as she entered the next pose: Floating Leaf. She'd missed this beautiful tyrant of a bird.

Nalia vaulted into the air, arms and legs outstretched, a pinwheel of motion and light. The golden shackles on her wrists caught the sunlight as the sun rose to the sky, blinding her. Nalia closed her eyes as her hands searched the currents of the wind. She stayed there, suspended above the sand, her body dipping with the gusts that swirled over the beach. When she landed, Thatur gave a grunt of approval.

They went on like that for nearly two hours, bruises blooming over her skin as the stick made contact with her body again and again. Magic hummed through her, obliterating all thought. There was only breath, and Thatur's watchful gaze, the crash of the sea upon the shore.

Finally, it was over. Nalia lay on the sand, her arms outstretched in the thousandth pose: Faithful Warrior. She held her breath in honor of the dead, the dead she had now burned, the dead who lived inside her, who she carried in her heart.

The dead she would avenge tomorrow.

When Nalia opened her eyes and let out her breath, Thatur was standing over her. This face, with the blue feathers around its eyes, this face that she'd never expected to see again after the coup, glowed with pride.

"Your best practice yet," he said. He gave her a slight bow. "My Empress."

"I'm ready," she said.

He threw the stick into the ocean. "I know."

Nalia wanted to see the look on Calar's face when she realized her enemy was using the very same secret passage as the one they'd walked through together four years ago, when Nalia had set Calar free. There was a certain poetic justice to that.

The tunnel through the western Qaf range—which began in Ithkar and ended in the bowels of the palace—was narrow and dark. Thatur had insisted on going first, followed by a small handful of Brass soldiers, then Nalia, Raif, Touma, Taz, Ajwar, and two more Brass soldiers. They'd decided to keep their company small, so as not to alert Calar or her guards. Once Calar and her soldiers knew of their presence, Ajwar would break the palace's *bisahm*, which would allow the whole of the resistance's army to descend upon the Arjinnan seat of power.

Nalia remembered the tunnel's musty, earthy smell from that night leading Calar to safety. She remembered the way her heart had beat so hard, she was certain her mother could hear it all the way at the other end of the palace. She remembered the stench of the Ifrit girl—of *Calar*—blood, urine, days of not being able to bathe, the sweat of pain and fear lying over her like a second skin.

Why did I do it, Thatur? she asked the gryphon. *Why didn't I just follow orders?*

Because you were meant to rule this realm, Thatur thought to her. *And if the coup had not happened, then the lote tree would not have been planted here. The land needed you.*

I have so much blood on my hands, she said. *Raif's best friend. Jaqar.*

Child, everyone in this realm has blood on their hands.

That answer wasn't good enough for Nalia. She couldn't help but feel unworthy of the crown she hoped to have on her head by the end of this night. It was infinitely easier to accept, though, knowing that burden would be shared by Raif. She took several deep breaths as she tried to center her *chiaan*. She was nervous. Scared. She knew her training would kick in when the time came, but Calar fought so differently from any of Nalia's enemies—she was too similar to the Ash Crones. And her shadows: Nalia had only heard of them. The thought of actually encountering the creatures made her insides roil.

Thatur slowed as they came to the end of the tunnel. "No matter what happens," he said in a low voice, his gaze on Taz and Touma, "do not leave the empress's or emperor's sides." They both nodded, solemn.

There was the sound of rock scraping against rock as Thatur moved the passage's hidden door aside. Dim light filtered into the tunnel. Nalia swallowed. This would be the first time she'd been inside the palace since the coup.

"You okay?" Raif whispered, taking her hand.

"I . . . don't know." She smiled at him in the close darkness. "It's hard, coming back."

He squeezed her hand. "You're back for good."

They came out into a familiar empty hallway lined with torches. To the right were the laundry and kitchens. Though no sound came from them, Nalia knew a servant could run into them at any moment. The palace smelled different—like campfire smoke, not the amber oil that had once burned continuously in its halls. Nalia wondered what else had changed.

Thatur turned to Nalia, his eyes boring into hers.

Salaa'Khim, My Empress.

Salaa'Khim, my friend.

Victory or death.

Thatur led the way to the throne room. They'd decided to go there first. When they reached it, Nalia motioned for all but a few Brass soldiers to remain outside the tall double doors that led to the heart of the palace. She knew the palace guards would be there any minute, making their rounds. She wanted to keep that battle away from what was going to happen with Calar. She needed her core fighters completely alert, not worrying about two-bit guards. Her father bowed to her, wordless, his eyes conveying his fear and hope. Ajwar turned and made his way to the tower, from which he could break the *bisahm* when the time came. Nalia watched him go, then faced the doors before her. Raif took her hand and his *chiaan* rushed through her, calm strength that burned away fear.

I am Ghan Aisouri.

Nalia wasn't prepared for the feeling that washed over her as she entered the throne room. Memory after memory flowed through her—ceremonies, celebrations, special audiences with the empress. And then, of course, there was the coup. The last time Nalia had been in the throne room, a battle had been raging between the Ifrit and the Aisouri, gryphons ripping out throats left and right, *chiaan* everywhere and still it wasn't enough, still the royals had been gunned down in a dark cell. The human weapons had echoed off the walls, deafening, terrifying. It was the first time Nalia had ever seen a gun. She could still hear the cries of the dead, as though the very stones had recorded them.

As Nalia moved down the central aisle that led to the throne, it became apparent the room was much changed. She'd expected it to be different, of course, but it affected her more than she thought it would. The once-beautiful carvings of the Ghan Aisouri's history had been defaced, with crude words and images over Nalia's ancestors. Though the elegant mosaic ceilings that arced high above the marble floor were still intact, Calar had replaced the Aisouri throne with a sinister seat made of Ithkar's volcanic rock, not unlike the one Nalia had been forced to sit on in the Cauldron.

And then she saw the bottles.

Nalia gasped, horrified. Hundreds of bottles lined shelves behind the throne, each one containing a jinni. It was so cruel, so twisted. All that pain and misery on display, the evidence of Calar's sick mind.

The jinn behind Nalia stared, silent, their collective *chiaan* heavy with sorrow.

Raif gripped her hand tighter and she could feel his anguish through her skin. The jinn trapped in the bottles hadn't noticed the arrival of Nalia and her small company. Part of her was terrified to stand before them. In the end, it was her fault they were there. Her fault the coup had happened at all.

Nalia moved closer as she noticed that some of the bottles had gone dark, the jinn inside them still, some of them little more than a collection of bones. Dead. She stared at the darkened bottles, grief and fury spinning inside her. She wanted to sob, to rage at the gods, but she had no tears left with which to mourn the dead.

Chiaan sparked at her fingertips, violet wisps of light that cut into the inky black that surrounded her.

"We have to free them," she said.

"There'll be time for that later," Thatur argued.

"No." Nalia shook her head. "I will not stand by and let these jinn suffer for one moment longer. I serve the realm, not myself. We will free them."

Thatur sighed. "So it would seem that you no longer wish this to be a somewhat stealthy operation?"

"Fuck stealth," Raif said. "We're here to free slaves. And these ones need freeing."

Pride surged through Nalia as she stood beside her husband, the first emperor of Arjinna. This was how she wanted to begin their rule—not with murdering a tyrant, but freeing her victims.

They lifted their hands at the same time, and when Raif glanced at her, a slow smile spread across Nalia's face.

"Remember how we messed up all those cars in Malek's garage?" she asked.

He smiled. "Yeah."

"Let's do that again."

Chiaan streamed from their fingertips and the bottles shattered, the walls of the jinn prisons falling away, freeing the captives inside. The throne room filled with their cries as they floated out of their bottles, full-sized jinn once more, their evanescence tumbling over the throne and into the cavernous room. The jinn were of all ages, most of them terribly ill. They stared at Nalia and the others, shell-shocked, just like the Brass Army had been when they'd been freed from their bottles in the Sahara.

Nalia turned to the few Brass soldiers she'd allowed into the throne room. "Help them get out of here."

"My Empress—" Touma began, but Nalia held up her hand. "Our group will be large enough for one jinni. Please," she said to the soldiers, "go."

Touma sighed, but bowed and stepped back to await further instruction. Soon the room was empty.

"Where are all Calar's guards?" Raif murmured. "I would have expected *someone* to come running at the sound."

"Gone, I suppose," Nalia said.

The entire Brass Army and what was left of the *tavrai* were stationed outside the palace, awaiting their signal. But there was no one to fight. So many jinn had been lost on the Godsnight, and the refugee camps in Ithkar were now full of former Ifrit soldiers who no longer claimed Calar as their empress.

"I see you've been admiring my collection," said a cold voice near the entrance to the empress's private chambers.

Nalia kept her hands raised as she turned to the jinni across the room. Pure white hair, blood-red lips, a *sawala* made of rich ruby and black velvet. The Amethyst Crown glinted atop her head. Nalia's violet eyes met Calar's crimson ones.

This was the jinni who'd killed Nalia's brother, butchered an entire caste, laid waste to her homeland. This was the jinni who grew powerful off the enslavement of hundreds of jinn, who frolicked with Mora and worshipped the darkness. The jinni who'd taken Kesmir from Taz.

"Your *collection*," Nalia said, "is no longer yours. And it never was." Nalia smiled, the kind of smile that Malek would have approved of. The kind he gave to men just before he killed them. "Did it make you feel powerful, Calar, having those jinn behind you?" She remembered something Taz had told her about Calar that he'd learned from Kes. He'd called it her weak spot. "Did it turn you on, seeing their pain?"

Calar's eyes sparked. "When I kill you it will be slow, and excruciating, and *I will love every second of it*."

"You mean *if* you kill me," Nalia said. She moved closer, feeling her training in every step, every move. She was a tiger about to leap, a dragon's claw, a storm tamer.

I am Ghan Aisouri.

Calar's hands flicked in the air above her, as though she were batting away a horde of flies. But there was nothing there.

"I want my crown," Nalia said, her voice even.

Calar smiled. "Then come and get it."

Nalia threw her *chiaan* at Calar's chest, the force of it knocking the Ifrit empress off her feet. Outside there were shouts and the sound of battle: Calar's meager forces had finally realized the palace had been breached.

Calar leaped to her feet, flames roaring toward Nalia, but Nalia flipped into the air, missing them by a hair's breadth. Raif and Thatur flanked Nalia as she vaulted toward Calar, but the Ifrit empress was faster.

She pulled the *yaghin* off her neck and held it up, triumphant. "*Sahai!*" she cried, putting her lips against it.

Raif threw a swirling ball of *chiaan* at Calar, but it was too late. The shadows inside burst from the stone, a lightning-fast swarm that flew straight toward Nalia.

49

NALIA LAY SLUMPED AGAINST THE BASE OF THE THRONE. Her eyes fluttered open as Raif called her name. But he was so far away.

Calar's voice was louder, though, and came from the deepest recesses of Nalia's mind: *Come, Aisouri, let's take a trip together.*

This time, Nalia didn't push back when Calar forced herself into Nalia's mind. She rode the wave of pain as though it were a fast-moving river that held Nalia in its blistering embrace, a current she could no longer fight. There was no *here*, no *there*, no boundaries. Just sensation and undulating light: pain, the light the color of her pain—blinding, searing red.

Then: a room.

No, *the* room. It slowly began to materialize around Nalia— the dungeon where Nalia and Calar had first met, when Nalia had watched her own mother torture the then-unknown Ifrit girl. Nalia remembered the way her mother had washed the blood off her hands, how the water turned pink.

"Familiar, no?" Calar said.

Nalia turned. The Ifrit empress stood behind her, wearing the same bloodied shift she'd worn that day, her face the same patchwork of bruises that Nalia's mother had inflicted on the delicate jaw, the small nose. Calar was barefoot and somehow that simultaneously made her seem both vulnerable and more powerful, as though in exposing herself, she had no intention of holding anything back. Just like that day so long ago, she showed no fear. Calar stared at Nalia, her bloodred eyes hungry, calculating.

Is this really happening? Nalia thought.

Does it matter? Calar answered.

There were so many levels to exist on—Nalia was familiar with these planes from her time in the Eye. Mindspace, dreamscape, memories of the past, visions of the future. She and Calar were suspended between the universe's exhales.

"I set you free," Nalia said. Her voice echoed off the cell's stones. "I don't understand—why am *I* the person you hate the most?"

"Because you thought it was enough," Calar said. She threw back her head and laughed, then twirled as though she were at a ball. "You thought you were good, yes, and merciful. Kind Nalia lets bad Calar go." Calar spit on the ground. "That's what I think of your benevolence."

This time the pain Calar unleashed on Nalia's mind was lacerating, as though every nerve ending that moored Nalia's consciousness to her body were being severed. She must have passed out, because when she came to, her body was slumped in the chair Calar had been sitting in that fateful day. Her hands and feet were bound with iron chains, the metal weakening her, stealing her energy. The room faded in and out of focus. The walls had begun to ooze—when had that happened? Thick, black muck slowly sank to the floor and Calar danced in it, laughing. A fetid stench filled Nalia's nose as the black poison came closer and she gagged.

"I danced in your blood," Calar sang out. "I danced and danced and danced."

The floor filled with blood and the room shuddered until it became, briefly, the room where Nalia had lain, riddled with bullets, under a pile of corpses. The chair Nalia had been tied to disappeared and she fled to a corner, as far away as possible from her Aisouri dead. Calar paid her no mind; it was as if Nalia weren't even there.

This isn't real, Nalia tried to remind herself, but there was nothing to distinguish it from reality. The smell, gods, blood and shit and fear. Nalia trembled, watching in horror as Calar's feet became stained red with blood.

"I danced," Calar sang, "and I danced and I dan—" Her voice cut off with a cry as the walls gave way to an endless plain scattered with obsidian and ash. Ithkar. The sky was filled with the noxious smoke the volcanos belched, but it was torn, as though someone had burned holes in it with the end of a very large cigarette.

And suddenly it began to make sense, what was happening. Calar was losing her mind—it was fracturing, burning up—and she'd taken Nalia along for the ride. A year with shadow creatures that fed on *chiaan* would do that. They'd infiltrated her energy, infused it with their own deathly vapors.

"This is *your* mind," Nalia said, "not mine." But Calar didn't hear her.

Nalia turned in a slow circle. How was she supposed to get out of here? Would she be trapped forever on this plane with Calar, waiting for the empress to die?

Calar was digging at the ground with her bare hands, her fingers bloody. "Where is it?" Calar screamed, tears falling down her face. She gave a cry of delight when she found what she'd been looking for: a roughly made doll. She hugged it to her chest. The face had been badly burned.

"They came in the night," Calar said, her voice soft. "The Aisouri. Fire. So much fire."

The sky darkened and the air filled with screams. Nalia remembered this, too. She wished she didn't.

Flames, everywhere. A village filled with Ifrit who tried to outrun the violet *chiaan* aimed at them. Nalia and the other Aisouri sat on their gryphons. The elder Aisouri ran down women, children. The gryphons' beaks filled with flesh and blood. Nalia could see herself in the farthest ring of Aisouri, sitting atop Thatur. She was only six summers old and her eyes were filled with terror.

Calar—as an adult, Calar in the present—was standing before a burning home. "No!" she screamed. She dropped the doll and tried to enter the hovel, heedless of the inferno. The flames licked her skin, but she was Ifrit, so she did not burn. A gryphon reared up and knocked her down.

Darkness.

The scene was swept away, a wave of nothing crashing upon the shore of Calar's memory.

"Please, please, make it stop, Kes, make it stop," she mumbled.

In the distance a volcano erupted, its red lava startling. Calar stared at it, hungry. The smoke that wafted toward them took on the faint green hue of *gaujuri*. It enveloped them in a cloud every color of the rainbow. Calar lay on her back, arms outstretched, surrendering to the drug.

"Thank you," Calar whispered.

The smoke cleared and Calar leaned over a crib, a dagger in her hand. Tears streamed down her face as she looked at the baby inside it. *Yasri.* Nalia froze; she couldn't move as Calar raised the blade—and let it drop to the rug at her feet. She reached inside the crib and picked Yasri up, holding the child to her, kissing her over and over.

"My baby," she whispered. "My sweet one. I'll never hurt you, I promise. Mama will never hurt you."

There was the sound of paper tearing, and Nalia and Calar were thrown from the room and into another.

They were lying on a bed now, the curtains around the four posters tattered and blowing in a breeze. Nalia had never been inside the empress's chambers, but she knew these must be her rooms. She recognized the intricately carved balcony, its recurring teardrop pattern. Soft candlelight filled the room, but the shadows in the corners writhed. Nalia lay beside Calar, no longer afraid of her.

"*Rohifsa, rohifsa,*" a male voice whispered.

Nalia scrambled out of the bed, blushing as Calar and a jinni with a scar covering one cheek began to make love, unaware of her presence. Nalia looked away, but not before she noticed the adoration in their eyes, his gentleness, how her head fit perfectly in the crook of his shoulder. It was the first time Calar seemed happy.

Raif.

She had to get back to him. Nalia ran to the balcony and stared up at the sky. The Three Widows beamed, all in different phases.

Calar let out a bloodcurdling howl, and when Nalia turned she saw what Taz could only have imagined: Kesmir lay on the floor beside the bed, his lifeless eyes open, a dagger inches from his hand. He was covered in blood. Shadows descended upon his corpse, feeding on his *chiaan*. Calar stared, her mouth open in a frozen scream. The shadows lifted off the corpse, satiated. Calar fell to her knees and crawled to Kesmir.

"Why?" she screamed. "Wake up." She sobbed, her hands covered in his blood. "Kes, wake up!"

But he didn't and so she lay beside him, pulling him closer, holding him for the longest time. Then she raised her hand, and the flames that stood suspended in a corner of the room rushed to Kesmir, covering his body. Calar keeled over as she said the prayer of the dead.

The sky began to melt then, like wax, and the balcony Nalia stood on fell away. Nalia screamed, and as she plummeted toward an unfathomable darkness, Calar tumbled past her, twisting in an invisible grip, eyes wide with terror. Nalia landed hard on the dungeon floor, pain shooting up her arm. She looked up. Calar was in the chair, bloodied, bruised.

The beginning.

The end.

"Pretty Aisouri," Calar trilled. She pulled against the iron chains that bound her hands and feet. Her eyes roved continually around the cell and a manic smile flitted across her face, then disappeared, like the sun passing behind clouds, then bursting out again. "Kill me. You want to. I know you do."

The walls began to crack, the openings between stones shot through with bright red light.

Nalia stood before Calar, uncertain.

This was the jinni who'd killed Bashil.

Massacred Nalia's entire race.

Forced Nalia into slavery.

Shut Nalia out of Arjinna once she was finally free.

This was the tyrant who had destroyed the realm.

If Calar lived, thousands more would die.

"Kill me!" Calar screamed.

Nalia's jade dagger appeared between them. She leaned forward and picked it up, then stood before her enemy, uncertain. She'd made the wrong decision the last time. She could make the right decision now. Shadows slipped through the walls, silent witnesses. Nalia stepped forward. Stopped.

Once again, she was filled with that same uncertainty that had made her choose to set Calar free, all those years ago. It was so unfair, all of it. Who would Calar be if the Aisouri hadn't burned down her villages, if Kesmir's love had been enough? Who would Calar be if she'd grown up in the palace, surrounded by beauty and privilege? And the darkness in her—wasn't it in Nalia, too? It was the same thing that had drawn her to Malek, the same thing that had made her kill Jaqar in cold blood.

"Do it!" Calar screamed. She closed her eyes, chanting in the old tongue. *"Mora sahai mundeer. Mordam jal'la."*

Mora wake my soul. Death, take me.

"No," Nalia said softly.

There had been enough death. She wanted to build, heal, grow. The only way she could do that, the only way Nalia could truly serve Arjinna and its jinn, was if she was willing to kill the parts of her that wanted to gut Calar. The Aisouri who had been trained to hate and oppress, that jinni needed to die, too. Nalia knelt before Calar.

"Dari ehakar mordam ne salaam," she whispered in the old tongue.

Sister in death as well as life.

Nalia raised the knife, its point directed at her own chest.

The room filled with song, faint at first, and then louder. Familiar. Calar went silent, her eyes filling with tears as shimmering light pure as snow fell through the ceiling, a cascade of glittering rain. The white phoenix swooped down and landed on Nalia's shoulder.

"I'm so tired," Calar whispered. "So . . . tired. . . ."

The phoenix's eyes were kind as they gazed into Nalia's, tangerine wells of peace. These were the eyes that had led her through the long, dark night.

And even death can bring new life, the phoenix sang.

Nalia faced Calar. The Ifrit empress's eyes were suddenly clear, all trace of madness wiped away. She was so very young.

And beautiful. And infinitely sad.

"It ends with us," Nalia said.

Something like peace settled over Calar. "It ends with us," she whispered in agreement.

Nalia plunged the dagger into her own heart.

50

"*ROHIFSA*, PLEASE WAKE UP," RAIF CRIED.

She was alive—he could see the slight rise and fall of her chest. The shadows had been unable to take her away completely—he'd never seen anyone resist them, but then again, he'd never seen a jinni do half the things Nalia could.

As soon as Calar had fallen to the ground in some kind of trance, Taz had pulled the *yaghin* out of her hand and said the word in the old tongue that Kes had taught him—"*Đæl*," *sleep*—and the shadows immediately fled into the stone. It now sat on the floor, forgotten.

This was the third time Raif had been forced to plead with Nalia not to leave him. First on a blood-spattered beach on Earth, then in a healer's tent in the Sahara, and finally, now, before the throne that was rightfully hers.

Her eyes moved frantically beneath her eyelids and every now and then she shuddered or cried out. An ear-splitting scream cut through the air and Raif whipped around. Calar still lay slumped on the other side of the throne, Taz leaning over her, eyes murderous. Like Nalia's, her eyes were closed, her body still.

"What are they *doing* to each other?" Raif asked. His helplessness threatened to choke him.

"I don't know," Taz said. "But we can't kill Calar yet—if she has a hold on Nalia's mind, it could take her, too."

Raif placed his hands against Nalia's heart and poured his *chiaan* into her, but he knew it wouldn't be enough. He could only hope that it would let her know he was here, that he was fighting for her. Raif picked up her hand and kissed each finger, rubbing his thumb against the tattoo that wound around her ring finger. He could now admit to himself what he'd known all along: Nalia had insisted on having the wedding as soon as possible for just this reason.

I heard a rumor that if you don't consummate your marriage, it's as if you weren't married at all.

Hot tears rolled down his cheeks. Suddenly she sighed, all the tension draining from her face.

"Nalia!" He screamed her name as he felt her go.

Blood bloomed over her heart, soaking her tunic, sliding to the floor. Her *chiaan* slipped out of her skin and wound itself around him, an amber-scented caress. It slipped through his fingers and he grabbed Nalia, pulling her onto his lap, his cries a wounded animal's.

She was gone.

It was like swallowing needles, hearing Raif's sobs. The young emperor screamed Nalia's name again and again, holding her to him.

Raif wasn't going to survive this.

Taz met Touma's eyes and they both began to weep, unashamed. They'd come so far, gotten so close. Taz could almost hear Raif's heart break. Thatur roared so loudly the glass burst from the windows all along the eastern wall of the throne room. It was the sound of their hope shattering, of an end to their new beginning.

Taz felt a hand on his arm and he shouted, jumping back.

Calar was awake.

Calar was alive.

Raif went silent. He stared at Calar, murder in his eyes.

Calar laughed when she saw him, not a cruel, maniacal one like Taz would have expected, but that of a small child who was utterly delighted.

"We danced and danced and danced," she sang. "And the phoenix said . . . the phoenix said . . ." Calar began to sing, her voice raspy and soft. *"And even death can bring new life."* She smiled at Raif. "She said it ends with us." Calar reached out her hand to him. "Take me to her."

Raif gently lay Nalia's body down, his eyes never leaving Calar's. He stood as he unsheathed his scimitar.

"Her crown," Calar said, sitting up. *"And even death can bring new life . . . new life . . . ,"* she sang.

Calar reached up and took the Amethyst Crown off her head. She smiled, pure and kind and peaceful, as she held it out to Raif. "Long live the empress."

A look of unspeakable sadness passed over Raif's features. The scimitar fell to the floor and he stumbled away, utterly lost. Taz took the crown and stood. He walked toward Raif, slow, gentle steps. Then he knelt beside Nalia's dead body and rested the crown on her chest. This was how she'd be burned. Raif crumpled to the ground, his sobs echoing throughout the room. Taz bowed to Nalia, then turned to Raif.

"My Emperor," he said. "What is your will?"

"I can't," Raif sobbed. "I'm done, I can't, I—"

There was a crack and Nalia burst into flames. Taz jumped to his feet, dragging Raif away from the fire. Raif fought him, reaching for Nalia, but Taz and Touma held him back.

Song filled the air, though Taz would never be able to say from where it came. The voice was unspeakably beautiful and its song fell on his ears like soft rain.

> *Awake, awake, the dawn is yet to come.*
> *The gods do look upon the brave with favor and delight.*
> *And even death can bring new life.*

Raif sagged in Taz's arms, all the fight gone out of him as Nalia's body disappeared in an inferno of violet, emerald, crimson, sapphire, and golden flames. It was as though she were being consumed by a column of *chiaan*.

Calar clapped her hands, delighted. "It ends with us, yes,

yes!" She turned to Taz suddenly, cocking her head. "I saw you in his mind. I saw you kiss him."

Taz stared. *Kesmir.*

"I saw him give you our daughter." She said these words without malice, feverish. "I burned him I burned him and ate his ashes I ate his ashes and they tasted like sorrow I ate and I ate and I danced and I danced *and even death can bring new life and even death can bring new life and even—*"

Without warning, Calar sprinted toward the balcony. Taz watched her, too full of despair to bother following. When she reached the railing she turned, fixing him with a radiant smile before throwing herself over, backward, her face to the sky, grinning as she plummeted to the rocks below.

The column of *chiaan* that had devoured Nalia's body evaporated, leaving behind a pile of shimmering ash. Raif knelt before it. He'd known this was possible, he knew no days were guaranteed them, and yet he'd allowed himself to believe they would have more time.

Nalia.

Raif could feel himself breaking. Something inside him cracked and he laid his forehead on her ashes, sobbing.

Thatur came to kneel beside him, tears falling down his face, liquid pearls. Their grief was a thick, weighty thing that twisted throughout the room, with Raif at its center, his despair radiating a power all its own.

Calar was dead and Raif didn't care. He could hardly breathe, the loss of Nalia so all-consuming.

Nalia, his heart cried, over and over. *Nalia.*

The first rays of dawn sunlight climbed across the lapis lazuli walls of the throne room, banishing the darkness that had lingered over the palace while Calar still lived. The light crept over the floor as the first prayer sounded, a Shaitan *pajai* calling from the pillar where the lote tree bloomed.

Restless goddess of the skies, send us your spirit on the wind. O Grathali, fill us with the power of your ever-changing, ever-shifting grace.

Raif sat up. *Grace—Ashanai:* Nalia's true name. It was as though they were singing just for her.

Raif stared at her ashes. Nalia would want prayers. He had to honor her before he joined her in the godlands. A drifting fleck just above Raif caught his eye. A feather, white as snow. It gently fell, landing on top of Nalia's ashes. Sunlight hit the amethyst crown that sat before the pile of ash, throwing violet shards over Raif. Was this her spirit's way of telling him the white phoenix had finally taken her to the godlands?

Why did she always go where he couldn't follow?

A breeze blew through the windows then, smelling of the sea and *widr* trees and vixen roses. And amber, that scent that would always be Nalia to him. It reached the pile of ash and Raif cried out as all that was left of Nalia was caught up in its swirl. The wind pulled the ashes up, a furious whirlwind, like evanescence. It spun around, faster and faster, a silent funereal dervish. Raif slowly rose to his feet. Suddenly he could feel her—*he could feel Nalia.*

And then the song he'd heard when Nalia's body burst into flame settled into his heart:

> *Awake, awake, the dawn is yet to come.*
> *The gods do look upon the brave with favor and delight.*
> *And even death can bring new life.*

Then he knew, he knew, he *knew*—

A glowing white ribbon of light twisted through the ash, mixing with the violet evanescence that tumbled toward him like a wave.

A hand.

The crook of an elbow.

An arched foot.

Lips he'd memorized long ago.

The smoke cleared and Nalia stood before him, clothed in dazzling white, head bowed, eyes on the crown at her feet. She knelt down and picked it up. Finally, her eyes met his, shining and alive, and he could drown in them.

The true empress of Arjinna raised the Amethyst Crown and placed it on her head.

EPILOGUE

THE PALACE GARDENS ARE FILLED WITH THE SOUND OF merriment. The jinn scattered throughout the opulent grounds wear the traditional harvest-festival animal masks and crowns of flowers. The palace gates are open wide and jinn from all over the land flock to the glimmering lapis lazuli castle high in the only remaining ridge of the Qaf Mountains. Threads of *chiaan* cut the sky over the palace like fireworks.

In one corner, a band of Djan musicians plays the *zhifir*, drums, and flute while wizened jinn sing the old serf songs. Though their shackles have long been gone, their songs tell their story, which will be passed down for thousands of summers to come. A story of war, a story of the gods and an empress who refused to die.

In the center of the garden, surrounded by glowing *calia nocturne* and vixen roses, is the dance floor. A large gryphon and the captain of the guard stand just outside it, neither looking amused, their eyes roving the premises, ever vigilant. In one corner of the dance floor, two Dhoma swirl, their arms wrapped around one another: a Djan with braids that sprout from her head like spring grass and a tall, elegant Shaitan in white healer's robes. They laugh and kiss as they make up their own dance. A Shaitan *pajai* and a tiny Ghan Aisouri dance beside them, the little girl holding her papa's hands, her bare feet on his as he teaches her an ancient series of steps. A few of her Aisouri sisters play in the garden, but only a few. It will take a long time for Aisouri parents to believe the palace is a safe place for their daughters.

Near them, the empress and emperor are serving *savri* to their guests, and every few minutes he leans close to her and kisses her neck. They wear matching phoenix masks, hers white and his red. He's been on Earth for several weeks, teaching a team of mages how to do the unbinding spell that will free the jinn on the dark caravan. He came back early because, though they've yet to tell anyone, the emperor and empress have a secret nestled beneath the folds of the empress's flowing gown. And he doesn't want to miss a moment of this.

"Raif, I won't be mad," the empress says as her husband refuses yet another glass of *savri*. "Go, drink. Dance! I'm perfectly happy." She nods toward the two Dhoma on the dance floor. "Besides, it looks like Zan and Phara could use a few pointers."

The emperor shakes his head. "Nope. If you can't drink, then I can't drink."

He smiles and holds out his hand. The musicians have begun a slow tune, a lilting one that reminds them both of the souks of

Marrakech and the dunes of the Sahara—and a jinn club beneath a restaurant.

"Dance with me, Nalia."

He'd said those words to her long ago, back when the empress was a slave, imprisoned by a human who would one day love her enough to die in her place. That was the night the emperor's heart knew—even if his mind did not—that he loved her.

The empress takes his hand and the jinn around them watch, smiling as the young couple—the first of their kind—take to the floor. The empress shivers as the emperor pulls her closer. She moves her lips close to his ear, drunk on his sandalwood scent, on the *chiaan* in the tiny life that grows inside her like a flower.

"You are the wish of my heart," she says.

The emperor brings his lips to hers, ignoring the gryphon, who never approves of such displays of affection. "And you," he says, "are the wish of mine."

When the music ends, the empress turns and leans her back against the emperor's chest and he holds her as she gazes up at the emerald stars, their hands intertwined over the soft swell beneath her gown.

"Nalia-jai, what are the stars?" Bashil is sitting beside her in the garden. It is late at night and they whisper quietly.

"The jinn in the godlands. They come to visit us at night," she says.

"How can they visit us if they're dead?"

"Well, no one ever really dies, gharoof." She runs a hand through his thick hair as she gazes at the constellations above.

"But I've seen the dead jinn burn!" he says. "There's nothing left. How can they watch us from the godlands without eyes?"

She laughs. "You are not your eyes or your ears, your mouth, or even your heart."

Bashil frowns and drops his chin into his hands. "What am I then?"

"You're the feeling inside you when you're happy. And when you love something. You're the part of you that looks at the stars and wonders what they are." Nalia pulls him against her. "Nothing can kill that."

He looks up at her. His eyes are golden and warm, and she wonders what he will look like when he is an old jinni and if he will remember sitting in the palace garden with his big sister, talking about stars.

"So we live forever?" he asks.

She kisses his head. "Forever and ever."

"Will I be a star too?" he asks.

"Of course, gharoof. You'll be the brightest one."

The empress's eyes scan the sky, searching for the brightest star. It winks back at her, then shoots across the aurora, free to roam where it pleases.

Pronunciation Guide

Jinni: JEE-nee
Jinn: JIN

JINN CASTES
    Shaitan: shy-TAN
    Djan: JAN
    Ifrit: if-REET
    Marid: muh-RID
    Aisouri: ass-or-EE

JINN GODS AND GODDESSES
    Tirgan: TEER-gah-n
    Grathali: gruh-THAL-lee
    Lathor: luh-THOR
    Ravnir: RAV-neer
    Mora: MOR-uh

CHARACTERS

Aisha: eye-EE-sha

Anso: AN-so

Bashil: bah-SHEEL

Calar: cuh-LAHR

Dthar: d-THAR

Fazhad: fuh-JAHD

Fjirla: FEER-luh

Halem: hah-LEM

Haran: huh-RAHN

Haraja: hah-RAH-ja

Jaqar: JAH-car

Kesmir: KEZ-meer

Malek: MAL-ick

Morghisi: mor-GEEZ-ee

Nalia: NAH-lee-uh

Noqril: no-KREEL

Phara: FARE-ah

Raif: RAFE

Samar: sah-MAR

Saranya: sah-RAN-yah

Tazlim: TAZ-leem

Thatur: thuh-TOOR

Touma: TOO-mah

Urum: oo-ROOM

Xala: DZ-AHL-la

Yasri: YAZ-ree

Yezhud: YEH-zhood
Yurik: YUR-ick
Zanari: zah-NAHR-ee

Glossary

Arjinna (ar-JINN-nuh) *The jinn realm.*

Ashanai (ASH-uh-nie) *Grace.*

B'alai Lote (BUH-lai LO-tee) *The Great Lote, a magical tree.*

B'alai Om (BUH-lai OM) *The Great Cauldron, an Arjinnan constellation.*

bisahm (bee-ZAH-m) *A magical shield used to cover an area in order to prevent jinn from evanesceing into it.*

chal (chuh-ALL) *Jinn tea.*

chiaan (chee-AHN) *The magical energy force that all jinn possess.*

đæł (D-AH-L) *Sleep; old-language word used to trap Calar's shadow monsters.*

Dhoma (DOH-ma) *The Forgotten—a desert tribe of jinn on Earth. The jinn are from all different castes and reside in the Sahara.*

evanesce / evanescence *This is the same word in English, but used differently. When jinn travel by smoke, they evanesce. The smoke itself is called evanescence.*

fawzel (faw-ZEL): *Jinn who shape-shift, usually from human to bird form.*

gaujuri (gow-JER-ee) *A hallucinogenic drug used in Arjinna.*

gharoof (gah-ROOF) *A term of endearment for children. Translates as "little rabbit."*

hahm'alah (HAHM-ah-lah) *The magic of true names, whereby jinn can contact one another psychically.*

hagiz (huh-GEEZ) *A jinni with mixed parentage, biracial.*

Ithkar (ITH-car) *Ifrit region.*

-jai (j-EYE) *A term of endearment used among family members; a suffix, as in Nalia-jai.*

jolip (JUH-ahl-up) *Moss that heals the brokenhearted.*

Kada (KAH-dah) *The jinn language.*

kajar (kuh-DZ-AR) *Plantation.*

kees (KEYS) *Bread dusted with sugar and spices.*

keftuhm (KEF-toom) *Blood waste. A term referring to male offspring of the Ghan Aisouri.*

lasa (LAH-suh) *Bird that causes jinn to fall in love when it sings.*

ludeen (loo-DEEN) *Tavrai home in the Forest of Sighs; jinn tree house.*

mundeer (moon-DEER) *Soul, in both kada and the old tongue.*

niba (NEE-bah) *The jinn currency.*

pajai (puh-JUH-EYE) *Temple priest.*

pardjinn (PAR-jin) *Someone who is half jinn, half human; seen as an abomination by the jinn.*

Qaf (COFF) *Mountain range in Arjinna.*

Qalif (kah-LEEF) *Hope.*

raiga (RAY-guh) *Wolf.*

rohifsa (roe-HEEF-sah) *Soul mate; translates as "song of my heart."*

sadr (SAHD-r) *Arjinnan prayers in the jinn holy book, comparable to the Christian psalms.*

Sadranishta (SAHD-rahn-EESH-tah) *Jinn holy book.*

sahai (suh-H-EYE) *Awake; word from the old tongue used to awaken and deploy Calar's shadow monsters.*

salfit (SAL-feet) *A derogatory term used by the lower castes when referring to Shaitan and Ghan Aisouri jinn, who mostly reside in the mountains. Literal translation: "goat fucker."*

savri (SAH-vree) *The favorite drink of the jinn, a spicy wine with hints of cardamom.*

sawala (sah-WALL-ah) *Traditional Arjinnan clothing consisting of pants and a long tunic. Worn by both males and females.*

sawal-hafim (sah-WALL hah-FEEM) *Formal jinn attire.*

Sha'a Rho (SHAH-ah-ROE) *Ghan Aisouri martial art, with similarities to yoga, tai chi, and kung fu.*

shirza (SHER-zuh) *Ifrit general.*

skag (SKAG) *Insult used for any caste, male or female. Loosely translates as "motherfucker."*

sula (SOO-luh) *Empress.*

sulahim (soo-luh-HEEM) *Emperor.*

tavrai (tuh-VR-EYE) *A member of the jinn resistance, similar to "comrade."*

vashtu (VAH-shtoo) *Ajinnan predator birds.*

voiqhif (vwah-KEEF) *A psychic power similar to remote viewing. Very rare among the jinn.*

widr (wi-DEER) *An Arjinnan tree, similar to a weeping willow. Has silver leaves.*

yaghin (yah-GEEN) *Magical necklace used as protection against and storage of Calar's shadow monsters.*

zhifir (zh-if-EER): *An Arjinnan fiddle.*

EXPRESSIONS IN KADA

Batai ghez sonouq. (buh-TAI GEZ soh-NOOK) *My family is yours.*

Batai vita sonouq. (buh-TAI VEE-ta soh-NOOK) *My home is yours. Used when visitors come to one's home.*

Ghar lahim. (GHAR la-HEEM) *Nice to meet you.*

Ghasai œɲæ. (guh-SEYE OON-ay) *Old tongue: We want your breath.*

Ghasai nëjër. (guh-SEYE nay-JER) *Old tongue: We want your blood.*

Ghasai zææ. (guh-SEYE z-eye-EE) *Old tongue: We want your bones.*

Hala dkar. (HAH-la duh-CAR) *All honor to the gods.*

Hala shaktai mundeer. Ashanai sokha vidim. Ishna capoula orgai. Hala shaktai mundeer. (HA-lah shock-TAI moon-DEER ASH-uh-nai SO-kah vee-DEEM EESH-nah KA-poo-lah OR-guy HA-lah shock-TAI moon-DEER) *Prayer for the dead: Gods receive our souls. Fill them with grace and light. Grant entrance to your eternal temples. Gods receive our souls.*

Hif la'azi vi. (HIF la-AH-zee vee) *My heart breaks for you. Used as a condolence.*

Jahal'alund. (JUH-hahl-uh-loond) *Gods be with you. Typical jinn greeting.*

Kajastriya Arjinna. (kuh-JAH-stree-yuh ar-JINN-uh) *Light to Arjinna.*

Kajastriya Sula. (kuh-JAH-stree-yuh SOO-luh) *Light to the Empress.*

Kajastriya Sulahim. (kuh-JAH-stree-yuh soo-luh-HEEM) *Light to the Emperor.*

Kajastriya vidim. (kuh-JAH-stree-yuh vih-DEEM) *Light to the revolution. Expression used among jinn revolutionaries, as a toast or battle call.*

Ma'aj yaqifla. (mah-AHJ yah-KEEF-lah) *I wash my hands of it.*

Mahan laudik. (muh-HAH-n lah-DEEK) *Many favors.*

Mora sahai mundeer. Mordam jal'la. (MOR-uh suh-HEYE moon-DEER MOR-dum jah-LAH) *Old tongue prayer for the dead: Mora raise my soul. Death, take me.*

Salaa'khim. (suh-LAH-keem) *Victory or death. Used among the Ghan Aisouri before battle.*

Shundai. (shoon-DIE) *Thank you.*

Vi fazla ra'ahim. (VEE FHAZ-la RAH-ah-HEEM) *You are a sword, nothing more. What tavrai say before a battle.*

ACKNOWLEDGMENTS

I will be forever grateful to my characters for choosing me to write this story, for allowing me to have a very big dream come true. Writing this series would have been one of my three wishes, had a jinni been around and in a mood to grant.

Just as with every book in the series, there are many people who helped me on this journey. First, Brenda Bowen, fabulous agent, who believed me when I said jinn are the new vampires. Donna Bray, my editor. Thank you for making a good home for the series and for your brilliance. This series—especially this book—would not be what it is without you. *Shundai* from the bottom of my heart. Big love to everyone from Balzer + Bray/ HarperCollins—thank you for beautiful covers and word spreading and copyediting and doing all those millions of little things that make a book.

My beta readers: thank you for the love you put into your reading: Jamie Christensen, Elena McVicar, and Brandon Roberts. Shari, Jen, and Leslie: thank you for being with me from the very beginning. My Allies in Wonderland for their endless support. My best friend, Sarah Roberts, for being my go-to girl for everything. Of course I'm gonna shout-out my husband, Zach, first reader and my partner on this crazy, life-changing journey (TS&TM&EO). Thanks to my family and friends for always supporting me and my work.

Thank you to all the bloggers—especially the Blogger Caravan—that supported me throughout this series. An extra hug for Sarah from What Sarah Read for all the cheerleading.

And thank you, dear reader, for coming along for the ride. May all your wishes come true.

Also by Heather Demetrios

BALZER + BRAY

An Imprint of HarperCollinsPublishers

www.epicreads.com

JOIN THE

Epic Reads

COMMUNITY

THE ULTIMATE YA DESTINATION

◀ **DISCOVER** ▶
your next favorite read

◀ **MEET** ▶
new authors to love

◀ **WIN** ▶
free books

◀ **SHARE** ▶
infographics, playlists, quizzes, and more

◀ **WATCH** ▶
the latest videos